FRIDA SLATTERY AS HERSELF

FRIDA SLATTERY AS HERSELF

ANA KINSELLA

SCRIBNER

London · New York · Amsterdam/Antwerp · Sydney/Melbourne · Toronto · New Delhi

First published in Great Britain by Scribner, an imprint of Simon & Schuster UK Ltd, 2026

Copyright © Ana Kinsella, 2026

SCRIBNER and design are registered trademarks of The Gale Group, Inc., used under licence by Simon & Schuster Inc.

The right of Ana Kinsella to be identified as author of this work has been asserted in accordance with the Copyright, Designs and Patents Act, 1988.

1 3 5 7 9 10 8 6 4 2

Simon & Schuster UK Ltd, 1st Floor, 222 Gray's Inn Road, London WC1X 8HB

For more than 100 years, Simon & Schuster has championed authors and the stories they create. By respecting the copyright of an author's intellectual property, you enable Simon & Schuster and the author to continue publishing exceptional books for years to come. We thank you for supporting the author's copyright by purchasing an authorised edition of this book.

No amount of this book may be reproduced or stored in any format, nor may it be uploaded to any website, database, language-learning model, or other repository, retrieval, or artificial intelligence system without express permission. All rights reserved. Inquiries may be directed to Simon & Schuster, 222 Gray's Inn Road, London WC1X 8HB or RightsMailbox@simonandschuster.co.uk

Simon & Schuster Australia, Sydney
Simon & Schuster India, New Delhi

www.simonandschuster.co.uk
www.simonandschuster.com.au
www.simonandschuster.co.in

The authorised representative in the EEA is Simon & Schuster Netherlands BV, Herculesplein 96, 3584 AA Utrecht, Netherlands. info@simonandschuster.nl

Simon & Schuster strongly believes in freedom of expression and stands against censorship in all its forms. For more information, visit BooksBelong.com.

A CIP catalogue record for this book is available from the British Library

Hardback ISBN: 978-1-3985-4922-7
Trade Paperback ISBN: 978-1-3985-4923-4
eBook ISBN: 978-1-3985-4924-1
eAudio ISBN: 978-1-3985-4925-8

This book is a work of fiction. Names, characters, places and incidents are either a product of the author's imagination or are used fictitiously. Any resemblance to actual people living or dead, events or locales is entirely coincidental.

Printed and bound in the UK using 100% Renewable Electricity at CPI Group (UK) Ltd

CONTENTS

1 Overture, 2005 — 7

2 *Bird* (John Reddan), 2006 — 19

3 *Graceland* (John Reddan and Frida Slattery), 2007 — 87

4 *Graceland* (John Reddan and Frida Slattery), 2008 — 117

5 Hiatus, 2008–2010 — 139

6 *Four and Ten* (John Reddan), 2011 — 215

7 *The Reason* (Tobias and Sara Lund), 2011 — 231

8 *Ripples on the Water* (John Reddan), 2015 — 261

9 Hiatus, 2017–2019 — 311

10 Exit strategy, 2019 — 367

11 The dark times, 2020 — 381

12 The auteur, 2020 — 411

13 *Frida Slattery Plays Herself* (Frida Slattery and John Reddan), 2021 — 443

One of two things happened each time Frida Slattery was waiting in the wings, about to step on stage. Sometimes she was consumed by it all: the role, the costume, the lights. The audience there in the dark, expectant. Her lines. Her make-up. Her character. Eaten up by it and disgorged, a new person, not Frida but Hedda or Juliet or, at the forefront of her memory, Maria in *The Sound of Music*, as she had been when she was still in school. This was the thing that usually happened. It was the thing that she loved most.

But sometimes it didn't go her way. Instead Frida remained obstinately herself – just Frida Slattery, refusing to undergo any meaningful dramatic change. As if some valve hadn't managed to open. Just an actress, on this occasion nineteen years old, wearing a long silver gown, standing on a staircase at the back of the stage, waiting in silence. Visible to the audience, though only barely. Frida was supposed to be a ghostly presence, one who hovered on the stairs while the play's two main characters, a man and a woman, moved around a rudimentary set made to look like a living room: a faded green sofa and matching armchair, a tasselled yellow lampshade, a painting of a whitewashed farmhouse on the wall.

An hour earlier Frida had been at home in the flat she shared with her friend Catherine in Rathmines, having finished a quick dinner of beans on toast with grated cheese and showered at breakneck speed, shaving her underarms and legs in record time, then looking for her leather jacket, her bike helmet, her keys, imagining that very soon she would stop being herself and start being the ghostly presence she had been cast as.

She cycled back into the city centre in the dark, a little rain dampening her curly hair en route. It took hours for Frida to get her hair right for this role. It seemed to take Frida hours to do anything – a personality defect that Catherine and the other student actresses she'd become friends with didn't have. That was just the kind of person she was, Frida thought. She and the other girls went for the same roles in these student productions and it was stupid, wasn't it, for Frida Slattery to think that this was going somewhere, that this was anything other than passing time. She was studying history of art and geography because she hadn't been accepted onto the acting degree. She was the ghostly presence and not the female lead because Catherine had gotten the female lead. Tonight Frida's role was to stand very still at the back of the scene, while the couple in front of her argued and laughed and cried.

She was trying to follow the play's dialogue passively. It was easy to zone out and end up surprised by the arrival of your own cue. But when her only job was to remain still, her thoughts inevitably started to wander. Her mind went to failure, to the myriad problems she knew existed within her, rattling around like ball bearings that had scattered into every nook and cranny of her. If she was a better actor, she would have been given the lead. If she looked like Catherine – tall and imposing, not short and mousy, pale and unfit – she would be speaking now, downstage instead of half-visible in the shadows here. If she had gotten into the acting course and not merely the cop-out arts degree she'd settled for after failing the auditions in her final year of school. If she was different somehow, took all of this more seriously. Acted like an actress. If she wasn't so worried about everything, about time running out, about what people thought of her, about all the other girls.

She was living with Catherine mostly because the two were inseparable but also because Catherine was rich and her uncle rented the flat to them cheaply. Before this Frida had lived at home, in the small terraced house she'd grown up in with her mother and older sister, Edel. Growing up, the atmosphere there had been thick with the miasma of Edel's anger and arguments with her mother. God, Frida needed to focus. She was not back in that terraced house. She was standing half in shadow at the back of a pub theatre, waiting for her cue. She was wearing the silver dress that was supposed to represent ghostliness, in a glamorous sort of way. She had dressed in the tiny storage room half an hour earlier and now she was sweating, heart racing. And for what? A monologue in another student play. Why had she chosen this life for herself?

All of these were quotidian problems, she thought, starting to feel the warmth of the stage lights. Rivalries with friends, the longing she had for better roles, for some kind of stardom or success: Frida wanted a better class of anxiety for herself, but this was what she was stuck with.

Downstage, Catherine turned to look at Frida. The black

silk robe hanging on her graceful shoulders, like a life model. Expectation all over her friend's face. The room was silent, and Frida could feel it, the way the audience was waiting for something. Their attention stretched tight as a drum. Something had gone wrong, Frida thought. Maybe backstage, or a technical fault. Someone had made a mistake somewhere.

One hand still resting on the banister, Frida stood still as ever. She stared straight back at Catherine. Then the male lead turned to look at where Frida stood on the stairs and made a concerned face at her.

It's me, Frida realised at once. I have made a mistake. Oh, God. The room's attention was straining. She heard a man at the back release a little nervous chuckle, and then, as Catherine and her counterpart stared with alarm, Frida stepped down the staircase and began, belatedly, the ghost's monologue.

On an upholstered stool near the Liffey side of the small room above the pub sat a man named John Reddan, his back leaning against the wall. The play was far too long, he thought, swilling the warm ends of his cider around the pint glass before setting it onto the ground beside him. And the actors, he thought. Even for students, they were amateurs.

His was a professional interest. Having recently had his first play at a real theatre, and not long graduated from university himself, John was a director now. He was looking for new actors to work with. For him, there was nothing remarkable about this particular production. Years later, it did not stand out in his memory; in fact it took comparing diaries and old ticket stubs for Frida and John to realise they'd been in the same room at the same time. Even then, it was as if John's memory had been wiped of this evening. This bothered Frida. She wanted confirmation that what they shared had been predetermined, that John had been able to recognise something in her even before they'd ever met each other. Of course, the ghostly presence who missed her cue! she wanted John to say, slapping his forehead. How could I forget?

But it wasn't like that. Instead John just shrugged. I saw a lot of plays back then, he said. I spent all my evenings in little theatres like that one. In fairness, Frida – the adult Frida, the real Frida – couldn't really remember it either, other than as part of the long, blurred procession of acting jobs she'd had from aged twelve, when she first attended an after-school drama class, until she was introduced to John Reddan in Kehoe's eleven years later.

1. Overture, 2005

You're down on your luck. This was what Frida Slattery's mother said every time they met in the year Frida graduated from college. This was Una's way of saying, This acting thing, this dream of yours, it might not be working for you. In the twelve months since entering the workforce, Frida had had two acting jobs: the lounge girl in the background of a soap opera (two days' shooting, standard Equity rates, no lines) and the Wicked Witch in a community-theatre production loosely based on *The Wizard of Oz* (many lines but no pay). To stay afloat, she picked up temp shifts editing entertainment listings for a local newspaper. Any free time Frida had on top of that was spent despairing. Could she not go full-time at the paper, her mother wanted to know. Or get a good job teaching secondary school, like her sister. Would Frida not consider something like that? Wasn't that what an arts degree was for?

The truth was that Frida was addicted. Every time she came off stage she felt like a prizefighter. The curtain fell in the community theatre and there she was rolling her neck, bobbing on her feet, flexing her prosthetic, wicked-witch fingers. Like she had been through eight rounds in the ring. Jab, bam, punch. Pow. She didn't know anything about boxing but she knew this feeling. Whatever role she had just played, whether she'd missed a line or soared through the performance, it was always the same thing. A bodily rush that she knew she couldn't control and wouldn't want to, anyway.

It had been this way since Frida was twelve, in the Thursday-afternoon drama class that took place in the airless community hall near her primary school. Had she ever expressed a desire to join this class? Her mother had signed Frida up to get her out of the house, because Edel, who was in secondary school, was at hockey then and it made sense to schedule both girls' activities to allow for one pick-up.

At first Frida thought the post-performance feeling would go away with practice. Even as a child she understood that things were scarier the first time you did them, that after a while they became easier. But acting wasn't scary. She loved when it was her turn to get up in front of the class, paired up with another child, running through a scene printed off and distributed by the teacher. Over time she came to think of the adrenaline that followed as a sign she was doing something right. It didn't go away, but it did become routine.

Frida had graduated from university and her days of being remarkable were long behind her. She knew she was one of so many young women like her; she could see this for herself at every audition she went to. Her CV was lacking in comparison to the other actors around her. Years of this had earned her barely more than a list of credits in student productions. At university she had done as many plays as she possibly could and now, in the sprawling open space of adulthood, she chased whatever work she could get her hands on. Dressing up as Jane Eyre for a group of secondary-school students. A music video for a friend's band, something nobody would ever see. The idea that she might still come off stage and have all that magic coursing through her – well, it was beginning to seem a little silly.

Frida wanted something else to happen.

The wanting was almost frightening to her in its magnitude, its depth. It coloured everything from the moment she woke up in her dingy bedsit until she fell asleep after a late shift on the paper. The wanting was about the capacity for transformation, and it made anything Frida already had seem wan and frail.

She talked about the wanting to everyone. She was engaging with what Edel called the law of attraction. Invite this something else into your life. Make space for it and it will arrive.

So Frida was in the pub telling Catherine, her old flatmate, about it. Catherine had stopped acting after they graduated, and Frida was grateful they no longer needed to compete. They'd both moved out of the flat on Grosvenor Road and Frida saw her friend was growing up. Catherine now worked as a writer for a TV soap and was buying a flat of her own with a generous mortgage. She owned an espresso machine and Frida lived in a bedsit. College felt like a long time ago. When Frida opened her mouth to explain, the words that came out sounded almost too pathetic to mean anything.

'I just want something to happen.'

Catherine nodded, brow furrowed, looking at Frida with a familiar concern. It was the same look she'd given Frida so many times throughout college, whenever Frida needed a dig-out, a lend of cash or a lift somewhere. It was painful for Frida to be on the end of this look. It felt like Catherine was scanning Frida's face in search of cracks in the edifice that might see the whole thing crumble and give way.

'I know what you should do,' Catherine said at last, taking out her diary. 'You should meet this guy I know called John Reddan.'

John Reddan was five years older than Frida and to Frida, at twenty-three, these years were crucial. John Reddan had had five more years to prove himself, to get established, to find out who he was and what kind of work he wanted to create. John Reddan had used those five years, Frida learned, to make plays. She realised that she had even seen one of them, at the Fringe festival. Reddan had reimagined *Julius Caesar* on a stage covered in dirt in which the cast walked back and forth, never looking at each other while speaking, stopping only between lines, not touching but simply miming their required actions. Brutus stabbing the air in the back. Frida had liked watching this production, thought it almost funny in its irony, shot through with anxiety though it was. But it was evident that not all of the audience agreed with her. The couple beside her booed at the curtain call. They did it with gusto, smiling at each other with contentment.

Reading reviews in old magazines before they met, Frida learned that opinion seemed to be divided on Reddan's work. Half the critics considered him pretentious, messy, his work banal in its attempts to shock. The other half considered it to be emotionally raw and honest in its examination of the anxieties of the era. John Reddan was quoted in one review she found, saying it was the actors that interested him most in any production. The muck, the choreography, the staging, was all set dressing. It was the actors and whether or not they could be truthful about who they were and why that was most important.

Frida was to meet John in Kehoe's on Anne Street South. Catherine had said he was always there, aim for 3 p.m. and you'll find him in the back room reading, nursing a pint. He knows you're coming. When Frida arrived just after 3 p.m. there was only one person in the back room; he was tall, rangy, putting on his black woollen coat with his back to her.

'John?' she called, and the man turned around.

'Aha,' he said. 'I was thinking you weren't going to show up.' He sat down again.

'Sorry. I didn't know I was late. Can I buy you a pint?'

'You're grand.'

His eyes flickered over her as she took a seat on the stool opposite. John Reddan had a prominent brow, aquiline nose, and a shock of brown hair that stuck up like a cartoon character's. He sat with one hand splayed on his knee; his limbs were unusually spindly, and overall he had the look of a marionette at rest. There was a strangeness about him that made Frida want to keep looking.

'Thanks for meeting me,' she said.

'Catherine tells me you're an actor.'

'Yeah. Or, I don't know. I haven't got much work lately and the stuff I have got, it's all crap work.'

'Crap work.'

'You know what I mean. Tiny roles, no lines, something

where they just need a young woman on stage for a few minutes. It's difficult, you know.'

'Yeah. It's supposed to be difficult.'

Frida blinked. 'What?'

'If it wasn't difficult,' he said, his tone verging on hostile, 'what would be the point?'

Startled, Frida wondered if there was a correct answer to his question.

'Well, maybe it could be easier,' she said lamely.

John's face broke into an uneasy grin. 'I need to run an errand. Will you come with me?'

Outside it had started to rain and Frida took a small, cheap umbrella from her handbag. John strode ahead towards Trinity, nonplussed by the shower.

'I saw your *Julius Caesar* a couple of years ago,' she said, trying to keep up. 'It was excellent.'

'Thank you.'

'The people beside me booed at the end. Did you get a lot of that?'

'Did I, or do I?'

'Either, I suppose.'

John glanced back at her over his shoulder and she noticed that his eyes were a very light green, almost golden.

'Yeah, there's booing sometimes,' he said. 'It doesn't bother me.'

'What are you working on now?'

'Something they might hate even more.'

'Are there any roles for women in their early twenties?'

They came to the traffic lights at College Green and she watched John press the button over and over.

'Is that how you think of yourself, Frida? As nothing more than "a woman in her early twenties?"' With his free hand he made air quotes around the tail end of his sentence.

There was a stab of panic in Frida's chest, like she'd lost her footing on a rocky path.

'I just—'

'I'm joking with you,' he said in monotone. 'I think you should think more of yourself.'

Frida's cheeks flushed. The pedestrian light turned green and John was off again, tearing down the wet road towards the river.

'Where are we going?' she asked breathlessly, one step behind him.

'I've to collect something.'

Across the river they passed the Abbey Theatre, then took a turn down a lane Frida didn't know.

'Why is work so difficult for you right now?' he asked, without looking at her.

'A lack of good roles,' she replied automatically.

'Yes. Sure. That's always the problem. But other than that, what has changed for you, Frida? You personally, I mean.'

Frida thought for a second. 'I used to know why I did this. I used to like the adrenaline it gave me, being on stage, being someone else. I think I was addicted to it. Acting felt so strange, so unlike anything else. But I'm not sure anymore. Now I feel like there's no magic to it. And if there's no magic, there's no point.'

John laughed at this, giving his large head a small shake. 'Magic. Is there supposed to be magic?'

She was confused, almost embarrassed. Kicking a discarded can of Coke with her toe, she asked, 'What else would there be?'

'I don't think it's about magic,' he replied. 'Not for me, anyway.'

'What do you think it's about, then?'

'I think it's about trouble.'

John turned down another narrow lane and Frida took a look around her. She had never been here before. It was like there was a shadow-half of this city she hadn't noticed, a mirror network of lanes and mews and yards. Parked cars with tickets on the windscreen, seagulls tearing open plastic bags of rubbish.

'Where are we going?' Frida asked again.

'Just a little further.'

A sudden gust came down the lane and Frida winced, one of her eyes starting to water. They stopped at a mechanic's garage in the lane behind a row of dilapidated houses.

'Wait here for me, please,' John said.

He disappeared behind a corrugated iron gate, and Frida stood gazing blankly up at the back of the Georgian houses beyond. Each building was in a different state of disrepair, one with a bin bag covering a broken windowpane, one with a tree growing from the chimney stack, another with a roof that was slumped and had shed its slates. She was thinking about how it felt to be in the company of John Reddan. His way of talking was weighty and imposing. His sidelong attention, how he spoke directly while barely looking at her; it all made Frida feel more real. And more urgent, too, how she almost had to run to keep up with him. She imagined being in a rehearsal room with John, or on a stage in an empty theatre, him sitting there in the middle of the second row. She pictured blood on the floor. Well, maybe metaphorical blood, she thought. Something about it felt exciting. Dangerous, and new.

He emerged from the mechanic's yard, the gate slamming behind him. As he crossed the lane towards her, Frida looked again at the shape of him. His was an odd figure, long and gangly, his joints moving loosely underneath his big black coat as he walked. It was easy to see why he wasn't an actor, anyway. There was something about his physical form, something almost repulsive, like he'd revealed some vulnerability of his too soon for comfort.

'Did you get what you needed?'

'I did,' he said, though his hands remained empty. 'I'll walk you back to the Spire.'

They turned down another corner and found themselves out on Parnell Square.

'I'm working on something at the moment, but I don't know if it'll end up being right for you,' he said. 'I certainly can't promise anything. But if it does work out, I'll be in touch.'

O'Connell Street was slick with rain and the road snarled in traffic. At the Spire, they stopped walking. John raised a hand to say goodbye and Frida watched him turn away towards the river, without looking back.

2. *Bird* (John Reddan), 2006

1.

John Reddan was fifteen when his mother died and nineteen when his father stopped speaking to him. At the time of his mother's death, his parents had been separated for five years. Following the separation, John and his brother, Barry, the older by three years, remained in the family home. Their father, Dermot, moved to an apartment in town. John's mother, Eileen, died of a kind of osteosarcoma, a cancer the consultant oncologist said was so uncommon they might see it only once in a career. She explained this to John and Barry while Eileen was receiving chemotherapy in a room down the corridor, and she said it in such a way that implied its rarity might soothe them somehow. It didn't soothe John in the slightest. When they left the consultant's office in the hospital in Waterford that afternoon, he walked down the corridor with the hood of his sweatshirt pulled up around his ears, certain that the world was so full of rare and devastating things that even the most unusual tragedies could be rendered commonplace. In the backseat of their neighbour Emer's car, the two boys sat in silence as they were driven home again.

Was it this early experience of grief that set John on his path? It would be easy to think so. It was true that, after his mother died, John Reddan began wearing black more often, began obsessing over Samuel Beckett and watching the films of Andrei Tarkovsky bought in video shops on trips to Dublin. It was true that the creation of his new self put distance between him and his brother and father. Dermot moved back into the house, a thatched cottage on the side of a busy road on the border of Wexford and Waterford, to look after the boys and almost instantly it stopped being a home so much as a space for three unhappy men to sleep and store their possessions. That was it, really. There was no real parenting to speak of, and once both Barry and John had been dispatched to college, Dermot sold up and sent them a cheque for their share of the sale price. It was not a huge amount of money, but it was more than John knew what to do with, so he put it in a savings account and pretended it didn't exist.

'You know we've no home now,' Barry said to John. Barry had gone to university in Dublin not long after the death of their mother. John had followed him to UCD when he finished school three years later. Away from home for the first time, he liked having someone he knew in the same city as him. 'You don't want to take that money and buy your own place?'

John shook his head. He was a student. He was content to bounce from one crappy flat to the next. It was what everyone did, wasn't it? And money in the bank meant options. In the end, Barry bought a little worker's cottage in Harold's

Cross and said John could take the spare room if he wanted. It was good to have options, John thought.

The grief that teenage John experienced evolved over the years. It never dimmed, exactly, but sometimes it was charged by other things. After Dermot sold the thatch, the grief was rippled with anger. On grey autumn mornings waking up for lectures, it condensed into an existential loneliness. It was separation, wasn't it, from those around him, something that marked him deeply like a red-wine stain on a tablecloth. It was never going to leave him, and that meant that the grief was also confinement, mortality, an eye to the terminal above all else. Maybe this was why he loved Beckett.

John had spent his teenage years watching movies, tracking down obscure videotapes, reading film magazines, tentatively writing things that might, he hoped, someday become films. At UCD, he reckoned he would try to make films. It turned out that it was difficult to make films. It was competitive, and there was a paucity of money, of equipment and of people with the skills to use the equipment. John thought about the money from the thatch, but spending it all on making a film when he didn't know what he was doing felt reckless in the extreme. It was suggested to John by Sinéad, the drama student from Mayo to whom he'd lost his virginity during their first term, that he might make plays instead. And John, with Barry's words still ringing in his ears, that he had no home now, thought that plays might actually help with that, too. With a theatre there was always somewhere to go, a building with people in it. John went along with Sinéad to a student drama and for the rest of the year he went every week, helping out with other people's plays. Sinéad fell off the radar after a few weeks, changing her course from drama to politics, but John kept coming back to the student drama centre. Through observing the other students he started to learn about dramaturgy and lighting and Chekhov. In his second year, following a summer alone in the city, John went back to the student drama centre with a script of his own. It was not much, really. He wanted to write a story about death, but was too nervous to write about cancer. So alone in his room at Barry's, with nothing to do and no money to spend, John wrote a script about a man who has a heart attack and who, in his final moments, lives and relives a series of decisive moments from his youth. He meets his wife outside a chipper, he quits a job where the boss is a bastard, he tells his dad he'd been a horrible father. The drama society took a vote and agreed to put it on, and when it opened in October, Barry sat in the audience and applauded. John found he couldn't look Barry in the eye, and afterwards dashed off to the student bar before he had a chance to get backslapped by his brother.

From that point on, it was clear: John was a writer of plays. He shuffled through his classes, but his mind was focused on the student drama centre. He was always writing. The notebook and biro became an extension of himself the way the black T-shirts, the cigarettes, the battered Dr Martens had been since he was fifteen. The other students commented on it. You're always writing, Reddan.

It was true. He couldn't stop himself.

Because if he was writing, he had something to do with his hands.

If he was writing, people would assume that he had purpose.

Because a man without a home needed to have something else, didn't he? He needed to have purpose.

The other thing, too, the thing that the films had been about in the first place. Maybe the writing could be a way to get away from his family.

If that was the case, then why did he keep coming back to this new draft: a script about a family not unlike his own. Two parents and a little boy, the long lead-up to a painful separation. Every month he bought new notebooks, intending to start afresh and get away from the draft, and yet he kept circling back to it.

In his final year, he won a prize for best student director in the country. The prize came with a commission from a real theatre to show at the Dublin Theatre Festival. It was a tiny budget to make an even smaller play – no parents, no boy. But that was enough for John. He leafed through the notebooks and made a short one-man thing that lasted about twenty-eight minutes. It did okay. The reviews were positive, and critics were excited about the new playwright John Reddan. John felt good about this. Now he had finished college, he wanted to do something bigger. A producer called Katie MacGowan got in touch, she'd seen his work and wanted to meet for coffee. John agreed out of courtesy; wasn't this what you were meant to do? When they met in Bewley's he found her to be intelligent and a bit frightening, and full of praise for him. She seemed much older than him, though she was only twenty-six. Katie wanted to know what he was going to do next. She wanted to be involved in it; she was part of a new theatre company called Madhouse who were looking for directors to work with. Leaning forward over the table, in the dark wood-panelled room, she tapped the table beside his hand. The sudden sharp movement unnerved him.

'John,' she said with urgency. 'You should be dreaming big right now.'

John thought, what does big look like? From where he sat, big looked like Shakespeare.

2.

A few weeks after Frida met John Reddan for the first time, she was in the pub on a Friday evening with the copy editors from work. She went to the bar to order the first round. Beside her, two men she didn't know were talking about theatre.

'It was the oddest thing I've ever seen,' one man told the other. 'And I'm not really the type to be going to these things, but you know how it is. You say you're not the type, and then you find yourself in the audience one day, watching a woman stab a man in the back.'

Were they talking about *Julius Caesar*? Frida thought, and took her phone from her pocket to check it. Nothing. It had been like this since she met John Reddan. She would be going about her business when something reminded her of him, and then he was stuck in her brain for hours. She had his number, sure, but the idea of calling him wasn't right. Instead she'd wander the city, she figured. Dublin was small, after all, and their social circles within it even smaller. Sooner or later, Frida would run into him again.

Was the feeling romantic? Frida worried it might be. She had that familiar looping feeling in her mind. The same questions rang through her head any time she went somewhere John Reddan might be. Did that make it a crush? But it couldn't be. She didn't want to kiss him. Frida knew what it was to have a crush. She had them all the time, recurrent and tenacious as acne. This time there was none of the giddiness or warmth. Just all the obsessive thoughts, the confusion. So what did that make it? She wanted to ask everyone she met up with, the girls in the newspaper office where she freelanced, putting together classifieds and cinema listings for the entertainment supplement. Was it possible to have a crush on someone you didn't want to kiss? What was that called?

Time passed and Frida kept floating onwards. In between her shifts she took new headshots, taught children's drama classes, worked as an extra on a soap opera. As a favour for a director friend, she shot a music video for a songwriter named Matt Culligan. Matt was tall and ambitious, in his late twenties, capable of composing pop songs that had an almost timeless melancholy. The piano in his flat took up much of the living room and when he played it for her after the shoot, Frida's face went red and she didn't know where to look. As she was leaving his place he took hold of her on the threshold and kissed her, one hand on her jaw. The whole way home Frida thought about the soft cedary smell of Matt Culligan, the way the collar of his linen shirt had felt under her fingertips.

After the first time they slept together, it became clear that Matt was a casual sort of guy. The type of guy who'd call her on a Tuesday evening and say, What are you doing right now? Do you want to come over here for a takeaway? Their relationship, if you could call it that, consisted of late nights in his flat, hungover brunches, rambling voicemails that Matt occasionally left while in the airport. That was fine with Frida. She liked casual. Or she could pretend that she did. It was casual when he told her he liked her outfit in the coffee shop, and when he gave her a spare key to his flat as they sat in St Stephen's Green with their cappuccinos. It was purely so she could keep an eye on the place when he was away for work, he explained. Don't get ahead of yourself, Frida could hear in his words.

Matt was often away for work, travelling to Los Angeles or London to sell songs to one starlet or another. The flat on Baggot Street was a nice place to stay in his absence. It was a hollowed-out floor of a Georgian terraced building, polished into something much more modern with much less character. It was clean, bright and a little soulless. Before he left, Matt showed Frida how to water the bonsai on his kitchen windowsill. It was pleasant, being left alone there. She liked the boring black-and-white abstract art on his walls, liked reading books on the tiny couch beside the piano, going to the café downstairs in her flip-flops in the rain. All of it gave her an illusion of stability, like she had propped herself up somehow. Still, though, she had the feeling that something was missing. Matt wasn't the type to call much when he was away, and Frida could accept that. But all that free time. She could feel her mind wandering, sitting by the window looking out at the street below. She was at a loose end, and wanted occupation. What was John Reddan doing, she wondered, what part of the city was he in right now?

Home from California for Christmas with a light winter tan, Matt took Frida to a dinner at a friend's house in Portobello. It was the day before Christmas Eve, and Frida was supposed to be at her mother's, wrapping presents for the extended family. But Matt insisted and anyway, she was keen to see him. See if anything had changed in his absence this time. In the taxi there, his arm slung possessively around her shoulders, Frida realised Matt had an image of the two of them that she didn't really share. In the image they were a shiny, interesting pair. Frida was an actress, after all, even if she was never in anything. It helped that she was pretty and young and wore nice clothes that she couldn't quite afford. But she didn't feel particularly interesting, and increasingly she didn't feel like an actress. She certainly wasn't really Matt's girlfriend. At the party that evening someone was sure to ask Frida what she did for a living. What was she supposed to say? I'm an actress but not the type you'd actually see in anything. I'm an actress but I'm still waiting for someone to give me something meaningful to do. What was the point in all of this? The last time she'd gone to Edel's for lunch, her sister had gently raised the idea of emigration. London, New York, they all have theatres too, you know, she had said. In the backseat of the cab, Frida leaned against Matt, thinking for a second that physical closeness might be enough to fill the gap inside her chest.

The house in Portobello was beautiful, with an elegant hallway hung with oil paintings of purple mountains and female nudes. Their hosts were Michael and Hannah, a married couple Matt's age. Michael was a political consultant and Hannah assisted a painter whose name Frida thought she was supposed to know. Michael took Frida's coat and hung it under the stairs. The rooms smelled of cinnamon and there was a tree glittering in the window, a log fire in the long dining room. Frida was awkward in her dark-green velvet dress, wanting to adjust her tights, wanting to go outside for a cigarette in the fresh air, though she noticed someone smoking inside. A man at the other end of the room, leaning on the windowsill, tapping into a small glass ashtray. John Reddan. Their eyes met and he raised a hand to greet her while sipping from a can of Heineken. How funny he looked, Frida thought, so much stranger than in her memory. In the time since they'd first met, Frida had imagined him to be more handsome than this. Now she looked at his face from across the room like it was a riddle, something she could figure out given the time. Was that fair? Before she could walk over to him, Matt pulled her aside to meet Hannah, who was beatifically pregnant and smiled at Frida condescendingly.

Seated for dinner, Frida found herself stuck between Matt and their host, who talked across her about the merits of various American airports as though she wasn't there. From the other end of the table where John Reddan was sat, she could hear snippets of a gossipy conversation about an older actress she vaguely knew and admired. This woman's husband had recently walked out on her and their two children. In the note he left he said that he couldn't go on living with an actress – 'someone whose job', John Reddan recounted to the table, 'was telling lies.'

His audience issued a chorus of theatrical gasps. Frida's end of the table fell silent in response.

'Sorry,' John said, his eyes on Frida. 'I hope you're not offended.'

She could feel everyone looking at her. 'Not in the slightest,' she responded.

'For what it's worth,' he said. 'I don't agree. I think he just said that as an excuse. Really he wanted to trade her in for a younger model.'

'Do you know that guy?' Matt whispered beside her, and Frida nodded.

'So you don't think that acting is lying,' Frida said to John. 'You're saying that this particular woman happened to have a shelf life.'

'You're asking me if I think acting is lying?'

Frida nodded. The other guests were silent now, and she was aware that this conversation was taking all the oxygen from the room. People she didn't know were looking at her, forming opinions about her. But it was worth it, she thought, to see how John Reddan would react.

John leaned back in his chair, one arm on the windowsill behind him. Frida held her breath as she waited for his response.

'I think that depends,' he said, 'on who's doing it.'

3.

After Frida left home, her mother sold the small house in Deansgrange and bought a one-bedroom flat in Dun Laoghaire, not far from the harbour. It was a tight squeeze for Christmas dinner, with Frida, Edel and Edel's partner, Ian, who was a few years older than her. Edel was heavily pregnant and Una delighted in it, sitting her eldest daughter down and not letting her near the kitchen for the day. Frida was grateful for the break in normality that Christmas provided, a reprieve from worrying about her future. At the dinner table Edel told long stories about ultrasounds and parking at the Coombe, and Ian nodded along blankly, a lightly dazed look on his face. Una added in stories of her pregnancies, reminiscing about mood swings and hankerings for pickle juice.

Una had Edel and Frida by herself, slightly later in life. When the girls were growing up, Una had always been very open and honest about how things had happened. She had never really been 'with' their father, Simon, who was ten years younger and an architect who worked with her in the county council offices. They'd had a quiet relationship that, by mutual agreement, they attempted to keep hidden from their colleagues. It led to two pregnancies in quick succession, and it ended decisively when Frida was in nappies. After that, Una had raised the girls almost entirely on her own. The way Una told it when the girls asked, there was no question whether or not she should have this man's babies. This was for two reasons. The first was that pregnancy itself had come as a surprise – she had been told by a consultant that her teenage struggle with anorexia had most likely left her infertile – and the second was that she had a lingering suspicion that abortion was sinful, despite going on the marches and voting in the referendums with her peers. Her age, also, was a factor – thirty-six when Edel was conceived. Una told the girls that she'd felt like it was either now or never.

Simon was 'Simon', never 'Dad'. He sent cards at Christmas and plenty of money to Una, apparently. Once a year, on a date halfway between Edel's birthday (August) and Frida's (September), he took the girls to Eddie Rocket's for 'birthday burgers'. He treated them with curiosity, like they were exchange students from another country, his first exposure to the culture of girlhood. This was good, Edel reckoned once they were teenagers. It meant he never told them what to do, or what he thought they should do.

Their mother told them what she thought they should do constantly; it was the soundtrack to life in Deansgrange. Edel was the difficult one, the catalyst for shouting matches, the slammer of doors. What a way to spend your teenage years, Frida used to think, watching the two of them go at it. Frida couldn't see why Edel didn't just stay away from their mother when she felt this angry. It was easy to avoid confrontation. Why didn't everyone do it?

Simon remarried when Frida and Edel were thirteen and sixteen. They were not invited to the wedding, but they looked at the pictures the next time he brought them for birthday burgers. Frida took a photo in her hand and stared at it for a long, long time. The woman who was now Simon's wife was called Christina, and she had dark hair in a pixie cut. She looked very pretty in her meringue-white dress.

'Does this make her our stepmother?' Frida asked.

'No,' Simon said, shaking his head.

Neither Frida nor Edel ever met Christina. At some point in Frida's late teens, Simon and Christina and their two young boys moved to Dubai. By this point, birthday burgers had been replaced by the occasional card, sometimes with a cheque for a couple of hundred quid folded into it. After the move, it was like they didn't have a dad at all, absent or otherwise.

Una came to expect Frida to fill the void left by Edel's anger. Frida was the good daughter, the uncomplicated one. When Edel left to study arts in Maynooth, it was as though the house itself breathed a sigh of relief. In her last year of school, Frida found that attending to her mother's moods was absorbing more and more of her energy. Was it because Edel was no longer there? Or was it that Una was feeling herself getting older, watching her daughters become adults? Una seemed to age faster than Frida's friends' mothers. Maybe it was something to do with her unhealthy lifestyle – she was so gaunt since she never really ate, she chain-smoked and never exercised. Frida herself moved out halfway through her first term at university, into Catherine's flat in Rathmines, and although she tried to visit her mother weekly, some weeks were busier than others. Some weeks seemed to go by in an instant at that age.

Now, though, Frida could see Edel's relationship with their mother was evolving into something else, something adult. Gone were the rages and arguments and in their place was something informal, intimate, almost cosy, even if not exactly typical. It was like an agreement Una and Edel had made without Frida's involvement. There was an understanding between mother and daughter that was borne out of all those bloody rows. As adults, it was as though they were on equal footing with each other at last. Frida did not have this with Una. Frida was Una's youngest, special daughter. Their relationship could only ever flow one way. Una came to all her first nights and often wore lipstick and her one pair of earrings. She waited for Frida to emerge after the performance ended and congratulated her warmly, kissing her on both cheeks, telling her she was wonderful and beautiful. And then she left, lighting a cigarette as she headed for the Dart. And Frida would feel guilty for reasons she could not understand.

But Frida tried not to think about any of this at Christmas dinner. The distraction of Edel's pregnancy meant that nobody asked her about work, or her love life. They ate and when it was time to leave, she gave her mother a big hug at the door and then clambered into the back of Ian's car. In the front, Edel and Ian settled themselves. Frida watched as Ian reversed out of the parking spot, her sister gazing hard-faced out the window. It was easy for Frida to sit in the backseat quietly, like a child, and be driven home through the city's near-empty streets.

4.

For the past year, John had been living in fear. The fear, lodged deeply within him and as immovable as grief, was that his last play had been a fluke. Unrepeatable. Also, that it was just a new staging of an old story: Shakespeare, and not his own writing. Writing was the thing that John loved most, obviously. And it was the first thing he'd done, when he had started obsessing over movies in the months after his mother's death. What fifteen-year-old boy saw himself as a theatre director? He hadn't even seen a play until he got to university, not a real one, anyway. As a teenager his knowledge of the world of theatre was mostly derived from watching reruns of *The Muppet Show*. No, John was a writer at heart. Everything else was set dressing. But for twelve months he had conceived of nothing new: no ideas, no words on the page.

How would John Reddan follow *Julius Caesar*? He had no idea. But it was what the people at the Central Theatre wanted to know, too. He knew he was lucky that anyone was even asking him this question. They had liked his *Julius Caesar*. Mark McCarthy, the theatre's literary manager, told John that his work was 'vital'. They were looking to commission him now, kept asking if he had any 'big ideas' in mind. Other directors, directors who were probably more intelligent and charismatic than John, didn't necessarily get opportunities like this.

The truth was that he didn't have any big ideas at that moment. Only the thing that had been in a notebook in his drawer for years. The thing that every few months he returned to again. He crossed some parts out, rewrote them to be a little weirder. He told Mark McCarthy that he had this thing and that it was small, but it could be big, maybe. That it might be difficult. John explained that it was called *Bird*. He almost wanted McCarthy to say, Look, it sounds interesting, but come back to us when you have something that isn't difficult. Honestly, John didn't really want to do *Bird* at all. Because *Bird* was about his childhood observation of the breakdown of his parents' marriage. He was supposed to be making things up, new things, not picking at the same old wounds over and over. Why would he want to stage this play? No fucking idea. But it would be nice to be working on something again. Feeling important. McCarthy said he trusted John, that there wasn't a lot of budget but that they'd love to have *Bird* on their stage in 2006. Brilliant, John said. For fuck's sake, he thought as he left the theatre, stepping out into another rainy afternoon.

John had passed the thing called *Bird* through many gauzy layers of allegory and expression. His mother had been dead years now and he barely even thought of his aul fella these days. Still, it needed to get further from them. It wasn't right, to make it about his family. After the meeting, John reversed the dialogue, turned the father into the mother. No. Didn't work. He put all three characters, mother, father, son, in a small box in the middle of the stage. He conceived of a rain machine that ran constantly throughout the first act. He thought it might be too expensive. He moved the characters around, shuffled identities. Daughter. Mother. Sister. He ventriloquised them. He thought: puppets? In the autumn he was ready to chuck the whole script and make it a mythic allegory, a retelling of the story of the Children of Lir that was in fact obviously about his childhood observation of the breakdown of his parents' marriage. Christ. No. Start it over. Rain. The box. A nest in a tree, a roadside shack. He made the parents into birds. He was getting closer. Early in November he called Katie MacGowan, who had produced his *Julius Caesar*, and who he suspected knew his work better than he did.

For some reason it felt like admitting defeat, waiting for her to pick up the phone. Explaining the mess he was in once she answered. It was oddly revealing, like inviting her into his home and revealing it to be a pigsty. But Katie listened and kept prompting him to say more.

'It sounds exciting, John,' she said once he'd gotten to the end. 'It sounds like you just need to figure out what it really is. Not what you think it should be.'

The next day she came over and they talked *Bird* to death. They mapped it out on Barry's kitchen table in string and drinking glasses, the salt and pepper shakers as the two actors.

'Make it smaller,' Katie said. 'Make it tighter. Get rid of

the child. They can be parents if you like, but the child is not on stage.'

She moved the salt and peppers forward on the table.

'Make it two actors, adults, in the small box on the stage. Man and a woman. The audience is the child. Make it about claustrophobia. I like your rain idea. Rain all through the second act. We can use hosepipes in the rafters. Make the audience feel unwell.'

Christ. Okay, then. He rewrote it all through that month, the dark of early winter encroaching on his afternoons. Katie was right, he thought. Now it was working.

There was a woman in the play. For a long time, John had assumed that she was older, the goodness in her worn away by years of this man who was not unlike his own father. Now he began to think that the woman could be younger. Not one of his parents, no, not part of the world of 'parents' at all. A little more naive instead, a little less hurt by the world. More like the girls he knew his own age. John thought the woman could look like Frida Slattery. He hadn't seen her act, but he knew from the moment she entered the back room of the pub that she was something he could work with. Cutting through the place in her little navy peacoat and ballet shoes. Like a girl from a Godard film. He had pretended to be leaving when she sat down. Knew he wasn't able to sit in the pub with her. Ended up taking her on a wild goose chase across the city because he'd had a few pints already, didn't think he could just sit across from her for an hour without trying to impress her. He had realised that as soon as she walked in. The way she moved through the bar towards him, the way her eyes searched his face looking for something, God knows what it was she was looking for. He would end up demeaning himself if he had to look this beautiful woman straight in the eye.

So off they went, him pretending he needed to pick something up. Thinking frantically as they walked down Grafton Street between the shoppers. Where would he take her? Over they went to the northside, to the garage where he'd brought Barry's car a day before. It was the only thing that came to mind. Went inside and asked for Alan, asked him when the car might be ready for collection though he already knew the answer. John tried to drag out the conversation, brought up football scores, traffic, the weather. He was thinking of Frida waiting for him outside, under her bockety little umbrella. Rain misting her fine blonde hair.

And after they parted at the Spire, John went back to Kehoe's and ordered himself another pint. He sat down with his *Bird* notebook and his pen and started crossing things outs. Begin the story earlier, he thought. The woman needed to be much younger. Prettier. Not unhappy, just backed into a corner. The audience was the child, Katie had said, and John liked that. The audience was the child. And the woman was Frida Slattery. He would write something that had to be for her and her alone. It was the only way to make sure he could get a hold of her again.

A couple of months later, after a few more rounds of revisions, he saw her in the Portobello dining room of his old college friends Michael and Hannah. Her hair a puff of gold in the winter gloom. The room all candlelit and soft, glowing faces. And Frida Slattery at the other end, in a dark velvet dress with fine straps that hung on her shoulders, trying not to meet his eye. He saw that she had a tiny gap between her front teeth that he hadn't noticed when they'd met. It made her look alluring in an off-kilter way, like a girlfriend of a member of the Rolling Stones. Star power. John thought: put that face on a poster and people will come to your show.

Over dinner she had a go at him and he watched it, how happy she was to make the rest of the room uncomfortable in order to connect with him. Ah, yes, it worked. It made him uncomfortable, being put on the spot, being challenged about women and their work and their looks. There was no way for a man like him to come out of that smelling of roses, was there? It worked, and he liked that too, how unafraid Frida Slattery was of pissing him off and being impolite to their hosts and ignoring the tall, good-looking guy she'd come with, sitting beside her in his stupid leather jacket.

The next day was Christmas Eve and he wanted to call her, to talk to her about *Bird*. But ordinary people spent this day with their families, didn't they? He had Barry, but Barry was in the office until 3 p.m. John opened his laptop and found the *Bird* document. He started to visualise it on a stage now, Frida as the woman, a little meaner than he'd thought.

Christmas Day with Barry passed as it always did in the years since their father faded from their lives after handing them the proceeds of the thatch. They were used to it now: a roast chicken in the oven and a slab of cans from Tesco. They watched the films they'd seen a hundred times – *Apocalypse Now*, *Goodfellas* – and crunched the empty beer cans between their fists when they were done.

After that, John waited. The turgid days between Christmas and New Year dragged on and, on the second of January, he called Katie and asked her if she knew this girl Frida Slattery.

'This woman,' he added, correcting himself.

And Katie did. Katie knew everyone, it was a character trait of hers. Katie said Frida was alright. She'd seen Frida in some short films and also in the pub; Frida, Katie reported, was a talented mimic. Good craic, nice to look at.

'But you can find better actresses in Dublin, you know. I get the feeling that she's not, you know, *serious*.'

'Serious?' John repeated.

'It's your play,' Katie said finally. 'You call the shots.'

Over the break, John had begun worrying that the certainty he felt about Frida was actually just sexual chemistry, the feeling he got sometimes around charismatic women, like it was inevitable that they'd fall into bed together. Was it simply that Frida was attractive and that he'd liked the way she put him down at the dining table? Embarrassing. But talking to Katie something shifted. For the first time he saw Frida from an angle outside his own. It was confirmation that she was a real thing, not some wispy figment of his overworked imagination. He decided to believe that there was something there. Regardless of what happened in reality, which was usually nothing, John thought you could probably run cities on the energy generated between directors like him and actresses like her.

'I'm going to call her about *Bird*,' he told Katie.

In *Bird* there was a man, too, but that was already taken care of. For some time John had been thinking about Chris Hammond. Chris was always around, a decent actor with a face for the pictures. John had talked to him about *Bird* already, bending the ear off him in Grogan's late one night after too many pints. Chris had nodded along, asked him questions about autobiography and memory. Now John could see Chris on the play's poster, too, if there was to be a poster. Thinking about a poster made it feel more real than staring at his Word document. When Chris wasn't acting he played the fiddle for the tourists in various Dublin pubs. He looked good in an Aran jumper. It was a nice juxtaposition, John thought: this handsome man in this weird little play. And it needed Frida to complete it.

On the 8th of January Frida Slattery came to the small room that the Central Theatre had given John for auditions. She was more petite than he'd remembered, taking off her navy wool peacoat and standing on tiptoe to hang it on the hook on the back of the door. She was pint-sized, a little curvy. That was good, John thought, for the role.

She took a seat on a high stool and read from the script, a page-long monologue from the Woman character. John let it drift over him while Katie took notes in the seat beside him.

The first time I met her she was down on her luck, John thought during Frida's audition. He was always doing this, narrativising things, pretending it was ten, fifteen years in the future and he was being interviewed about whatever was happening in the present moment. Someone in the future cared about the first time he met Frida Slattery. And the first time I met her, he imagined, she was being her usual cruel self. Ah, it wrote itself, he thought, breaking out of this daydreamed dialogue. Of course he had no idea about Frida's usual self, whether that self was cruel or otherwise. But it sounded right. It felt right, her sitting up on that stool, putting acid into the Woman figure's words, but then glancing back at him, a little teasing in her eyes that he thought was just for him and nobody else. It was magic. Beside him, Katie murmured that the other girl they'd wanted to see had texted and couldn't make it today.

'Can you come back on Friday?' John called to Frida. 'That way you can meet Chris and we can get started on this thing.'

The following evening, John and his brother headed into town. Barry had just broken up with his girlfriend, Elaine, and he wanted to drink a rake of pints and not talk about it. He was thinking about moving to Cork with AIB now that he was a single man. It would be easy for him to transfer, apparently.

John pretended to care about Barry's plans. He waited for several rounds while they talked about Arsenal, work, the news, Cork, the few friends they still had from home. John was waiting to talk to Barry about *Bird*. *Bird* hadn't been truly autobiographical since about seventeen drafts ago, but that wasn't to say that there weren't some core remnants of similarity. John and Barry's father was indeed a quiet man, prone to long silences punctuated by monthly bursts of rage. John and Barry's mother had also been five years younger than her husband, marrying him while not long out of school. Frida's and Chris's characters, however, were not their parents. They might not even be parents at all. There was ambiguity there. *Bird*, as John tried blearily to explain to Barry, was an alternate story, a path where the decay that led in reality to their parents' separation set in much earlier, not long after marriage, and combusted wildly before the two boys had a chance to be present. It wasn't easy to talk about any of this. He was shouting over the music in the pub. He could see Barry's eyes trail off over his shoulder to the football on the screen behind him; his brother wanted to get up, go to the bar for another round and come back to the table with something new to talk about. The brothers never talked about their family. They hadn't spoken about their mother beyond a stray sentence or two since her funeral thirteen years earlier. Shite luck in this family, Barry had said after the funeral, and that was the end of it. John didn't usually bring her up because he thought it might upset Barry, though he suspected that Barry might have been thinking the same about him. Now in the pub on Wexford Street, John was diving in, albeit cushioned by a number of pints of stout. He didn't just want to tell Barry about his play. He wanted Barry's approval.

'The aul lad isn't dead,' Barry said to John.

'Yeah,' John replied. 'But when did you last see him? Six, seven years ago?'

'Same as you, whenever that was. When he gave us the cheques.'

'Yeah, exactly. We're as good as orphans.'

Barry didn't say anything for a minute. 'Still,' he said. 'I don't know if that means you should put our family on stage.'

'That's not what the play is. It's different. It's—' John hesitated, hating himself. 'Art, you know.'

'Art,' Barry repeated flatly.

'And it will only be you and me who see it as our family history. Nobody else will be offended.'

'It's not about being offended. I'm not worried about you getting into trouble.'

'Then what are you worried about?'

Barry screwed up his mouth. 'You're the one who knows about this stuff.'

'Just say it.'

'I mean it, I don't know anything about what art is and that stuff. That's your bag. But I don't know. Is this worth it? Will whatever you get from this be worth what you're doing with our story?'

John hadn't an answer for him. He was thinking of the last twelve months of nothing. He shrugged and told Barry he'd email him a copy of the script to read for himself, then he stood up and went to the barman for two more.

They persevered together until just after 2 a.m., when Barry got sick on the way to the chipper and John decided they should head home and make a sandwich instead. He was getting Barry into a taxi on Wexford Street when he saw the guys coming towards him. They were saying something to him and John couldn't hear what it was but it wasn't good. He ignored them, which they didn't like, so one of them boxed him on the nose. That was how he remembered it but in fairness, John had had the same number of pints as Barry. Maybe if he had had fewer he would have found the whole thing a bit distressing, but the reality of it was he woke the next morning with a hangover and a black eye and it was almost funny, the idea of it happening to him. But his face was bloody awful to look at. Swollen and horrible, like stage make-up for a man playing a monster. He thought about ringing Katie, seeing if she had any way for him to hide it, folk remedies or special creams. John sat on the couch with a bag of peas on his head and called for a takeaway instead. He relied on Katie too much during the week to be calling her about his black eye as well. The swelling had eased by the time he got to the rehearsal space on Capel Street two days later, but the purple ring around his eye was still there.

'Well,' Frida said when he entered the room. 'Don't you look sexy? Like a Victorian pugilist.'

Frida was sat on an ottoman in the middle of the room, untying one of her Dr Martens. Compared to his groggy state, she looked clean and fresh, rosy-cheeked and smiling in a striped men's shirt and black leggings; John noted as she pulled her boot off to massage her big toe that the end of each legging went around the sole of her foot like a stirrup.

'Thanks,' John said. 'You should, eh, see the other guy.'

'Really?' Frida said, blinking as she stood up.

John couldn't think of what else to say. Chris arrived

through the door in a rush, out of breath and with his bike helmet still on his head.

'Hey,' Chris said, unfastening the strap underneath his chin. 'Sorry I'm late.'

'You're grand,' John said, turning to face him. 'I only just got here.'

Chris winced at the sight of John's face. 'Ouch. How's the other guy?'

'Was there actually another guy?' Frida interjected. 'Or was this a trip-and-fall sort of thing?'

'Ah,' John said. He felt the creep of self-consciousness as the two of them peered at his face. 'Yeah, I got walloped on the way home from town the other night.'

'Jesus!' Chris said. 'Did they take anything?'

John shook his head. 'Just one of those random acts of violence, I guess.'

'This fucking city,' Frida muttered.

'Should we just start?' John said, clearing his throat.

And the thing was that he had still never really seen Frida act. He was still relying on Katie's testimony, that Frida was decent in something once, and on a sense of sureness he couldn't remember ever having before. It was killing him, though, and he had to see it for himself. John had long admired Chris's acting, the way he could focus himself and allow the intensity of his performance to build over the course of a scene, rather than announce itself the moment he walked on stage. He was a slow burn. Chris had read earlier drafts of the script, the back-and-forth versions John had been working over recently. He had given John notes, quite useful ones, along the way. Now, in the rehearsal room on Capel Street, Chris sat down on the couch and said that he had a few more notes before they got started. John watched Chris actually take out a little notebook. He may as well have been donning reading glasses. Chris explained that he thought his character was too rough around the edges. He thought that it needed to be clear to the audience why this man was appealing to his wife in the first place, before things started to go wrong. (John had been hoping that Chris's broad, handsome features might help to make this obvious.) Chris said, with an air of certainty, that the man and woman needed to have chemistry if they were to be credible for the audience.

Frida was watching with amusement, one leg crossed over the other on the ottoman. Chris suggested, gently, that if indeed there were autobiographical elements in *Bird*, that there might too have been a hint of loathing, deep-seated or otherwise, in John's depiction of his play's father figure.

'Just saying,' Chris said with a shrug. 'Don't want to get psychoanalytical on you or anything and in fairness I myself grew up in a house with no shouting at all. But I'd say it's pretty tough going to see your dad shouting at your aul one all the time. I'd say you might come out of that with a bit of a chip on your shoulder.'

John, leaning against the wall by the window, didn't say anything, just took a long sip from his cup of instant coffee.

'I mean it's up to you, man,' Chris added. 'You can tell me that the script is the script if you want. But if you do think there's something there, maybe we can make some changes as we go along.'

'Maybe let's just see how we go today to start with,' John mustered. 'Let's get set up, anyway.'

Don't want to get psychoanalytical on you, John repeated in his mind as he bustled around the small rehearsal room, straightening the few chairs and the table by the ottoman. The two actors were settling themselves, and John wished he had another room to disappear into for a minute with his thoughts while they did so. He did value Chris's opinion, he thought, raking the flimsy yellow curtain to one side of the window and looking out at the street below. But maybe he hadn't been prepared for how exposing it would be to do something like this; how much of himself was being dragged to the surface from the murky waters of his brain, his memory, and would soon be tossed to the waiting crowd for inspection.

He couldn't keep thinking about Chris staring into his soul. John thought about Frida instead. Frida hadn't had as much time with the script, and if he was honest, John wasn't interested in her feedback in the same way. The two actors were bringing different things to this play. That was how John thought it worked. Frida Slattery was even less of a draw than Chris Hammond and while John had wanted her badly for this role, he knew he didn't need her in the way he needed Chris. If Frida didn't like the script, well, he thought, he could always find another actress.

But would he want to? Of course not. He remembered the surprise of her, sitting down at the table in Portobello, the plus-one of that musician guy, challenging John in front of his old friends.

Here she was now, retying the lace on one of her black leather boots, shaking her lovely fair hair out of the back of her shirt collar. Perched again on the ottoman in the centre of the room. Script in her lap. Her boot was still bothering her, there was a stone in it or something. Impossible to imagine this woman as his mother, but that was the purpose of the play. Parents were just humans, weren't they? John had gathered up his own memories and funnelled them into different vessels. It was what he'd said to Barry the other night. Before he got punched in the face. He hoped *Bird* was a way of showing that these experiences, these old wounds, were malleable and not particular; they could be known universally, they could be acted out by anyone, even this short blonde woman with the sleepy blue eyes and fizzy limbs, and this Hollywood-handsome man who people would pay good money to see take his top off.

'Frida,' John called. 'If you're happier without your shoes, that's fine. We'll start with a read-through, so however you're comfortable.'

He went to the far corner of the room and fiddled with the storage heater, switched it up to the highest setting. When he turned around, Frida had taken both boots off and was sitting on the chair with her legs folded under her. Her eyes followed him around the room like they were playing chess, and she was waiting for him to make a move.

5.

When Chris said to John Reddan that he thought there should be chemistry between the Man and the Woman, Frida wanted to blush. She tilted her head down, pretended to be removing a stone from her shoe. Moments like these she wanted to crack a joke. In school she had been the class joker until she realised that she could act. Maybe it was true, what the maths teacher who hated her used to say: Frida Slattery, all you want is for everyone to look at you. Well I hate you too, Mr O'Connor. And look at me now. Chris Hammond was a real actor, although like everyone else Frida knew, he had multiple jobs, many of them boring. But he'd been in the Gate, and the Abbey too. If Chris said they needed chemistry between them, well, Frida would bat her eyelashes and bite her lower lip all day long. The day she read for the role, John had said to her, Frida, I hear you're a wonderful mimic, and Frida couldn't help herself. She'd always been a good mimic, had learned as a very small child that if she could parrot the voice of another person, someone on the radio or a neighbour, she could make her mother laugh. And she'd realised that she loved to make her mother laugh, more than anything.

So Frida said his words back to him, in his very voice. *Frida*, she said to John, aping also his bad posture, the slight stoop of his shoulders, the way he balled up one fist and rapped the knuckles of it with the flat of his other hand.

Frida

she said

I hear you're a wonderful mimic.

And John Reddan snorted with pleasure at this, like it was the confirmation he had been waiting for. Frida smiled at him and he smiled back. Yes, maybe all she wanted was for everyone to look at her.

After rehearsal she walked to Matt's flat on Baggot Street in the eternal sideways rain that came off the Irish Sea and turned directly into air. Matt was home for once, sat at the piano with a bottle of red wine, and he wanted to know how the play was going.

She said, 'Do you know Chris Hammond?'

Matt shook his head.

'But you remember John Reddan, from Michael and Hannah's dinner?'

And Matt said yes, though Frida didn't think he did, because Matt never remembered people unless they were engaging with him specifically – it wasn't selfishness, she thought defensively, it was self-preservation, Matt met so many people, did so many favours. How could he be expected to remember someone like John Reddan?

'It's a good script,' Frida said, 'and I play the woman, and there's also a man.'

'A love story?'

'No, not at all. The opposite. A falling-apart story.'

Matt looked at her over the piano. 'Even a falling-apart story has to start with a coming together. You can't write a sad song without a love song inside of it. Do you want a drink?'

But she didn't want a drink. She wanted to make dinner and stare at the script, find the love story within the falling-apart story. She knew what it meant, what Chris was trying to say when he said they need chemistry. She wanted to talk to John about this. Frida put dinner on, supermarket ravioli dancing in a pot of boiling water, and texted John.

> Do you think Chris was right? About the need for chemistry

John didn't text back for hours, during which time Frida and Matt had dinner and smoked a joint and put on records, danced around a bit, watched the rain fall down the windows, and eventually went to his bedroom and had sex. When Frida checked her phone again, going to set an alarm for the rehearsal in the morning, there was a reply.

> Do you?

Beside her Matt was already drifting off to sleep. She stared at the message and typed a reply.

> I think chemistry can always make thing more interesting

It was the late hour, she thought. It made her feel bolder. Frida didn't expect John to reply, but as she was turning off the bedside lamp, she heard her phone vibrate.

> I think you're right, Frida. So let's give it a try in the morning.

Matt had already left for the studio when Frida woke up. She wanted to get everything right today: she ran a bath and put on a favourite outfit, a floral tea dress she had been wearing a lot lately, black tights, and leather ankle boots. She brushed her hair and pinned back the wispy bits by her ears. It didn't matter what she did. Her hair would frizz by the time she'd walked through the rain again.

The boys were already in the room above Capel Street when Frida arrived, drinking instant coffee and rolling cigarettes. She apologised for being late, but John told her she wasn't, they'd just arrived a little early. And then she was newly aware of it, the imbalance, that perhaps the two men had intended to arrive ahead of her, that John respected Chris more deeply than he did Frida. Chris and his feedback. Chris and his strong jawline.

'Where are we starting today?' she asked.

'The second scene,' John said.

John went to the middle of the room and moved the table so it was oblong between the two chairs. Then John moved the chairs so they tilted slightly towards each other and slightly towards the ottoman against the wall, representing the audience. Frida on one side, her script in her lap and Chris on the other clutching his copy.

6.

John had written a script in which all the scenes were fundamentally the same: the two actors sat on either side of a kitchen table, talking. Today he wanted to start with the second scene, in which the Man and Woman argue about how their lives have changed since they first met.

'Let's run through it,' John announced, raising a hand above his head and cocking it to indicate Go.

    You looked beautiful last night.

    What about tonight?

    Don't push it.

    Some husbands treat their wives with respect, you know.

    Shut up about respect. What would you know about respect.

John was waiting for what Chris had said he wanted, what Frida had felt compelled to text him about.

He could see Frida trying to muster the chemistry up. The way she telegraphed it, big eyes roaming. He could probably see her longing from space.

And yes, John thought, he had been right: Chris was handsome in such a way that invited chemistry, even if it wasn't there.

'Frida,' he said, raising a hand to stop the pair of them. 'Can you try it again? But with more subtlety.'

And this time Frida was much more subtle. She lowered her eyes. She had such long eyelashes. She glanced sidelong at Chris, who sat up straight, like such a small, gentle glance could hurt him and must be deflected with strength.

Oh, yes, John thought. Very, very nice.

'*Some husbands treat their wives with respect, you know,*' Frida said.

And Chris's lip curled with just a hint of pleasure, something that both husband and wife could share together. It was as though a memory of something better was passing over Chris's face and John suddenly remembered moments with an old girlfriend from college where the teasing was fun and part of why they liked each other.

'*Shut up about respect,*' Chris said to Frida, teasing her so delicately. '*What would you know about respect?*'

And Frida looked at Chris like she wanted to eat him up, and John wanted to punch the air with his fist but settled for slapping his knee lightly instead.

They were finding their way, mostly. It worked best when John focused on it, didn't think too much about it but just watched the pair of them. It worked best when he let them take his script and bend it lightly over the tops of their knees, solder it, agitate it just enough to see what kind of sparks could fly out of it. All week he watched them do this in the small rehearsal room. He had long since stopped thinking of this script as a Mother and Father at the kitchen table. Man and Woman was enough instead.

Friday afternoon came. They were tired, ready for a break. John's face still hurt from the incident of the previous week. The bruise had gone yellow. He noted a smell in the room that wasn't there before lunch, like stale bodies. It was distracting. It made him think of bedsheets. He stood up, went to the window.

'Do you mind if I open this?'

Frida shook her head.

'Okay. Let's go again.'

'From the top?' Frida asked.

'No, just keep going.'

Frida looked down at her script. *'You're not the man I thought you were,'* she said to Chris, downbeat.

'You're not much of a woman. You give me nothing to work with.'

Frida let out a little laugh. *'I don't think you know me at all.'*

'Stop,' John called. 'Frida. What's this? Why are you laughing? You're hurt. You're not being vindictive. You're sorrowful.'

'Am I? I read it as having a little dryness in it. I read it as her being pissed off at being trapped with him here.'

John looked down at his own copy of the script in his lap.

She was right, he thought, that was what was there on the page. The Woman's thin streak of malice coming to life under pressure. He had thought he knew that woman well. It had been easy to get her down on the page. And now it wasn't what he wanted.

'No,' he said, aware of Chris watching closely. 'There's time to be pissed off later. Let's do it again, but with sorrow instead of malice.'

Frida crossed her arms. 'No.'

'What do you mean, no?'

'I think malice trumps sorrow here.'

'How can malice trump sorrow?'

She sat forward, raking a hand through her hair, and fixed him a knowing smile.

'Let me put it this way. I've been in her place; I've heard men who are supposed to care about me tell me all sorts of trash about myself.'

'So you know better than I do?' John countered.

'I just have a different perspective.'

'But you're not the director here, are you?'

Frida frowned uncertainly; it was an expression he had not yet seen on her face.

'No,' she said. 'I'm not the director.'

John shifted on the ottoman. Frustration rose up within him. With one hand he rolled up his script and batted it off his knee.

'In fact, Frida, you're just some random actress. And now you know the script better than the guy who wrote it and who, let's not forget, hired you in the first place.'

'Hey, hey,' Chris interjected.

Frida ignored him. 'It's not about who knows better than who,' she replied cautiously, her voice much softer. 'All I'm saying is that I feel like I recognise this woman. I know her.'

John folded his arms and looked at her. He wanted to throttle her. Or at the very least, fire her. 'And so do I,' he said. 'She's sorrowful, not malicious.'

'In fairness,' Chris said to Frida. 'He did write the script. It's his ma, after all.'

'Fuck's sake, Chris,' John barked, standing up from the ottoman. 'Shut up. It is not supposed to be my mam in here.'

Chris gave a sheepish grimace and pretended to zip his mouth shut.

'Malice doesn't trump bloody sorrow,' John went on, reaching for his coat. 'Look, I need to go and get something for this fucking bruise. Let's take ten minutes.'

'I've got ibuprofen if you want,' Frida said, leaning backwards on the two rear legs of her chair. He ignored her and pushed open the fire door.

Outside on Capel Street rain was falling in thin, invisible film. It was like gauze, a layer of wet grey haze through which one had to squint to see the city. John walked down towards the Liffey. It was ridiculous. Malice shouldn't trump fucking sorrow. He knew that woman better than Frida ever would. Didn't he? What a fucking farce. What was an actress for, exactly? Did she go through life like this, telling people how to do their jobs? Saying that she knew men who put women down. Waving it in his face, her romantic past. How did she manage to get any work in the theatre? He supposed that maybe she didn't, really. John supposed that he had been the only one to take a chance on Frida Slattery. Perhaps that had been a mistake. The rehearsal room was not meant to be a space where he was overruled or made to feel unsure of himself. He wanted to call Katie to complain, but couldn't let her know that she had been right about Frida Slattery. Yes, Katie, he could have found plenty of better actresses in Dublin.

And then there was Chris. Don't want to get all psychoanalytical on you, man. In his mind Chris was wearing tie-dye, long hair pushed back and smoking a massive joint. John hadn't invited anyone to get psychoanalytical on him, actually. He wanted to be the artist, the guy who said what they were doing. He wanted to be in charge for one fucking moment. It had been easier with *Julius Caesar*. People trusted him then. Why, who knew, but they had. Young wunderkind. And now this, twenty-eight years old. God, his face still ached. There was no chemist between here and O'Connell Street. Katie had only paid for the room until five o'clock and they hadn't made it through one whole scene yet that afternoon. He was wasting precious time now, leaning on the river wall on the quays, palm of his hand covering his sore temple. Frida had said she had ibuprofen in her bag. John turned back.

When he re-entered the room, Chris was standing at the window, one big hand on the frame above his head. Frida was smirking, God almighty, like a schoolkid who'd managed to make the teacher break down in the classroom. That was enough for John. For the first time he saw how young she was, here in her first proper theatre job. She was a child, he thought, someone who nobody ever bothered to listen to. If he remembered that, then he could surely take control of this room once again.

'Alright,' John said, taking his seat on the ottoman. 'Malice trumps sorrow. We try it your way this time.'

Frida leaned forward on her elbows, fingers intertwined. John noticed her thin wrists, the lumpy bone prominent on each side. 'That works for me,' she said.

'But one other thing,' John continued. 'The woman doesn't want to hurt the man, necessarily. The woman just wants to win.'

Slowly she nodded. At the window, Chris turned around to face them.

'Yeah?' John asked, rapping his knuckles on the table. 'That okay?'

'Yeah, I get it,' Frida said. 'We'll do it that way.'

7.

Did Frida like working on *Bird*? It felt like a new school year. Those first weeks in rehearsal were unlike anything she had done before. She moved through her days with a new confidence, an energy that came from thinking constantly about the work she was doing, the world they were building together. Sometimes she and Chris would walk through the city centre after rehearsal, not quite in character but not out of it, either. It came so easily, their connection, and on tough days it meant that Frida hated Chris because of everything that passed between the Man and the Woman. In general, though, she liked Chris. He connected with her in a very honest way, like he wanted nothing from her but her time and company. It was not something Frida was used to with men. She thought of him as a plug with a different adapter.

At home, Frida wanted to talk to Matt about her work all the time. It was the thing about being with another artist, wasn't it? It was why she'd all but moved into his place. The very image of it. The two of them sitting in the living room with a bottle of red wine, talking about what they'd done that day and how it made them feel. Matt was often away, though. And when he was home, he was always preparing to go somewhere, or playing the piano with the door closed. Was it possible that Frida was more alone with him here than she was on the rare occasions she went back to her empty bedsit in Rathmines? What a stupid way for things to unfold. On those sorts of evenings, Frida sent a lot of texts. She texted John quite a bit, angling for an invite to the pub or whatever his evening plans were. The more time Frida spent with John, the more she liked him. She liked how he pushed her and Chris in rehearsal. How discombobulated she could feel under his gaze. How he made suggestions (or were they orders?) that surprised her, unravelled her, made her aware of how little she knew about the Woman and indeed about love and its collapse.

Everything about *Bird* made Frida aware of how young she was. Not just green, inexperienced in theatre, but inexperienced in all of it. There had been boyfriends in college but nothing serious, and now there was this thing with Matt. Could you call it serious? They were living together, yes, but really she was camping out in his flat. He'd not met her family, nor she his. In fact, she rarely mentioned him around Edel. Matt was another part of Frida's life that would make little sense to her family. She was keeping up the rent on the bedsit because it was so cheap. She kept her things there. It was easier and anyway, she and Matt didn't share anything. Why would they? They'd been together about six months, and he'd had a whole life of his own before she met him. At times she didn't even know how she felt about him, really. It hurt, of course, when he was evasive with her about who he'd been out with. When he reminded her that she was such a small part of his world. But did she really want it to be more than that? Sometimes when Frida was with a man, lying beside him in bed, one hand resting on his chest, she felt so sure of herself. So necessary. She felt that it had been fate that led her to this place. But with Matt in recent weeks, the whole thing seemed so contingent that she was afraid to look too closely at the small things that propped up their relationship, that were keeping their life together afloat.

After Bird, she told herself. *You can figure all these things out after you've finished* Bird.

Sometimes when Frida left the room on Capel Street, stepping out into the dark evening, she found she could walk for streets and streets before she remembered who she was, or where she was going. This is John Reddan's doing, she thought when she eventually snapped out of it.

8.

On opening night John found Frida sat in the dressing room that was reserved just for her. Chris had graciously agreed to use the small backstage toilets to get himself ready, giving Frida a measure of privacy fitting for a leading lady. It was her first time in a proper dressing room in a proper theatre. It was the first time she hadn't had to share the mirror.

It was the first time, John realised, that he had been alone with her since they'd started rehearsing. There had been plenty of texts, yes, but not this. He closed the door behind him and cleared his throat. He looked at Frida in the mirror – they locked eyes for a minute, and then she smiled broadly. She looked beautiful. Bird-like. Her curly hair combed out and hanging down to her shoulders. He pulled up a small plastic stool and sat beside her. How could it be, that they hadn't sat together like this before? He was worried now about the door he'd closed behind him. What message it sent to the others backstage, to Chris and Katie and Katie's assistant, Aoife. The two of them in a room together with the door closed. But he was allowed to do what he wanted, John told himself. Frida was looking at him expectantly in the glass.

'How are you feeling?' he asked her.

'Are you allowed to ask that?'

'Do you mean is it bad luck?'

'Maybe,' she said, giving him a sly grin.

He leaned back on the stool. 'I don't believe in that stuff. You're far too good in this role for bad luck to enter the equation.'

'Stop. You're just plámásing me now.'

'What else would I be doing? I'm your director, aren't I?'

She turned away from the mirror to look at him straight on. 'Give me a pep talk,' she said. 'I am nervous, you know. I haven't done anything like this, of this level, before.'

'Ah, Christ,' John said, thinking. 'A pep talk. Look. You're going to be great. You know this woman better than anyone. You know her better than I do, and I wrote her. You made her into the thing she is now, the thing you're about to show everyone. You have that within you. And you can always fall back on that, if something falters. But you won't falter. It's in here.'

He took her hand, circling her fine wrist with his middle finger and thumb. He paused for a moment and then it felt like time was slowing down.

'It's running right through your veins, Frida. You're an actor. You're the real thing.'

He could feel her pulse beneath his thumb and had the startling thought that she was trying to tell him something with the beat of her blood.

'The rest of this,' he carried on. 'Me, the stage lights, the set, the audience. It's all surplus to requirements. All that's needed tonight is for you to walk out on that stage and show the room who you are.'

Gingerly she extracted her wrist from his clasp and slid her hand over his. Her skin was smooth, cool.

'You're ridiculous, you know,' she said, but she was smiling at him.

He blinked. 'Of course I know that.'

At the last minute, John decided to sit in the audience. Hanging around in the wings he felt too much like the director. He wanted to feel like he had paid to see this show. He knew too much, of course, to be able to take it in the way the audience would. But it was better this way. He pretended he was invisible sitting in the back row, by the emergency exit. He pretended he was just there to see Chris Hammond and Frida Slattery in this new play *Bird*. Ah, yes. At last, he had seen Frida Slattery act! He loved to watch the pair of them. Loved when Frida came in a beat late on a line. More than a beat. She came in two beats late. If this was rehearsal he'd be up on his feet, palm on the table, asking her what the fuck was going on. What's the hold-up, Frida? Get to the point.

But sitting in the audience, he loved this break of hers. This foolishness.

Chris was there beside her and he said, *You know what this is, don't you. You know that this thing is going to kill us.*

Caesura. John remembered the word from university.

Yeah, she said, a second too late. *Yeah, I understand.*

God, he loved that tiny pause. It was the thing that made it feel human. It was why Frida was so good, if indeed she was so good. He could never direct that. He could never make that happen, for all his bravado and his posturing and his desire. John loved that he could hear her mind working, whirring, even though her face didn't betray a thing. John loved that the audience around him didn't know anything was happening. Loved most of all that Frida Slattery just kept on going, like it was nothing at all.

But that was only for John. For everyone else in the audience this was something different. There were certainly people sitting in the theatre who didn't like *Bird*, but for those who did, it was something entirely new. It had been right to remove the child from the script. Because as Katie had said, you became the unseen child sat at the top of the stairs while downstairs your two parents fought. You could watch them without being seen. Like you were sitting in the dark of a theatre. These two people on the stage were not your parents but perhaps they were, perhaps you could see the resemblance. Perhaps you wondered, as the lights came down at the end of the play, if this man and woman, their names Chris Hammond and Frida Slattery according to the cast sheet in your lap, were in fact a real-life couple. Though they were young, you wondered if either of them had children of their own. How they knew to act in this way. These were two ordinary people, so ordinary that you almost recognised them as your neighbours or colleagues or the parents of classmates. You recognised them because parents, after all, were the first thing you ever knew. For this reason, you were struck by *Bird*, and when you left the theatre that night, pressing open your umbrella against the rain, conscious of the slippery wetness of the cobblestones beneath your feet, you felt certain that you had seen something real, lasting. Indelible as raw childhood memory, the loneliness of sitting on the top step during an argument downstairs that seemed, to your child's mind, like it might go on forever.

Afterwards, John lit a cigarette. It was raining still, and he stood under the pub's striped awning to stay dry. Upstairs there was a party going on. Standing here, he could watch people arrive without being seen. He had gone backstage once the curtain was down, pulled Chris in for a sweaty hug. John's eyes were wet. Chris was soaked from the second act's rainfall. Frida's gone already, Chris had said. She wanted to shower. We'll see her at the party.

John told Chris to go on, that he'd follow him there. Alone in the dressing room, John sat at the mirror and found some hair gel in a box of toiletries, pushed it into his hair and slicked it back. It looked better this way, he thought. He should do it more often.

He wanted to be the last person to arrive at the party, but he hadn't seen Frida go up yet. Maybe she was already there, having entered through another door. It would be stupid to spend all night in the rain. It was his night, he thought. He headed upstairs.

The room greeted him with cheers when he entered. He felt like a soldier returning from battle, except better, cleaner – nobody had to die for this applause. No real pain. John thought that *Bird* must surely be a success. He quickly found he was uninterested in finding out information more specific than this. A drink was thrust into his hand, a hand was clapped onto his back in appreciation. He was ferried from one corner of the room to another to be congratulated. He looked each person in the eye as they delivered their praise for his play, and he didn't listen to their words, just nodded and thanked them as sincerely as he knew how.

Frida arrived late. It must have been at least an hour after John's arrival. Two pints at any rate. She was with a man so tall he had to stoop gently to get through the doorframe. The musician who had been with her at that dinner. She had changed into a short blue dress, a shiny material that made her look like a Quality Street chocolate, with her black leather jacket. Her face was flushed, and she had applied a pink lipstick that he hadn't seen before. She was perhaps a little overwhelmed. The musician was wearing a similar leather jacket. Cheekbones, he had very nice cheekbones, John thought. He remembered a song of his that got a lot of radio play. A song about religion that was also about addiction and also something very rude, a sort of innuendo? John tried to remember the lyrics. It sold a lot of copies, he recalled, whatever it was.

Now he noticed Frida looking in his direction. She and the musician started to make their way across to the bar. Frida beelined for John's arms and they hugged quickly, her small frame tight against his torso.

'You were perfect,' John said quietly into Frida's left ear. He felt her nod into his shoulder.

'This is Matthew,' Frida said as she stood back, pointing upward.

'Matt,' the tall man said, extending a hand to John. 'Pleasure.'

'We've met,' John said. 'At Michael and Hannah's house.'

Matt's face was blank, but he nodded.

Chris was beside them, leaning against the bar. 'I feel like we've already met,' Chris said, and hummed a few bars of Matt's religious hit. Matt grimaced.

'Christ, Chris.' John said. 'How are you, Matt? What did you think of Frida tonight?'

All three men turned to look to Frida, who was agitating herself at the bar, taking off her jacket, folding it over her arm, then shaking it out and putting it on again. John wanted to go to her and embrace her the way he did backstage with Chris, sweatily and with deep affection. He wanted to pull her aside, so they could debrief properly.

Matt draped an arm around Frida's shoulders and gave her a little squeeze.

'Really great,' he said. 'Interesting stuff. The bit towards the end, where they've said everything they have to say – where they're just sitting there in silence for ages and ages while the light fades and changes. The way they're facing the audience then. It really felt like it contained all the years yet to come between them, whatever it was they decided to do. Right?'

John rubbed his chin. 'Yeah, yeah,' he said. 'There's a lot going on there.'

Matt smiled stiffly. John remembered seeing him being interviewed on *The Late Late Show* a year earlier, remembered that he had been tense in the armchair and hadn't seemed to love being asked questions.

'What are you up to these days?' John asked.

'Ah, you know. This and that. I'd no real interest in touring and recording myself after the first album. I realised that what I like most is writing, producing. So I'm doing that, mostly, for other people.'

'I'm gonna go for a smoke,' Frida said, zipping up her jacket and wrapping a little pink scarf around her throat.

'Cool,' Matt said, his eyes still on John.

'I'll join you,' Chris offered.

'I didn't know you guys were going out,' John said abruptly, as Frida and Chris disappeared downstairs.

Matt leaned forward on the edge of the bar, looked sideways at him. 'Yeah?'

John felt a wave of embarrassment pass over him. 'I mean that Frida didn't mention having a boyfriend, when we were rehearsing.'

'I don't know if *boyfriend* is the right word exactly,' Matt said, raising his eyebrows at John. 'We haven't really put a label on things.'

'Oh right. Okay.' John tried to redirect the conversation. 'Well, it's funny. You spend so much time with someone when you're in rehearsals that you come out thinking you know them. But really all I know about Frida is how she plays her role in the play.'

'She plays it well.'

'Absolutely. She's talented.'

'I've seen her in a few things now, short films and so on. This was the best she's been. Don't tell her I said that.'

John looked at him. 'You think she wouldn't want to hear it?'

Matt took a swig of his pint. He seemed tired of the conversation. 'No, I mean, look. I think she's a little in awe of you. I think she might assume that if this is the best she's ever been, it's because of you and not because of her.'

'It's because of her,' John said.

'Well, I know that,' Matt replied.

'I'm gonna make the rounds,' John said, and put down his pint glass. 'Nice meeting you.'

John got talking to an older couple for the guts of an hour. They kept buying wine, they wanted to know what John Reddan was going to do next. Would he do a film? Fuck knows, John thought. I literally just did this. I am still doing this. Yeah, film sounds good, John told them, nodding with enthusiasm. Who knows, he thought, maybe they'd finance it.

Frida appeared at his side from nowhere. 'I want to tell you something,' she said into his ear. She had the smell of the rain outside on her, her breath wet on his neck.

'Excuse me,' John said to the couple, rising from the table. Frida had him by the cuff of his jacket. She pulled him out to the landing where it was quiet and they stood alone by the threshold of the lounge. She let out a long, deliberate exhale.

'What is it?' he said.

'It's funny,' she said, looking up at him. 'I just realised how comfortable I feel around you. Like I can unclench my shoulders and be myself.'

John's lower lip curled into a smile. 'And who is "yourself", Frida?'

She laughed. 'Ugh. I don't know. I just . . . in there I feel like I'm playing a role.'

The landing was dimly lit and Frida had a warm glow, like she had carried some part of the stage lights with her after the curtain fell. John fought the urge to reach forward, brush a piece of curly hair behind her ear.

'What did you want to tell me?'

'Hang on,' she said. 'Do you have any notes for me?'

'Notes?'

'From tonight. Did you have anything?'

It was as though the question had only just now occurred to her. John's eyes fell to the cuff of his jacket, where her small hand was still holding on to the fabric. There were two ways this could go, he thought. He could treat her like he would treat Chris, he could find faults that were visible only to him and zoom in on them. He could pick through Frida's performance for an hour, until the bar closed and it was time to go home. Or he could just tell her what he wanted to tell her. That was another kind of truth, wasn't it? Her expectant face was waiting for his answer.

'Frida,' he said. 'I thought you were superb.'

She gave him a disappointed look then, like that wasn't enough, like he owed her more and she was being short-changed. It was such a delicate and tender thing, John thought, to take someone's work in your hands and to hold it there, like a small, scared animal, its heart racing, until it figured it could trust you and it settled.

'I really don't want to tell you that. I want to tell you all sorts of things you need to change,' he said, trying to keep her gaze on him. 'But I couldn't fault you. I sat in the back row, you know, watched it from there. And I thought you were brilliant.'

'I don't believe you.'

'It's true.'

Frida's face softened then, and she let go of his cuff, slapping him lightly on the upper arm.

'Couldn't have done it without you,' she said wryly.

'What was it you wanted to tell me?'

Through the door beside them, Chris was taking hold of a fiddle being passed to him. In the next seat, Matt steadied himself, clearing his throat. John watched Frida's eyes drift over to her boyfriend. The music started up, the violin first, then Matt's baritone that sounded generations older than him. Matt beckoned for Frida to join them.

'It can wait,' she said to John, and started to move over to them.

The room reorientated around the two men and their music. John was left alone at the other side of the lounge. It was like a scene on a stage, viewed from a dark corner of the wings where he remained outside the action. Their first song, a sad one, ended, and the onlookers cheered and clapped. Frida was smiling, her mouth freshly lacquered, her fingertips pushing her hair out of her eyes as she made her way through the throng. A woman with a familiar face stood up beside Chris, offering Frida her stool. Frida's older sister, John assumed. Frida took a seat beside Matt.

She can't sing, John thought.

But how would he know? He had never seen her sing. Had

never asked her if she could sing. All their time together had been in the service of *Bird*. He hadn't even thought about whether or not she had a boyfriend, hadn't put two and two together and connected the man he'd seen her with before with the men that she alluded to when they were thrashing out the script together on Capel Street. For now Frida didn't open her mouth, just sat beside Matt, swaying with the music a little, smiling blankly at him after he finished a verse. Opposite them a man was stamping his foot. Another was clapping gently. They were doing a faster one now, and John tried to focus on Chris. He liked when Chris played, had always liked it, the ease with which he moved the bow, the way he closed his eyes and tilted his chin and seemed to disappear into the sounds he was producing. If John focused on Chris then it was like Matt and Frida mattered less; Matt and Frida were just addenda.

What had Frida wanted to say to him? He wanted to go over there and grab her lightly but firmly by the arm. March her out of here and down to the rainy street. Stand with her under the awning and hear it. Was it something good? Must be something good. He thought about the two of them in the dressing room earlier that night, a million years ago now. He thought about Matt, the sly look he'd given John as John had said he hadn't known Frida had a boyfriend. Like, Oh, so you thought she was single? No, he hadn't thought Frida was single. He just hadn't really considered it at all. He hadn't put together the Frida he'd met at the dinner and the man who was sat next to her. John had heard vague gossip passed on by Katie, something about a rich man who owns his own house.

Katie knew everything about everyone in Dublin. Katie had a mind like a galaxy. Pity he'd never wanted to sleep with Katie, John thought, sidetracked, she was too practical, too sturdy, not his type. But no, Frida had never mentioned a boyfriend in all their hours in the little upstairs rehearsal room. So, no, John hadn't thought that Frida was single. If he had thought anything at all, it was that whatever was going on in her personal life couldn't matter much to her.

Now she was clearing her throat, too, opening her mouth to join Matt in song. She came in on a line about a big boat that would take the song's author away. John had been right. She couldn't really sing. But the room was looking at her now, not at Chris or at Matt or certainly not at John, who was signalling to the barman for another pint. The barman nodded, but he too was transfixed by the woman in the blue shiny dress, the pink of her mouth, the bright patch in the dark corner of the room, the words she sang and the way her eyes were closed, smiling, a reverie that John thought must have resembled how she looked when she was in bed with someone she desired very much.

John tried to run through all the things Frida might have wanted to say to him. When she walked in with Matt earlier, he had thought: boyfriend. Then: she doesn't love him anymore. These thoughts had come to John instantly, almost instinctively, as they had crossed the room to where he and Chris were leaning against the bar.

How could he possibly have known that? Apparently he was wrong about the boyfriend part, anyway. John remembered the way Matt's face hardened as he'd said, well, we haven't really put a label on things. John was realising more and more that his life, his world, was full of wide blank spots of ignorance. He didn't know how people worked. Unless they were people like Katie or his brother, Barry, people who were open and forthcoming with him about most things in a way that seemed innate. Otherwise, they didn't really give John any information about themselves. They kept such important parts of themselves hidden. So why did it feel like he knew Frida better than anyone else in this city? How did that work? It was the hours spent in the small room with her and Chris and John's words on a piece of paper in front of them and John's opinions (no, fuck that, not opinions, his convictions) about where the two of them should stand, what they should do with their faces. About when they should breathe and when they should pause.

It would have been a lie if John said he didn't like the power he had when he was directing. But he saw now that the power was not real. It was just a mimeograph of power. It just looked like power. A neon sign that read POWER. It led nowhere good, or useful. The power was far removed from what was going on in the other corner of this upstairs room off Grafton Street, where three good-looking young people were making music that was causing a grown woman in a brown fur coat to weep quietly, wiping her cheeks with the back of one hand.

And Frida can't even sing, he thought.

John supposed that he had thought the power – all the time spent together in that little room for so many afternoons – would get him something. It would get him closer to her somehow. Not necessarily sexually but also, not definitely not sexually, either. No. He didn't want to think about that, it made him feel grubby for wanting it. He'd just thought it would get him closer. Now she was singing on her own, 'The Wild Rover', of all things, Matt's turn to close his eyes in a hazy stupor beside her. Frida's voice was turning thin and weak at times, like something being stretched. John wanted it to stop. Wanted her to just fucking say it, tell him whatever it was. He turned, went to the door, downstairs and out to the wet street for a cigarette. He realised, once he was out there, that he could just leave, call it a night, go home.

On Saturday morning, early, John's phone rang. It was Frida.

'You said you live in Harold's Cross, right? Whereabouts?'

John sat up in bed. 'Why?'

'Is it Armstrong Street? I think I might be outside.'

He opened the curtains and looked out. There she was at the end of his street, wandering around the pavement with an armful of newspapers.

Grabbing his robe, he went down to let her in. Three days had passed since opening night, and they'd barely exchanged a word other than about the show.

'Reviews!' she said, dropping the papers on the couch. 'Put some coffee on?'

John ran the tap for the kettle. 'Why are you up this early? How did you even get here?'

'I walked.'

'From Baggot Street?'

'From Matt's, yeah. It's not that far.'

'Well, it's not exactly close.'

'Did I wake you?'

'It's not even eight o'clock. I'm surprised you found somewhere open to sell you the papers.'

'I was excited,' she said.

Sitting down at the coffee table, John handed Frida a mug. 'Okay,' he said, running a hand down over his face. 'Let's see what they say.'

She paused. 'Matt and I broke up last night,' she said, her fingers splayed across the front page of the *Irish Times*.

'What?'

'He's moving to New York for a bit. He's going to do some producing. He's a bit of a prick, don't know if you noticed.'

'I don't know him. We only just met the other night.'

'Yeah, well.' Frida knotted her hands together in between her knees. 'He's a bit of a prick.'

John looked at her. He was so rubbish at this stuff. 'Did something happen?' he asked slowly.

Frida stared at her hands for a second, then looked up at him, a placid expression on her face. 'No, nothing like that. It was me who dumped him, actually. Let's look at these papers.'

Frida had bought three different newspapers, but it turned out that only two of them had covered the play. John asked Frida to read them first, in case they were awful.

'You're a coward,' she said, then stuck her nose into the first.

Both were full of praise for the visual elements of *Bird*,

the interesting production design and the rainfall, calling it 'haunting' and 'beyond immersive'. The first review mentioned Chris by name but not Frida. The second review was longer and by a critic named Andrea Doyle, who they both knew and respected. It was devoted almost entirely to Frida.

'John Reddan is one to watch, and Frida Slattery a star already on the rise,' Frida read aloud, folding the paper over and handing it to him.

'Jesus,' he said, reading it for himself. 'Look at this.'

He meant it more as exultation than direction, but Frida scooted over nonetheless, curling her small frame up beside him on the couch. Newly he was aware of his grubby dressing gown, his various morning smells.

'We should call Chris.'

'John, Chris'll be asleep.'

'I was asleep, you know.'

'But it's worth waking up for,' she said, resting her head on his shoulder. 'Isn't it?'

He nodded and he couldn't help it, he turned towards her and kissed her lightly on the top of her head.

Frida sat up then, leaning forward and looking back at him. She hid her face in her hands and laughed.

'John,' she said.

'What?'

'Maybe I should let you get on with your morning.'

'Yeah, okay.'

The two of them stood up, and he took a step back from her. He felt her gaze slide to his skinny, hairy shins sticking out of the bottom of his dressing gown, his bare feet on the clammy lino of Barry's living room.

'I'll see you tonight,' Frida said, heading for the door.

'Tonight?'

She looked back at him. 'Work, John. I'll see you at work.'

3. *Graceland* (John Reddan and Frida Slattery), 2007

1.

Graceland is a small room, a dark stage. It is a woman's bedroom, a stool in front of a dressing table that faces the audience. Where the vanity mirror should stand on top of the dressing table, there is instead an empty frame, lined with fairy lights. Grace – a small-framed woman with highlighted hair and pale skin – sits here facing us. Once she comes through the door, dressed for the end of a night out, hanging up her coat and her bag and taking off her high shoes, Grace sits down on the stool and starts talking to the room while she takes off her make-up. The audience watches her through the space where the mirror should be. She talks about what happened to her that night at the party, how something bad happened, something she couldn't quite name, and how it caused her to spiral, thinking of everything that happened between them.

Graceland was John's idea. Wasn't it? It was hard for John to tell. After *Bird*, he took some time off, took some meetings, did a little work for a theatre in London. He sat on panels and assessment boards. He started dipping into the thatch money to pay the bills while he cycled through many bad ideas for new work. He discarded one draft after another. All he could see was that Frida should be there.

He remembered the last time they did *Bird*, him standing in the wings, watching her during the second half's rainfall, her wet hair, her T-shirt sticking to her back. He saw, from this vantage point, that the audience could not take their eyes off her. He remembered that review: Frida Slattery is a star on the rise. He felt a sensation like sand running through an hourglass, and he thought he had to get Frida in something new before it was too late. Before she wound up with a recurring role on a soap, or something that took her from Ireland altogether. The thought of it. In the months after *Bird*, they spent days together when between projects, sitting in pubs, talking shit over a pint that they stretched out for hours. John sat in front of Frida for whole afternoons while she talked about her life and the sky outside grew dark. The world turning as he watched her face change in the light. The image of her sitting at a dressing table before the audience was the first thing that lodged in his mind, and *Graceland* grew from there.

Since that moment in John's living room after *Bird* opened, the two of them had danced awkwardly around the prospect of a relationship. Instead of doing anything about it, they called each other up on their afternoons off. They went to the theatre and the cinema and then eventually to the pub, where John bought Frida pints with the money from his nest egg. He noted that Frida tended to adopt a sardonic, cynical tone with him. Like the two of them shared the same battle wounds or something. Like they were forced to sit together in the dim upstairs of the Library Bar on sunny afternoons because for some reason they had been kicked out of polite society.

She was newly honest with him, after *Bird*. She told him about her family, how she and her sister had been raised by their mother alone. She made their household sound like a sort of women's utopia, like the two girls had sprung forth fully grown from their mother's head like Athena from Zeus. Frida told John about how the thing with Matt Culligan ended, that she'd finally realised they didn't love each other. He was moving to New York for work and wanted her out of his nice flat on Baggot Street, and so she'd said there was no point in them continuing to pretend they were a couple, then. He'd looked at her then like she was stupid, she said. As soon as he got to New York, the first thing Matt did was post pictures on his Myspace of the beautiful woman he was now living with. Frida talked about the men she'd been seeing since then. John asked his questions carefully. He tried to keep his private life to himself when Frida asked questions of him in return. Not that his private life was all that interesting, one short-term relationship to the next, woman after woman breaking it off and telling him they thought he had commitment issues. Probably he did have commitment issues. He just couldn't picture it, moving out of Barry's and in with a woman, attending other people's weddings together. The same way he couldn't picture himself with a real job, a reason not to sit in pubs with Frida all afternoon long.

John didn't tell Frida that he was writing something for her. He felt it would be strange, for her to know. The pressure.

It might make her less comfortable with him, less honest about her life. He was waiting for the day Frida realised what he was doing, why he was always listening so attentively. He also feared that eventually she'd probe him deeper, ask him why he lived the way he did, why he was so afraid of commitment or if his grand plan in life was to sublet a room in his brother's house and fiddle around with little drafts of plays that wouldn't ever get made.

He kept the early drafts of *Graceland* to himself. His idea was that he would get it to a decent state, a palatable state, and then he would show it to her. Would ask her if she'd like to collaborate, fully this time. *Graceland* was not just a work of his. It was something the two of them could make as equals.

Then they'd go away somewhere, borrow a friend's house in the country for a week and bash it out. Complete rewrite. He had the bones, but he wanted Frida to choose how they fleshed it out. Do it together. Co-writers, credited as such.

He wasn't just being altruistic, of course. He knew that *Graceland* would be more authentic with a female writer involved. Who was John Reddan to know what went through women's minds? All he had were those hours in the pub listening to Frida. No, it needed a woman's name on the sheet. Frida Slattery & John Reddan. It was only fair to let her name come first.

Frida and John were upstairs in the yellow room in Kehoe's. The only people there. It was April, unusually bright out, and golden streaks of sun were streaming through the window onto where they sat, on a pair of bentwood chairs by the fireplace. He took the script out of his leather record bag, the handful of white A4 sheets comprising a single long monologue and a few meagre stage directions. He handed it to her with a caveat.

'I want you to write this with me,' he said, a note of reproach audible even to him.

'I don't write,' Frida said, flicking through the pages, eyes scanning the text.

'Look, read it first, then maybe we can talk. I was thinking that you give me notes on the character, and then we could redraft together.'

She said nothing, turning back to the first page and beginning to read in earnest.

'Please don't read it here in front of me,' he said. 'Jesus. Take it with you, spend some time with it and let me know what you think.'

'I've never given notes before.'

'That's fine. We can figure it out.'

Frida texted a few days later and said that she'd read the script and was ready to talk about it. They agreed to meet in the café at the Irish Film Institute. John arrived early. He was anxious and had been running through Frida's possible reactions all morning. Sat at a table in the corner, waiting for her, he wondered if he looked like a man on a first date. It was sort of how he felt – the butterflies in his stomach when he saw her enter the room. She was wearing black skinny jeans and an oversized blue-and-white striped T-shirt. With her hair pinned back, he thought she looked like Jean Seberg.

She sat down in the seat opposite, fixing him with a happy smile. That did it. The nervousness John had been feeling dissipated.

'I've no notes for you,' Frida said with a glimmer of triumph in her voice.

John stared at her blankly.

'I mean it,' she continued. 'I think Grace is intact, she's credible. And I can see myself being Grace, if that's what you had in mind.'

'Yes, Jesus Christ, of course,' he replied, nodding furiously as if he might otherwise lose his lead actress.

'I just get it. The end-of-the-night rush of emotion, the catharsis of talking to oneself, to an imagined audience, when you're worse for wear.'

She didn't say, and John was grateful, that it was obvious John had worked parts of their conversations about Frida's relationships into the play. She let that go unsaid, and John felt cowardly for how relieved he was by this.

He told her that he had a grant to bring something of this scale to the Edinburgh Fringe, off the back of the awards won by *Bird* a year earlier. 'It would be a very DIY-type thing,' he explained. 'It would be sleeping on a couch for the guts of a month.'

'It would be fun,' she replied, and he wanted to lean across and kiss her in that moment, the sudden rush of delight he felt that she was up for it, that she thought their work together worthwhile.

It was not a couch in the end, but a small guest bedroom belonging to the mother of a friend of John's from university.

It was their only option, given the circumstances. John was struck from the moment he left the airport how much he hated being in Edinburgh. Perhaps that was just the Fringe itself, and not the city. But within days he associated the look of the place, and the air, colder and windier than Dublin's, with all he despised about the festival. The stand-up comedians wandering the streets, begging for attention. Worse, the burlesque artists, the buskers, the clowns, the people on stilts. He hated all the particularly British brands of comedy – the women with wry smiles joking about the size and shape of their breasts, the men, clearly all very depressed, talking about their fathers. The clipboards, the flyers, the walkie-talkies, the branded T-shirts. When he and Frida walked down the Royal Mile together he sometimes held an arm around her, as if they were two retirees who'd turned down the wrong street in a dodgy part of the city and were intimidated by what they'd found. He hated with all his heart people who attempted to be funny.

'Why are they trying so hard?' he asked Frida one morning as they walked through town after breakfast, past cabaret dancers and stand-up comedians.

Frida snorted. 'Why did you come here, if you hate all that stuff?'

He didn't really have an answer for her, other than the grant. John followed the money like a dog smelling sausage, powerless over the direction in which he might go next.

John and Frida had not rehearsed *Graceland* as much as they had rehearsed *Bird*. His impression was that they both viewed it as a bit of a whim, albeit one that had taken up much of the last few months of their lives. It was a fun experiment, and one that was occurring somewhere so remote and far from Dublin – Scotland, of all places – that it might as well have not counted as reality.

But it turned out that it did count. In its first week, the show won a prize awarded by a broadsheet newspaper that was basically a guarantee of at least a few sell-out shows. Journalists came knocking. John discovered how much he hated talking to the press. His hands shook while he waited with Frida for each reporter to arrive. He drank too much coffee and vibrated lightly during interviews. Frida said she could almost smell the spikiness in him.

'It's like you want to be difficult with these people,' she said after the first interview, and he agreed with her, he did want to, and he didn't know why that was.

There was one journalist who seemed determined to give them a hard time. They sat with this man, who was younger than both of them and had a Home Counties accent, at the bar where *Graceland* was running, and listened to him talk. He told them their play had no good jokes. (It's not a comedy, John informed him.) He said it was unclear if Grace herself was supposed to be English or 'foreign', due to her accent, which was essentially Frida's own accent. He said it was boring for an audience who had come expecting something a bit more upbeat. There are a lot of comedy shows out there, the man pointed out. Then he said the script was probably sexist, and gave Frida a pointed look, like it was her fault.

'Are you planning on asking us any questions?' Frida asked him.

'I thought your play was dull,' the man announced.

'Were you expecting more explosions, or...?' John interjected.

'I think people come to the Fringe looking for a good time, not a lecture on sexual politics.'

Frida gave him a winning smile. 'Maybe you're right. But we've sold out tonight's show and tomorrow's, so I'd let the audience decide for themselves.'

After the man left, John went to the bar and ordered two whiskeys. He sat down beside Frida.

'If it's okay with you,' he said, 'I'll let you do the rest of the press.'

After that, Frida and John's roles became more clearly defined. She was Grace. He was the facilitator of *Graceland*, the play's enforcer. Frida would talk as much as she needed to, and John would lurk in the shadows with his arms folded, ready to shut things down if necessary. Frida said it was never necessary. Frida, he was quickly realising, could talk her way into or out of anything.

Maybe that was why the play was a sell-out for most of its run. People queued outside in case of unfilled seats. John didn't mention this to Frida backstage, though obviously she was aware. Frida's a racehorse, he thought. You do what you must to avoid spooking the racehorse. The press, it seemed, had started to assume that *Graceland* was a work of memoir by Frida Slattery. Since his early retreat to the shadows, many of the reviews barely mentioned John Reddan. One described him not as the play's writer or director but 'a sort of steward of Frida Slattery's own truth'.

Frida laughed at this. 'Because I'm a woman and Grace is a woman it's got to be about me? Ridiculous.'

John knew it wasn't just a raw fact of gender. It was the way Frida played it, the way she seemed to delve within herself each night and extract something, slap it down on the stage beside her to show the audience. Look, she seemed to say, look at what I have throbbing and bloody inside of me.

2.

The first time Frida read *Graceland* was in the small Belgrave Square bedsit she'd moved back into after breaking up with Matt months earlier. From the opening lines she could see Grace clearly, which was to say that she could see herself. The stage in her mind was the same as her bedsit, a map made to fit the territory, and when she looked up from the page she was startled to see her room in reality, her possessions arranged around her like a set.

The second time she read *Graceland* Frida did so aloud, acting the role from the beginning. She began by going out to the dank stairwell of her building and putting her key into the door of her flat, pushing it open as per John's stage directions.

The effect of it was uncanny. The sense of dislocation, of disembodiment. But Frida wondered. What were the rules of all this? Where had John found Grace? On the third read, she took a pencil and marked the sections that she thought were lifted verbatim from conversations she'd had with John.

Very soon, the pages were littered with her notation.

All those conversations. So many days when she had been

trying to apply for jobs or to read and she'd received a text from John that said, Pub? Why had she always gone? Had she nothing better to be doing? After *Bird*, her job at the paper wound up and Frida went on the dole. The rent on her bedsit apparently hadn't been raised since 1994, plus she had a credit card and an overdraft, and most of the time it seemed like she might be about to get a decent acting job. She'd recently signed with an agency on Grafton Street, had headshots taken. She did a little voice-over work for radio ads. After her and Matt broke up, her life had taken on a funny kind of isolation, and she liked that. She had a handful of friends, people she knew from college and from theatre. Every couple of weeks she went out with them on a Saturday night and got stinking drunk, kissed someone she shouldn't have. Other than that, she saw Una once a week for lunch, Edel and her new baby girl around the same, and didn't get up to much else. Some of her college friends had gone abroad, but Frida could see no point in emigrating and starting over in London right now. When she wrote it down on paper, she thought it looked like she might be depressed. But in practice she felt the very opposite: a strange, hopeful kind of contentment. Since Matt, and since *Bird*, her life seemed to be perpetually on the brink of change, always at risk of suddenly improving wildly.

She knew John was interested in her as an actor and as a woman, too. At any rate, he clearly found her intriguing. He was always asking questions, and Frida supposed that she liked the attention. Attention was a form of currency, after all. Maybe that was why she answered his texts. She liked it when a mutual friend or acquaintance passed them in the pub and said, Ah, you two are here, like it was an inevitability, like they owned the place or were married to it. Yes, she liked how John's attention felt. She thought he was the real deal. He was the first proper director she'd worked with, after all, the first person who took what he did so seriously that it made her want to take herself seriously, too. And they were peers: John wasn't twenty years older than her, wearing a suit and with some big institutional backing.

When sooner or later he got a big job, moved to the West End or Hollywood or whatever, Frida wanted John to take her with him. Sometimes they talked about themselves in the future like it was inevitable they'd become famous and successful. They'll write books about us, Frida, John said one day in Kehoe's, swilling the ends of his pint around the glass. Behind him was the framed poster of Irish Writers that hung on the walls of so many Dublin pubs: all of them men, all of them dead.

So of course Frida had told him about her life in the way she did. And now there was this. Whole half-pages marked up in Frida's pencil, delineating where he had taken her words and used them as Grace's. Should she have been angry? She didn't know that she was. John had asked for her input on this script, but what was the point if he'd already gotten it without her doing a thing?

The other thing was that the script was good. The second time she read it, when she acted it out with the pages in her left hand, Frida lost herself entirely. It was like being in school again, undergoing an almost metaphysical transformation during a performance of *A Midsummer Night's Dream* or *The*

Crucible. Almost embarrassing. The edges of herself became blurred, feathered, smudging into the world beyond her. There was Grace, and so there was no Frida.

This is it, she thought. This is why I want to act.

By the time they got to Edinburgh, Frida knew Grace's meltdown back-to-front. She knew that Grace was not a lost cause. John liked to say that the play was about the disintegration of the self, that was why Grace was taking off her make-up throughout. In Edinburgh, Frida watched him explain this to various journalists from London and Dublin, sitting beside him while he said these words and sometimes even found herself nodding, her hands folded neatly over her knees. The journalists always requested interviews with Frida alone, but she insisted on bringing John with her. It was John's play, after all. And also she loved agreeing with John. It made her feel safe, and ten times bigger than she was. It felt like there were two of her.

But really, Frida thought Grace wasn't disintegrating on stage so much as becoming more like herself. She was telling the room something about herself that she could never have said at the party. Frida wasn't to know, the first time she sat as Grace on stage in the basement theatre in Edinburgh, that she would remember this play for decades, that she would someday be twice the age she was now and still thinking of *Graceland*, wondering could she reprise *Graceland*, or direct it. And wondering too, if what John had done to create *Graceland* was right, or fair, or was actually Frida's fault all along.

The work in Edinburgh was draining. Draining for Frida

to perform every night, and for John to watch her. For the two of them to share the narrow double bed in Leo's mother's house, coming home late, often after a few drinks. Usually Frida tried to pretend John wasn't there in the dark, lying beside her. One night she couldn't get comfortable, kept shifting from her left side to her right. John asked her to stop, and Frida said that she was trying, but she couldn't settle. So he pushed one of his arms gently under her back, and then wrapped his other around her front. Then he was over her, really, closer than she'd known that two people could get in one bed. It seemed logical that they would kiss. But almost immediately she pushed him away.

'John,' she said. 'If we do that, then what happens to everything else?'

'Yep,' he said. In the dim light he looked resigned. He knew she was right. Suddenly Frida found she was more comfortable than ever, falling asleep almost immediately.

Most mornings Frida was keen to try to see other shows before theirs was scheduled, but John refused. He wanted to stay focused on *Graceland*. But when he told her the next morning that he thought she should avoid these shows, because they might affect how she performed, she caught his eye in the mirror and smiled.

'You're not the boss of me,' Frida told him, exactly the way a teenager would say it.

There was a belief that Frida thought they shared, that what they had – these two plays, the first in Dublin and the second here in Edinburgh – represented something precious. Frida tended to think of it as a rare bonsai tree, something that had taken time to cultivate thus far and still had years left to run. It was long-durational work, this friendship of theirs, and to put sex between them now would be like watering the bonsai with 7 Up. There had already been one close call, the morning she'd gone to John's house with the *Bird* reviews. She thought of that moment as a path forking in the woods, and she'd chosen the route that had led her here, to a narrow bed in Edinburgh, to an armful of good press in the British papers. And to John, of course, John as enduring presence, not flash-in-the-pan, not a great story for the pub, not a sweet love affair that would inevitably sour over time, the way they all tended to. John as a mathematical constant. John and Frida, two boxes ticked on a list. Two plays down, how many more had they to go? They were still young. Careers were so long. And she knew that sex was not a reward for hard work. Sex could always be found elsewhere. Here she was, once again at a forking path.

For the remaining nights in Edinburgh, John slept on the floor beside the bed in a nylon sleeping bag. He woke up each morning drenched in sweat, his joints aching, his hair a mess.

3.

For its debut in Dublin several months later, John planned to extend *Graceland* by about twenty-five minutes, making it too long for Frida to sit simply at the mirror and take off her make-up while she talked to the audience the way she had in Edinburgh. He redrafted the script over the course of one frenetic week in September, He wanted Frida to start by making herself a cup of tea, fussing around the kitchen, then he wanted her to take off her party clothes – a fake-fur bomber jacket and a little stretch minidress – and change into pyjamas. Frida said no to the pyjamas, since she believed that on stage they were inevitably infantilising to a woman, and he conceded defeat. She found a beautiful silk kimono in Jenny Vander's vintage shop and told him she'd only do it behind a screen. It was early days, he said, with regards to set design. They could sort that out later.

The removal of the make-up at the mirror would still comprise the bulk of the action, but it would be broken up with Grace moving around the one-room flat represented on stage, making herself her tea, sorting through some piles of dirty laundry. Frida thought they could give Grace a cat, but John worried about the unpredictability of a small and unfamiliar animal. Frida thought that was fair. She didn't like improv or ad-libbing. The first time they did a whole dress rehearsal of the new *Graceland*, Frida felt like she was returning to her old school to show off just how nicely she'd turned out. She'd spent time after Edinburgh in a small role on Catherine's soap opera and doing the odd low-budget Irish film. But she still knew *Graceland* so well. She never made the mistake of thinking she was Grace. She'd learned that lesson from doing the press at Edinburgh. But she indulged in the pretence of it sometimes, like when she left the theatre to head home after that first dress rehearsal. Frida was still wearing Grace's horrible bomber jacket, her minidress, lighting a cigarette on the corner and giving one to the man outside the Centra who asked her. That's the kind of thing Grace does, she thought, handing it to him. That's just the kind of person she is.

In making *Graceland* almost double the length, Grace would need to reveal more about herself, her last relationship that drove her to the brink. Frida could see that as the script grew longer, it was hinging closer and closer to her own life. Conversations she'd had with John about how things had gone with Matt Culligan the year before were floating to the surface of the new *Graceland*: the coldness of that relationship, the way Matt had been making it abundantly clear that he'd wanted her gone and the way she just hadn't realised for so long, had kept thinking she could make things better between them until it became impossible even to try.

'I think, looking back, I had no self-respect then,' she'd told John once. 'I didn't know anything about myself.'

She had meant that before *Bird*, she hadn't known who she was as an actor, and as a woman. But John took these sentences and added them to the script, almost word for word. The play began as Grace arrived home from a party, and now it was a party where her callous ex-boyfriend had shown up, a fellow artist riddled with toxic insecurity and arrogance.

Should Frida have stopped him? She didn't know how. She loved seeing how John's brain worked. He could turn anything into a story, and turn any story into something that moved people, that made them leave the theatre blinking into the night, one hand over their heart, aching to go to the pub with whoever they'd come with and talk about what they'd just seen. If he wanted to use chunks of herself in the new *Graceland*, who was she to tell him not to? There was a part of her that was excited, honoured even, to pour her own life into what he was making. It was his work, sure, but it was hers, too. The week before the play opened, Frida spotted an ad for *Graceland* on a hoarding on O'Connell Street. Both of their names were on the poster. Equal-size font. In a way wasn't that the deal she'd made, when she hadn't kissed John after *Bird*, and hadn't slept with him in the narrow bed in Edinburgh? In return for the absence of romance, both of them were inching closer to the artistic lives they wanted for themselves. Both of them would get the chance to make something truly great.

Graceland
Peacock, Dublin
★★☆☆☆

A young woman comes home from a party. It's late, she's drunk and she's on her own. She's a little upset, and she's talking to herself, under her breath at first, while she settles herself in her flat. Then she's talking louder. She's talking about the party, which means she's talking about her life, and her life, she tells us, isn't too great.

This is the plot of *Graceland*, John Reddan's one-woman play, which debuted at the Edinburgh Fringe last summer to acclaim in the British newspapers. Now expanded for this production at the Peacock, *Graceland* stars Frida Slattery, the rising star we can take to be Reddan's muse. On stage, Grace rattles around her studio apartment, brought vividly to life in its student bohemian squalor. She makes tea, sorts her laundry and lasciviously performs a near-striptease behind a pitifully inadequate folding screen. While she does this, Grace prattles on about her famous ex-boyfriend, his jealousy of her and how their relationship ended. Reddan succeeds in making this play about more than one young woman's drunken melancholy – *Graceland* serves as a comment on the alienation of young people in romantic relationships, and the difficulties so many Irish people seem to have around intimacy. This is partly down to the raw magnetism of Slattery's performance, which feels like unalloyed honesty brought to life.

But there's something not quite right about what

Slattery and Reddan have made together. Reddan's script begins to feel a little more like spiteful gossip or petty jealousy when one considers the lead actor's real-life relationship with the musician Matt Culligan (the pair have been seen on red carpets together). In his use of Slattery's talents, as well as her near-naked form at one point, Reddan's directing feels almost exploitative, were it not for the fact that Slattery seems to be complicit in her own exploitation. It's the second time Reddan and Slattery have worked together, following on from the award-winning *Bird* at the Central Theatre a year and a half ago. Slattery is a talented actor, but it would do well for her to move away from this particular collaboration and spread her wings elsewhere.

4.

A week after *Graceland* finished its short Dublin run, Frida received an email from Matt Culligan.

Since Matt had left for New York, he'd sent her the odd email. Their arrival tended to make Frida want to roll her eyes – hadn't he said he wanted a clean break? His correspondence – which he wrote from a place of casual indifference, not romance – seemed to suggest otherwise. Matt acted like he and Frida were old friends. She suspected he liked the possibility of having her there, a ghost in his inbox, a book he could pick up and leaf through whenever he wanted.

Sometimes Frida replied to these messages, always matching his friendly tone. Why did she bother? Mostly she was glad they'd broken up. Frida knew they weren't compatible, he liked the idea of her – the actress, the pretty face – and not the reality. She wanted other things for herself. But sometimes she thought about him still. The version that had existed outside her emails. His physical form and the smell of him in bed with her, in his old flat on Baggot Street. Last time they'd spoken, he'd been in the process of selling that flat.

She opened his email now. It was short, comprising just a link to a recent review of the play along with a single sentence of text:

Good to see what you've been up to lately.

Now a shiver of dread went through Frida. It had nothing to do with Matt. The point was that Frida hated this review. She hated thinking about the *Graceland* redux, which had been a damp squib, three winter nights of half-sold seats and scattered applause. She hated the idea of Matt imagining what the reviewer said to be true.

Don't read the reviews, John had said on the phone to her the Saturday after the play opened in Dublin. Don't even get the paper today. He explained that *Graceland* simply hadn't translated well from the intimacy of Edinburgh's pub venue to a real stage, a real theatre. It was fine, he said. These things happened.

Oh, she wrote in reply to Matt's email. None of that is true, you know.

He wrote back quickly. I know, I know. Come to New York for a week. If you're free?

Frida had never been to New York. For years she had assumed she would eventually work there, though nowadays, when she thought of America she thought that at twenty-five, she was already too old. The day after Matt's email she went to Sunday lunch at her mother's flat with Edel, who was pregnant again. Frida sat in the armchair with little Sophie on her lap turning the pages of *The Very Hungry Caterpillar* and Una stepped out to the balcony to smoke. Frida loved her niece, loved the idea there would be another little girl here in a few months, repeating their own strange family with a second set of Slattery sisters.

After lunch, Frida and Edel took on the washing-up together in the kitchen. Hands in the sink, Frida gave Edel a rundown of the situation: the bad reviews, the email from Matt and his invitation.

'You know, I never really knew what you saw in him,' Edel said.

Frida chuckled. 'Really? The tall and handsome musician with his own flat.'

'Oh, come on. You know what I mean. I just don't really think he treated you all that well. Do you still like him?'

Frida's eyes roamed around the room where her mother had made a home for herself in the years since the two girls left. 'I don't know. But I don't not like him.'

Edel nodded. 'I get it.'

'Would you go, if you were me?'

'New York?' Edel laughed. 'God, yeah. Just don't be stupid about it.'

It felt like all her life Frida had been trying not to be stupid about things. The seven days in New York passed stupidly, though. She and Matt didn't bother to talk about work, or plans. Mostly they had sex in his apartment, a one-bedroom in the East Village he was subletting. He wouldn't tell her who owned the place. Apparently he'd signed a non-disclosure agreement. They walked around Manhattan for hours. They went to Central Park and Chelsea and down Broadway from top to bottom. They rented movies about these places and watched them in the apartment before going back out to the street and walking to various hip restaurants that he said were key parts of Manhattan lore. Frida thought she'd packed all the wrong clothes for this trip, it was February, much colder than she anticipated, but she didn't have anything that was both warm and alluring at the same time. She worried she was embarrassing Matt; he did not introduce her to a single person all week. Even when they'd been approached by people he knew, people who looked famous but whom Frida couldn't quite place, in bars or hotel lobbies, Matt said nothing about the curly-haired Irish woman who sat across from him.

Frida wasn't surprised. It was in keeping with who Matt was in her life now, or maybe who he'd always been – the casual guy, the bit player, the person she should know better than to expect too much from. Anyway, it was sort of nice, she thought, to be nobody at all. It was a bit like being on stage, except without any audience to speak of, let alone a director glowering at her from the wings.

She barely thought about John Reddan all week. And it didn't even cross her mind to go and see a show.

On Sunday afternoon Matt drove her to the airport. In the car, crawling through traffic on some freeway heading east – they all looked the same to Frida – he explained to her that he never drove to the airport, that going to and from the airport was his least favourite thing about living in this city.

'Do you think you'll ever come back?' she asked him.

'To Dublin? Probably not.'

Frida looked at herself in the wing mirror, noticing that she looked older now, in need of concealer under her eyes and maybe a haircut too. Then the bright, low winter sun shifted as the car rose up a gentle slope and dazzled her, and she shut her eyes.

Frida's flight was delayed. The gate was crowded with noisy families, sullen business travellers. She took out her phone to check the time and noticed a new text from John.

> Hope NYC is good. Can we chat when you're home?
> Also, when are you actually back?

She typed a message back.

> what time is it there?
>
> Pretty late, I'm just in the door. where are you
>
> in the airport. flight delayed. what do you need to chat about

John didn't reply immediately. Quickly Frida sent another message.

> you can't just say 'can we chat', it's scary, makes me feel like i'm in trouble
>
> You're not in trouble Frida. It's just work stuff.
>
> good stuff or bad stuff?

> Hehe. It's nothing big. I just want to run something by you. What time do you land? I can pick you up from the airport.

He was waiting at arrivals when Frida emerged blinking into the morning light. He pulled her into a one-armed hug, his chin brushing the top of her head. She could smell the familiar scent of him, cigarettes and damp wool.

'For a second I thought you'd be tanned,' he remarked.

'It's New York in February,' Frida said. 'I barely saw daylight.'

'Pity. How was your flight?'

'Fine, long. I slept a bit.' They walked across to the airport car park together. Outside Frida was cold, pulling the sleeves of her cardigan over her wrists as John fumbled in his pocket for coins to feed the ticket machine.

'Tell me what it is,' Frida said as he hefted her suitcase into the boot of the car.

He chuckled softly as they got in. 'Do you like this car?'

Frida looked around, shrugging. 'It's a car. Please can you tell me what you wanted to ask me now.'

'I could probably take better care of it, I guess. It was old when I got it.'

'What are you talking about?'

'What I mean is, would you like to spend a few weeks with me in this car, Frida?'

John started to explain as they pulled out of the airport and onto the M1. There was traffic, and Frida flinched at how his nerves were visible on the busy road, how he gripped the gearstick like he was worried it'd get away from him. He had received a grant from an arts-education charity to bring *Graceland* on a three-week tour of secondary schools around Ireland in the spring. While Frida was in New York, he'd gotten the script back down to its bare bones – just Grace and her make-up bag again, a stool and an empty frame – so it could be performed in half an hour. Half an hour on 'stage' (a space cleared at the front of a classroom, John reckoned) followed by half an hour of questions with the students, rinse, repeat in fourteen counties over three weeks. They would collect a brown envelope with a few notes in it as they left each school.

'It might be an experience,' he said.

'I'm not sleeping in your car for three weeks, John.'

'Ooh, the fancy lady, back from America with all her notions. No, Frida, we've a budget for B&Bs.'

Frida thought back to her conversation with Edel. Don't be stupid, Frida.

'Okay,' she said. 'What else am I doing this spring?'

4. *Graceland* (John Reddan and Frida Slattery), 2008

Frida anticipated that the boys' schools would be worse. It was a stereotype left over from her convent education: that boys, when left to their own devices, were uncouth and smelly, prone to hooting and rudeness. It took the presence of women to soften their coarse edges. But the first stop on the *Graceland* schools tour was a Christian Brothers school in Tipperary that surprised Frida. The boys waiting for John and Frida were a small group who had been studying theatre in their free time, putting on their own productions of *Hamlet* and *Death of a Salesman*.

'They're an interesting bunch of lads,' said their teacher, leading them through the building, which was more modern than any school Frida had ever been in. The teacher spoke with the air of a parent who'd accidentally produced a musical prodigy and was doing everything he could to keep up with his child. They were indeed an interesting bunch, and unexpectedly career-minded – asking Frida surprising questions about funding art and the value of her degree, whether it was better to accumulate other skills that could also be of service on set. Most of their questions were addressed to Frida, not John. This turned out to be a theme throughout the tour. Frida put that down to the fact that she was a young woman and charismatic and that the students had just seen her talking for half an hour before the Q&A session began. But sometimes John didn't even sit down for the sessions, loitering in the doorway as if he might need to leave suddenly and take a phone call or drive someone to the hospital. Frida didn't mind. It was just like Edinburgh. They both had their roles here. Driving to their B&B one afternoon during the first week, John started rattling off thoughts about her performance that afternoon – not notes, just thoughts. She was acting to one person, not to the room. She was too quick in certain parts. He thought the boys lost track of the monologue at one point, when she was recounting what happened at the swimming pool. Also, the thing she did with her legs, the right ankle was—

Frida cut him off, waving a hand. 'I prefer it, you know, when you're not watching every single performance.'

'Sorry.'

'You don't need to apologise, it's just weird. We're in these classrooms, packed with all these children and we have to just go on with things as if we were on a stage. If we were on a stage you wouldn't be here, though. It's different in the schools. I don't really enjoy it. No, that's not true, because I like the questions at the end.'

'They had plenty to say to you today.'

'Yeah, to be honest I wasn't expecting to be asked about my bank balance by a teenager.'

'They're not immune to the headlines, I guess. They're thinking about their futures in a way we probably didn't have to at that age.'

'I don't think I remember being that age anymore,' she said.

John didn't say anything. It was starting to rain, and he clicked on the wipers. The guesthouse they'd checked into earlier that day was coming into sight on the left.

'You don't like talking to the students,' Frida said.

'I don't really like talking to anyone,' he replied.

'But you like talking to me.'

'Yeah,' he said, looking across at her with a funny smile. 'I like that.'

It quickly became clear that their evenings would be the same everywhere: dinner in Supermac's or at the local carvery or sometimes just a sandwich from the nearest petrol station, tuna mayo eaten while stretched out on the two twin beds in the B&B. Reading, or watching a torrented movie on John's laptop. They'd started *The Wire*. On their weekends off they drove around the countryside and went for walks in the rain, then sat in the pub until dinnertime, reading the paper. Frida was beginning to feel she knew him so well – the good and the bad. It was as if they were two components of the same system. It was a pleasant feeling, a kind of romance, maybe. She wondered if this was what married couples felt, after years of togetherness. In the girls' schools, the students sometimes asked Frida what her parents thought about her career. Career, Frida thought. Was that what this was? Driving to Galway one morning in their third and final week, John explained to Frida how the arts-education grant had landed in their laps. They were at the stage of just talking at each other without even noticing if the other person was listening.

'You decide to start thinking of yourself as an artist and then as a result you have to start applying for things,' he said. 'You don't think, when filling out the application on your laptop in some coffee shop in town, that some of them will result in you spending a wet dark March driving into the midlands and beyond, explaining to sixteen- and seventeen-year-olds that no, your parents don't always understand what it is you're doing with your life but that there's been no complaints yet anyway, we'll see what happens around the Christmas table this year.'

'There will be other chapters in your career, Frida,' John added, turning into the driveway of that day's guesthouse.

Frida believed him, because that was what she always did.

Their destination in Galway was a girls' school in an old Victorian building just outside the city centre. It was highly regarded, apparently, and selective, with small class groups. Turning down the drive, Frida started to crane her neck, searching for something out the window.

'What are you looking for?' John asked.

'The statue of Mary. There's always one. Haven't you noticed?'

'I don't think this school is religious. It's one of these post-convent schools.'

'Doesn't matter,' Frida said. 'I have to find it. I feel like I get points for each one I find.'

'Hunting for Marys,' John murmured. 'Now do you reckon that would be spelled Marys, with a y, or like Marie with an s. Maries would be more grammatically correct, but it wouldn't read right, would it?'

'I think it would be better to avoid the whole thing. Call it something else.'

'Hunting for virgins.'

'John, you're definitely not allowed to say that.'

He turned into an empty parking space. 'Fair enough. What would you rather we call it?'

'Hunting for Madonnas,' she suggested.

'Ah. That's actually the name of my next project. A documentary about the queen of pop – and about her many body doubles.'

Frida snickered. John was biting his lip in the way he did when he was trying to make her laugh.

'Imagine you making a documentary.'

'Anyway,' he said, turning off the engine. 'I see her over there.'

In a small alcove beside the front door of the school, dressed in blue with softly rosy cheeks, face turned downwards and hands outstretched, the blessed virgin mother.

The story of *Graceland* made more sense in a girls' school, the idea of putting on and taking off make-up in the company of other girls was something that had cultural resonance, fluency, in a way that it did not when performed only in the company of men. Something about the male gaze, Frida thought in the small cloakroom that had been appointed their green room. The way they looked at you, even though they were just teenage boys, sometimes felt so much like an attempt at control.

Susan Gallagher, the English teacher co-ordinating their visit, said on the way from the staffroom that she herself had seen *Graceland* and told her class about it. There was an active drama group in the school, she explained, and recently she'd shown her Fourth Years the episode of *Culture Review* where John had been interviewed about *Julius Caesar*, and the class had discussed it afterward. Frida noticed a colour rise in John's cheeks.

The classroom was small and bright. Susan Gallagher had the thin blinds rolled down, to keep the low afternoon sun out. Frida smelled chalk dust and sweat, and for a second as she entered, she couldn't see John. Then, as she sat down with the heavy sigh that marked the opening of *Graceland*'s monologue, she spotted him in the back row, long limbs crammed into a plastic school chair, incongruously male among the rows of girls.

It was a funnier performance than usual. It was always odd how that worked, but Frida didn't question it. She preferred it when people laughed at *Graceland*. They'd cut some of the more risqué elements for this school-tour version, but for whatever reason, Frida found herself adding back in the lines about trying to hold back your own hair when crouched over the toilet bowl, about the indignity of walking home from a guy's house in the cold light of the morning.

She never looked at John during a performance, but she could hear him react. He was chuckling along with the rest of the class.

They were a good bunch of girls, and curious. When it was time to ask questions, hands shot up all over the room. One belonged to a tall, striking girl with a long and angular face.

'It's a question for the director, actually,' she said.

Her voice was deep and husky. Frida straightened her back and leaned forward in her chair.

'Go ahead,' John said.

'Why were you drawn to this play about a woman? Why

didn't you make the same kind of play but about a man, instead?'

'Ah,' he said. 'What a question. It's complicated, but I think when I had the chance to work closely with Frida here on the script, it became clear that we'd make something about the experience of someone more like her than like me, you know?'

The girl had her arms folded and a slight smirk on her face. She looked combative but engaged. She looked, Frida was surprised to realise, like she was flirting.

'But why didn't you let Frida make a play about Frida,' she went on. 'And you make a play about John.'

'I'm not a director,' Frida interjected. 'Or a writer. I'm an actor. It made sense that I'd work with John. I wouldn't do it alone.'

'Yeah,' John said. 'That's sort of how this stuff works.'

'So you're the director,' the girl said to John. 'And she's the actor.'

'Yep,' Frida said.

'And together you make whatever John Reddan decides you should make.'

'No, no, no,' said Frida, although she wasn't sure. 'Not like that.'

'What's your name?' John asked the girl.

'Róisín.'

'Do you want to direct?'

'Are you offering?'

Other girls in the room began to laugh, and Susan Gallagher cleared her throat.

John leaned forward, speaking as if he and Róisín were

alone in the room together. 'That's what I was going to say. Nobody is going to invite you to make theatre or movies. That's not how this works. Nobody is going to come up to you and say, hey, this girl seems like she has a lot of talent, let's give her a chance to make a movie. If it's something that you want to do, Róisín, just go and do it. Just find a story, and find someone to be in it. And go from there. You've got to show them what you've got.'

'Thanks,' Róisín said lightly. 'Good advice.'

Frida couldn't tell if the girl was being ironic, although she remembered being seventeen and not always knowing when she herself was being ironic, especially when talking to adults.

'That's the most I've ever heard you say in one of these,' she said drily to John. It was meant to be funny, but the class didn't even notice she'd said anything.

At the sound of the bell marking the end of the day, Ms Gallagher left them to go do some marking and Frida and John stayed with the small group of older girls. They were asking questions about studying in Dublin, how much was rent anyway and was it hard to get into television. Róisín was among them and Frida watched her move away from the rest of the group to a seat in front of John.

'So,' Frida heard Róisín say to John. 'How do I show them what I've got?'

Frida turned away from them, back towards the other students.

Outside the tall windows of the classroom, rain had started to fall and it was beginning to get dark. The radiators had long since clicked off.

'Jesus, the time,' Frida said. 'Should we go, John?'

The girls started gathering their things, talking of German grinds and hockey practice. Róisín stood up and stretched her arms above her head, like she'd been sat down for a hundred years.

'Walk us out on your way?' John asked her.

She nodded. 'I don't have grinds. I do French, not German.'

Out in the hallway, the other girls ducked off in conversation, heading for the lockers. The corridor leading to the school's entrance was narrow, and Frida fell into step behind John and Róisín.

'Where are you going tonight?' Róisín asked him.

'Oh, our B&B. It's not glamorous. We've got two schools in Limerick tomorrow, then we're back to Dublin tomorrow night.'

'Where's the B&B?'

'On the Dublin road.'

'I live that way.'

'You want a lift?'

Frida paused as the two of them turned to look at each other.

'Frida?' John said, calling back to her over his shoulder. 'We can give Róisín a lift, right?'

For a second Frida was thrown. Was there a correct answer here? John was almost twice this girl's age. The two of them were looking at her, waiting for her response. It had been a long day. She couldn't bear another moment in their company.

'I'm actually going to walk,' she said. 'I need to go to the chemist on the way.'

'Oh,' John said. 'Are you sure?'

'Yeah, really. I need the air. I've a headache from being in that classroom all afternoon.'

Róisín smiled sympathetically at her. 'It gets really stuffy in there.'

'It was nice to meet you, Róisín. See you later, John.'

Outside Frida zipped her coat up to her chin and set off down the tree-lined driveway. Something uncanny about being on school grounds after dark. It was windy now, the branches of the oaks and elms along the avenue waving overhead. John's white Fiesta beeped as it passed her, and she waved a hand in salute. She could see Róisín's shiny dark hair in the front passenger seat.

That's my seat, Frida thought, petulant as a child. Róisín was impressive, confident and very funny, and pretty in the almost glamorous way of some teenage girls. Frida had noticed how she had made John laugh with her jokes about private school boys and Patrick Kavanagh, and how each time he laughed his manner had softened and he became more comfortable with the whole group of girls. Frida remembered herself at seventeen: awkward, unhappy, only at ease when on a stage. At seventeen she was Maria in *The Sound of Music*, her last role before university. That had been when she'd realised what the stage did to her, how it wiped her clean.

This Róisín, she thought now. This girl. I'm not threatened by her.

In the chemist Frida examined the shelves. She picked up little crimson nail varnishes. She had last painted her toes when packing for New York: she'd had a vision of herself barefoot in Matt's place, breakfast in bed together, lying in the rumpled sheets more beautiful than usual. She'd wanted to have her photo taken there, maybe on the street, the light in the city somehow flattering and atmospheric, and Matt had taken a few on his iPhone, but Frida never saw them. They hadn't spoken in a while; there had been a few emails between getting back to Dublin and setting off with John. At the till Frida bought tampons, ibuprofen. She had been embarrassed to say that she had cramps. Headache was easier, she thought, walking back along the main road towards the guesthouse.

When she turned into the gates of the house, the bright motion-sensor lights flicked on at her approach. The Fiesta wasn't in the driveway.

Róisín's house must be further out the Dublin road, Frida thought. Or perhaps they'd hit traffic somewhere. Entering the bedroom she tipped herself forward onto the bed without turning on the light. There was nothing to eat. Maybe John would bring back something for them, takeaway chips and curry in a metal tray, two plastic forks. If she ate another on-the-road meal she would die. One more day of this, she told herself. Two more schools, one more day.

Frida hadn't noticed herself dozing off but when she woke

up the small clock on the bedside table said 23:03. The room was still empty. She heard the crunch of wheels on gravel outside and sat up as the front door of the house closed quietly and someone padded down the hallway. John opened the bedroom door.

'What happened?' Frida asked. 'Are you alright?'

'Yeah, yeah. Of course.'

'Where did you go?'

'Oh, we had dinner. We drove around for a bit, Róisín wanted to show me something.'

'Show you something?'

'Wittgenstein's cottage. In Killary.'

Frida spluttered with laughter.

'Sorry. She wanted to show you Wittgenstein's cottage?'

John switched on the light and the room looked newly ridiculous, all flowery textiles and pink doilies. He sat on the edge of the other twin bed with great fatigue and leaned down to untie his laces.

'The cottage where Wittgenstein used to stay. It's a hostel now, or something. It's in Killary on the water, about an hour out. It's where her family is from.'

'Has she ever read any Wittgenstein?'

John turned to face her. 'Have you?'

Frida raised an eyebrow. 'And you ate there?'

'Yeah. We stopped in a pub. Like a tourist place.'

'With Róisín in her uniform?'

'I gave her my coat.'

'Oh my God.'

'It was nice,' John said, standing up. 'We had a nice time.'

For a split second Frida saw his face change, like some light was passing over it. He looked much younger, and happier. She was embarrassed to see him like this.

'Okay,' she said, sitting up and swinging her legs off the bed.

'I'm going to shower,' he said, hand on the knob of the en-suite door.

'I'm going to bed.'

They didn't talk on the drive to Ennis the next day. Frida flicked through the radio stations, unable to settle on one that didn't annoy her. She had the map open in her lap to provide directions. John didn't ask for them. Frida was thinking about all the schools they'd visited, about how tired she was of Grace and *Graceland*, how long it had been since she first performed this play, almost a year ago now. How little John had had to do these last three weeks, other than sleep in unfamiliar guesthouses and drive the two of them down motorways and through service stations. I could have done this alone, Frida realised. Didn't she write most of the script to begin with? John was almost extraneous to proceedings, a name on the marketing materials, someone to help with funding, yes, but Frida herself was *Graceland*. That was how the students treated her, in every classroom they visited. And yet here the two of them were, on their way to yet another secondary school where John would be greeted by the teacher as the play's brain, the engine, and she just the rosy-cheeked face of it. His genius on one hand, and her charisma on the other.

'Did you get her number?' Frida eventually asked John as they approached a roundabout.

'What?'

'Róisín's number.'

'Number, no. I gave her my email address.'

'She's too young for you, you know.'

John didn't reply immediately. 'We got on well,' he eventually said. 'She's an interesting girl.'

'"Girl" being the operative word.'

'She's mature for her age. She's eighteen, you know. It's not what you're thinking, Frida. I gave her my email to help her find work experience when she moves to Dublin.'

Frida turned to look out the window. She started making a mental list of things she had to do back in Dublin: call her sister, make a doctor's appointment. Get a new job.

'Do you know the name of the street?' John asked, indicating to pull off the main road. 'The exact name. Some of them are very similar.'

Frida looked down at the map in her lap, laying her finger on the building marked School.

'It's just here up ahead. The second left.'

The first school of the day was a big and modern mixed-gender comprehensive. Half the students were out sick with flu and the other half were suffering from what their teacher described as seasonal malaise. Frida went through the motions of *Graceland* for the eight or so students in attendance. Everybody looked bored, even the teacher. *Graceland* didn't feel like a play to Frida anymore. It felt like the safety demonstration flight attendants did as the plane taxied to the runway. Afterwards, the students had no questions, apparently, so the music teacher stepped up, asking John about what he'd studied at university and whether he had ever had writer's block. In her mind, Frida was elsewhere. It was like her own school days, daydreaming, her gaze drawn to any patch of sunlight on the wall. She was back in Dublin, sitting in a pub somewhere, telling Catherine or her sister the story about John and the eighteen-year-old.

Can you believe it, she imagined herself saying. I walked home in the rain. And when I got back to the guesthouse, the Fiesta wasn't there.

But there was no way to tell this story that made it funny, she thought. It just felt a bit sad. A grown man, thirty-one years old, and a teenager, driving through Connemara in the night. What kind of a story was it, really? Romantic? Any way Frida might possibly have spun it would make her seem like she cared just a little too much about what John Reddan did, and with who.

After a chicken-fillet roll eaten in the car, John drove to Limerick to the next school. It was set back from the main road, behind a tall brick wall, a girls' school of the same religious order as the Galway school of the previous day, the one where they'd met Róisín.

'You're to stay away from the young ones here, John,' Frida said as he reversed into a parking space. 'Even if she tells you she's read the collected works of Plato.'

'Even if she claims to know where Karl Marx went on his holidays?'

'Especially. There's nothing more dangerous to a man of your standing than a teenage girl who knows more about Karl Marx than you do.'

'You sound a little jealous,' John retorted, turning off the engine.

The humour left the car like a popped balloon. Frida reached into the footwell for her bag and got out.

'That was a joke,' John called to her. He went to get the frame from the boot, but she didn't wait or offer to help him. At the school's entrance were two teachers waiting to meet them, and Frida strode across the car park to get things under way.

The taller, younger woman was Ms Keenan, the English teacher, and the woman standing behind her with the short white crop and thick red-framed glasses was the principal, Ms O'Dwyer.

'We heard you got on well with the girls at the Ardscoil yesterday,' Ms O'Dwyer said after they made introductions at the door.

'Yes,' Frida said quickly. 'Ms Gallagher was very good to us, and they were a lively bunch.'

Ms O'Dwyer eyed John, who was gripping the frame tightly with both hands.

'I wonder, Mr Reddan, if you might join me in the staffroom while Ms Keenan here shows Frida to the dressing room.'

'Sure,' John said, handing the frame to Frida, who slipped it onto her shoulder.

The principal ushered John down a corridor and out of sight. Ms Keenan beckoned for Frida to follow her up a flight of stairs.

The dressing room was a small bathroom upstairs, beside the classroom she'd soon perform in. By the time Frida applied the thick layers of make-up that turned her into Grace, there was still no sign of John. When Ms Keenan poked her head around the door and asked if Frida was ready, Frida said that she was.

'Good,' Ms Keenan said. 'We're all waiting for you.'

'Is John in there?'

Ms Keenan led Frida out to the corridor, which was cold, damp. 'He's in the staffroom talking to Ms O'Dwyer. Now, I'll go ahead and introduce things, and when I'm finished I'll sit down and you can begin in your own time.'

Frida watched the teacher enter her classroom, leaving the door to the corridor open so Frida could see. Why was John in the staffroom? What had Ms O'Dwyer meant when she mentioned the Ardscoil? Frida thought of Róisín, alone in John's car. It wasn't exactly appropriate. What if something had happened to her? If she'd told her teachers this morning about the long drive to Wittgenstein's cottage? Frida was thinking of the Marys now, a wide network of them stretching across the country, in silent communion with one another.

Ahead of her, Ms Keenan stretched out a hand to gesture to Frida, then took a seat among the students. Frida nodded at her, shook her head as if to clear a sneeze, then entered *Graceland* once more.

John remained in the staffroom for the duration of the play and the questions. Frida felt herself click into autopilot, the way she always did if he wasn't watching her perform. It didn't matter if she was good or bad or great if her only judges were a bunch of teenage girls. They asked about Frida's favourite plays, about how she'd done in her Leaving Cert, about what her ambitions were. After the final question she smiled and thanked the girls for having her, then returned to the bathroom where she'd gotten dressed.

'Should I go find John?' Frida asked Ms Keenan once she was back in her street clothes and ready to go.

'Oh,' the teacher replied. 'I've been told he's waiting in the car park for you.'

Outside it was raining sideways. Frida pulled her scarf around her hair and ran to the Fiesta, where John was sat behind the wheel. He started the engine as she neared the passenger side door.

'That eager to get home?' she shouted over the rain.

'Have you got your things?'

'Yeah. Have you got the frame?'

'It's in the boot.' He reversed out and gave the engine a tiny rev as they started towards the school's front gate.

'Where did you go? I'm not used to doing all of it alone, you know.'

'I was in the staffroom.'

'Why?'

'I needed a break.'

'Did I not need a break? Jesus, I'm exhausted.'

'You've got one now. No more schools, ever. I promise.'

'Did they tell you not to go into the classroom?'

'Who?'

'That old witch. The principal.'

'Why would she do that?'

Frida didn't say anything. Wasn't it obvious why they might? The last time John was in front of a group of teenage girls he ended up bringing one of them to dinner in a Connemara pub.

'I needed a break, Frida. They made me tea, we talked about the Abbey.'

She gave him a sideways look. She hadn't ever thought of John Reddan as a liar. But didn't pride make men do funny things?

At some point on the drive back to Dublin, Frida fell asleep. When she woke up, they were in traffic at the crossroads in Terenure, and she had an awful furry taste in her mouth.

'Sleep well?' John asked her.

She glanced at him and he looked hardened, older now, like the two of them had been on a three-day bender.

'Like a baby,' Frida replied.

5. Hiatus, 2008–2010

1.

A three-part drama on a submarine. Frida played the only female member of the crew. Only a handful of lines, mostly in the script for reasons of diversity in commissioning, or else to be the butt of jokes when she was not even on screen, the target of a certain kind of maleness that came about when sixty of them are crammed into a single tin can underwater. Frida didn't have to go anywhere near water, thankfully. The drama was shot entirely on the submarine set, built in a warehouse outside Manchester. Five days of filming, a vast system of almost frightening order and fluidity, that she quickly realised she could slot right into. At home, John was doing *Hedda Gabler* at the Abbey. A short run, and his first time on the Abbey stage. He had told Frida he wanted her for the lead, but between the jigs and the reels something seemed to get lost. Her agent, Madeline, claimed she never had a call from casting. The production would be starting when Frida was in Manchester anyway, so it probably wouldn't have worked. When she returned, the first thing Frida did was go to see *Hedda*. Hedda was played by an actress Frida hadn't seen before, a woman named Audrey Lennon who was slightly older than her. Frida had to admit that this other actress was a good pick. There was a glimmer of destabilising vulnerability within Audrey at all times, the caged bird who nevertheless couldn't stop singing. Maybe Frida wouldn't have been quite right for the role. After the curtain fell, Frida left the theatre and stood alone outside on the pavement, listening to the traffic hum by on the quays.

After *Hedda Gabler*'s run ended, Frida wanted to see John. She texted him the following day.

> **Hedda was great!** she wrote.

> A couple of hours later came his reply: **Thanks Frida!**

Something about his text made Frida feel embarrassed and pained. She wanted to see him so badly that she thought she saw him everywhere. Cycling down Camden Street she could have sworn she passed him waiting at the pedestrian lights in a black turtleneck. Browsing the new fiction in Hodges Figgis she heard his voice laughing at the tills and turned to find nobody there at all – just two sales assistants sharing a joke. Where was John? Why weren't they talking? There was no work around, for Frida or for anyone, and the city seemed to empty out. Dublin was missing something vital in an uncanny way, like a building paused in the middle of demolition, the sides blown off, offering a view of the home or office in cross-section. The winter stretched on as an endless parade of dark days, grey mornings, no news from anywhere. Half of Frida's phonebook had emigrated, including Catherine, who had moved to London to pursue work writing for the BBC after her Irish soap was cancelled. Frida lost interest in doing the things she usually did. Her mind kept coming back to John's car, all the hours they'd spent together there earlier that year. The damp smell of the Fiesta, the heater that never worked, the chequered woollen rug she kept pulled over her knees against the springtime chill. John's iPod plugged into a cassette adapter in the tape deck. Playing Fleetwood Mac and Townes Van Zandt. That was the place she felt most connected to John. Him sitting beside her in the driver's seat. His gangly legs so close to hers. Why didn't she just call him? What was this new feeling she had in her chest when she thought about him? Maddening, infuriating John Reddan. Exasperating and surely unappealing John Reddan. What she wanted, most of all, was him to call her. Frida wanted him to say, Look, I've got something for you, I'm working on a script, it's another thing for you and me to do together. I've got a reason for us to be close once again.

And you couldn't force that, apparently. You had to wait.

While she did so, Frida passed the time by looking after Edel and Ian's little girls. Most mornings she cycled to their house in Crumlin. Rain pants over her jeans, pedalling through the school-run traffic. Edel had gone back to work part-time when Sinéad was eight months, picking up substitute teaching jobs. Frida had a key to their house and let herself in, did some laundry, then picked Sophie and Sinéad up from crèche at lunchtime. If the weather was dry, she'd take them to the park. If it wasn't, she let them loose in the living room, helping Sophie turn the pages of her alphabet books. Edel came home to relieve her around 4 p.m. They couldn't pay Frida much, a twenty- or fifty-euro note here and there, but it was all welcome. Anything beyond her rent Frida spent on cinema tickets, cheap pints, enormous plates of vegetarian food at Govinda's.

Edel and Ian were supposed to take the girls to the Canaries in early March, but Ian had to stay behind to work. There were pay negotiations stuck at an impasse at the pharmaceutical company where he worked, and Ian was shop steward. Would Frida like to join instead? Edel said she could use the extra set of hands with the girls, if Frida didn't mind sharing a double bed for a week. Sure, what else would she be doing?

Tenerife in March was bright and breezy, more sunshine than Frida knew what to do with. She ran out of suncream on the second day. Pushing the double buggy down the waterfront with Sophie and Sinéad in their sun hats, their little pink sandals. The four girls ate dinner early – pizza cut into squares, lots of chips, a beer each for Edel and Frida. Everyone loved little Sinéad, the waiters standing back and applauding her when she pulled herself from Edel's lap up onto the white plastic table on the terrace.

On the morning of the third day, they were packing bags to go down to the swimming pool when Frida's phone rang. Her agent, Madeline, was on the other end. Frida stepped out onto the patio for quiet, sliding the door closed behind her. Madeline had been trying to reach her all morning. The agency on Grafton Street was closing, effective immediately. The receivers were on their way in now.

'I'm sorry to tell you like this,' Madeline said. 'I thought we had more time.' She sounded like someone in the middle of a long list of bad phone calls.

'No, I understand totally,' Frida said. 'It's a bad time.'

'I don't know if you're owed any money by us. I can check after lunch.'

'I doubt I am. I haven't worked since *Submersible*.'

'You know, a lot of people are going to London at the moment. If you wanted to go, I could try to set up some meetings for you.'

'London,' Frida repeated the word like she was hearing it for the first time. 'I hadn't ever thought about it, really.'

Edel was in the swimming pool with a firm grip on Sophie; Frida sat on the lounger in the shade with Sinéad on her lap. Frida recounted Madeline's call to her sister.

'What are you going to do?' asked Edel. 'Can you get a new agent?'

'I don't know. If they're shutting up shop, there's about to be a lot of agentless actors floating around the place.'

'Hmm.'

'But she mentioned London,' Frida continued. 'She said she could set up some meetings for me there.'

'That's nice of her. Would you do it?'

'It's weird. I didn't really think it was the right time to leave Dublin. But things are so crap here. I haven't worked in months, and even my old job at the paper is gone. They don't work with freelancers anymore.'

'Conditions of pay negotiations, I'd say.'

'You'd be the expert.'

'I think I'd go to London if I were you. For a little while, anyway. See what the meetings bring about. You've got friends there, don't you?'

Frida nodded. 'You know I handed out like thirty CVs last month. While *Submersible* was airing, I was going around every shop and café in town. And I've heard nothing.'

Edel shook her head. 'It's not good at the moment.'

'And at the same time you've got John Reddan winning awards for the first play he does without me in it.'

'Awards?'

'Last week at the Theatre Awards, for *Hedda Gabler*. Best director, best production.'

'Have you spoken to him recently?'

'Not really. I guess we don't have much to say to each other if we're not working together. And every week I'm going to another leaving drinks. Spending my pennies toasting another person's escape from all of this. It feels like I've been cheated. It's so unfair.'

'Babe, you can't think that way. It doesn't get you anywhere.'

'I know, I know.'

'If you have this opportunity ...' Edel mused, '... I think you should be jumping at it right now.'

Frida reached over and took a new bottle of suncream from her bag, squeezing some onto Sinéad's little arms. 'I'd miss you lot, though.'

'Sure you'll see us all the time. You'll probably see me more often than you do now.'

'Hmm.'

In one smooth movement, Edel swung Sophie up and out of the water, lifting her to sit on the edge of the pool. 'You know what you need to do, Frida. You're someone who needs to keep moving.'

Edel packed up the girls' things and took them both up to the flat to make lunch. Frida stayed by the pool, dragging her lounger back into the sun. The way her sister said it made London seem like the only choice. There was a part of Frida that agreed: Now was the time to do something big. Something different. Did that have to mean London? And what might life there be like for Frida? Closing her eyes behind her sunglasses she saw a street of red-brick terraces, big leafy trees, a red bus driving by. She saw herself shutting the front door of one of these terraced houses, stepping out onto the street, walking to the corner shop. She had been to London twice, both short trips, once with a drama group she was in as a teenager, once in college to see three plays in two days. The city, as she remembered it, seemed sprawling and anonymous; part of Frida had liked that about it, the freedom it could promise her. A place where nobody knew her. Would that be nice?

After lunch the girls went down for their naps in the bedroom, and Edel and Frida sat on the adjoining balcony, the striped awning down, two cans of Mahou sweating on the table in front of them. Edel was talking in a low voice so as not to wake the girls, telling stories about the lives of people she knew. Frida sat on a plastic chair beside her, listening passively. This man cheated on his wife with his best friend from college. This wife walked out and moved in with her colleague, but they didn't tell their other colleagues for over a year.

'Is everyone at this stuff?'

Edel nodded. 'All of them. Every street, every workplace, every friend group in the country has this stuff going on. You go past the wedding phase of your friends' lives directly into the scandal phase.'

Frida squinted. 'Do you ever worry?'

'About Ian? Jesus, no. The only thing Ian might abandon me for is golf, and his club is closing down at the end of the year anyway. They've to sell off the land to the bank.'

'It's funny,' Frida said. 'It's like, you hear these stories about people. You gasp and you're shocked, you can't believe it. And then you just go on about your business, trusting people, building lives with them.'

'What else are you going to do? Withdraw from it all, live like Mum does?'

Edel didn't tend to bring up their mother's personal life. It was, after all, personal.

'What do you mean?' Frida asked.

'Haven't you ever thought it was weird? Her and Simon, like basically a secret affair that produced us, and then after that she just put a stop to anything like that in her life?'

'She doesn't feel she needs a relationship,' Frida said carefully. 'Some people are like that.'

'Okay, sure,' Edel said, shrugging. 'So unless you're like that, you need to accept the fact that people are mental and cruel to each other.'

Frida felt the conversation start to wear on her. 'Should we go inside, I can feel my legs starting to burn.'

Edel and the girls went to bed early most nights, despite the afternoon naps all four of them seemed to take. Frida had more energy than she knew what to do with. After dinner that night, she quietly slid the patio door open, took a seat with a bottle of beer and a new notepad she'd brought from home. She opened it to a blank page and wrote

Two couples

Carefully she underlined both words. Then she closed the notepad again. Why was she doing this? She had never tried to write anything before. It was embarrassing to imagine what anyone who knew her might think, if they ever saw it.

But here in the dark, at the edge of the ocean, nobody was going to see it. Tentatively she reopened the notepad. She was thinking about Edel telling her to keep moving. The stories they'd been telling each other earlier circled in Frida's head. Everyone loved a gossip, didn't they? A group of friends, a spaghetti junction of relationships. Bad decisions that overlapped again and again. Chance encounters that changed things forever. Two couples who switched allegiances, who hurt each other in the process. Four people who went through something awful together, something that left a mark on each of them.

If she wrote it well enough, maybe she wouldn't need to go to London after all.

And if she wrote it well enough, well, then, maybe she could write John Reddan back into her life. Frida stopped writing then. It was a stupid thought. They had barely spoken for months, and the break had been welcome. But now she was aware that she missed him. How would John react to the idea of her as a writer? Would he laugh at her audacity? Or would he be curious, and want to see what she had? She tried to imagine what he might think about this thing she was attempting to get down on paper.

Complicate it, Frida. Don't let this be so easy. Make it a little weirder, make it a little worse.

If you're going to do this, she thought, it needs to be really good. It needs to make doing this the only solution.

At the end of the week she returned to Dublin with sunburn and a few pages of notes, written in the dark on the balcony each of the last four nights. To call them notes would be too generous, she thought, waiting to disembark the plane. Edel and the girls had slept for most of the flight, but Frida's mind had been whirring the whole time. Character sketches, a woman called Aoife, an amalgam of all the women Edel had told her about, and all the women Frida was friends with, too. And another woman called Orla, older, not wiser, still making the same mistakes she had been making her whole adult life. The way Frida herself felt. Walking through the airport, pushing the double buggy, a new clarity came over her. It didn't matter that she wasn't a writer. She had something here, and maybe it was enough. Maybe she could hand it over to John and he could do the rest.

2.

When John picked up the phone the following morning, he heard the excitement in Frida's voice immediately. He liked that. It sounded like she was outside, somewhere windy, shouting to be heard. She said she wanted to see him soon.

'Where are you?' he asked.

'I'm with the kids. We're in the playground.'

'Oh right. What kids?'

'Edel's kids! I've been childminding recently. Look, when are you free?'

They met the same day, early that evening in a pub on Baggot Street. It had been some time since they'd seen one another. Not long after *Hedda Gabler*, John's dad had died of a heart attack and despite their estrangement, there had been one logistical task after another for him and Barry to wade through. An exhausting and depressing few months. It was nice, John thought, to be seeing Frida again, play that other role of his once more.

Frida was late, bustling in in a big pink jumper and blue skinny jeans. She was flush with suntan. She bought the first round; she said she had something she wanted to talk to him about. Carefully she slid a small blue notebook out of her handbag and onto the table. John reached for it and she pulled it back towards her.

'I was in Tenerife last week,' she announced. 'Have you ever been?'

John frowned. 'No.'

'I was there with Edel and the girls, and it's a funny place, like it's designed for holidays like that, nothing there except beach and hotel and bar and pool. But that's good, because it's not easy to deal with a little kid and a baby 24/7 in a foreign country. Anyway one afternoon Edel and I were talking about people, adults, you know. All the things they get up to. And I got thinking, and basically, please don't laugh at me. But I started writing something.'

'About adults?'

Frida nodded. 'About adults. About ... relationships. I mean, when I say writing, all I'm doing is jotting things down. But I don't know. I was just thinking the whole way back – the flight is long, you know, almost five hours – about working with you.'

John leaned back in his chair, watching her. With one hand he gestured for her to continue.

'I think there's something about how we work together,' she said. 'Do you know what I mean?' She didn't wait for his answer. 'I don't know how you feel. But I think that when we work on something together, it becomes like, what's the phrase ... a sum greater than its parts.'

He nodded slowly at her.

'I just have this feeling,' she continued. 'I can't explain it really. Like if I bring you an idea, even something rough that doesn't make any sense yet, we can do something with it.'

'Alchemical,' he offered.

'No, I'm not saying it's magic,' she said.

'No, I know. But it's like when we have an idea together, we can turn something kind of shitty into something almost golden in a way.'

Frida looked at him, smiling.

'That's it. And what I'm saying now is that I have this thing, and it's probably not very good, but I think it can work if we do it together. And I want to write it with you.'

John reached again for Frida's notebook. 'Can I see what you have?'

She nodded, and he opened it, running the fingertips of one hand over his mouth as he read. He didn't need to look up from the page at Frida. He could sense her discomfort with his reading. He himself never allowed someone, even someone he trusted the way he trusted Frida, to read his work in his presence. What she had here was not a script, not even a synopsis. It was a little bit of a mess, some characters, some diagrams explaining how they were linked, a list of possible scenes, things that might happen, not in chronological order, and a name. Frida wanted to name this new play *Four and Ten*.

'Why do you want to call it *Four and Ten*?'

'I don't know what it means. I just wanted to call it something that didn't feel stale, that people could make their own minds up about. I like that it's ambiguous.'

'Okay,' he said, turning the page in her notebook.

She came back from the bar with two more pints and sat,

waiting for John to finish. When he had gone over everything a second time, he looked up at her.

'Yeah, okay,' he said lightly. 'I get it, I think.'

They stayed until closing time, two packs of cheese-and-onion crisps and some peanuts instead of dinner. It was so easy. They were talking like they always used to, trading ideas, augmenting each one for the other person, merging things, making rapid-fire jokes that referred back to comments said three or four minutes earlier, interrupting each other with bits of gossip. Her company was a salve for John, like it always was. With her he could forget about everything else, except for art and having a nice time. When they stepped outside, the night was surprisingly mild. John took out a packet of cigarettes, offering her one and they smoked together, leaning on a bollard. It was a Tuesday night, and the street was quiet.

'It feels so early still,' Frida said. 'It feels like we just got here.'

'Could we go somewhere else?'

'Where's open?'

'Good point. It's balmy enough, we could just walk home for a bit?'

They pointed themselves in the direction of the canal and started walking.

'You used to live around here,' he said, remembering suddenly.

Frida stopped, pointing behind them to a narrow Georgian terrace with a coffee shop on the ground floor. 'That one. But I don't know who lives there now. Matthew sold it.'

'Do you still talk to him?'

Frida shook her head. 'That's done now. Are you seeing anyone?'

'Not currently,' John said slowly. 'It's been a funny few months.'

'Do you mean it feels like the city is dying a slow and painful death? Because that's how I feel.'

He nodded, eyebrows raised. 'It's like everyone I used to know has left. It's like every morning, I wake up and it's even greyer outside. You know the last time I was in a packed theatre was the closing night of *Hedda*. Since then every room has been half-full. Half-empty,' he said, correcting himself.

Frida laughed. 'Yeah. Half-empty is definitely the mood, isn't it? You know my agency closed down last week?'

'What the fuck?'

'They went bankrupt. Like, literally open one day, shut the next. Did you not hear this? I think some clients are going to be seriously out of pocket.'

'What are you going to do?'

'I don't know.' They reached the traffic lights and crossed onto the bridge. Frida paused and leaned her bum back against the wall. 'I was thinking I'd go to London. But now, I want to write this thing with you instead.'

John rested one hand on the wall beside her so their hands were close, almost touching.

'Then write it with me.'

Frida was looking up at him, smiling nervously in a way he hadn't ever seen before. Frida Slattery nervous. The thought of it.

She released a breathy little laugh. 'You think I shouldn't go?' she asked him quietly.

'Do you think I'm going to tell you what to do?'

'Yes. That's what you usually do.'

'Fair. Okay then, Frida. You're going to stay here in Dublin. You're going to write *Four and Ten* with me and we'll find a way to put it on. We'll get a loan from the bank, we'll produce it ourselves, you can do the hair and make-up, and the costume too, probably.'

Frida tilted her face up towards his. Now they were really close to each other, and her voice was very small. He could feel the warmth of her breath.

'And what are you going to do, John?'

His own breath was tight and high in his chest. Suddenly John had a strong feeling that it was just the two of them left in the city, that they'd stayed long after all the lights had been turned out. There was nothing else to do, was there? So he did it. He leaned down, and for the first time he kissed Frida Slattery.

3.

John looked ludicrous in Frida's small bedsit. In the morning she couldn't stop laughing at the sight of him cramped in her narrow bed, his big shoes a trip hazard in front of the bathroom door.

'I never realised how small it was in here,' she said, running the tap for the kettle. He had dressed and arranged himself on her single chair, waiting while she made tea.

'You never realised before now? Frida, this room is tiny. The shower in that bathroom. I hit my head three times.'

'You're quite a bit taller than me, you know.'

He looked around the room in consternation. 'We won't be able to work here. We'll work at mine, Barry's house.'

'That's fine with me.'

John puffed his cheeks and exhaled through a corner of his mouth. 'I don't know how you live like this.'

'I've barely spent any time here in the last few years. The rent is nothing. Well, not nothing, but you know what I mean. You find something like this, you don't let it go so easily, you know?'

The warm weather of the previous night had dissipated, and when John and Frida stepped outside onto the main road, a strong breeze sent litter and dried leaves flying down the pavement. Frida winced and tilted her head backwards. The gust passed, and when she looked down again she saw her hand had found John's. She felt butterflies in her stomach. It was entirely new, and yet it was also as if they did this all the time: left her flat together in the morning, walked to the coffee shop together. John said he wanted to go and pick up his laptop so they could start working immediately; she countered and suggested they get takeaway coffees and bring them back to Barry's.

These unemployed midweek days had always felt to Frida like skipping school. Like there was somewhere else she was supposed to be instead. As if any minute now, a car carrying some authority figure was going to slow to a stop beside her and roll down the window. Ask her where she thought she was going. Today she almost wished for it to happen, against the odds. She wanted to lean into the window and shout, I'm going to John Reddan's house to write a play!

One by-product of the city's desolate emptiness was that it was easy for John and Frida to sequester themselves for a little while. Nobody around to miss them. Frida arrived with an overnight bag she'd packed while John was in the shower, but each morning she decided to stay for another day, and another, doing laundry in Barry's kitchen, hanging her cotton underwear on the clothes horse by the back door. They'd set up a work station at the coffee table in the living room and stayed there all day while Barry was at work. When he came home, they migrated upstairs to John's small bedroom. Frida was aware that Barry hadn't asked for this, for this woman, familiar only from his brother's plays, to be padding around his house in her bare feet, using up all the hot water to wash her hair.

She texted Edel to ask for a couple of weeks off babysitting. Edel was curt in her reply, saying she'd have to ask her elderly neighbour Maud to pick the girls up from crèche. Everyone knew Maud was an old witch. Frida looked at the text and replied: Sorry xx needs must.

Yes, needs must. In John's bed they stayed up until all hours watching Bergman films, clips of old Beckett productions on YouTube, smoking hash, batting around ideas until Barry texted John and told them to keep it down. They slept late. They made love in the morning, and from the first, Frida was obsessed with the newness revealed in John Reddan's body: the way the skin on his back was smooth in parts, rough in others, the dark wiry hairs on his shoulders that she hadn't known about until now. It was like she'd never seen him shirtless before, though of course they'd been sharing bedrooms for work since Edinburgh. It was like she'd never allowed herself to look, she thought, watching him bend down to pick up a sock, his long limbs even spindlier than she'd imagined. She revelled too in John's attentions, the way he buried his face in her stomach and breathed her in, a muffled ecstatic God! coming from her abdomen. He looked at her in wonder when she got out of bed, standing naked in his room. It made her want to pose like a Greek statue. It made her want to have him take her photo like this, capture the moment for her future self to wonder at.

About half the time they went to bed together, though, something went wrong for John. Frida knew it was half the time because for a while it was literally one on, one off. Every second attempt ended in John lying on his back, palms pressed into his eye sockets, apologising.

'It's okay,' Frida said, again and again. 'It's a bigger deal for you than it is for me.' It *was* okay, provided Frida didn't try to analyse it too much in her head. Didn't pretend to puzzle it out internally with a trusted interlocutor, imagining herself in dialogue with Edel or Catherine. It was easier for her to stay focused on everything else: the thing they were writing together. That was the engine, she thought, the thing that powered all of this.

Their days together moved from sex to movies to work with such ease that the things blurred into one another. Frida would come back from the shower, wrapped in one of John's thinning towels, and he'd already have the document open, transcribing notes from his notepad onto the laptop. Then she'd dress and join him and they'd write for a bit, padding out one character or another, and then suddenly his hand on her thigh instead of the keyboard and then they were back at it, undressed again.

John had a taste for films where the director and the lead actress were *'simpatico'*, as he described. It was crucial, he said, for everyone to really understand each other. It was where a good movie became a great one. He liked movies where you couldn't imagine another actor in the role, where it was like God had ordained it this way. It was how he liked to work, too. Together in his bedroom on his laptop, they watched *Blue Velvet* and *Persona*, and every single John Cassavetes and Gena Rowlands picture. Frida was transfixed by *A Woman Under the Influence*, the way Gena Rowlands moved erratically around the room like she was possessed.

'I hope you're taking notes,' John said at one point, leaning across Frida for the ashtray.

'I don't need to,' she said. 'I know you're doing it for me.'

They downloaded a BBC documentary about David Lynch and Isabella Rossellini and when it was over, Frida rested her head on John's chest and wrapped her arm around him.

'Do you wish we were like them?' She asked.

'No,' John said. 'I think we are like them already.'

'Really?'

'I think we're better.'

'Do you think we could still do this when we're old and grey?'

'What, make plays together?'

'Yeah,' Frida said. 'Well. I guess I mean all of it.'

'If you will, then I will.'

God, Frida liked that idea. She turned her head so that her left temple lay on his chest. She could hear the tapping beat of his heart under his skin. She could picture it, the two of them somewhere in the future, a nicer bedroom, maybe. It didn't actually matter where they were in this picture, she realised, or how nice the bedroom was. What mattered was that they were still in each other's heads, for a really long time, the same way they were right now.

'I will,' she said, closing her eyes.

Was the thing they were writing any good? Frida couldn't tell. She was far too close to it, living too much inside of it to see it. Like how one couldn't identify the unique smell of their own home. She couldn't separate herself from the page, from John, from the movies they were watching and the four walls of the terraced house they'd barely left for over a week. They lay in bed with his laptop open and moved the characters around the page. Aoife paired first with Michael, then with Steve. No, the other way around. John had no end to his ideas on how to improve Frida's draft.

'You've got jealousy between this pair,' he said, scrolling through pages of text. 'But jealousy is only so powerful. What about betrayal? There's nothing more powerful than betrayal, is there?'

Frida watched him delete a raft of text and started retyping quickly. Words filled the screen. She had a memory of playing dolls with Edel as a little girl and, when her sister wasn't looking, making the dolls kiss.

'Right,' John said on Saturday afternoon when they'd just finished breakfast. Pages were scattered all over Barry's table. 'We're going out today. We need some daylight on our faces.'

Showered, shoes on, wearing clothes that needed a wash, they started walking towards town. The whole way down Clanbrassil Street John talked about *Four and Ten*, about how he thought the couples should change earlier, midway through the first act, shifting allegiances in a way he had seen before in real life. It happens, he said. Betrayal is a hell of a drug.

In Temple Bar he led Frida upstairs to a tiny café she hadn't been to before, a room no bigger than the kitchen in Barry's house. Seated by a window overlooking the Liffey, they ate chicken wraps and sad side salads. John leafed through Frida's notebook with blue pen in hand, striking through sentences she had written and replacing them with ones of his own. She was fascinated, watching him do this. The fluidity of it, like she could see his mind's processes working in real time, like his brain was a machine with its parts on the outside, cogs turning, sparks igniting and setting new things alight. She almost forgot to say goodbye to all her little sentences, struck through with his firm line.

Outside the sky was azure, the river reflecting the colour upwards and making the quays look like they were lit professionally, like the cityscape was in fact a stage set. It was good to be outside on a day like this, Frida thought, invigorating, standing on the pavement with a man who understood her, who believed in her talents and her brain. The man in question lit a cigarette now, turned to her and said, Pub?

Could it really always be like this? The two of them fizzing with excitement, with desire for each other, and the sun shining as they walked through Temple Bar towards the pub they always chose, if they had the choice. The one where they'd first met, with the elegant yellow upstairs lounge and the bright flowers in the window boxes. Frida was just filled with it. The feeling of potential that spring brought each year. The endless yearning of the new crush, wanting badly to be with the person even when you were already with them, wanting the moment you were in never to end. John took Frida's hand and together they dashed through traffic across Suffolk Street onto Grafton Street, heaving with shoppers, and she was out of breath, laughing at something he'd said when suddenly he dropped her hand like it was burning him.

'Hey,' John said to a man and a woman who'd stopped in front of them. Frida recognised the woman. It was Katie MacGowan, and a man Frida didn't know.

Katie looked between John and Frida. 'Hi, you two. What are you up to?'

'We were at the Chester Beatty library,' John replied, lying with such alacrity that Frida blinked, feeling her brow furrow. 'We were doing research for something I'm writing.'

'Oh, you're writing something?'

'Yeah, ha ha. Early days yet.'

'What is it?'

'Sort of a love story, but for four. A complicated love story.'

'Got a name?'

'*Four and Ten*. Working title, obviously.'

The man beside Katie shuffled.

'Sorry,' Katie said. 'This is my boyfriend, Ed. Ed, John Reddan and Frida Slattery. We all worked together on one of John's plays.'

Frida cleared her throat. 'We're on our way for a pint now, if you want to join us?'

Ed shook his head and looked down at his feet.

'You two and your pints,' Katie said. 'Would you ever get

some work done? Nah, we're heading to the Dart now. We're actually late already. Look, John, whatever you're writing I'd love to read it when it's ready. I'm mostly in London now, that's where the work is, but Ed's here so I'm back every couple of weeks.'

Frida looked between John and Katie, in search for the thing that wasn't being said aloud. Some imbalance of power, some *sub-rosa* conversation that she wasn't privy to. She couldn't see what it was exactly but she could sense its vague, feathery outline.

'Sounds great,' John said. 'I'll let you know when I've got something viable.'

Katie nodded at him. 'Frida, it was good to see you.'

Ed and Katie disappeared into the crowds at the pedestrian crossing. Frida turned to John as they continued to make their way towards the pub. 'The Chester Beatty library?'

'It was the first thing that came to mind.'

'It sounded rehearsed.'

'Why would I rehearse saying "the Chester Beatty library"?'

'I don't know. Probably the same reason why you stopped holding my hand the moment you saw Katie.'

John didn't say anything.

'And just so I can get our story straight,' Frida continued as they reached the door of the pub. '*Four and Ten* is your script?'

'What do you want to drink, Frida?'

'Just a pint is fine, John.'

Frida climbed the stairs to the yellow room and took a seat by the fireplace. She thought of her notepad in the inside pocket of John's jacket, his blue pen markings all over it. She thought of Katie MacGowan's eyes roving from John to Frida and back again, searching the two of them, of the readiness with which John dropped Frida's hand. Why did it matter what Katie MacGowan knew about them?

John appeared at the table, setting down two pints of lager. He looked anxious, walking with a slight jerk in his step.

'Frida,' he said, sitting down opposite her. 'Look. Sorry for what happened with Katie there. I'm not really very good at this stuff. Relationships. I was thinking ...'

His eyes drifted to the corners of the room, like he was looking there for a good excuse.

'I think I was worried about you, really, about whether or not you wanted everyone to know about us.'

Frida blinked slowly. What she wanted to do was roll her eyes at him, but she was trying to be mature about this.

John went on. 'Because we haven't talked about it, have we? About us, I mean. You know, are we ready for this, for people talking about us in that way. Because you know as well as I do that they will talk, and—'

'Stop, John,' Frida said. 'Everyone's thought for years now that we've been sleeping together. I don't know why you're so worried about it now.'

'Yeah, okay.'

'Okay? Okay, what?'

'You're right. It's not a problem. Whatever we're doing here, it shouldn't be a secret if you don't want it to be.'

Frida's jaw tensed. Who said she didn't want it be a secret? Who said she even wanted it to be a thing?

'Look, John, I'm not saying that ... I just thought it was

weird, how you acted with Katie. But it's not a big deal. Let's stay focused on the script.'

'Cool.'

'Our script,' Frida added. 'Because I'm clear that it is our script, right?'

'Yeah, of course.' John reached inside his jacket, pulled Frida's blue notepad from his pocket and placed it on the table. 'I've never slept with Katie, you know, if that's what you're worried about.'

They stayed in the pub until the sky started to grow dark, writing and rewriting dialogue, saying every sentence aloud across the table. It was like tennis, Frida thought. Frida hated tennis. When they grew hungry they made for the bus. John suggested a takeaway pizza. He wanted to keep on working when they got home. Frida curled on the couch, watching him type on his laptop. The beginning of period cramps flickered through her abdomen. She thought of her flat, mostly empty for the last two weeks.

'Do you have any Solpadeine, John?'

'I don't think so. Paracetamol, maybe.'

She stood up and reached for the kitchen cupboard closest to her. 'Where would it be?'

'I don't know, Frida.'

She wanted him to ask her what was wrong. She wanted an argument, if she was to be truthful.

'I can't find any,' she announced.

John sighed. He tilted the screen of his laptop down and looked at her over it.

'Go to the shop, if you want. It's open until ten.'

'I think I'm just going to go to bed,' she said. 'If that's okay.'

'Sure. I'll follow you once I'm finished this. It might be a little while.'

John's bed without him in it. These sheets should be changed, Frida thought. The room aired out, maybe. A smell not unlike something curdled, just past its best. She put on an old black T-shirt of his that had a print of *Eraserhead* on the front and got under the duvet.

Frida woke earlier than either of them had in days. Heartburn. She had a deep desire not to be in John's house anymore. Once dressed, she lay down beside him in the bed again, over the covers, stroking the angle of his jaw with her fingertips. He started to stir.

'What time is it?' he asked through sleep.

'Early. Only nine. I'm going to go back home for a little while. I really need to do laundry and see Edel and the kids.'

John yawned and sat up. He scanned her face in search of something. Then he nodded.

'Sure. Maybe good for us to take a break with this anyway. Give me a call whenever you're ready.'

Days passed. Frida slept late and brought her laundry to the laundrette in her battered old suitcase. She went to the yoga studio in Ranelagh for their pay-what-you-can classes. How long could she make him wait, she wondered. At what point would he be the one to pick up the phone and call her? Every time she thought of *Four and Ten* she thought of John saying to Katie: working title, obviously. Under his watch it was becoming less and less like the thing she'd thought of in the Canaries. The spaghetti junction of bad relationships. And the thing was that Frida didn't even mind that so much. She wasn't angry at John for making those changes, or at herself for letting them happen. She just didn't care about it anymore. All the fervour she'd felt that first night in Toner's pub on Baggot Street, the subsequent wonder at the new dimension of their relationship – all of that was cooling now.

Checking her email four days into their hiatus, Frida saw an email from a name she didn't recognise. A freelance casting director called Shona Reynolds in London who said she knew Madeline. Shona was working with an Irish director on a play at the National Theatre and they wanted to see Frida for a part. The director, whose name Shona didn't share, had seen Frida in *Bird*, as well as in *Submersible*. They wanted to know if she could be in London the following Monday. Frida looked up the cost of flights. Of course she could.

Frida cycled through the list of directors she thought it could be. She'd have been keen to work with any of them. And at the National Theatre! Shona sent her two short scenes to prepare. It was a small part, she explained to Frida, the younger version of the female lead role, who appeared only in flashback. She signed off her email by saying that she was really looking forward to meeting Frida.

Can I come over tonight? Frida texted John. Need to chat about something

An audition was nothing. Frida thought, in fact, that she was made for auditions, built for twenty minutes of dynamic and exciting first impression, the freedom of knowing you were not yourself at all in that room – *you* were the character, or you were your interpretation of that character. There were many roles Frida hadn't got, of course. But for whatever reason, she couldn't muster the kind of shame and regret that actors were supposed to have about missed roles, the bitter feeling that seemed to corrode so many actors' ambition. It's my interpretation, she thought. It's just not my problem if that doesn't align with the director's interpretation.

So she had no instinctive anxiety about this particular audition. What she was worried about was telling John. She cycled to his house in a cornflower-blue dress he'd complimented before, and white tennis shoes. The evening was mild, the Irish idea of summer unfolding itself gently over the city. Along the canal there were shirtless men drinking cans of beer from supermarket plastic bags at their feet. She'd forgotten her helmet, and her hair bounced at her shoulders in the breeze.

When John opened the door to Barry's house, he pulled her into a deep hug. He was wearing a dark-blue linen shirt that needed an iron and his usual black skinny jeans. Just for a second, Frida's heart skipped at the sight of him.

'I hope you enjoyed your brief reprieve,' he said, in the voice another man might use to say, I missed you. There was the smell of seafood through the house, tealights glowing on the sticky kitchen table. Frida sat, taking the glass of wine John proffered and drinking most of it in one go. John was making risotto, and in between stirring he was opening cupboards to show her things he'd bought that he thought she might like. Boxes of camomile tea, chocolate biscuits.

'I think we're almost there with this draft already,' he said, spooning risotto into her bowl. 'There's pepper there if you want.'

Frida took the pepper canister in both hands and held it tentatively. 'John, I need to take a bit of a break from this.'

'What do you mean?'

'I've got an audition in London the day after tomorrow. It's a play at the National Theatre.'

'What's the play?'

'I don't know yet. I know it's an Irish director who's seen my work before.'

'Your work,' John repeated slowly.

'Yeah.'

'And you don't know who?'

'The way the casting director phrased it, I imagine it's someone pretty established.'

'Can I see the email?'

Frida frowned. 'Well, I don't have my laptop with me. I probably can't stay past tomorrow morning, by the way. I need to prepare.'

'And you're really going ahead with this?'

'Of course I am. It's an incredible opportunity. It's London, John. And it's not like there's any other work around at the moment. I'd love to make money for something that isn't minding my nieces, you know.'

John said nothing. He screwed up his thin upper lip and stared at her.

'The script will be here when I get back,' Frida added.

'I mean, will it?' John asked. 'If you get this role.'

'I'm most likely not going to get the role!'

'It's not even the point, Frida. Do you really think the world is just going to stop and wait for you to do whatever the hell you want?'

'John,' she said. She pushed her plate forward an inch. 'I think I should go home.'

Her heart was beating fast in her chest, making her feel unsteady as she laced up her shoes by the door.

'You're going to leave,' he said, standing up. 'You're not even willing to talk this out. I don't think you ever really cared about this play, did you, Frida?'

'Oh my God, John, it was my script in the first place.'

'But you brought it to me. You said you wanted to work on it with me.'

'I did! I do, still. I'm just taking a break for like, two days.'

'Two days, two weeks, six months. However long you need. I'll just be sitting here, won't I, waiting for you to return.'

'John.' Frida was trying hard to modulate her voice, to make herself sound amenable and not hostile. 'You told me yourself that scripts can take ages. So don't you think it might help if we got a bit of distance from it, for a little while? We could return with fresh eyes.'

John rubbed his forehead with index and middle fingers. 'Sure.'

'It might even be good for us, too,' Frida added, her hand on the handle of Barry's front door. 'To have a little space.'

4.

When Frida wasn't preparing for her audition, she was trying to figure out who the director might be. She thought she had it narrowed down to Killian Schaeffer, an acclaimed Irish-German writer and director in his late fifties. The night before her audition, when Frida was waiting to board her flight at Dublin Airport, Shona confirmed this by text. She asked Frida for her discretion – it had been many years since Schaeffer had a new play open in London.

The story was pretty simple, if devastating: A couple in their fifties are rocked by the death of their two children in a car crash. Frida's character was the younger version of the female lead, seen briefly in flashbacks to when the couple were first married and considering having children. One of the scenes bore thematic similarity to *Bird*, and Frida suspected this might have been why she was called for the audition.

Her flight arrived in Heathrow late on Sunday and she passed the long journey on the Piccadilly line rereading the two scenes. Frida was glad she hadn't told John any of the specifics, or shown him the script. The idea of him watching her run through something from another writer made her feel hot and uncomfortable and stressed, like her recurring dreams of running through airports for flights she was sure to miss.

She'd made arrangements to stay with Catherine. It had been some time since they'd seen each other, though they still texted often. Catherine had spent about a year trying to get writing work in London before giving it up. Now she'd moved on from drama entirely, working in HR at the BBC, 'doling out disciplinaries to strong-headed newsreaders', she said. A funny thing, life, Frida thought, brushing her teeth in Catherine's small bathroom. To see your peers – the people with whom you once passed nights of your life in the bar's smoking area, gabbing away until the lights came on – now engaged to an Englishman chosen almost at random, living in the small two-bedroom flat he owned in a converted Victorian terrace eight stops from Oxford Circus. Catherine had been the glorious wildcard in their student drama society, the beautiful but obstinate girl who always had a ridiculous feud going on with some boy or other, wanting to hatch some madcap plan to show him what he was missing. All of that seemed to dissipate once they left university. How ordinary Catherine's life seemed now. What Frida wished she could ask was how her friend had known when to cash in her chips.

Frida's audition was scheduled for noon the next day. It was raining as she hurried from the tube station to the address, an old brick building just south of Waterloo. When she entered the blank white room, a tall woman with a cold demeanour introduced herself as Shona. As she stood to shake

Frida's hand, Frida thought she saw pain in the woman's eyes, like her back was in spasm. The man seated next to Shona was indeed Killian Schaeffer. He was grey-haired and quiet, bearded, light blue eyes set above bulbous cheeks. He directed Frida to stand in the middle of the room.

'Frida,' Killian said. 'Pleasure to meet you. I saw you in something years ago, and Shona speaks highly of you as well.'

'Thank you, I'm happy to hear that.'

'What did you think of the scenes we sent you? What did you think of young Moira?'

If John Reddan had been asking her this question, Frida thought, he would have wanted to hear something that chimed with his own opinions. A surprising answer to this question would have set John Reddan's teeth on edge, she knew. But she was not standing in front of John Reddan.

'I think I understand young Moira,' Frida said slowly. 'Her uneasiness with her new husband, with the life she is making for herself. She doesn't know what her role is, really, but she knows what it isn't. And in order to be who she is, she has to hide certain parts of herself. That's the crux of it for me. That's the interesting thing, how to show or obscure those certain parts of herself.'

In front of her Shona was staring her down, in a way that felt almost physically aggressive. Killian Schaeffer's face was completely blank. He gestured for her to begin.

'We'll do the first scene, then.'

After Frida finished, Killian and Shona turned to each other and talked in low voices that Frida couldn't make out.

'Again, I think, but this time slower. You said earlier that you thought Moira isn't sure of herself in some ways. So let's try it with a little more of that in her voice.'

For a second Frida felt like her brain was stalling, like a car that cut out at the traffic lights. Everyone could see. Then she took a deep breath and started again.

'Fine, that's good,' said Shona. 'Thanks for coming in, Frida.'

During the forty minutes she was in the audition room, the rain in Waterloo had stopped. If I lived here, Frida thought, walking along the South Bank, what version of myself might I be? She was thinking of the clutter in Catherine's kitchen, the fridge magnet shaped like a sheep from a holiday to Scotland, the orange Le Creuset casserole in which Catherine had cooked dinner the night before. What did Frida even own? Some old clothes that she didn't particularly like, and a bunch of second-hand books. From a distance things in Dublin felt flimsy. Shored up by lollipop sticks and an over-dependence on her sister and tiny nieces for a sense of self. Frida thought she wouldn't get this job, but increasingly she felt she'd get some other job and end up in London anyway. There were Irish accents here, people passing her on the riverside with warm, familiar voices. What Frida wanted was the same thing she had always wanted. Didn't success inevitably involve leaving home? Put like that it had the ring of Greek myth, and Frida liked that: herself as Odysseus, not Penelope. It had been so long since she really thought about what she wanted from life. Now she pictured the entrance to

Catherine's flat, the colourful rag rug, the coats hanging on the wall. A little dish for keys and a heavy stone paperweight on top of the day's post. She imagined having these things for herself. It was inevitable, wasn't it, that she would have to turn away from Dublin sooner or later. Who had it in them to stay put forever?

Passing through passport control in Dublin Airport the following day, Frida thought for a minute that John would be waiting for her. They hadn't spoken since she'd left his house a few days earlier, quietly shaking with anger and confusion. She would need cash for a taxi; joining the queue for the ATM, she saw she had a voicemail. It was Shona. They were going with another young Moira, but would Frida be interested in understudying?

Well, she thought with excitement, that's something that hadn't ever crossed my mind. Her mouth curled into a smile.

5.

Acting was pretending. Understudying involved an additional layer of pretence. From the opening night of *The Other Side of Silence*, Frida realised she would have to pretend constantly that she was going on stage as young Moira, even though she knew that in all probability she would never go on stage as young Moira. I agreed to do this, she reminded herself. They are paying me to do this. Nobody put a gun to my head.

At rehearsal, nobody talked to the understudies. Frida and four others, understudying for a total of six roles, sat at the edge of the room and observed with a script in their hands. They listened for the notes that Killian Schaeffer gave, and they wrote down notes of their own where necessary. Frida found it mind-numbingly dull. She launched into wild, spiralling daydreams about the actor who played young Moira (a younger woman from Belfast who had attended RADA) falling down in the street, having a psychotic break, becoming suddenly addicted to heroin or simply – Frida's favourite – quitting on the spot. Albert, in his sixties and the alternate for the lead role, passed the time backstage by doing sudoku. He liked to recite names. Anthony Hopkins, Laurence Olivier. Shirley MacLaine, Carol Haney. Donald Sutherland. Actors who understudied for other actors, all of them famous.

Frida wanted to tell Albert to knock it off. He didn't notice that she didn't care.

'Everyone does it at some point on their way up,' he explained to her. 'That's my point. It's part of the system.'

Then why are you still doing it, she thought to herself unhappily.

Nobody wanted to do this. Nobody grew up attending drama classes, thinking, someday I'll get my chance to be an understudy. Nonetheless, it was the National Theatre. Enough to make John Reddan feel sick with envy, probably. Even if it was just understudying, it was, as Catherine kept on saying, great for the old CV.

Catherine had helped to find her a sublet, a friend of a friend's small one-bedroom flat in Finsbury Park, and that part of things was all fine. She liked the busy street, the late-opening corner shop, the trees in the park just starting to turn from green to orange. The girl whose flat it was had departed for New York to do a master's and left her bike for Frida. Frida cycled down treacherous roads towards the heart of the city every day on her way to work, gliding over Waterloo Bridge like she was starring in a movie in which a girl steals a bicycle. The city was rewiring her brain. She barely registered the sirens now. But sometimes she heard them and thought, Are they for me? It was like being on fire all of the time. It was late summer, and she couldn't imagine ever being cold again. She drank iced coffees from Pret that made her feel like she'd taken speed. She was smoking more than ever. She found herself unbearably attracted to every sexy person she saw, male or female, college student or old-age pensioner. Wanted to give the whole world her number. On her nights off, she was spending her wages on boozy dinners in Soho restaurants with Catherine and her BBC friends. Frida borrowed the clothes the girl had left behind, belting wide-leg jeans high on her waist, wearing a crop top to work like she was an errant Spice Girl. To call it liberating would be a cliché, but it turned out there was nothing like being twenty-seven years old and living alone in London for the first time.

She and John had been emailing. He started it, sending a message that was written like they'd parted on good terms. Frida had responded in kind. It was so much easier than nurturing a grudge. She missed him, sometimes, the happy feeling of being alone with him, in his bed or walking down the street together. Like it was just the two of them in the whole world. But she found that the romantic part of their connection didn't make as much sense now that they weren't working together. Frida encouraged him to keep working on *Four and Ten*; for now, she didn't want much to do with it. Or more than that, she didn't have the time, the space in her brain. There were so many things! Which to choose? For years now it had felt like John Reddan was, in a way, an externalised part of herself. A hard drive she could download pieces of herself onto, as a back-up. So if he was to take *Four and Ten* and finish it himself, make it into a John Reddan production, wouldn't it still remain somewhat hers, anyway? It would always contain traces of her DNA. After all, there was a female role made for her. In fact, there were two. She could have her choice.

Frida almost never interacted with Killian Schaeffer. He breezed into the rehearsal room like he was heading to the beach. He didn't even see her. He had the actors doing all sorts of games with each other, but the understudies were not involved. She got used to this quickly. There were other learning methods, she thought. Just watching the actors at work, with their drama-school educations, their decades of real-world experience, showed her all the different ways one could be an actor. In her emails to John she elided this, though. Instead she told him about the boredom, the bone-numbing uncertainty, the feeling of purgatory unique to the understudies' green room. She didn't mention Killian Schaeffer himself, his cool disregard for her. I will never talk to John about working with another director, she decided. The reality was that really, there was nothing to say.

I'm looking forward to *Four and Ten*, she wrote to John in one email. This experience has made me miss the smaller rooms, the ones with you in them.

On the second night of *The Other Side of Silence,* Frida came to work visibly hungover. She entered the green room where the understudies congregated and took her time taking off her denim jacket, her long woven scarf. Albert was already seated with his book of sudokus in his lap. He watched her.

'Alright?' he said as she took a seat in the worn brown armchair.

'I've been better.'

'Big night?'

Frida had gone out with some of the cast for celebratory drinks and they'd ended up in the American Bar at the Savoy. It was the first time she'd ever had a martini, and then it was the second, and maybe even the third.

'Sort of,' she admitted. 'You know how opening night can be.'

Rolling the biro across the front of his sudoku book, Albert prepared to say something.

'You're not taking this seriously.'

Frida swallowed. 'I am taking this seriously.'

'The thing about this job, Frida, is that you must be ready. Always be ready. Don't come here looking like crap, smelling like an ashtray. There is no time to not be ready.' Albert stood up, pointing towards the corridor. 'This place is a big deal.'

'I know that,' she said.

He continued, ignoring her. 'There's a stage out there, with people who paid lots of money to see this, people who paid some proportion of their daily income to sit here for two hours and have us entertain them. That's no small thing. As well as that, there are people like me, like you, like the ushers and the stagehands and the cleaners who are here to make this work, who get paid to do this and thus need it to have some value for them, so they don't go home feeling like complete shit. It's a livelihood. You can't fuck this up for everyone because you're not ready.'

Frida nodded, running her hands over her knees. 'I am ready,' she said, not quite believing it.

Albert gave her a wry smile. 'I'd hope so. Your girl looked hungover in the dressing room earlier as well. Tonight could be your night.'

It was doing something to Frida's brain. It did not suit her, this uncertain kind of work. While she tried to focus on the prestige, the 'big deal' theatre that Albert had mentioned came as little comfort in the green room. Sometimes she soothed herself by looking at her picture in the programme. A headshot, out of date, that Madeline had emailed her one day saying, You might need this. A picture of her, just like the pictures of the actual cast, like they were all the same. She envied the cast, not because they got to act every night, but because they got to have a degree of certainty when they woke up in the morning.

By closing night Frida was the only understudy working on *The Other Side of Silence* not to have gone on at least once. She made her peace with this. It was a form of apprenticeship, anyway; something that gave her skill and experience through close observation rather than actual practice. She was aghast to think how things could have worked out, had she landed the role of young Moira. Showing up for rehearsals without having done a play outside of Ireland. A bare-bones CV and her agency bankrupt. It made Frida feel unwell to even consider it.

She decided to stay in London a little while longer. She invited John to come over once the play finished. She wanted to pick up the thread of *Four and Ten* with him, and she assumed that their relationship would resume along with it. Frida bustled around the little flat in Finsbury Park, imagining John in the yellow kitchen, the small, bright bedroom overlooking the garden. She had the vague, silly idea that she was different now – a different kind of actor from her experience understudying, and a different kind of woman, too. She was trying to imagine the next chapter of Frida Slattery's life, and doing so felt pleasantly poignant.

In Frida's final week understudying, Mel McMorrow entered her life. Mel was a talent agent who had just seen *The Other Side of Silence*. She told Frida on the phone, the first time they spoke, that the play had done nothing for her. Too miserable. Not her thing. She thought the actors were well cast, though, which meant she found herself engrossed in the programme on the way home. This was how she came face to face with Frida's out-of-date headshot. Mel was looking for an emerging Irish actress for her roster. She said this to Frida straight away, with no compunction about sounding like a mercenary. An Irish actress called Penny Hegarty had recently broken out thanks to a very raunchy BBC adaptation of *Persuasion* and now everyone wanted one of their own, especially if she had a sexy little overbite or a set of dimples like Hegarty's. Frida had a gap between her front teeth, and this, Mel said, was what caught her eye.

'But you didn't even see me act,' Frida said, sounding like a child who couldn't get their head around how adults can break the rules.

'Doesn't matter,' Mel responded. 'Well, no, of course it does. But I know Shona Reynolds. I asked her to send me your CV. She's cast some of my other clients and I trust her. Can we meet this week?'

Frida was impressed by Mel. She was maybe in her early thirties, very well groomed, and she carried an expensive Prada handbag. Frida had been wearing the same jeans for most of the autumn. Sometimes she worried that the jeans were becoming a part of her, like a smell she couldn't get rid of. They were sitting outside a coffee shop on Monmouth Street and Frida couldn't stop looking at Mel. Mel was gay and had grown up in Sunderland, but now lived in Peckham, she explained, where she'd bought a house the year before. (A *house*, Frida thought.) She also spent half the year in LA and said this to Frida in a way that sounded, to Frida's ears, like it might be an invitation.

'What do you want from your career, Frida?' Mel asked, pushing her big sunglasses onto the crown of her head.

'You make it sound like I could have anything.'

'Who says you couldn't?'

'I'm an understudy, and I'm almost thirty. I've barely been on television.'

'So what? Who cares?' Mel asked, tapping a cigarette into the ashtray. 'For one thing, you're twenty-seven ... twenty-five on a good day, I reckon. You haven't answered my question, though.'

Frida turned away from her and looked down the street, at a group of tourists taking photos of a building painted bubblegum pink. If John had been asking her that question, she would have known exactly what to say. I want to make the kind of work that makes people believe in theatre. I want to do that with you, because I think you're the one person who knows how to push me, how to get the best out of me, and because I think there's a good chance we might be in love with each other.

'Ah, you know,' Frida eventually said. 'I guess it'd be nice to go to Hollywood.'

It helped that Frida and Mel got on so well. Frida had never met a proper northerner before, only posh drama-school graduates who claimed to be from Yorkshire but sounded like they'd gone to Eton. It turned out that Mel liked to have a good time. She was always inviting Frida to the pub or to a friend's house party, and Frida would show up to find Mel half-cut, rolling cigarettes, someone's toy poodle on her lap and the contents of her handbag spilling onto the floor.

Frida told Mel about John Reddan, who after all was responsible for more than half her CV, and was surprised that Mel did not seem particularly impressed. In advance of John's arrival, Frida suspected it would be best to keep the pair away from each other. At least at first. They were two live wires that were not supposed to touch, she reckoned. When John arrived he unpacked his laptop and thick sheafs of paper along with his clothes and shoes. They were print-outs of the latest draft of *Four and Ten*, he explained as they headed down to the cheap and cheerful sushi restaurant two doors down from the flat, and he wanted Frida to read through the latest draft before he started taking meetings with commissioners from the Royal Court and Donmar Warehouse about it.

'I didn't know we were at that stage of the script now,' Frida said once they were seated at her usual table. 'I had thought that we were going to get back into the writing together, now that you're here.'

'It's pretty much done, to be honest.'

'Really?' she asked.

'Yep.' The way John said it felt like a riposte, or a challenge. 'Some tweaks, see what the commissioners say. But that's it. Did you think I was just going to put it aside while you were off in the West End?'

'It wasn't the West End.'

'You know what I mean.'

'I didn't think you'd put everything on pause. I was just curious. I've been looking forward to working with you on it.'

John dipped a piece of salmon nigiri into the soy sauce and they both watched the rice fall away from the chopsticks. 'You will work with me on it. When I get the commission, I'll cast you as Wendy.'

'Who's Wendy?'

'She used to be Aoife. I changed some names and details, since it's not going to be set in Ireland anymore.'

He was happy for her to read every new draft, review each tweak he made to dialogue or stage direction. But Frida quickly became aware that John no longer wanted any real input from her on this play. He wanted nothing more than for her to tell him it was looking good, it was getting better with every alteration. On his arrival in October, John told her he would stay in London for a week, but soon it became clear that he had no immediate plans to go home. It happened without them even talking about it, the same way their sex life had resumed again. One morning at the breakfast table

Frida mentioned that she needed to pay rent, and John said, without looking up from his laptop, that he'd pay half for this month if she wanted him to. Soon it was Christmas, and Frida went home for a few days to see her family. When she returned to Finsbury Park, she realised on entering that the flat smelled like John, because he lived here, too. They were living together now, like real people in a real relationship.

Frida told Mel none of this. Despite their frequent phone calls, Mel knew simply that John was around, that Frida referred to him mostly in oblique terms as a sort-of ex-boyfriend who she was sort-of still seeing, and who was sort-of developing a new play. Mel didn't care. The plays Frida had made with John were small fry. Mel had big plans for Frida, even if they were going to take a while. She sent Frida to a hairdresser she liked in Chelsea who understood curly hair. Frida left the salon blonder than she'd ever been. Mel was talking to people about Frida all the time, she told her one Friday evening in the pub, it was just a matter of time before the auditions started rolling in. Just then Frida's phone rang with a call from John, wondering what she was up to.

When she hung up, Mel rolled her eyes.

'What does he want this time?'

'He's just out of a meeting at the Royal Court. He might come by for a drink.'

Mel exhaled a thick plume of smoke. 'Fab. Here comes the misery man.'

'Mel, he's my friend. I mean, well.' Frida stopped to think about it. 'We've worked together for a long time.'

Mel hadn't seen *Graceland,* or *Bird,* though she was aware of the good critical reception *Graceland* received at Edinburgh two and a half years earlier.

'Yes, vital, important work, truly groundbreaking stuff,' Mel said, adopting a plummy accent.

Frida took a sip of her cider. It had been a while since she and John worked together outside of writing in his living room, and the passing of time was starting to make her feel a little embarrassed about those plays. Their relationship had changed since she'd left Dublin. The first time they'd gone to bed together, it had felt inevitable to Frida, and for that reason it had been pleasing. A little revelation, another part of their relationship unfolding before her. For a while, then, it was as if John was the answer to her every question. But as time went by, their sleeping together here in London started to take on an anxious edge. If they had this, then what else was there? How much time did they really have left together?

When John arrived, Mel made space for him at their table. Frida introduced them and they eyed each other with the suspicion of two people who'd heard a lot about each other, and had already drawn their own conclusions.

'Now,' Mel said while John got settled. 'How are they all at the Court today?'

He attempted a laugh. 'They're all fine, I suppose.'

Mel gave him a pointed look. It was as if she thought John was far too serious and pretentious for a humble Sunderland girl like her, but that wasn't right. Mel had clients who made work that was ten times more pretentious than John's, and Frida didn't think she acted this way around them. John, for his part, didn't know how to act around Mel at all.

'What are you working on now?' Mel asked John.

For a second Frida was fearful that John would say something about *Four and Ten*, her involvement in it, the part he believed he had written for her.

'Ah, I don't know how much I should be talking about it,' John said. 'Until we get a definite commission. I'm a bit superstitious, you know, about spooking the horses.'

'But your agent seems to think it's viable, right?' Frida said. 'Like, nothing is 100 per cent, but it feels like they're going to produce your play.'

'I mean the artistic horses,' he said.

Across the table Mel could barely contain herself. 'Spooking the artistic horses,' she repeated. 'What a lovely turn of phrase. What a lovely image. I could never come up with something like that, John. But that's why you're the writer. That's why they pay you the big bucks, isn't it?'

John stared at her over his pint. 'Yeah, Mel. That's why, alright.'

Other than that, Frida loved Mel in an uncomplicated way. It was not often that she had experienced friendship with a woman in this way. It came as a surprise, this far into adulthood. There was no jealousy, no attempts made by one to possess the other. Frida and Mel talked on the phone most days: sometimes about work and potential jobs, but mostly about their lives, what had happened to them that afternoon and what they'd wear the next night, their childhoods and their worries and something funny they'd both seen on the internet that day. Even with John, who she had spent so much time with these last few years, things had never been this easy. Frida loved John, and hoped they could make many more plays together over the years, even if Mel managed to get her to Hollywood in one piece. But in London there were times when the fact of him – his presence in her bed, his mannish smells, his obsessive neurosis about their sex life, or his drafts waiting for her on the top of her chest of drawers – felt more like a burden than a partnership of equals.

Frida knew that Mel couldn't have friendships like this with all her clients. She had too many on her books to be yapping on the phone all day long. That fact made Frida aware that their working relationship had something else to it, some deeper level of understanding. She realised this all at once, waking up early one morning with the knowledge that she trusted Mel now, trusted her profoundly. Mel had professional expertise, but also a growing understanding of who Frida was as a person. Frida got out of bed, leaving John asleep, and went to the toilet with a sense of existential urgency. Looking in the mirror as she washed her hands, she said aloud, like it was a mantra: I'm just going to do whatever Mel thinks is best for me.

It turned out that what Mel thought was best was a series of auditions for car ads, small parts in independent films with acclaimed directors, some episodic TV jobs. Frida got more call-backs than actual roles. But there was a day here or there in the background of a BBC drama, a single line in a movie by an esteemed British film-maker. Then there was the audition for a director who Frida greatly admired. Rebecca Jenkins had made a string of critically acclaimed films that were connected by a vague feminist slant. People liked her work, and the actors she worked with often went on to bigger and better things. Frida had high hopes. When it was her turn, she entered the room to find Rebecca Jenkins sitting with a man and a woman, deep in conversation. All three turned to look at her sharply, like she'd rudely interrupted them.

'I'm Frida Slattery,' she said as she took a seat in front of them. The panel said nothing. The silence while they met each other's eyes was unsettling. Frida was about to start her monologue anyway when Rebecca Jenkins raised her hand.

'Wrong look,' the director said flatly. 'Thanks for coming in.'

Frida cycled home miserable, anger and despair in every push of the pedals. It was the repetition of it all, she thought, locking her bike in the hallway. It was how much you cared, and how quickly that dissolved once someone got a look at you. And it was the fact that none of it seemed to be getting any better. Who was it who said that the definition of insanity was doing the same thing over and over and expecting a different result? And yet here she was.

John was in the kitchen when she opened the door to the flat.

'Hey. What's wrong?'

Frida felt hot tears stinging in her eyes, like she was a little girl. 'Rebecca Jenkins thinks I have the wrong look.'

'You auditioned for her today?'

Frida nodded.

'You should've told me.'

'Sorry.'

'And she said you had the wrong look? Well, that's not too bad as criticism goes. That's just the luck of the draw.'

'No, it was worse than that.'

'How?'

Frida blew her nose. 'It was the way she said it. It was horrible.'

'Oh, Free. Come here.' He enveloped her in a hug. 'You don't need to dazzle everyone.'

'Yes I do.'

'No, listen to me. You're not going to be able to walk into every single room and be everything to every person. The only people who can do that are boring people. And you're not boring.'

'I just feel so tired of all of this sometimes. I'm tired of feeling so unremarkable.'

'Frida, Jesus.' John held her shoulders at arm's length so he could get a proper look at her. 'Unremarkable? Don't ever let me hear you say that. Never.'

He was deadly serious, and she had the urge to laugh to break his focus, but she resisted it.

'I mean it,' he said. 'Do you think I would want to work with you if you were not remarkable?'

'I suppose not,' Frida said, wiping her eyes on the sleeve of her jacket.

John rested his chin on the crown of her head, so she could feel him talk all through her skull. 'You're more than remarkable,' he said. 'I think you're an absolute showstopper, Frida Slattery.'

At last Frida did laugh then, leaning against John's chest, the two of them shuddering with laughter until all of it was out. It was true, she realised. He wanted her to be remarkable even more than she did. In one way, that made him feel like home. In another way, though, it could only ever feel like pressure.

At any rate, Frida could no longer pretend that she and John weren't a real couple. In the spring, they attended Catherine and Toby's wedding together. It was a pleasant day – the ceremony at the registry office on Upper Street followed by pictures taken under a cherry blossom tree, then a big meal in a French restaurant for about forty of them. Catherine beautiful and teary-eyed in a bias-cut white slip dress, ten times better looking and more interesting than her new husband, Frida thought. It was a funny thing. Frida spent the day swinging wildly from a feeling of total happiness for her friend – a kind of pride in Catherine, she thought – to another feeling, the complete certainty that Frida herself did not want anything that looked like this.

A few weeks later, Catherine sent her a link to an online gallery of wedding photos. She attached one particular photo to the email with the message: You guys are so adorable. Maybe you two next? Xx

The sight of herself and John made Frida flinch. In the photo they were under a canopy of pink blossom, John looking down at her with one arm wrapped around her small frame. His blue suit was slightly too big for him, the only one he owned. This had annoyed her so much on the day, that he couldn't scrub up the way she could. But in the photo the two of them were gazing at each other so intently, him with his familiar half-smile etched on his mouth and her looking back up at him, clutching a glass of prosecco. It was like they were sharing a moment in private. Catherine was right, Frida thought, closing the email. If Frida hadn't known the couple in the photograph, she would have said they were adorable, too.

Mel sent Frida to read for a new American network drama, a procedural thing with a twist made by a married couple who were of vaguely Scandinavian extraction, who wanted someone totally different, someone with a 'regional charm', for the female lead of the hard-boiled criminal lawyer.

'You're perfect,' Mel promised on the phone as Frida walked to the hotel in Kensington where the couple were holed up. 'Tell me everything the moment you come out.'

In the lobby, in the mirror by the lift., Frida fixed a thick strand of her hair, blow-dried straight with great care that morning. When she'd left the flat earlier, she'd told John she was going to meet Shona Reynolds for a catch-up. As the lift spirited her up five storeys, she couldn't figure out why she'd lied. Maybe she feared what he might say.

The hotel room was a minimalist white palace, gauzy curtains and early afternoon light pooling all around. Sara and Tobias Lund sat on a bouclé cream puff of a sofa, chic and dressed entirely in black. There was a cluster of empty espresso cups in front of Tobias, who was tall and doughy, not particularly attractive but sort of interesting to look at. Sara was elfin with white-blonde highlighted hair and scarlet nails. She had milky skin, like she had never been exposed to the sun.

'Welcome,' Tobias said, his vowels long and languid. 'You are...'

'Frida Slattery,' Sara said, reading from the laptop in front of her in a mid-Atlantic accent.

Frida nodded. 'Yes, thanks for having me.'

Frida read the script for them – unremarkable, barely memorable – and when she was finished Sara held up one small hand and asked her to sit down on the white plastic Eames chair in front of them. Sara asked Frida what her favourite role had been, and Frida thought about the question for a little while.

'I'd been in plays in school and college,' she began. 'But the thing that felt like the beginning of my career as an actor was a play called *Bird* that I did about five years ago. You won't have heard of it. It was in a little theatre called Dublin, and some people truly hated it. But I played a woman who was going through a separation, and was losing part of her sanity in the process. And every night I got up on stage, where the stage manager pelted us with rainwater and flashing lights, and I forgot that I was me. That I was Frida. There was something about that experience that I come back to when I look at a project now. Is there enough there, I ask myself, when I'm getting to know a potential role, is there enough in this person for me to forget about the Frida Slattery-ness of me? Because that's really all that matters.'

'And is there?' Tobias asked. 'In what you have before you. In Katherine Richards, the tough lawyer.'

And Frida knew that he was testing her, and that the rest of this audition didn't matter if she didn't answer correctly. So she smiled at him and said, 'Oh, yes. I think there is.'

In the lift back down to the hotel lobby, Frida shut her eyes tight. Was it really necessary to prostrate herself before the altar of American network TV? What about *Four and Ten*? It was going to be a chance for them to go again, to create something from nothing together. She walked out of the hotel and headed for Knightsbridge station, head buzzing with embarrassment. This had been Mel's idea, not hers. This was just a bad day at the office, she reassured herself, albeit one in what was beginning to seem like an endless string of bad days. As she reached for her Oyster card to tap through the turnstile, her phone vibrated with a call from Mel. They really liked you, she said. They want you to stay close to the hotel, while they talk some things through, and they'll call you then.

So Frida turned around and left the station, went to the pub across the road, ordered a gin and tonic and waited for things to change.

6.

John and Frida walked along the old disused railway line, the dirt path dry and dusty underfoot, talking about work. It was early summer in London, and the city was in the midst of a heatwave that was refusing to break. For weeks John had been waiting to hear from his new agent about finding a home for *Four and Ten*. He expected there to be another round of development, but he could cross that bridge when he came to it. In the meantime, he was thinking about Frida.

'If you could do anything for your next job,' he asked. 'What would you pick?'

'Fuck knows. The last few months have been so weird. Mel just keeps sending me on things, and I keep going without even thinking about what they might be like.'

'Sometimes you have to follow your nose. A while back, I thought I'd make a documentary. I thought I had to go where the funding was.'

'Christ almighty. You never told me that.'

'It was going to be about this guy, this boxer who's hoping to go to the Olympics. I met him four times, I really sold it to him. One of his sisters thought it was going to be like *Keeping Up with the Kardashians*. I had to break it to her gently.'

Frida kicked a stone with the toe of her sandal. 'I cannot imagine you doing that.'

'He's a really interesting guy. Multi-faceted. Maybe I'll still do it. Olympics isn't for another two years. There's time.'

Nine months earlier, John had received a bursary to write his next play, and after that, the documentary idea went out the window. He'd spent most of the money on these last few months in London, wasting time, tinkering with *Four and Ten* while he waited for it to find a home.

'That attitude,' Frida continued as they walk. 'That thing of going where the funding is. It's so grim. Don't you find it depressing?'

'I think it's the reality of it sometimes.'

'Sometimes I just wish we could forget about money, about commissioners, and just try to do something for the love of it, you know? Like when we did *Graceland*.'

'*Graceland* was the depressing thing. And look, I'm doing *Four and Ten*, once it gets signed off.'

'I know.'

He reached for her hand. 'We can keep doing this, you know. For as long as we want to.'

'I know that too, John.'

'Anyway,' he said, teasing. 'Who are you to call me a sell-out? Didn't Mel send you on an audition for a car ad the other week?'

She smiled wistfully. 'I would've been so good. But they said I lacked the right maternal energy.'

'I bet the money would have been nice, too.'

'Do you ever wonder why we're still doing this?'

John paused to lean on a tree stump, taking off a shoe to shake out a stone. 'Yeah, all the time. But then I think how terrible it would be not to do it. To just go and get a real job? It would feel like giving up on a dream.'

Frida snorted. 'I think that's bullshit.'

'What's bullshit?'

'Your talk of dreams. I think we're like junkies, you and me. It's impossible to get us off the teat. I think if we tried to stop, go cold turkey, we might die.'

'You think we like the attention.'

'I don't think we like it. I think we need it to live.'

John had been in London for almost eight months. It was silly to think about now, but when he'd arrived at Frida's flat he thought he'd be there for a fortnight tops, enough time to get her to read through the latest drafts of *Four and Ten*, and get them sent off to the commissioners who'd expressed an interest in his work. But then he was courted by an agent. *Hedda*'s awards had done the trick, sending a small but exciting flurry of messages into his inbox. Growing up, John had been more Broadway-minded than West End (indeed, more arthouse cinema than theatre at all, but theatre's door had proved a lot easier to lean on thus far), but nonetheless he wasn't immune to the city's charms. He met Alice Greer for lunch in a restaurant on the Strand that she assured him was 'the heart of the action'. She wooed him over champagne, oysters, a good steak and a promise that she could get his work in front of all the right people. He was impressed by her, no doubt. She was ten years older, had an expensive haircut and talked obliquely of her two toddlers. Three times, their lunch was interrupted by people who came to greet her – actors, directors – and she introduced John to each of them in a way that implied that he was the important one in the equation. He knew it was a ruse, but it was fair to say that it worked on him.

Since he'd signed with her, Alice had barely called. He sent her the best version of *Four and Ten* and left it to her to find it a home. He'd never worked on a script the way he had worked on this one. Since sending it off, he'd spent most of his time rattling around Frida's flat, trying to write. He didn't tell Frida that the script was in limbo. He didn't want to risk dragging her back into the writing of it, the way they had been a year earlier. That phase was over. He'd trusted her with so much, and then she'd left him in the lurch. He would continue to work with her, but only as an actor, he thought. Anything else would be too risky.

Now each day felt like the two of them were sat in a waiting room together. He was sure they were both a hair away from something big. Every time John checked his email he braced himself for the message that would bring new promise, an opportunity, the prospect of money. This was easier and less painful than simply sitting down and writing something new, like Alice had advised him to. Meanwhile Frida was out every day, auditioning, meeting people, going to movement classes or hair appointments. She had a new agent too, an abrasive woman named Melanie who she seemed to revere. Melanie had Frida dye her hair much lighter, and John liked that, it made him think of Tippi Hedren in *The Birds*. Frida was always on the phone to her, laughing away while painting her toenails or making dinner.

A slim, tense part of John worried that he was cramping Frida's style. She had been in London for almost three months before he'd arrived on her doorstep. Frida had a burgeoning circle of friends, and a favourite pub down the road with its shady beer garden and intimidatingly trendy young bar staff. Even without any work lined up, she got up early in the morning and went and did things. John didn't have this ability within him. If John wasn't assiduous about it, he could easily waste the day dicking around with *Four and Ten*, browsing Twitter, smoking out Frida's bedroom window, doing nothing until she returned. So he made up meetings with producers and agents, research trips to libraries that would fill the afternoons. In reality he wandered around, sometimes sitting in a coffee shop on his laptop, sometimes queueing for returned tickets at the National Theatre box office. It was all work, he reminded himself. It all counted.

Except that Frida's dry spell was starting to feel portentous to John. Melanie McMorrow had designs on Frida's future, and they didn't involve highbrow theatre. That car ad was just the latest in a long line of potential gigs that were getting glossier and glossier every week. In Dublin what John did, the work he made, made sense. Here he felt like an amateur. Why had nothing happened with *Four and Ten* yet? What was his life? Crashing in Frida's flat, sleeping with her just enough to make it feel like actually what he was doing was 'living with his girlfriend', like a normal adult man of thirty-three. While he waited around for her to come in from wherever she'd been all day, he decided to start doing the things that people in relationships do. He could buy groceries and have Frida's favourite meal ready for when she arrived home. He could kiss her, ask about her day. Did he feel like a hausfrau? Yes, a little, but maybe at this juncture, that was better than feeling entirely useless.

'White smoke,' Alice said when John answered her phone call the day after his walk with Frida along the track. 'The Court are in. There will be a bit of a process from here – workshopping, development. But they're game, and I think it looks good. They're sending a contract over now.'

A jolt went through John like he had just taken a shot of tequila. With his free hand he made a fist and banged it lightly off the kitchen table. 'Ah, Alice. You've made my day.'

'My pleasure, John. I think this might be the beginning of something quite exciting, you know.'

Four and Ten felt like it had been a long time in the making now. He needed to tell Frida. She was so busy these days. Sometimes it felt like John was competing for her attention. He wanted Frida for himself, but that was mostly because he wanted Frida to be great. He knew she could be great. They could be great together, and hopefully for a long time to come. Wasn't that why they'd decided to get into bed together the year before? Now here she was, coming into the flat in her denim cut-offs, slightly out of breath, her bike helmet dangling from her wrist.

'Guess what?' he said, rising from his chair to kiss her.

That night after dinner he and Frida went down to the local pub.

'It's such good news, John,' Frida said as she sat down at the table with two pints. 'Congratulations.'

'Well, it's good news for us both, is it not?'

'Sure,' she said, laughing a little. 'Congratulations to me too.'

John frowned. 'This was your play to begin with.'

'Yeah, well. It definitely feels like yours by now. So much has changed in the last year, hasn't it? And of the two of us, you're the writer. You've always been the writer.'

'Okay, but ... no, I guess you're right.'

'It's been a long time in the making, it feels.'

'Frida,' John started. 'You're still in, right? I mean, you still want to be in *Four and Ten*?'

She blinked, setting her glass down. 'Of course I do. Just as long as the timing works out.'

'Why wouldn't it?'

'Well, I had an audition today.'

'You did? I didn't know.'

'Sorry. It was for a TV show, like an American crime drama-type thing. It's one of three lead roles, actually. And I think I'm going to get it.'

'Wait. Really?'

'Yeah, they called me back almost instantly and we just talked, me and the two showrunners, for an hour or so. I've got a call-back next week, a chemistry test.'

'Jesus. But how's that going to work? When would you be filming?'

Frida shrugged. 'Fuck knows. I've never done anything like this before!'

John stared at her with confusion. 'Frida, *Wendy*,' he said, pressing on the name Wendy like it was a doorbell. 'How can you do both this new thing and Wendy?'

Frida's eyes lit up suddenly. 'Wendy, John! Wendy! You know in my version, she was supposed to be called Aoife. Like, come on. How do you get Wendy from Aoife?'

'Aoife would never have worked, Frida, not if we're doing it in London.'

'But are we? I gave you my draft over a year ago. Look how much our lives have changed since then.'

'It is going to happen. And anyway, I wouldn't call what you gave me a draft.'

'Stop. I think that's unfair. You know I'm not a writer.'

'That's how we work, isn't it? We work together, you and me, Free. And so it doesn't work if you just pull out and fuck off to America to make a – what did you say it was? – a procedural crime drama.' He said the last words like he was tasting something rancid.

'Well, maybe we shouldn't be working together on this play, then.'

'What?'

She folded her hands in her lap. 'I mean, you did such a

good job without me on *Hedda Gabler*.' She sighed, and neither of them said anything for a long time. 'Look, John. I don't even have the part yet. At least give me a chance. At least let me tell you about it.'

Frida's crime drama was called *The Reason*. It was the brainchild of a Swedish-American couple who had cut their teeth working on all sorts of lowbrow nonsense that John obviously hadn't seen. In the pub, Frida and John looked at their IMDB pages on John's phone and Frida told him what she knew about the show. It was going to be smart and sexy. It was the kind of show people would want to talk about. It might even twist the genre a little, push some boundaries. And the part was a good one, the female lead, really, opposite two men, all three of them lawyers. There would be a long-running plot, a romance between co-workers as well as short-term stories to fill an episode or two at most. Frida was enamoured with it, John could tell. He suspected that Mel was blowing smoke up her ass. Back in her flat that night, Frida opened her laptop and started playing an episode of a murder-mystery miniseries that the Lunds had written.

'I think they've got a sense of humour,' she said, laying her head on John's lap on the sagging grey couch. 'And you definitely have to agree that their work is sexy.'

'Do I?' John said. On screen, a freckled young woman too young to be a detective was getting into a very large car. 'I think it depends how you define sexy.'

'It's the Florida Keys, imagine how sticky it is there. I feel like it has like a noir streak to it.'

The word noir made John think of *Chinatown*, Faye Dunaway coming down the stairs as the plot unravelled before your eyes. John loved Polanski, even though you weren't really supposed to anymore. It was basically impossible for John to imagine Frida in an American network drama. She could possibly be a detective in a Scandi-style noir, maybe – a woman with problems and a couple of skeletons in her closet. He had seen a clip of the British submarine drama, and while she only had a few lines, she was very good as the Northern Irish navy officer, the tomboy among the lads. But it was outlandish, the idea of Frida visiting California, a place neither of them had ever been. He imagined her bathed in golden light. He imagined her with her teeth fixed, the little gap cemented over. If she got this role, she would be made American, he thought. But surely she wouldn't get it.

It would have been ludicrous, unthinkable, for anyone to say that John was jealous of Frida. Such jealousy surely couldn't exist between them, considering their different disciplines. And yet there was at times a meanness to his thoughts. He wanted her on stage in London, yes, but partly because he wanted to direct in London. Sometimes he wanted the two of them to be one of those couples, the director and the actor who shared an entire life, two halves of the same whole, inspiring each other to make new work, giving interviews together about their latest projects. It was one thing when she'd gone to understudy at the National Theatre without him. That was respectable work. But American TV, he thought in bed that night, after Frida went to sleep. It just wasn't the right path for her. At times like these, he sometimes noticed his thoughts about Frida becoming more critical. Her range wasn't great, he considered. She would become wooden in a role like that, forced into the same interactions and situations over and over. The procedural format definitely wouldn't suit her. She was at her best when she could laugh and cry and rage against the world. And she was good at nuance, and those shows left no room for nuance. Also, he thought, looking at her sleeping beside him in the late-night half-light, she probably wasn't thin enough for American television audiences.

What was the problem? What was it that had changed between them? Which part of their relationship had gone haywire, which limb atrophied? John had never felt less like sleeping. He lay awake and ran through these thoughts over and over.

Until *Hedda Gabler*, John had feared that all the plaudits he'd received in the last few years had been for Frida's work, not his. He was keenly aware that it was his work with her that had cut through the most. When making *Hedda*, the Abbey's casting director told John that Frida Slattery wouldn't work, she was too young, and also he didn't like her. He thought she was too poised, too tense. John was struck by panic. He thought, almost superstitiously, that he would be doomed to failure without her. He had said this to his brother over pizza in Harold's Cross and Barry had slapped the table with his palm.

'You've got it all wrong,' Barry had said. 'It's upside down. It's not doomed. It's an opportunity. You have a chance now to prove yourself wrong.'

It was rare that his brother would come forth with such wisdom. Fuck knows where it had come from. John missed his brother, which was embarrassing. They'd been living together for years, and three months after *Hedda* they'd had a call from a cousin of their father telling them that Dermot had died of a heart attack. After the small funeral in Waterford, Barry had turned to John and told him in a low tone that now it really was just the two of them. Barry had a girlfriend, Joanna, who had been staying in the house in Harold's Cross since John had left for London. Lately John found himself braced for the phone call from his brother that would tell him to pack up and move out so Joanna could move in.

But maybe that would be fine. Maybe this was the start of something else now, here, in London. Alice's words on the phone came to him again. The start of something really exciting. Frida was still sleeping beside him. Her bad attempt at toasting his success earlier that night, her immediate pivot to some news of her own. A ridiculous thought crossed his mind then, right as sleep began to come: he saw himself driving a very nice car, a little dark-green sporty number – the kind he could never afford – and driving it away from here, away from the tiny outline of Frida standing on the curb behind him, disappearing in the wing mirror.

7.

Seeing the two lines on the little window was just so reasonable. As soon as they appeared, Frida was certain there could have been no other way for this to go. The nausea she had had all week, the sense of profound unease within her own body. Something entirely new for her. It all felt concrete now, and impossible to ignore. The pain in her breasts was the final giveaway. On the Tube on her way to her call-back with the Lunds, she gazed at her shadowy reflection in the carriage window. In her white Oxford shirt her chest looked like it belonged to someone else. Buy a test on your way home, she thought.

From Boots, Frida walked through Soho until she came to a hotel on Berwick Street where she'd once gone for drinks with some actors she knew. She beelined through the lobby to the ladies' loos and locked herself in a cubicle. Frida felt a kind of relief – like she'd been running and running from danger for so long and now, suddenly, the threat had passed. Perhaps the threat had just caught up with her at last. Crazy to think that two people could have been as lax as Frida and John and get away with it. Lax with everything, she thought, standing up from the toilet seat, not just the issue of getting pregnant. In a way she'd assumed that the casual nature of things, compounded by the fact that half the time they tried to have sex, John was let down by his anatomy, meant that they didn't need to take things so seriously. She took a final look at the pregnancy test before forcing it into the trapdoor of the sanitary-waste bin. What was their relationship? They'd been having sex on and off, for a year now. They'd started living together without ever even addressing their situation in actual words. They'd never 'gone on a date', nor told anyone in their lives that they were together, nor even told each other that they were together. Things had felt even more piecemeal, ramshackle, since he'd moved in with her. She thought suddenly of Una, the way she'd kept her relationship with Simon secret from their families and their co-workers, and felt that inheritance rocket through her. The idea of trying to explain this to her mother hurt doubly. Were she and John together? Frida had kissed one of the actors from *The Other Side of Silence* at cast drinks one night last November. Now she and John could literally bring a child into the world if they wanted to. They were standing together on that threshold and neither of them had even been aware of it. She imagined Edel laughing at her for being so naive. What did you think would happen, Frida? His sperm would take one look at your egg and think, Well, in fairness, they've not really *defined* their relationship. No, she couldn't tell Edel about this, either. The whole thing from start to finish was beginning to feel to Frida like an accident – like they'd gone too far while rehearsing one day and ended up killing someone. Like they forgot, somehow, that the things they did with each other took place in the real world and not simply in a rehearsal room or on a stage.

She left the bathroom shaking her head. Outside on Berwick Street, Frida emerged blinking into the daylight. It was like seeing the world clearly for the first time, like when she'd been prescribed reading glasses a year earlier and saw the words falling cleanly into place on the page before her. It was all so obvious now, and it made sense that she would sit down that evening, tell John what happened, tell him what it was that she wanted to do next.

But he had been such a shit about *The Reason* the week before. So snobbish about the decisions Frida was making for herself. He'd tried to rein it in, but Frida could sense it there, just behind his eyes. He was biting his tongue. He wanted to say, This is beneath you, Frida. More than anything, she knew he wanted to tell her what to do. It was what he had always done, from the very first time they'd met. It was the bedrock of their relationship, wasn't it? It was what connected them to begin with. Frida at a loose end, in need of guidance and John happy to pick her up and point her in the way he thought was best.

And so if she went to him and told him this and wasn't 100 per cent certain in her voice, in her body language, in how she stared at him – how would he react? What might he tell her to do?

When she came home, John was there at the stove, cooking spaghetti bolognese. He'd made a mess of the kitchen. The smell of the minced beef wafted right through the flat and

Frida winced. He turned to face her, an expectant look on his face.

'How did it go?'

'Just fine,' she said. Her voice was high and tight.

He opened the fridge and pulled out a bottle of supermarket cava. 'Are we celebrating?'

'Yeah. I think we are.'

John poured two glasses and sat across from her at the small kitchen table. 'That's good.'

'Well, yeah. I haven't signed a contract yet. But apparently that's all in progress as we speak.'

He forced a smile at her. 'Congratulations, Frida. When will shooting begin?'

'They're aiming for October. Georgia first, then the studios in California.'

'You'll need to find somewhere to live.'

'Mel is good at that stuff. She spends months out there, she knows loads of people.'

John sipped his wine, checked the time on his phone.

'It is temporary, you know,' Frida said. 'It's not a forever thing.'

'Okay.'

'Don't be like this.'

'I'm not being like anything. If you want to go, you should go. I've never said otherwise, not once.'

Frida stood up. 'I'm not really in the mood for wine. You can have mine.' She crossed the kitchen, heading for the bedroom. The door closed behind her and she lay down on the bed.

It was not like she had to tell John anything, if she didn't want to.

In the kitchen she heard him bustling around with pots and pans, draining the pasta.

His voice came through the bedroom door.

'Frida?' John said. 'It's ready when you are.'

6. *Four and Ten* (John Reddan), 2011

John could barely remember the first time he slept with Kitty Adams. He knew that it had been the end of *Four and Ten*'s first week at the Royal Court. A couple of sell-out shows, some good reviews. They'd been celebrating. Kitty was the play's assistant costume designer. There was drink taken, he knew that, and he also knew that they'd been in her flat in Peckham, which she shared with four other girls. Four other women, he corrected himself. He found that out later. Kitty was five years older than John. They'd swapped numbers before he'd gotten a cab home at the end of the night, but he didn't text her. He'd been busy with the play, which was getting good reviews.

Frida had left for California at the end of the summer, almost six months earlier. They hadn't spoken much recently. At first John had received the occasional email that glossed over the painful way they'd left things, instead containing dispatches from Hollywood, queries about John's progress on the play and invitations to visit in the future.

Winter sun, Frida promised. John told her he'd think about it.

He didn't tell Frida that *Four and Ten* was now an entirely different beast from the script she had walked out on. After she'd left, John stayed on in the Finsbury Park flat by himself. He would pay the rent on his own. It was good to be alone. Something about the isolation changed him, set him alight.

It was freeing: the anonymity, the lack of expectation. The Royal Court wanted him to make the script weirder, and John wanted that as well. Days passed and he barely moved from the kitchen table he'd dragged across the room to the window. It had become his desk now, and he sat there for hours smoking cigarettes while typing endlessly on his laptop.

He was trying to push himself. Could *Four and Ten* be about a messy foursome, and also about the end of a relationship not unlike his and Frida's? In his new version, the first act remained close to what they'd written together: the two couples betraying each other in turn. But the second act he ripped up. He started over, took down the walls of the set, made it so the stage looked like a theatre, the play set in a theatre and featuring a writer and an actress talking to each other over the corpus of the thing they were working on. Then the first half's actors re-emerge, start circling the Frida- and John-like figures, asking them questions, probing them to tell the truth about who they were and what they'd done to each other. God, it was almost too much. Wasn't it? When he finished his first draft, John read back through the new pages with unease. Nobody is going to come out of this well, he thought. A flicker of satisfaction passed through him.

This was the version that ended up on the Royal Court's stage, and of course this version had only John Reddan's name on the billing. The work he did with Frida had receded in memory – the time they'd spent together was a mirage in his mind, something that couldn't be held in place without disappearing. By the time *Four and Ten* opened, John was capable of going days, even weeks sometimes without thinking about her at all. Occasionally he went on dates; occasionally, as with Kitty Adams, he slept with women in his social or professional circles. These circles of his were growing the longer he stayed in London.

John hadn't been expecting to hear from Kitty, when she texted almost three months after opening night and asked to meet up. Of course he remembered this part: walking around a freezing Peckham Rye on a Sunday in late March with Kitty, tall and striking in a long, bottle-green velvet coat. She had a face like a Russian ballet dancer's, the kind of profile they might write song lyrics about. John had a faint inkling from when she met him at the station what she was going to say. He had the impression this wasn't meant to be a romantic afternoon. Kitty waited until they'd gotten their coffees, left the noise of the street behind as they tramped around the common. Kitty was pregnant. It was John's, she said, and she'd be keeping it. She told him that she'd thought long and hard about whether or not to tell him at all, and she delivered this part in such a way that John could infer she believed she was being generous.

'What are my options here?' he asked her as they stopped at a bench to sit down.

Kitty gave him a cold look, like she was warning him of something very grave. 'John,' she said. 'I did say I'm going to keep it.'

'No, no,' he replied. 'I know that. I'm wondering if you'll let me be involved.'

Her face changed, like a light had just switched on

overhead. 'I hadn't considered that,' she said softly. 'The possibility that you might want that.'

It was the right thing to do by her, he thought on the train home. It wasn't, as Kitty had said, a possibility he'd considered for himself, either. But why not? Here was a chance to make something else of himself. To do better than his own father had done. And also, he thought, what was the alternative? (Part of him deemed it also a sort of cosmic recompense for a night of what had been slightly heartless behaviour on his part.)

And so John and Kitty's first date took place at her twelve-week scan at King's College Hospital. John watched Kitty wince at the cool jelly of the ultrasound on her stomach, and he held her hand as they marvelled together at the bean-shaped blur on the monitor. What a world he had found himself in. When they left the hospital after the appointment, he saw his phone had a missed call from his agent. He dialled his voicemail at the bus stop while they waited for the number 35. *Four and Ten*, Alice Greer reported, had just been nominated for an Olivier for best new play, and he another one for best director.

'Jesus fucking Christ,' he said, hanging up the phone. Kitty was beside him in her blue high-waisted jeans, looking at him inquisitively, waiting for him to explain.

They started making plans to move in together. He saw no reason not to give it a go. John found there was an unexpected degree of comfort around the idea of fatherhood. The logic of it gave his days a newfound rigour, and it was pleasant to think like this: it made sense to him that if Kitty wanted to do this, that he would be involved, too. It was what a good man would do, and that made the decision simple. Telling Barry on the phone was an entirely new sensation, the pure delight of it, the lift in his brother's voice down the line, like the two of them had won the lotto together.

All of that was fine. What John was unsure about was how to build a life with someone you barely knew. John wanted to do this right, but that meant doing the whole thing at speed – introducing Kitty to his friends and meeting her family, learning what she liked to eat and what she didn't at the same time as managing her pregnancy nausea and sudden cravings, building all the flatpack furniture from Ikea as fast as he could. In London they viewed a series of small two-bedroom flats together around the city. In Brighton, where Kitty's parents lived, he tried to match her father for pints of ale and failed, stumbling to the gents' during the second half of the football to get sick. John's own parents were both dead now, something Kitty assumed must be a source of trauma. But he was surprised by how much he didn't think about them, now that he was going to have a child of his own. He felt guilty about this, like there was something wrong with him. It was only when the curtain fell on one of his plays that he thought of his parents, that he longed for their presence in his adult life.

Together they flew to Dublin to visit Barry and Joanna. John showed Kitty the room in Harold's Cross where he'd written *Graceland* and *Bird*, now a home office. On the bank holiday Barry drove them all to Howth for the day and like children they ate ice creams at the harbour in the sunshine, dodging diving seagulls and stumbling around on the stony beach. Kitty liked Dublin a lot – its size, its theatres, its proximity to sea and mountains both – and on the plane home suggested they give living in Ireland a try instead. John said he wasn't sure it made professional sense for him. John wanted to look to the future. When he was in Dublin, he was reminded of the plays he had once made there, the pubs he used to drink in and who he used to drink with.

'Let's stick to what we know for now,' he said, taking her hand and kissing it lightly. Behind her, through the plane's window, he saw the city's coastline as they left it behind.

Often, lying awake at night, he tried to remember the night they had conceived the baby now growing in Kitty's belly beside him. The memory was hazy, though he recalled Kitty's bedroom, the stacks of clothes folded on every surface, the framed poster from *Vertigo* opposite the bed. He recalled how funny it had been to him, that for weeks he'd barely noticed the strange and quiet English girl in the costume department, and now here she was, naked in front of him in her dimly lit bedroom.

Had he enjoyed it? Depends how you defined enjoyment. He was aware that he should marry Kitty next, if they were going to go the whole hog, but there was something stopping him. Work was so busy now, and anyway, wouldn't it be better once the baby was here? Give her the day he assumed she'd always dreamed of. Champagne, friends, dancing.

Kitty was regal in pregnancy. John hadn't ever been close to a woman who'd had a baby, not close enough, anyway, to see her body grow and change over the full nine months. All of it was new to him. But he did know that not all pregnant women carried it the way Kitty did. From early on, just a few weeks after that first ultrasound, Kitty had been the size of a house, resplendent in dungarees, constantly reclining on a sofa or a bed while eating yoghurt or on the phone to her mother. She'd had her hair cut into a sharp bob, and it suited her, made her look like a flapper from the 1920s. And she looked so happy, even when he knew she was physically uncomfortable. John didn't yet know if you could call it love, but he certainly found himself unbelievably attracted to her, her new curves, her glowing complexion. He loved the animal smell of her, the heft of her when they embraced. Did it help that he barely knew her before she became pregnant? Now he couldn't picture her without this facet of herself, this doubling, this future child of his she was carrying.

High summer coincided with the height of Kitty's pregnancy. While John logged hours at the theatre, Kitty was at home in their new flat off Blackstock Road, sweating in the bathtub. She kept texting him, asking him what time he might be home for dinner. In April *Four and Ten* had won both the awards it was nominated for, and off the back of that got another run at the Theatre Royal on Haymarket. John was working every day. He was afraid to stop for even a moment. There were so many people to meet. They wanted to translate his play into French, German, Italian. The second run sold out. Kitty was on bed rest for the last two months of her pregnancy, and John found himself split down the middle. The play needed him so much, and he was at work all the time. He had to keep *Four and Ten* going. It was a divine chance in a man's career, after he'd worked so long. It was a window, a chink in the curtains, through which he could see some golden promised land. Also, it was currently earning him enough money that they would be able to afford a wet nurse if that was what Kitty wished for. A sleep coach. All the high-tech baby gear she could desire. Whatever Kitty wanted she would get, he figured, sweating on the Tube to Piccadilly Circus in August. It would be worth it. He just had to keep going a little longer, and she had to understand that.

In this way, John Reddan's life changed so quickly, so inexorably, that it was hard to see it happening at all.

Just over a year earlier he had been in Frida Slattery's sublet flat, hoping she wouldn't notice him, wondering if he should pack it in. Now they wanted him to adapt *Four and Ten* for the screen. Jesus Christ, he thought, I should have got a better agent. By the time Ruadhán was due in early September he'd agreed to transfer *Four and Ten* off-Broadway the following spring, though he soon learned that he wouldn't be there to see it through. Little Ruadhán. Born a week after his due date, his mother's contractions starting the day after his father's play wrapped in the West End. Three days of labour and John would close his eyes for years after and still see Kitty's blood on the floor, on the walls, on the ceiling. And yet Kitty had come out of it intact somehow, and given him this infant, this tiny, tiny purple thing with a thick whorl of jet-black hair. Those tiny fingers. Ruadhán had a problem with his heart, the doctors said, the two main arteries were for some reason reversed. He'd have to stay in the hospital after Kitty was able to leave. He would need surgery in Great Ormond Street, and provided that went well, monitoring for life.

John closed his eyes. The image of his tiny son's tiny insides, the thing the size of a tiny infant's fist beating away in there, trying to keep him alive. All the wires and machines the little lad was hooked up to. And Kitty, who John was sure he loved now, lying ashen in the bed he sat beside, half-woman and half beeping medical machinery. So yes, New York was off the cards for a little while. The show would go on without him.

What followed in its wake was bewildering. Once Ruadhán was finally home, the small flat morphed into a newly formed republic, some chaotic land created through bloody rebellion and sheer will. John was a father now, and he never seemed to sleep. There was barely a moment to spare for checking up on *Four and Ten*, let alone thinking about making new work. The boat had left the harbour and he hadn't even had the chance to wave it off. In the end he put an out-of-office on his email and asked Alice Greer to give him a few months. Parental leave, he called it. He received occasional missives from the front – *Four and Ten* touring to Chicago and San Francisco without him, earning positive reviews for its translated versions in Paris and Berlin – but it was as though they were dispatches from a soap opera he only faintly followed. Just keep going, he kept telling himself. If he stopped to think about it, between hospital appointments and sleepless nights and petty arguments with Kitty about nappies or shopping lists, he would realise how little of himself he still had a hold of. His old life, the theatre life, would be waiting for him on the other side of this first, harsh year, he assured himself. Ruadhán's doctors said that despite his early setbacks, the trauma of his time in the NICU, their boy would most likely go on to have a long and normal life. It would pay off, then, John and Kitty knew. Kitty coped better with the uncertainty of it all. She knew how to talk to doctors, how to soothe Ruadhán in the middle of the night, what to do when the whole household came down with a fever and stomach bug at once. John tried to give her what she needed. That was the best way he was capable of helping. Sometimes what she needed was space. She had moods, of course, and they argued, but he never saw her cry, never heard her shout or swear. He liked that about her. It was the opposite of his own upbringing, together with Barry.

In the meantime, John earned more money in a year than he knew what to do with. More money than he had ever had in his career, all the other earning years combined into one. The tax bill his accountant showed him made his eyes water. They bought a slightly run-down house in Tufnell Park, with a big garden where Ruadhán could play once he got bigger. Kitty started the long, slow project of renovation. She had such impeccable taste the job fell naturally to her, and John watched with amazement as mosaic floors went into the bathroom, a glass-roofed kitchen extension took shape at the rear of the house. Light pink roses climbed up trellises as if placed there by an act of God himself. When it came time to move, they paid movers to do the work for them while they went to Brighton to Kitty's parents' house for the weekend. It was the beginning of June again and they were having a drink in a pub by the pier, talking idly about getting a nanny, about Kitty going back to work part-time. Kitty elegant and mysterious in sunglasses, jiggling Ru in the pram with her sandalled foot. Red polish on her toes.

John remembered Howth a year earlier. He had had two beers, and no lunch, and lately he had been thinking about writing again. Making notes on his phone when up at night with the baby. The beer, the sunshine, made him want to talk to Kitty about it. It was funny, he thought, that the entirety of their relationship had run parallel with this period of him not writing. He didn't say anything to her. They'd never really talked about his work before. He smiled at her and said, Yes, of course they'll get a nanny if that's what she wants. Get through the summer, he thought to himself, and then Ruadhán would turn one and you can begin again.

They went to Ireland for a week at the end of August. Then they came back to London and John found himself in the new house filled with energy, a kind of back-to-school feeling that had been lying dormant within him for so long. He invited Alice Greer over for dinner and they sat in the overgrown, lush back garden of their home, still something of a building site inside. She held a squirming Ru on her lap while John started to outline some early ideas. Alice nodded and encouraged him, and said, 'Look, you have everything now, you have so many options, you just need to choose what it is you want to do and then the rest will follow from there.'

And then after she left, John and Kitty stood in the kitchen cleaning up from dinner, the remnants of the evening light coming in through the glazed roof. Ruadhán was at last down for the evening, they hoped, and Kitty turned to John at the sink and with a steely, distant look in her eyes told him that she was pregnant again.

'Brilliant,' he said uncertainly, and hugged her. His arms were wrapped tight around her shoulders, and he felt the edges of her shoulder blades digging into him, as if they were trying to leave some indent on the surface of him.

He hadn't considered another conception an option, not any of the times they'd had sex in the last few months. Ruadhán was surely enough for the two of them. Everything he had tried to write over the summer had been, dismally, about awkward relationships and sick babies. None of it would work, he was as sure of this as he was of anything. He needed distance. Kitty was worried that this pregnancy might be tough for her. She told him this in bed that night, said these words with a vague air of reproach.

But he was always dreaming of work. When he went to sleep he dreamed of being in an empty apartment in a foreign city where he did not speak the language, where he could shout out the window and nobody looked at him, where he could smoke at his desk and tap ash on the ground if it made him happy, and in the dream it did, it did make him so happy. He smoked the cigarettes solely to tap the ash onto the carpet, and to smush it in with his shoe, and it felt good, and he woke to the sound of an infant crying at 4 a.m. and forgot for a moment, standing up, reaching for the frayed towelling of his dressing gown, not to be happy.

One year had surely been enough. One year, and now eight months more, and then there would be another child, too. Two times all this. John's mind was always racing. When he went to bed it was at its worst, even when he was exhausted from the daily chaos of their lives. He was thinking of everything he had to do, counting the months since his last play opened, reciting emails from his agent and his producers verbatim. There was a way he had of calming himself, though. He pictured things differently. He was not proud of this. But John pictured a life in which, when Kitty met him on Peckham Rye, he had withdrawn instead of turning towards her with palms facing upward. A life in which he had offered her money instead of building a family from the ground up with her. In this imagined life, John was free to make the work he wanted to make. He could shut himself in his room for days if he wanted to write, and nobody would knock on the door. He could travel, smoke cigarettes. He could sleep with any amount of women (taking all necessary precautions, obviously) and in the morning he could leave and move on. Usually, running through this fantasy helped to slow his racing thoughts enough that John could finally fall asleep.

7. *The Reason* (Tobias and Sara Lund), 2011

1.

Frida sat in the comfortable backseat of a nice car, being driven through the commercial business district of a city in the Pacific Northwest. She wanted to rest her head against the window, but she had already spent an hour and a half in hair and make-up and she could imagine the greasy mark that would be left on the glass. What was it about being driven through the downtowns of North American cities? All that interchangeable steel and concrete, smoky glass covering tall office buildings, the same stores and signs everywhere, the same people wearing the same clothes walking down the same pavements, while she moved passively by. It made her feel sad, and dreadfully alone.

It didn't help that Frida was jet-lagged. She had arrived from Ireland early that morning, straight back to work after two weeks visiting the whole family. The fatigue, the time difference, the displacement – it all served to put her firmly into stock-taking mood.

On the one hand, she had this: the comfortable backseat, the nice car being driven through traffic from one hotel to another. Her needs taken care of, and all of it because she was going to her well-paid job. *The Reason* had just wrapped its third season, and had been renewed for three more. Today she was on her way to a television convention. First she'd sit on a panel with Tobias and Sara Lund, and after lunch, she'd have her photo taken with fans of her show. In the evening, she'd be driven back to the hotel and that would be it. For a day's work, plus travel time, she'd be paid enough to cover a couple of mortgage payments on the bungalow she'd bought earlier that year in Los Feliz.

On the other hand, there was everything else. All of the things that Frida had jettisoned in order to get here. She wasn't usually in the habit of weighing things up like this – Mel always told her, when the two of them were drunk in some hotel bar, that you couldn't look back – but the trip home had brought some things to the surface. Not the trip home, Frida thought, correcting herself. It was the trip back to the US that had done it.

It was her first time home in over a year. Five years had passed since she'd left Dublin for London, and four since she'd made the decisions, all the decisions, that had gotten her to Los Angeles. A fortnight with Edel and her gang, and her nieces had grown so much. Frida had been grateful, and surprised, to be left alone for the guts of two weeks, not much to do other than go look around the shops with Edel and the girls in tow, or walk in the mountains with the whole family, Una and Gus, their cocker spaniel. She felt restored, tired in the best way possible, as the plane started down the runway to depart from Dublin Airport. It was when she pulled the in-flight magazine from the pocket on her business-class seat that she came face-to-face with John Reddan.

All the buzz around *Four and Ten*. Even in California, even filming in rural Georgia, its impact had been palpable. Awards in London. Texts from friends in Dublin who didn't know that Frida and John had parted the way they had. Did you see this? Were you not going to be in this one? Christ almighty. Then she'd heard it was coming to New York, translated into French for Paris. This she'd heard from someone who didn't know about her and John, someone who wasn't even Irish. Greg Rachlin, an American actor in a recurring role on the show who thought of himself as a bit of an artiste. Juilliard, the Atlantic Theater Company. A guy who was regarded as difficult to work with, but who Frida thought was quite admirable, the way he approached things with such intensity.

'Hey, Frida,' he'd said one day when they'd finished and were heading to their trailers to wash the mountains off them. 'Do you know anything about this Irish guy, John Reddan?'

After that she'd started tuning it out. On the phone to Edel she'd told her sister in a laboured voice that it was painful to talk about John, that she didn't want to hear about him. Frida had felt silly saying this, like she was hamming it up for the camera. But wasn't it true? It was painful to talk about. It wasn't just the play. Thinking about what could have been between them, had she told him about the pregnancy rather than simply book a GP appointment without telling anyone. It was the feeling of the road not taken, and it felt so close to regret. She heard Mel's voice in her head whenever she thought of this – never look back. Mel was the only person she had told about everything that had happened then.

What Frida had learned from Greg about *Four and Ten* was that it was partly her script but largely not. It was about an actor and a director who are in love until suddenly they hate each other, and their lives are ruined.

'Stop,' she'd said to Greg at the time, 'genuinely, please stop telling me about this play. It's not my kind of thing at all.'

On the flight, Frida had shut the magazine before she could read it. Just thinking about him, about what had happened, tended to make her feel claustrophobic at times – trapped in her own skin. She had slipped it into her buttery brown leather carry-on. I can read it when I'm back on solid ground, she thought, and tried her best to fall asleep.

Now she carried that bag under her arm as she got out of the car and entered the hotel where the convention was taking place. An assistant brought her up to the ninth floor, a suite where she'd wait until it was time for her panel. A make-up artist appeared within seconds, dusting translucent powder over Frida's face, then left just as quickly. Perhaps it was safe now. She pulled the magazine from her tote. There was a picture: black turtleneck, hair sticking up, leaning towards the camera, elbows on knees, hands clasped together. It was a good photo. John looked a little older, a lot more polished. Frida hadn't seen a new picture of him in years: she didn't really use social media and the one time she'd googled his name, she'd found herself too self-conscious to click any of the links. She knew that he'd stayed in London, but they had stopped speaking about six months after they'd gone their separate ways. It was not a break-up, exactly. It was more complicated than that. Things had escalated, and then had arrived at a point where they had to stop. She couldn't remember now which of them had sent the last email to the other, which of them had stopped replying first.

And until now, Frida hadn't read any interviews with John. This one seemed pegged around a new project. *Ripples on the Water* was a dark comedy with a surreal edge about a man who buries his brother. But the brother wasn't ready to be buried. In the play's London debut, one of the brothers was being played by an Irish actor she knew called Conor Quirke, a theatre actor a little older than Frida who'd overlapped with her at college. They were bringing it to Broadway the following spring. She gathered that there were no roles for women in *Ripples on the Water*.

John said it would be harder to justify these big international projects once his eldest started school, and Frida blinked. He had two children now, with his wife, Kitty Adams Reddan, a costume designer. On the second page there was a smaller photo of the two of them. A sunny bay window, hung with red-velvet stage curtains. A terrace of pretty Victorian houses on the street outside.

The journalist asked about John's early work in Dublin theatres – it was, after all, an Irish-interest in-flight magazine – and he spoke about the shoestring projects, the sense that anything and nothing was possible during the strange, desolate days of the crash. 'The little rooms above pubs where dreams were made,' he said. John left the nostalgia trip there, and the article didn't name any of that early work.

There was a time, Frida thought, when articles about John Reddan mentioned Frida Slattery as well. She wondered if he had mentally expunged her from the record of his own life. Memory was so much like a draft of something that got pulled apart by too many rewrites.

John Reddan was lucky that anyone was interested in the arc of his career. Frida could certainly envy him that. When she sat in hotel rooms for endless press junkets, all anyone cared about was whether or not she was in a real-life relationship with her on-screen boyfriend, Peter Wright. During interviews in Ireland, it was the old chestnut of whether she'd ever move home. Frida wished they'd ask her about more interesting things. Every person had certain stories about themselves that they loved to tell. Frida told these stories to herself while cleaning her bungalow or driving across Los Angeles. But she knew that if any journalist or magazine ever cared enough to ask her about the very beginning of her career, she would have to tell the truth. Yes, of course. There was John, and he opened the door.

Her terminal honesty, Mel liked to call it. Mel had sat in the room for her first rounds of press for *The Reason*, when she was still green. Mel would raise her hand and say, 'Actually we'll stop there,' if Frida started to get too direct in her answers to questions about diet or boyfriends or which make-up brands she liked best. If the journalist was from a particularly prestigious publication, Mel would pretend to leave the room and hide in the adjoining bathroom, sitting on the floor with the door open and her recorder going. She gave her a lecture before the interview commenced while the journalist waited downstairs in the lobby. No brand names, no boyfriends, no sexy anecdotes, and no swearing. No complaining. There was potential, Mel said, in Frida's career. Potential for them both to make a lot of money through brand sponsorships. But that was dependent on Frida Slattery being clean and friendly, pretty in a sundress. And her tendency towards terminal honesty could very well stop all of that in its tracks.

The more money Frida could make while contracted to *The Reason*, the faster she could get back to making theatre or interesting cinema. Hence the Marvel movie, the conventions. Money was freedom, after all. She had told Mel to go into her recent contract renegotiation with all guns blazing, eager to squeeze the Lunds and the network. It was nice to have an agent. It meant Frida could hang out with her showrunners, get high beside the firepit in the Lunds' Malibu back garden, go to Tahoe with them for holiday weekends, while back in Hollywood her agent tried to drain them for an extra ten grand per episode with total impunity.

Also, shutting up in interviews had resulted in what Mel had promised. Frida wasn't exactly a cover girl, but from time to time there came an invitation to endorse a particular brand of shampoo or perfume (or her personal favourite, a high-SPF sunscreen suitable for the pasty Irishwoman in southern California) in exchange for payment. There were red carpets, dresses borrowed from designers. There were parties. Things that people broadly spoke about as opportunities, although in her most mercenary moods Frida was unsure what these opportunities were for. She tried to wring every drop from things, since she knew that fame was fickle, even the strangely shaped modicum of fame that she'd been allotted. She let herself be photographed on red carpets. She engaged a stylist for awards season, and the two of them created moodboards. She allowed herself to be seen in what Mel called 'a fashion context'. Sometimes she even came out on top in the blog posts about who wore it better. She always went out of her way to be introduced to casting directors and the more interesting producers at parties. Networking. She sought out the people who worked on what in Hollywood were regarded as 'weird projects'. And she agreed to conventions like today's, to keep the whole endeavour afloat financially.

Could she have ended up here if she and John had made different choices? Alone in this hotel suite, waiting for a runner to come and bring her downstairs? Obviously not. It was a handful of little plays, after all. It had barely been a relationship. It was John's breakthrough without her that hurt Frida now, that made her torment herself with these questions. What the two of them shared had resulted in John getting what he wanted: critical acclaim, commercial success, the respect of his peers. What had it gotten Frida? A complicated visa status that allowed her to work in the US, a contract she felt locked into like a pair of lovely handcuffs. A burning desire to never see John Reddan again, a desire that had faded into a sense of injustice that she knew meant he still mattered to her.

When she looked at everything she had now, whatever 'everything' was, Frida thought that she should probably just get over it. Youthful folly, or whatever. The John Reddan who couldn't bear the idea that Frida would make her own decisions was someone she couldn't stand to be around. But he was the same John Reddan she still thought of whenever she read a script for the first time. They didn't need to work together, or even to be on speaking terms, for him to take up this space in her mind.

After three seasons, the Lunds had basically given up trying to direct her. She'd become a different sort of actor under their tutelage, a more boring one, but a more efficient one, too. Frida prided herself on getting almost everything right on the first take, and the three of them seemed to work wordlessly together. At least, that was how it would look to an outsider. For Frida, there was always John inside her mind, sitting with his arms folded beside the monitor, appraising her performance.

Did he ever think of her? Impossible to know. He was married now. He had two children. Maybe, she thought, he found *The Reason* on TV late one night, looking for something mindless to watch. Oh, she liked that idea, John in his grubby T-shirt, the remote control in his clammy hand. She pictured him on the sagging grey couch in her old flat in London, bowl of pistachios in his lap. Where was Mrs Reddan in this fantasy? In bed, or attending to the children upstairs. With a jolt she remembered John in the pub years before, quoting someone old and dead, when they'd heard that an older actress, someone they knew and admired, was pregnant with twins.

'The pram in the hall,' he'd snarled. 'The enemy of art.'

'Just because there's a quote about it doesn't mean it's true,' she'd replied.

Every year on Frida's birthday, Mel took her to the Beverly Hills Hotel and bought her a martini and a steak.

'Don't tell me this is the year you want to have a baby,' Mel had joked after her second drink this year. 'You know I've just bought a new house.'

Frida didn't know what she wanted. She didn't regret her decision four years ago – regret wasn't the right word for it. She wanted to live many lives, stacked on top of each other like so many contradictory stories of the same events. What John had said in the in-flight magazine, about planning work around your child starting school – well, Frida liked having her independence. She couldn't imagine any other way. But wasn't she supposed to want something else? It helped that there wasn't anyone in her life to facilitate the having of a baby. She'd dated a guy named Justin the first year she'd moved out here, but after ten months and four holidays together he'd told her he wasn't ready for commitment. She'd just asked him to attend a cousin's wedding back home in Ireland. In the end, she pretended to have the flu and didn't go at all. Mortifying. Since then, there had been dates, of course, guys who worked in the industry who she had been fixed up with, or who she met at parties. None of them remarkable. There had also been a quiet, month-long fling with a set designer named Anne, a very elegant, steely woman from New England who seemed to be descended from one of America's first families. That had petered out after Anne told her she didn't like to get serious with girls who hadn't been with girls before. The experience hadn't made anything more clear in Frida's mind; if anything, she knew less now about who she was and what she wanted.

There was no one special, despite what she tended to tell the magazines when they asked ('I'm seeing someone but I'd like to keep it private,' with a smile coy enough to imply that yes, it could well be her tall and handsome on-screen boyfriend Peter Wright). Mel was clear that Frida's potential for romance with Peter Wright was powerful enough to keep fans watching *The Reason*.

The panel was an hour behind schedule and when the knock finally came, Frida was ushered down from her room by a smiling assistant. For fifty minutes she sat at a long table on stage with the Lunds in an enormous conference room in front of an audience and laughed and joked and performed. Peter had been invited, but he didn't like doing these things, especially if they involved travel. Frida thought Peter was lazy. He didn't bother to jump through the hoops that the rest of them did, and he got away with it. The Lunds started the conversation by saying that sadly he'd been ill. Peter got away with missing these things, Frida thought, because he was a man and because he'd been a star before the show. He had been the heart-throb on a paranormal teen drama a few years earlier, playing the teenage Samson until long after he was passable as a teenager, so now he came with superfans of his own. His casting was the reason, really, that there were conventions for Frida to go to. Also, he got away with it because he did not have much personality, other than his boyish good looks. He did the photoshoots, but Frida was the one who was capable of holding a crowd. The audience liked her accent, and they liked what Mel embarrassingly referred to as Frida's 'moxie'. Moxie, Frida had gathered, came down to a sharp glance along the table, a brusque Irish accent, a quick retort when Tobias Lund talked about her in the third person. I'm right here, Tobias, you can say it to my face, you know.

Moxie was a performative version of Frida's terminal honesty, something she'd honed carefully until it had taken a more useful shape. It was snappy zingers that cut through the Hollywood bullshit of being so grateful to be here ('Yeah, I'm definitely grateful for the three hours in hair and make-up this morning, sure') in a way that made her fans feel like she was one of them. And she did it with a smile, because she actually was grateful to be there. It would have been so easy for none of this to have worked out, for Frida to have wound up in her thirties still in Dublin, looking at Edel and Una over her mother's kitchen table. Where the only question being posed to her was, 'Would you not think about getting a real job, Frida', while the pair of them loaded up the civil-service careers portal on her laptop.

The thing about the conventions was that she wasn't Frida Slattery, as Mel had reminded her on the phone that morning while she had been in the make-up chair. She was Kathleen Richards, the attorney who couldn't seem to get a break. Luckily Frida liked Kathleen Richards. The pilot script had offered Katherine Richards, and it hadn't delved into her background, but Frida had asked Sara and Tobias if she could play Katherine as Kathleen, Irish-American who'd wound up in the South, daughter of a cop and a nurse, lapsed Catholic and riven with the usual intergenerational guilt and shame.

Sara had laughed awkwardly; Tobias had just stared – both typical reactions for the pair – and they'd agreed that Frida could give it a go.

It had worked. Now the fans queued up to see Kathleen Richards. They asked Frida questions about what kind of person she thought Kathleen was, about her secrets and her crushes and her career goals. And what surprised Frida the most was that she almost always knew the answer. Kathleen's dream holiday destination was Hawaii. Kathleen had her eyes on the DA position, unless she pivoted to more human rights legal work. Kathleen would definitely be open to getting a puppy in the next season, that sounded like a fun idea. Any questions that really stumped Frida could be redirected back to the Lunds, who held the keys, after all, to Kathleen's psyche.

Before they'd shot the first season of *The Reason*, Frida, the Lunds, Peter Wright and George Liu, who played Peter and Frida's boss, had spent a weekend together in a Santa Barbara hotel. The Lunds wanted George, Peter and Frida to really get into the script with them. In a sunny room with a view of the coastline, the five of them sat around a table with the scripts for the first five episodes in front of them.

Frida had arrived in Santa Barbara thinking she'd be undertaking a crash course: all of the others present had ten times the television experience she did. The idea of it had set her nerves on edge. The night before she'd had dinner with Mel.

You must remember, Mel had warned her, that if they smell inexperience or fear, they won't ever be able to respect you.

Maybe Mel was wrong, Frida had thought at the table in Santa Barbara. Sara Lund was several years older than Frida, but she looked at Frida like they were friends already. Tobias was harder to figure out. She wasn't sure what Sara saw in him. He was sort of a brute. At least, he presented himself as one: he wore a brown suede jacket that had seen better days and heavy leather boots, and his light hair was long around his ears. He was tall and thick-limbed, and he threw his arms around when he spoke. Maybe he was sort of sexy, Frida conceded. When he talked about his work, he oscillated wildly between playing the serious auteur and the money-making grifter, happy to direct any ad for a quick buck. Sara and Tobias had been together for ten years, since she'd met him as a student in his directing class in a New York degree-mill film school. Tobias had shot a handful of music videos in Europe, enough to make a name for himself, and Sara had been impressionable, by her own account. They had worked on a laundry list of prime-time dramas together, plus a couple of indie films, and *The Reason* was a chance for them to gain mainstream approval. They'd been given a decent budget and a relatively big name in the form of Peter Wright.

'The female lead isn't necessarily the main character,' Tobias had explained. 'The female lead is there, and she's important, but mostly as a foil to the men she works with.'

Frida had examined the script, not meeting his eye.

'You don't have to like it, Frida,' he had added.

She remembered Sara looking at him. 'Well, that's not how I wrote Katherine,' Sara had said in a clear voice.

Katherine Richards had been a passion project for Sara

Lund, Frida would learn. Years of Sara's life had poured into this fictional lawyer, this woman riven with internal demons who just wanted to be taken seriously. Throughout that first season, Frida had spent her time on set figuring out how to push Katherine – Kathleen – in a way that Sara would permit. Frida had to push her character, because if she didn't, Tobias Lund's crap about female leads would end up winning out. He may have been the dominant force on set, but Sara and Frida had something he didn't have. There were two of them. After they'd wrapped the first season's finale, Frida had a sense she and Sara had won.

It was after 6 p.m. when Kathleen Richards could leave the convention and become Frida Slattery again. Back in her room in a nicer, smaller hotel downtown, Frida eased off her shoes and hung up her dark-green trouser suit. The layers of make-up came off, and in the mirror she examined her pores carefully. In an hour she'd have dinner with Mel and the Lunds. Mel was on her way back from a string of meetings in Vancouver and she'd decided to stop off and meet them after the convention. This was the time of day when it would be nice to call someone, to hear a warm voice on the other end of the line. Sometimes it felt like it was Frida's fault that there was nobody like that in her life. She closed her eyes. She thought of John Reddan coming through the door of his terraced house in London, stooping to pick up one sticky child and then the other. Why did it feel like the pair of them had struck some cosmic deal back in London?

The restaurant Mel had chosen was just a few blocks

from the hotel, and Frida decided to walk. Outside it was raining and the pavements were slick and grey. That strange, thick North American rain that was so different to the ever-present mizzle of her childhood. She had changed into a blue dress and white sneakers, and on leaving the hotel, paused underneath its striped awning. Perhaps the rain would stop soon. She'd either have to run through it, one arm held over her hair. Or else go out to the street and flag down a cab. Apologise to the driver for the short journey. Tip him heavily. When she got like this, paralysed by indecision, it was like there were two tracks at work in her inner monologue. There was the part of her that went through her life, acting and reacting to the world. Then there was the other part, who watched the first part. This part was the director. The director saw her in the round, stalking around her like the black-clad Auditor in Beckett's *Not I*, the play John Reddan first told her about years earlier. She remembered watching the black-and-white film of Billie Whitelaw's mouth moving haltingly on John's laptop in the *Bird* rehearsal room. Unnerved by it, by what being an actor might end up doing to Frida Slattery.

Usually the director in Frida's mind was John, though sometimes it was Tobias Lund who fed notes into her ear as she moved through the day. (It was never Sara.)

Wait under the awning.

Turn to the doorman, give him a quick smile. Does he recognise you? Probably not, but that doesn't matter.

You've never been someone who feels the need to be recognised.

You're just another woman on a pavement, after all, wanting the rain to stop.

Now go. One arm over your head. The other holding your handbag to your side. Run down the pavement, around the corner, another block, through the rain.

Frida was the last to arrive at the restaurant. It looked like a nice place: big glass windows, wide booths, a shiny bar in the middle packed with good-looking, wealthy people. Their party had been sat to the side of the room, affording the rest of the restaurant a good look. Tobias stood to greet Frida, but Sara and Mel stayed seated.

'Oi,' Mel called jokingly. 'What time do you call this?'

'Oh, let her,' said Sara, Mel's humour gliding past her. 'She worked hard today.'

'She always works hard,' Mel remarked.

'That's why we keep her around,' Tobias said, arching one fair eyebrow.

When they were together like this, Mel and the Lunds had a tendency to talk about Frida in the third person, like she wasn't in the room. It was irritating.

'Sorry I'm late,' Frida said, stooping to kiss Sara on the cheek. 'It's raining outside.'

The others had dressed up more than Frida, Sara in a slinky black dress – both Lunds always wore black, like a pair of self-conscious artistes – and Mel in a bright blue suit. Frida slid into a seat at the head of the table, between Sara and Tobias.

Sara placed a hand on Frida's forearm. 'How did you find today?' she asked her.

'Exhausting,' Frida said. 'It's so tiring to be on all day. It's almost like doing a play.'

'You're good at it.' Sara filled Frida's wine glass, clasping the wine bottle with both of her small, delicate hands like it was oppressively heavy.

'Two more weeks now and we'll all be in Georgia,' Tobias said, raising his own glass in toast.

'God, already,' Frida said.

'I don't know how you guys do it,' Mel said. She was typing on her phone, her brow furrowed.

'You work harder than we do, Mel,' Sara pointed out. 'It even looks like you're working right now.'

Mel placed her phone down on the table and gave Sara a dazzling smile. 'Money never sleeps,' she said, making her northern accent sound richly Californian.

Sara flinched slightly. The two women were so aesthetically different that Frida almost had to laugh. Mel preferred high-maintenance make-up, and wore her ombré hair in crunchy Hollywood waves, while Sara's ghostly pallor and thin, geometric, white-blonde bob gestured towards what Frida thought was pretension, or at the very least a vitamin deficiency. Tobias and Sara had a fundamental disdain for Mel that was obvious to Frida, but if Mel knew, she didn't seem to care.

'I view these things like ringing in the new year,' Tobias said. More wine arrived on the table. Frida thought of the kale salad she'd had for lunch eight hours earlier.

'One season ends, a new one begins,' Tobias went on. 'We should celebrate, and also we should reflect.'

'So Scandinavian of you,' Mel said sweetly.

Tobias ignored her. 'So I want us to say what we're hoping to achieve this year. For me, I'm thinking an Emmy. We deserve it this time.'

'You always think we deserve it, Tobias,' Sara said. 'I just want to get through filming with no major disasters, and then I want to have a proper vacation. Frida, what about you?'

Frida closed her eyes. 'I'd like to do some theatre,' she said.

'That isn't really what I meant, Frida,' Tobias said. 'I meant for us, for the group.'

Sara laughed. 'Oh, Frida. You're so cute. What does Mel think of that?'

'We'll see how her calendar works out,' Mel replied automatically, her eyes scanning another email on her phone's screen.

'Well, we're filming for ten weeks, right?' Frida said, trying to count dates in her head. 'And then we have a block of time off. I think it could work.'

'Let's talk about this another time,' said Mel.

'She keeps you on a tight leash,' Tobias murmured into Frida's ear, and she expected to feel a shiver of discomfort, but it didn't come.

'We work well together,' Frida replied. 'We always have.' The wine was all through her head and her hands, a gentle numbness that she knew could tip over at any point into something sloppier.

Across the table, Mel stood up. 'Frida,' she said, 'walk me to the ladies'?'

In the bathroom, Mel stood in front of Frida with her arms folded.

'I don't want to be a bitch, Frida,' she said. 'But come on. You think the Lunds are your friends. They're your employers. So don't speak to them like you can trust them. Want to chat about your dreams and regrets? Talk to me. I'm your friend! Or even better, get another friend. Someone, radical as it sounds, who you don't work with.'

Frida glanced at her reflection in the mirror behind Mel. Her hair was still stiff from the morning's blow-dry, and she needed her colour done. 'You think I can't trust them?'

'I think they could drop you like a hot potato if they wanted to. The script can change at their will.'

'But I have a contract. Don't I?'

Mel turned and leaned into the mirror, reapplying her red lipstick. 'Look, my point is this. You act like you're the golden child. And, sure, the Lunds do like you. But the things we've worked for can all go in a flash, and where will you be then?'

'Free to audition for theatre work,' Frida muttered, rummaging in her bag for her own lipstick.

Mel laughed at her reflection in the mirror. 'Yes, Frida, free to go back to understudying at the National Theatre, if that's what you want.'

2.

Four weeks on location in the foothills in Georgia. Sticky weather. Very early mornings. Hours spent in hair and make-up, and half of it slid off Frida's face by the time the cameras started rolling. In Georgia there was no time for contemplation. There was no time for anything, really: not to exercise, or to call home, or to lie on her side in bed staring at her phone. All day long, and well into the night, Frida was Kathleen Richards. It was unbearably humid on set, and Frida was off her game. Every time the cameras stopped she chugged water. Every time Tobias yelled *Action!* she thought she needed to pee again. The Lunds there, the pair of them, standing by the monitor, eyes focused on that screen. Peter Wright visibly frustrated every time Frida needed a second go at a line.

It was like being pregnant, though Frida knew that wasn't possible. A good few months since her last date, and anyway, she'd been on the pill since she moved to California. It was like her body was trying to tell her something. Get out of Georgia! Contractually, that wasn't an option.

The Lunds' directing style was to offer her nothing.

Everyone involved in *The Reason* worked like a robot. The only notes they ever had were technical: Frida, turn your body to this angle so we see the light on your face. Frida, we can see the line of your panties through your skirt. Can you take them off for this scene? They worked on the assumption that she could deliver her lines and get through every scene without any deeper directorial guidance. Was it unreasonable, then, for Frida to have assumed that they trusted her? No, but maybe the unreasonable part was Frida assuming that trust went both ways.

Three more weeks here. Then two weeks off, and then back to the studio in California for the rest of the season's filming. Frida counted down the days. She was thinking of going to New York for the break, seeing if she could take some meetings about theatre, seeing some shows on Broadway if she had time. In Georgia the hotel was becoming more claustrophobic by the day. Eating in the same restaurant for breakfast and dinner. At least when she was on set, she wasn't at risk of running into a co-worker off duty. She saw the hotel's swirling navy-and-cream carpets when she closed her eyes, heard the ever-present hum of its air-conditioning system all day long. I am Kathleen Richards, she repeated to herself whenever the old worries cropped up.

In her mind there were two types of directors. The Lunds and John Reddan. It made Frida feel foolish to think she had barely worked with anyone else. The two eras in her career, the Reddan era and the Lund era, and a handful of small jobs in between. On those other jobs, she felt disposable, like she could be swapped out for any other actress at any time.

Maybe one actor wasn't so different from the next, except in terms of how much people liked being around them. On the plane home from the convention, Frida had taken a picture of John's interview, and sometimes she opened it and zoomed in on the picture of him and Kitty in their lovely home. John was allowed to be unlikeable and difficult to work with and still he had not only a career and the power to make or break actors – he also had a *wife*. And two children, apparently.

Frida had never been bothered by the fact that John was regarded as difficult to work with. She'd felt close enough to him that she was insulated from all that. She remembered sleeping in the same narrow bed together in Edinburgh when they made *Graceland* and now she thought: eye of the hurricane. She was never sure of how much she wanted him as a romantic partner. For a long time back then, she'd suspected that really she would prefer him in the rehearsal room than in her bed. That was why it had taken so long for them to get to that point. The luxury of options, she thought now. That was the feeling that had most characterised those years of her life, the Reddan era – the sense that there were abundant possibilities. It could be Hollywood or Cannes, the West End or the Abbey Theatre. It would be fine, if she was doing it with John.

At least the Lunds were more fun than John, Sara in particular. They too could be difficult. The fact that they were a couple sometimes spilled over into the atmosphere on set.

Tobias made jokes about women, including Sara, though not usually about Frida. He talked about women as baby-making machines, obsessed with pinning down a man for the sake of procreation. He pointed at a female extra coming out of hair and make-up and said Sara, sometimes I wish you looked like her. Tobias thought his jokes were admissible because he was such a great feminist; he and Sara mentored women writer/directors, and they always tried to hire women for the more technical roles so often dominated by men. The idea that Tobias might have actually been guilty of sexism – it would make him spit out his coffee. He was Swedish, wasn't he? Sexism was something only for Americans, and perhaps the Danish.

Once, in Georgia, when Frida bungled a line three times in a row, he called from his director's chair that she might be better off in the adult-entertainment industry if she couldn't deliver her lines right. Nobody laughed, then finally, Sara did. It was a performative laugh, designed to make Tobias feel like an idiot, and Frida couldn't help herself. She laughed at Sara's delivery, and then the whole set broke down laughing, clutching each other, doubled over, except for Tobias, of course. Tobias stood up then and swore at them all. He stormed off, reaching for his cigarettes. Once he was gone, Sara and Frida looked at each other like they'd just made a mistake. Let's take five, Sara said, redundantly, and Frida went to go chug some cold water.

When Tobias came back, he was smiling like nothing had happened. Sara intercepted him and from the other side of the set Frida watched the pair exchange quiet words. Sara was warning him, or admonishing him, and Tobias, twice her size and with hands like shovels, took her little face in his hands. He kissed Sara on the top of the head and she shrugged, throwing one hand in the air, and they both turned to their chairs by the monitor.

But off set and off duty, the Lunds were fun. Sometimes, after a long day shooting, Sara would knock on Frida's door with a joint in her hand and the pair would smoke it on the balcony. They'd complain about Peter Wright and discuss which crew member was sleeping with whom, whose drinking was getting to be a bit much, and what they'd eat once they got back to Los Angeles. It was easy, Frida thought, to get on with people, not make a fuss, keep her head down and have a nice time. It blocked out all her other thoughts. It was the easy thing to do, even if it also made her realise that John Reddan had never once told himself to do the easy thing, and look where he'd managed to get himself as a result.

The last week in Georgia, Frida found she couldn't sleep. She was waking up throughout the night, aware always of the clock creeping towards her 4.45 a.m. call time. One day on set there was a pain in her side that swung wildly from stabbing to dull. In the hotel that night she tried to think when it had started. Today, yesterday? She couldn't remember. Dull, then stabbing, then back again. It got worse by the hour, though at first she kept on saying to herself that it would pass soon. She thought of how she might describe this pain, but could only grasp words like *ice pick*. What was an ice pick, exactly? In the bathroom she vomited into the avocado-coloured toilet bowl on her knees, hands gripping the plastic seat. The front desk brought her paracetamol and a hot compress, but with her palm on her forehead she started to wonder if she had a fever. The pain was awful now, beyond her powers of description. She called the front desk again and asked for a doctor.

The Georgia of *The Reason* was deep in the Appalachian foothills, on the verge of a national forest. The nearest hospital was over an hour away, but when the local doctor saw her, he said she should go now. The pain was worse and worse by the minute, it seemed, and she started to think of things she had heard about childbirth. She counted the seconds between waves. She thought about what the word *unbearable* meant. The waves started to run into each other. She was lying down in the back of the car, but who was driving? Not the doctor, surely. She wanted Una to be here, to stroke her hair. Frida tried to sit up and saw the back of Sara's bob, her hair the only light thing in the dark of the night. The pain pushed her back down into the seat. Frida heard a grotesque moan, like the noise an animal made at the end of its life. It was coming from her own mouth.

Mouth and abdomen. That was all that Frida was on the long drive through the night. In the front seat Sara asked if she could put on a CD and Frida didn't say anything. She saw Sara's eyes flick over to her in the rear-view mirror. The opening bars of 'Second Hand News' by Fleetwood Mac started up, and Sara was humming along, red painted fingernails tapping on the wheel of the car. In the backseat, Frida tried to turn her body over.

The doctor suspected that Frida's ovary had twisted on

itself. The hospital knew she was coming, and the staff were ready with a trolley on the tarmac. Frida's eyes flickered as the staff snapped into action around her. Sara was not here now, nor Una either of course. A new person appeared in her eyeline, leaning over Frida, saying that she was a surgeon and Frida needed to have surgery immediately. Frida nodded. Then a little spike in her arm, nothing compared to the pain in her stomach, and all faded into darkness.

When Frida woke up, pressed in between the sheets of a hospital bed, she was down one ovary. That's how I'll tell it, she thought, after the same surgeon left her bedside debrief a little while later. Sara and I were driving through Georgia in the dark one night, and the next thing I knew I was in a hospital bed, down one ovary. She was numb through her lower body now, sipping water through a straw. Production had been paused, she assumed, though the idea of ever being on set again felt like a fever dream. When Sara and Tobias came by at visiting hours, they brought a bag of clean clothes and toiletries. They told Frida not to worry in the slightest, that the show would go on and she was to concentrate on resting and recovering for now. She watched the two of them, their pale faces, their uneven height. They were her friends, she thought, they knew her so well.

8. *Ripples on the Water* (John Reddan), 2015

1.

The first night John was in New York, he put his bag down in the flat his producer had arranged for him and went out to smoke a cigarette. Across the street a man got out of a taxi, wrangling a tuba with him. Cars honked. A young woman in a fluffy coat and a tight turquoise T-shirt strode past him on the phone. 'I just told him I miss the like, giddy thrill of being in love,' she said to the person on the other end of the call. Me too, John thought with a rush of recognition. But had he ever felt it? He struggled to remember. New York was like getting to a restaurant, being handed a menu at the very moment you realised just how hungry you are. How long it had been since you ate. Everything around him looked good, smelled even better. It was the smell, he thought, of being a living person, a man in his thirties with so many options. On the subway he glimpsed his first poster for *Ripples on the Water*, and the sight of his own name made him feel dizzy with ego.

At the theatre, everyone wanted to talk to him about *Four and Ten*. 'I loved it,' his stage manager Amy told him, one hand on his forearm. 'Lo-o-oved it.'

'Thanks,' John said. What else was there to say?

A teenager who was apparently on work experience from the film school at NYU wanted John to explain what he thought happened to the couple after the curtain fell.

'Nothing,' he said. 'That's where the play ends.'

'I know,' she said, 'but do you think Wendy and Ed really end up together?'

Four and Ten, to John's mind, was the same age as Ruadhán, and Ruadhán would be turning four this year. *Four and Ten*, his other first son, had ricocheted off around the world without him, and here John was now, away from his family, still just trying to catch up with his own career.

After tech rehearsals, he and Conor Quirke smoked a cigarette in the alley behind the theatre. They watched the flow of people on the street perpendicular, streaming out of the subway station and towards Midtown's bars and theatres. A tall woman in loose striped trousers pointed at them without slowing her pace. 'You guys make a really cute couple,' she called and kept going, not waiting for a response.

Conor broke into laughter. 'Did you ever think this would be your life?'

'I try not to think about it,' John replied. 'It's one of those things. It's like being in an airplane. It's fine, until you stop to consider how high up you are, how you're just sitting there in a little tin can in the sky.'

'Oh yeah. You're totally at the mercy of the universe.'

John looked sideways at the other man. It was nice to be around people who got it, who understood this bargain you had made with your own life. You were here, and you were not here, and you wanted this, and also you dreaded it, because when you had it between your hands, as John did now out in the alley behind the theatre, the slippery thing you'd always wished for, you were forced to contend with the idea that it had been you all along that was the problem.

'You ever get recognised?' John asked Conor.

'Christ no. Not here. In Dublin, yeah, in certain pubs. The barman will squint at you, you know. But no. Brendan gets recognised. And I think he loves it.'

Brendan was the good-looking one, the more famous one, but John thought Conor was the better actor. Conor was seven years older than Brendan and his CV was less starry than his younger brother's. Brendan had awards nominations, an A-list girlfriend, a brief foray into a profitable comic-book franchise. But Conor had been the first one on board in the play's London debut. Brendan had read for the role, but had to pull out due to scheduling conflict. Now John had both of them in New York and could compare and contrast. Conor had a lumpen profile, an uneven nose that bore the marks of being broken too many times on the rugby pitch. Brendan was almost girlish by comparison, his high cheekbones, piercing light-green eyes and pronounced cupid's bow.

It had been Kitty's idea. She had worked with Conor Quirke on a production of *A Portrait of the Artist as a Young Man* at the Young Vic, before she and John had first met.

'Conor's a legend,' she'd said. John always enjoyed his wife's attempts at Hiberno-English fluency. 'You should do a *Waiting for Godot* with the pair of them.'

Ripples wasn't Beckett, but it was a departure for John. That was what the critics were saying, anyway. It had started in the

Notes app on his phone while looking after Ruadhán when Kitty was pregnant with Fionn, and it had grown rapidly when he'd left for an artist's residency in a forest in Germany when Fionn was four months old. It had been over two years since he'd written anything more than five pages long. He had to go to Germany: Alice Greer had almost given up on waiting for his next project, and with the new baby in the house he no longer had a desk. Also, lately he had been feeling like if he didn't produce something new, he might stop being John Reddan. Kitty had been apoplectic with his decision to leave. She called him a coward on the dark early morning he was leaving for the airport. She said in low tones in the hallway in her silk dressing gown that he was a selfish man and a bad father. Was that fair? Was it true? She was just angry, he told himself in the taxi to Heathrow. Pissed off that his work had to come before the childcare. It all boiled down to issues of practicality, and so it was fair if she was upset. But hadn't she been attracted to him in the first place because he was sort of successful? And one of them had to earn some money. What had she expected of him, truly?

In the woods, John began to think that Kitty was being unfair. Wasn't this the way their family worked? This was his job. It paid for their life. He made creative work for a living. It was impossible to make good work without some degree of sacrifice. Surely she knew this, surely she had been aware of this from the very first moment they had talked about setting off on this path together that day on Peckham Rye. Families like theirs did find a way. It just involved the artist having some degree of freedom, some of the time.

Anyway, put the art aside, and you had the fact that she was just so much better at parenting than him. The day before he'd left for the residency, the four of them had gone to Alexandra Palace and gotten caught in a sudden downpour. John had been in just a T-shirt and shorts and was soaked almost instantly. Huddled together under a tree, John watched Kitty unpack two little raincoats for the boys from her backpack, raincoats John had never seen and didn't know they'd owned. Ruadhán stuck his tongue out at his mother while he held out his arms, and Kitty kissed him lightly on the nose. She was a natural mother. It was an issue, John thought, mostly, of practicality.

At first all he'd done in the forest in Germany was write emails to Frida Slattery that he knew he wouldn't send. It was part of his process, he told himself. In the past, almost everything had started with an idea told to Frida. On the third day, though, he began to feel foolish. He hadn't spoken to Frida Slattery since 2010. He closed the tab and opened a new one, wrote this time to Barry instead. The forest was thick with strange noises in the night, and John couldn't stop thinking about ghosts.

After he'd come home, John and Kitty had shuffled awkwardly around each other for weeks, running through the domestic minutiae of each day as a team of two barely on speaking terms. He tried to do more. He brought up getting help again, and Kitty agreed this time. It was possible, he was sure, for families like theirs to do this. It was just a question of doing it without resenting each other at the same time.

Anyway, it had worked. He was here now in New York,

Ripples on the Water in previews and John Reddan levitating clean off the pavements – sidewalks – with happiness about the whole thing. At home, Kitty and the au pair, a pretty Swedish girl named Katarina, taking care of the boys. It was a clean trade, and John was astonished that he'd managed to pull it off.

The night *Ripples* opened for previews, he and the Quirke brothers went on the tear, foolishly. From the very beginning of the evening John was concerned, asking would they really be able to act the next day with sore heads on them. Brendan laughed and slapped a hand on John's shoulder.

'John, I'm even better with a sore head on me.'

'You're the bad influence here,' John said to Brendan. 'I want that on the record.'

Ripples hadn't always been about two brothers. It had started unsteadily, in that cabin in the forest, in the emails John wrote to his own brother that he knew he wouldn't send. *Ripples* was about fear, and being a man and a husband and a son and a father. But once he met Conor Quirke, it became clear that it would be about being a brother most of all. Conor had liked the script and he'd thought that Brendan would be game, if he could find time in his packed schedule. The two had been meaning to do something together for years. John had received a standing offer from this particular theatre, after *Four and Ten* had transferred there in 2012. New York theatre, Conor had noted at their second meeting, would probably be enough to tempt Brendan away from Hollywood for a few weeks.

The two Quirkes had arrived in New York like they were on a J-1 summer visa, hopped up and delighted with themselves. They were subletting flats side by side in Williamsburg and were seldom on time for rehearsal, rolling into the room John had rented in Times Square bleary-eyed and clutching deli coffees and bagels. They'd witnessed a fight on the subway, they told him, or Brendan had been spotted by some schoolgirl fans and they'd had to pose for photos. One morning they'd seen a flotilla of muscle cars blocking the junction at Broadway. They showed John pictures on their phones. Something about their fraternal camaraderie made him feel old in comparison. When they weren't actively rehearsing, the Quirke brothers were pummelling each other, dissolving to the ground in a puddle of wrestling moves.

'Guys,' John, the schoolmarm, called across the room. 'Can we get started now please?'

Once they got into it, though, the Quirkes were pros. This was their first time working together in years, they said, since Brendan was a student. 'And still my big brother is the one getting me parts,' Brendan lamented.

'Shut the fuck up,' Conor said, waving an arm with intent to wallop.

'Jesus,' John muttered under his breath. 'The pair of you are like kids.'

But when they eventually opened the script, it came naturally. John had feared the brothers would be competitive with each other on the stage. They weren't. Instead he watched them slip into the man and his brother's ghost, circling each other warily, swinging at each other like ageing fighters at last orders. Conor and Brendan turned the rehearsal room into a boxing ring high above the city and the drama of it, the light and dark of these two brothers living and dead, came out in gaudy, delightful streaks in their acting.

Now they were in the bar around the corner from John's studio apartment, celebrating a job well done. The thing about going out drinking with actors was that they tended to attract attention. The bar was a dive and they'd chosen it for its dark corners, but nevertheless John watched a stream of young women approach the Quirke brothers, trying to start conversation.

'The Quirke brothers take New York,' Brendan Quirke said. 'I'm starting to think taking this job was a good idea. My agent thought I was mad.'

Conor raised a glass in John's direction. 'I always knew it was a good idea.'

'Shut up, Conor. Lick-arse. You're only saying that because you never get any decent work to begin with.'

'Look,' John said. 'It all worked out, right? We're here, we got through the first night.'

'You're a tough nut, John Reddan,' Brendan Quirke said.

Brendan Quirke was drunk. There was less of him to hold the alcohol. His narrow build and thin hips – he was a slender vessel that had been filled up with cheap beer and picklebacks. He stood in front of John and wavered lightly from side to side, his phone glowing in his hand.

'Jesus, Bren,' Conor said. 'Know the one that's one too many.'

'That's what everyone said to me,' Brendan went on,

ignoring his brother. '"John Reddan is a tough fucker." I hadn't seen your work but I knew your rehearsal rooms were brutal, everyone knows that. You make actors cry! But when I told people I was doing this play—'

'Shut up, Brendan,' Conor commanded.

'I've never made an actor cry,' John said, though he was unsure if this was true.

Brendan ignored the both of them. 'When I asked people in Ireland should I work with you do you know what they said? They said, Yeah, sure, if you can bear to be around him for six weeks! People said, You know there's a reason he never works in Dublin anymore. They said, John Reddan, he's a terrible arsehole. But you're not as bad as they say. I think you're actually grand.'

'Christ almighty,' Conor said. 'Actually grand, you hear that, John? High praise from this cunt.'

Brendan nodded with steady enthusiasm. 'Personally I don't mind working with arseholes.'

'What a compliment,' John said dryly. He kind of wanted to deck Brendan Quirke.

'I'm going for a smoke,' Brendan announced, eyeing a group of girls at the bar.

John pushed a hand through his hair. It felt thinner every time he did this.

'Sorry about that,' Conor said. 'You should ignore him. People chat a lot of shit at home. I wouldn't worry.'

'I don't even live in Dublin these days. I haven't for years.'

'I mean, that's probably why. You know, they see you as successful—'

'It's grand, Conor, don't worry about it,' John said. He picked up his bottle and downed what was left in it. 'Who gives a shit?'

'I want to sit in the audience tonight,' John told the stage manager, Amy, the following evening.

'Good,' Amy said. 'There's no need for you to be back here every night, you know.'

John was hungover. He remembered trying to get his key into the door of his flat and it taking ages. He'd slept long enough that he'd gotten through the headache and the nausea, but now the world seemed to be encased in jelly, and he was dimly attempting to move through without disturbing it.

I have poisoned myself, he thought. And everyone here resents me.

Also, he'd missed his chance to FaceTime with the kids that afternoon and Kitty was now texting him frostily. The energy backstage, which was no different from a normal night – props being moved around, voices calling down corridors, crew members with clipboards in a hurry – it all felt hostile. He didn't want to be here. Anyway, as Amy said, there was no need for it. Some directors would simply leave town entirely. Maybe none of these people wanted him here, anyway. Why did he stay? He could go back to London. Tonight he wanted to be in the stalls, in the dark. He wanted to dissolve into the fabric of the theatre itself. This was all Brendan Quirke's fault.

The evening's show was sold out – as far as he knew, the whole run was on the verge of selling out – but front of house managed to secure him a seat on the balcony. He waited outside by the stage door until the last possible moment, then entered the theatre through its main entrance. The show proceeded without incident: the audience laughed and gasped at all the right moments. The two Quirkes were brilliant, thankfully. They got better each time he saw them. Brendan was right – you couldn't tell he'd been drinking until three in the morning, but John could see the hint of it in Conor Quirke. Conor, defeating his brother's ghost in a duel with toy swords. Grey around the gills, voice straining as it reached its heights. Looking much older than he should. But maybe it was okay, John thought. Maybe John was the only one to notice.

He'd intended to return backstage for curtain call, so he could be dragged on for a round of applause if necessary. But somehow time sped up during the final act and he missed his chance. As the curtain fell, John was stuck on the balcony. Below him, the two Quirkes led the cast out for their bows. John had never seen this part from such an angle. The audience were on their feet for something he'd created, and he there among them. It felt like time itself was being pinched between forefinger and thumb, creating a tiny apex in the fabric of his own life. A thing he might want to remember. He stood with the rest of the theatre, no different from them for once. He too clapped like a sea lion. Down on the stage, Brendan Quirke caught John's eye and gestured up to him. The audience turned then to see John, and John bowed gently, respectfully he hoped, on autopilot. Applause, applause. His head ached and he was happy, for once. As he straightened up again he saw a familiar woman with fair hair in the stalls below, looking up at him and clapping obediently. It looked for a second like Frida Slattery.

Kitty and the boys arrived for a long weekend, four nights camping out in John's little apartment. Katarina had flown with them, but was going to stay with friends in Brooklyn for a few days and then travel back to London with them. Their visit marked the midpoint of John's time away from home. When their car pulled up outside his building, John could see Ruadhán's face pressing up against the window. Behind him, Kitty, and little Fionn in his car seat. Kitty's hair was longer than he remembered, grazing her chin now, and she was wearing a dark plummy shade of lipstick. He pictured her in the backseat of the taxi as they drove into the city, checking her appearance in her phone's camera while Ruadhán clamoured across her, reaching for the forbidden screen.

Ru tumbled out of the car and directly into John's arms, and John kept firm hold of his little boy, like he might have slipped away and into the city without him. When Ru grasped him like this, John was reminded of those treacherous first days in the hospital. How much his newborn son had looked like Kitty, and how John, sleep-deprived in the NICU, had stared through the glass and thought that maybe it had all been confused, maybe he was not the father of Kitty's child after all and another man should be here, standing in the antiseptic corridor listening to the beeping of the machines. John didn't like thinking of the version of himself who had had those thoughts. He handed Ruadhán back to Kitty and took Fionn from his wife's arms. Sweet Fionn, still sleeping somehow at the end of his long journey. The younger boy looked more like him. It was the birth of Fionn that had established John as a real father, not the scared and sceptical man he'd been in the hospital two years earlier. A transfiguration, Fionn's birth had been, for all of them – quick and efficient, Kitty's waters breaking right there on the threshold of the maternity ward.

'Think he needs changing,' John said to Kitty. He led the way upstairs to his apartment, weighed down once again in the ephemera of toddler parenthood.

Inside, Ruadhán dove straight onto the double bed. Kitty stood in the kitchen of his studio apartment.

'I didn't realise it was this small,' she said, looking around her for somewhere to put Fionn's changing bag.

'It'll be like camping,' he said. All four of them piled into the bed that night. John woke the next morning and was happy. Reviews in the papers were coming in, and *Ripples* was good. The cloud of tension was beginning to lift from his head. All week he'd been hanging around backstage, watching the show from the wings. Still the worry turned over and over in his head, that everyone around him in the theatre thought he was an arsehole. The next night, having left the boys in the flat with Katarina, Kitty and John would sit in the best seats in the house. Kitty insisted that they dress up, John in his black wool suit and her in a deep-blue Japanese dress that took ages to get into and out of. Looking in the mirror before they left, he pretended then that he was a real person, a man of substance and charm who people were keen to get to know and to be around.

'We look good,' Kitty said, slipping her arm through his.

Ah, at least he had Kitty. Mother of his boys and believer in his worth. His wife's frostiness over John's recent lack of communication had softened now that she could see the work close up, and even the tumult of his leaving them to go to the woods had faded. The work would save him once again, he knew. Leaving the theatre that night, Kitty told him that she thought *Ripples* was his best play yet. Yes, he thought, at least there was this.

John took the rest of the weekend off and they passed the time mostly the way they would at home in London. The four of them went to the zoo on Saturday morning, ate sandwiches in the park and exhausted themselves running around in the usual out-of-towner fashion. Racking up miles of steps and driving the boys to meltdowns at the playground. It was all pleasant, of course. It always was, in small doses, with time limits. He took photos of the kids on his phone and he held Kitty's hand as they walked down the street. He pointed out the things that had become, in the space of just a few short weeks, meaningful to him in some small way. The coffee shop where he only went when he was running late and couldn't go to the better one two blocks away. The subway station where he'd bumped into his old friend Chris Hammond on his honeymoon with his husband, visiting from Dublin. After the boys went to bed on Sunday night, John collected takeout from the noodle place around the corner and got a bottle of good wine and he and Kitty sat on the couch and talked the way they did at home in Tufnell Park, albeit in hushed tones.

But as Kitty had noticed on her arrival, the studio

apartment was small for two adults and two small children and when his family left on Monday morning, their taxi disappearing into the rush-hour traffic, John felt more than a little relieved. He went back upstairs and rolled a joint with the weed Conor had given him at the tech rehearsal. He smoked it and took a very long shower. It was like a tightrope walk, trying to hold these two roles of his in his hands at the same time. That Kitty was somehow able to look after both boys on her own, corralling them to the airport and onto a transatlantic flight with just Katarina to help, astounded him. He was beyond grateful for what she did. He could barely understand it. Then again, he thought, she had been the one who wanted all this for them.

Out of the shower, he wrapped himself in a towel and sat down on the edge of the bed. He would text Kitty, he thought, something nice and heartfelt about how much he'd enjoyed the weekend. Something meant to make her smile in the backseat of the cab. When he picked up his phone, he saw a new notification waiting at the top of the screen. It was an email from Frida Slattery.

To: John Reddan
Subject: (no subject)

John,

I hope you're keeping well. I'm in New York next weekend and hoping to see your new play. I hear it's impossible to get tickets! But don't worry, that's not why I'm emailing. I wonder if you'd like to meet for a drink, or a coffee, if you have the time. Am sure you're incredibly busy, but it would be nice to see you while we're in the same place.

Yours,

Frida

John had not thought of Frida Slattery in a long time. Maybe that was not correct. Of course he thought of Frida Slattery often. She crossed his mind constantly. But he did not think of the reality of her, of her existing in the same place as him. At present she was someone who existed on television. John knew all about Frida's TV show. It was the thing she'd left him for, after all, and he found himself surprised that it had lasted. Frida was lucky, he thought, to have stumbled into something with legs. It wasn't the kind of thing that he'd ever admit to watching, obviously, but he had seen it all. He'd found it on Netflix late at night when he was up with Ruadhán, and Kitty was in bed. He had managed to see every episode over the last couple of years. Some of them twice. Some of them were alright. He couldn't get his head around Frida's accent, the twang of it, and he could see there was something different about how she acted now. Some of the wild edginess she'd had before, the controlled intensity they'd once tried to cultivate together, was gone. Of course he'd had to watch *The Reason*. It was Frida's getaway car, and he had had its licence plate memorised the way he had his own date of birth.

But Frida existed also within John's memory. He still wrote rambling emails to her that were left unsent. Whenever he stopped to consider it, it was obvious that they weren't meant for Frida Slattery. They were intended for a version of himself that John kept close, a memory of his own youth that was preserved in aspic.

2.

They arranged to meet at a diner near the theatre an hour before curtain up. It was John's idea, both time and place. For a moment, leaving the theatre to meet her, he worried that he was trying to make himself look important. The slender hour of his schedule, the location so close to his work. Then he looked up at the marquee with his name on it and thought, Well, maybe I am important.

It was the last weekend in March and though the sun was out, John felt a chill in the air outside. Frida Slattery. Would she have a Californian tan? Walking down the block he could see that she was there ahead of him, seated in a red leatherette booth by the window, looking at her phone. He paused outside, wondering if she would look up and see him through the glass. Only a few metres separated them, and five years, of course. Her curly hair was longer than he remembered, piled up on top of her head and tied with a scrunchie. She was older, obviously, and so was he. But she looked better than she did in his memory. That was money, he reckoned as he pushed the door of the diner open. The money that women in her industry were obligated to spend on their own upkeep if they wanted to remain employable.

'Hey,' he said, sliding into the other side of the booth.

Frida looked up from her phone and her face broke into a smile. 'John,' she said. 'You're here.'

'Of course,' he said unsteadily. Was there anywhere else he would have been?

A waitress appeared clutching a Coke for Frida. John asked for a coffee. She nodded and glanced between the two of them, then smiled conspiratorially at Frida.

'Oh God,' Frida said. 'This is weird, isn't it?'

'I don't think so,' John said, though he wasn't sure. 'How've you been?' A stupid question, he thought.

Frida ignored it. 'I read an interview with you on the plane not too long ago. I didn't know you had a family now.'

'Yes. It's been so long, I suppose.'

'Yeah, the last place I thought I'd learn of your children's existence was the Aer Lingus magazine.'

John shifted, embarrassed. 'I find you end up revealing stuff about yourself in these things, if you're not careful.'

'Don't remind me. I've to do one with *Vanity Fair* tomorrow. Mel used to call it my "terminal honesty". She likes to sit in when I do them.'

'You're still with Mel. How is she?' (Why did it feel like one of them had gotten out of prison, John wondered. Maybe because there was a reason they hadn't spoken in five years.)

'Literally the same. Richer, maybe.'

'You too, I reckon.'

'Oh hush. It's nice to not have to worry, yeah. But how long does it last? It's different from your work, you know.'

'How's the show going, anyway?'

Frida screwed up her face. 'Not great. Well, we were filming the fourth season in Georgia a few months ago. And I got sick. And so they wrote me out of the second half of the season.'

'Sick?'

'I'm fine now. I needed to have surgery, and it didn't exactly gel with the shoot schedule.'

'Callous of your director. Sorry to hear that.'

'It's okay. I was recovering for four weeks, it really wouldn't have worked. The Lunds say I'll be back next season.' Frida smiled. 'Apparently Kathleen Richards is on secondment to the UN at the moment.'

John stirred his coffee.

'Kathleen Richards is the character I play.'

'Of course,' John said, feigning ignorance. 'Do you like Kathleen Richards?'

'Ha. Nobody's ever asked me that. I mean, she's fine. You get to know someone pretty well over the course of four seasons.'

'Three and a half.'

'Right, thanks for the reminder. Three and a half. Tell me about *Ripples on the Water*.'

John leaned forward, gave her the comprehensive patter he had honed in recent weeks. The ghosts in the woods in Germany, the brothers, and now New York. The feeling of a new chapter, the writing that resonated with audiences, 'the best work of my life'. He felt Frida's eyes on him at this last point. He wondered to himself if her story about surgery was the truth, and if the Lunds wanted to get rid of her. The story sounded like something he'd make up about an actor with whom he wished to part ways.

'Has Barry seen it?' Frida asked.

John smiled, remembering his brother at opening night in London. 'Yeah, I think he actually enjoyed it. I was apprehensive but he ended up seeing it twice. He said he thought it was funny, which I didn't expect.'

'God, I miss theatre,' Frida said wistfully. 'That thing when you get so absorbed in something, and then someone tells you what they think of it and their reaction comes as a total surprise. You don't get that in TV so much.'

'Can't imagine you do,' he said.

'I was thinking of using this break to line up some more interesting work, for once.'

John caught the eye of their waitress behind the counter for a second, and briefly she started to move towards them, like he'd requested something. Then she stopped and moved her gaze from his. He was aware then of how he and Frida looked. The serious man dressed in black and the pretty actress, the red leatherette seats of the booth ensconcing them. She a minor celebrity, depending on who you asked. He looked at her and thought of Max von Sydow playing chess with Death in *The Seventh Seal*. Broadway was just beside them, on the other side of the window. The whole thing like a mid-century painting about ennui. He was aware also that the two of them looked like cliché writ large.

'I didn't know you were thinking about the theatre again,' he replied.

Frida blinked. 'I never stopped, really. It's always felt like this TV thing, Hollywood, it's just temporary. Just something to do while I get back to the thing I love.'

This is what it is to have the upper hand, John thought. The diner's clock had its numbers etched in phlegmatic red neon, like everything else around here. The time was edging closer to curtain up for *Ripples*. The upper hand was a surprise for him. Frida was LA now. John had his share of the stage, but she was the Hollywood sign, the coast, the smog, a Cadillac with fins, a house in the hills. And that wasn't enough for her. It turned out that she wanted what John had, too.

John signalled for the cheque and took a cluster of crumpled bills from the pocket of his jeans. 'The time,' he said. 'I need to get back to the theatre. Walk with me?'

Out on the street he led the way down the block. It was a warm evening. Two taxis honked alongside them, and Frida flinched.

'I wasn't aware you wanted to do more theatre,' John said again. 'I mean, of course, I've followed your career.'

John wasn't going to tell her that he had seen *The Reason*. It was too revealing to do so, like inviting her into the living room where he sat watching Netflix alone, still always appraising her work.

'Yeah,' Frida said slowly. 'I've definitely been lucky. But, you know.'

Outside the stage door of the theatre, two stage hands smoked. They nodded to John as he approached.

'John,' Frida said, 'do you think you and I could ever work together again?'

He had known that this question would come, and still he wasn't sure what to do with his face. Part of him wanted to turn her down. A larger part of him wanted to keep a hold of her, keep connected. Oh God, John had missed her. That's why he kept watching her stupid show, because it meant she was there, on his screen, in his living room. It meant he could pretend to be directing her, giving her notes, arranging her into the positions he thought best.

'Yeah, probably,' he said. He knew it was a fudge of an answer. 'I don't have anything I'm working on at the moment that really suits. And there's talk ... oh, I don't know, I shouldn't say.'

'No,' she said. 'Go on.'

'There's a theatre in London and they've asked me about the artistic director job. If that comes about, it'll be less writing, you know. More big thinking, planning, whatever.'

Frida's eyes widened. 'Congratulations, John. That's amazing.'

'Oh, it isn't confirmed yet. It's early days.'

She smiled. 'Of course. Well, you know I'm always open to working with you. It doesn't need to be something you've written. You know I'll give anything a try.'

'Yeah, I know.'

He thought about an episode of *The Reason* where Kathleen Richards and Peter Wright had broken up, again, and yet they had to work together on a grisly murder of a mother and child. The moment when Kathleen reviewed the crime-scene photos was supposed to be poignant – Kathleen on the verge of tears for once, her hardened affect at risk of crumbling – and yet John saw Frida on screen almost hamming it up, pressing a hand over her mouth as her eyes filled with tears. It was ludicrous. Entertaining, yes, but how could the audience stomach that? It made him wonder: had Frida ever been as good as he'd wanted her to be?

'Come on,' he said. 'You should meet the boys.'

For a minute she looked confused and John saw that she thought he meant his kids. He gestured to the stage door and nodded then.

'Sure,' she said, and followed him into the bowels of the theatre.

3.

Frida's seat in the stalls was on the aisle, and for a solid ten minutes before curtain up she was standing up, sitting again, letting ticket-holders by. She never went to the theatre in LA. She hadn't even been during any of her trips home recently. She had forgotten about this: the bustle of bodies crowding into a single space, the fizz of anticipation, the stale air in the poorly ventilated auditorium.

This, of course, was John's life, had always been John's life. The remarkable way he had managed to get exactly what he'd wanted.

Talking to him in the diner had required the switching off of a certain part of her. Watching him, his fingers playing with a packet of sugar, his top lip curling into his faintly sinister smile, it had taken her back to a time in her life that was now long gone. It could easily make her long for other things from her life, if she wasn't careful. It was funny. She knew that John's life had moved on, and yet when they'd been together in the diner, it had been like looking into a portal to the past.

Sitting in the stalls, she attempted to empty her mind

of these thoughts. As the play began, she tried to focus on *Ripples on the Water*. John had brought her to meet the Quirke brothers backstage, the two of them shirtless in pancake make-up. Now they were peacocking under the bright yellow lights. It was impossible not to think that this was the proof of John's life – the proof of the path he'd chosen, and the one that she had not. Frida felt like a joke. He had used his time to do all the right things: marriage, children, art. And she had been allotted the same portion of time and had used it to dick around on television, rack up a string of failed relationships, a distance from her family and a literal hole in her reproductive system. Was this what she wanted? The audience's collective hush, the stakes high, the tension that held the room together. Or was it proximity to John Reddan that she was missing? The part of her that was always acting to him, even on set with the Lunds. Did Frida just want to turn the clock backwards? She knew it was impossible, and yet weren't lives long, and wasn't she still young? She was thirty-three. Perhaps she would be allowed another act. Plenty of actors had careers that twisted, that dipped, that circled back on themselves. Plenty of women she knew found themselves married at thirty-five to a man they'd slept with a few times in college. She thought of Catherine and the path she'd taken. Frida and Catherine hadn't fallen out, but they never had reason to speak anymore. That was life, wasn't it? John had always told her he'd never put a ghost in his play, and yet she was about to watch one jousting with his living brother on stage. What had changed? Oh, God, she thought. Maybe she didn't know John Reddan at all. But it felt so much like she did. It felt like she had a right to some part of him even now.

Frida paid close attention to the audience around her through the first act. They laughed on cue, were rapt and quiet at other points. She listened to them cough and shuffle in their seats. Frida was slightly wishing for *Ripples* to end. Not that it was dragging, but the boys, as John called them, had invited her to cast drinks at a bar around the corner after the show. She had tried to watch John's reaction to this, to measure if he wanted her there or not. But she figured she would go for a drink. She had come all this way, hadn't she? She was on holiday. Conor was basically an old friend from college. She'd met Brendan Quirke once before, at a party in Hollywood. Hadn't liked him. Pretended to, of course. But he was smug and a little misogynistic, and acted like he knew he was pretty, too. He reminded her of girls from school who were mean, but who thought they were conveying such a nice image that nobody would notice.

At the interval Frida bought a glass of wine and drank it quickly in the queue for the bathroom. When she sat for the second act, she could feel the alcohol in her system. The curtain rose on the Quirkes in a swordfight with toy swords and it took Frida a few minutes to realise that Brendan's character, the younger brother of the pair, was already supposed to be dead. She had been wondering since the play began when the ghosts were going to arrive on the scene. He had been dead the entire time, she realised, feeling stupid. From then on, it became somewhat difficult for her to follow the action. At the end of the swordfight Conor thrust a cardboard sword into the space between Brendan's ribs and his arm, asking him why he'd bother to spend all his afterlife haunting his own brother. Bit pathetic, isn't it? Don't you have anything else to do than relitigate your old sibling rivalry?

And Brendan replied in a voice that Frida thought was pure John Reddan, Well, that's the thing about the living. They can only ever see us in relation to their own sorry selves.

Frida wondered where John was now, at this very moment. Was he backstage? Could he see Frida from his spot in the wings? Or was he off having dinner, calling his wife and children? When she'd emailed him to ask to meet up, she had been planning to tell him about what happened almost five years ago, when she was leaving London. The pregnancy test, the termination.

For years, Mel had been the only person she'd told. Then at home in Dublin a few months back, she'd told Edel. A glass of wine in the Horseshoe Bar, and then Frida had mentioned it in passing, as if Edel already knew. She hadn't told her before because she knew it would only make Edel dislike John more. Edel had always treated John with suspicion. The things that had once drawn Frida to John were things that Edel found pretentious, or rude, or just wilfully eccentric.

'Sorry,' Edel had said in a low and serious voice. She set her wine glass down on the table in front of them. 'Did I hear that right?'

Frida stiffened instinctively. 'I made the decision that was right for me at the time.'

'No, I know that. Of course, Free. That's not what I meant. Why didn't you tell me?'

'I don't know. Things happened quite quickly, it was right before I moved to LA.'

'What did John say?'

'I didn't tell him.'

Edel's eyebrows shot up. 'Frida . . .'

'You don't know what it was like,' she protested. 'I was trying to make decisions for my future. And he would have—'

'He would have told you to do something else?'

Frida didn't want to be here anymore. She wanted to be in Los Feliz, alone on her patio. 'Not like that. It's just that I was very used to having his input on things by that point.'

Edel shook her head slowly. 'Christ almighty. What a dickhead. Well, I'm glad you've moved on from him, at any rate.'

Great, Frida had thought as they'd left the bar. Now we're all mourning something.

Frida didn't know what had changed, but she had come to the belief that John should know too, that he had a right to know. But in the diner, the idea of telling him had felt ridiculous. It was unnecessary, she thought. He had a life of his own, a family. What did she have? She didn't need to go sharing her own secrets and make them his.

On stage she watched Conor Quirke bounding about. He had been lovely when she'd arrived backstage, in contrast to his brother. Delighted to see her after so long. Frida wondered if he was single nowadays. John wouldn't like it, she thought, if she went home with one of his actors. In fact, that was exactly the sort of thing that John didn't like at all. She remembered making *Bird*, years earlier, with the tall guy, Chris. The two of them had had a little chemistry and Frida could tell it rankled John. It was like John thought people should only share what he allotted to them, and nothing else. It had been years since Frida last worried about the possibility of upsetting John. But the impulse returned easily.

When Frida arrived at the bar, the specifics of *Ripples on the Water* had already left her brain. She leaned in and kissed John on both cheeks.

'A triumph!' she whispered into his ear in a voice both mocking and deadly serious. Her mouth so close to his ear, she felt him flinch nervously. The two Quirkes pulled her in for a sweaty embrace, and she could sense John's gaze on the back of her head.

'Next time,' Brendan Quirke said to John over her head. 'Next time write one for all three of us, yeah?'

A few martinis. A few glasses of wine. A lot of shouting. A joint, ill-advised, with Conor Quirke in the sticky back alley of the bar. She was telling him about her surgery and saw him cringe at the words *ovarian torsion*. She thought, Oh I've gone too far again. I am always doing this! Inside, John leaning over the jukebox. 'Marquee Moon'. Eleven minutes of it.

'John, you fucking shit,' Brendan shouted. 'Put on something we can dance to.'

But they danced anyway, the four of them banging into each other.

'How do you keep up with those two?' Frida asked John,

but she herself was floundering, wobbling on her feet, starting sentences and forgetting where she was going with them. She should've had dinner. John could tell, she knew. The Quirkes were ordering another line of shots, four little chalices of quivering vodka arranged with precision along the bar.

'Oh, no,' he said to the brothers, slapping a hand down on the bar. 'No, no. I'm taking this lady for a cheeseburger.'

Back to the diner, then. Frida explained on the way to their booth that she never drank like that anymore. The same red neon and leatherette inside. Different waitress now, an older woman, didn't make eye contact this time. Something almost demonic about the diner's red coherence. Briefly Frida thought, How would I know if I was in hell? It was a question she'd asked herself on the drive to the hospital. Two cheeseburgers. Onion rings. Set down on the table in front of them. Oh, lovely onion rings.

'Mel would hate this,' Frida said, diving straight in.

'What?'

'Me eating onion rings with you.'

'Are you not allowed onion rings?'

'Ah, you know,' she said, swallowing. 'No. But also, I didn't tell her I was coming to see you.'

'She never liked me.'

'True. Plus I don't think I'm in her good books at the moment.'

'What did you do?'

Frida pointed down at the space in her abdomen where her ovary used to be. 'I "jeopardised my own success".' She made air quotes with an onion ring.

'By having emergency surgery? Bullshit.' He smacked the table with an open palm.

She liked this. John on her side now. For once. He had burger sauce halfway down his chin. She reached for it with a paper napkin.

'I'm supposed to do an interview tomorrow where I tell them how I almost died. So the Lunds can't fire me next season.'

He squinted at her, reached for a chip. 'Did you really almost die?'

Frida thought about this question.

'Yes,' she decided.

John was chewing, nodding, his eyes wide. 'Jesus, Frida.'

'I know, right. Life without Frida Slattery. Not worth living!'

'My little boy was sick. Ruadhán. He'll be four this year. His little heart.' John made a fist with his hand and looked at it.

'Ah, John, I'm so sorry.'

'He's okay. The surgery worked. But it changes you, doesn't it?'

Frida nodded. 'Oh yeah. It changes you.' She picked up another onion ring. 'Do you ever think about moving home?'

'Ah, fuck knows. I don't think they'd have us.'

'Shut up, John. You? They probably think you're the king. They've probably got the snug saved for you in Toner's.'

'I'm happy where I am.'

'It was in a bad way when we left, wasn't it?'

'I think it probably still is.'

'It's getting better now,' Frida said. 'Every time I go back ... there's money there again.'

'And isn't that what it's all about? Money, money, money.'

'You know what I mean. Money is important. Can you do what you do without someone with deep pockets paying for it?'

John put the sopping end of his burger down on his plate. 'Yeah, Frida, I guess you're right.'

'Sorry,' she said, shrugging. 'I thought that was just how it works.'

'Yeah, it is how it works.'

'Even for the artists among us.' She was pushing it now, cheeky, verging on rude.

'And are you not an artist anymore? I seem to remember a girl in Dublin who thought she was the second coming of Ingrid Bergman.'

'I am the second coming of Ingrid Bergman,' Frida confirmed.

She had assumed the diner would be open all night, but the waitress was coming over to them with the bill.

'"The check,"' Frida said.

'I've got no money,' John announced.

'And you a famous director.' Frida opened her handbag to dig around for her wallet. When she looked up again, John was staring at her, his eyes locked on her.

'It's funny,' he said. 'I'm not even tired anymore. I think I could talk to you forever.'

She couldn't help herself. She grinned at him. 'We don't have to go home,' she said. 'Maybe we can find somewhere to sit.'

'I really want to tell you about what I'm working on. I miss telling you about what I'm working on.'

'Do you talk to Kirsty about your work?'

'Kitty. Yes, I do.'

'That's really good.'

'It is.'

'It's so important.'

'Do you have anyone, Frida? Like anyone in your life like that.'

They were getting up to leave the diner now. John holding out the arms of her jacket for her to slip into. She turned around to face him and lay a hand lightly on his chest.

'Yeah, I do,' she said. 'I have you.'

'Ah,' John said. 'Not really what I meant.'

'I know. But do you remember? What we were like.'

'Yeah, Christ. Of course I do.'

'We were something,' she said, her brow furrowing.

'And I'm saying I've missed that,' he said. 'I don't think you can have that many times in a lifetime, you know?'

'I know, yeah.'

'So, I've missed that.'

'My hotel is down the block,' she announced.

'Down the block,' he repeated.

'Down the street, whatever. Just come and have a drink and tell me about the thing you're working on.'

Out on the street it had rained, and the city smelled damp and sweet with pollution. John was lighting a cigarette. The door of the diner creaked closed behind Frida. With him she felt twenty-four again, completely green. The power of that inexperience. Jesus, you could do anything under its cloak. Then all at once it lifted and was gone and you were here, on the sidewalk, a decade on, a different kind of woman, and John Reddan walking a stride ahead of you in the dark. Even though he didn't know where it was you were taking him, he was trying to lead the way anyway.

With him, Frida felt safe.

With him, Frida felt like she was on stage, or in a rehearsal room, or was sat at a table with a script in front of them.

He walked a stride ahead of her the whole way down the block. There was a stone in Frida's shoe, and she stopped to remove it, balancing with great care on one leg.

John paused outside what he thought was her hotel, and he turned around to face her.

'Is this you?' he asked, angling his head to the door.

And Frida nodded, and she followed him inside.

The lift was small, and they were close together. She could smell John's breath as she leaned across him to push the button, and the scent was so familiar. Frida tried to remember what the surgeon had said about sex at her last check-up. Shit, Frida, she thought. She stopped herself. She forced herself to look down at John's hand, where a thick silver ring sat on his third finger.

'Tell me more about Ruadhán and Fionn,' she asked him.

He looked down at her, smiling uneasily, a curl of his lip that she recognised as desire. 'No,' he replied, taking her hand in his as the door slid open.

4.

John fell asleep hoping that he woke before Frida did in the morning. He knew the best thing to do would have been to leave before sleep came, go downstairs and wait for the Q train back uptown. But it hit him all at once, the tiredness, and the sheets of her nice hotel bed were so inviting. In the morning he woke with the sun, and here was Frida, still curled up. She was as beautiful as she'd been the night before, as beautiful, almost, as when they'd first gone to bed together years earlier. The night before, he'd seen the tiny scar on her abdomen, the incision site. Only then did he really believe her. He had wanted another chance with her. He had known that the moment he saw her waiting for him in the diner. What had he said last night to make this happen? He tried to remember. What had he plámássed her with? Talk of the old days, probably. Talk of the future. Had any of it even been necessary? Probably John could have just snapped his fingers and Frida would have been there by his side. Maybe it had always been like this. Maybe she had always been waiting for him. She was asleep now, one hand curled over her belly. Jesus, what a mistake, he thought. What kind of man was he? He remembered with a flash what she'd said, right before they'd gone to sleep. When she had gotten the part in *The Reason*, she had been pregnant. She had had an abortion. Jesus Christ. She said it so lightly, like she was telling him the plot of a TV drama of which he'd missed an episode. He pulled on his jeans and the shirt from last night and headed out, closing the door behind him as quietly as possible. Outside, the wet humidity of the previous evening had dissipated. Now John shivered in the cool morning air.

How easy it had been to conceive Ruadhán five years earlier. And Kitty the last woman he had slept with. And now Frida, for whom there was apparently already proof of concept. Stupid of him. Reckless. He walked down the block towards the subway station on the corner. It was early still, the edge of rush hour, and John longed for his home in Tufnell Park, the kids and Kitty in it. It was as if he chose to make things difficult for himself. Last night he'd enquired about a condom, knowing he didn't have any (he was married, after all, and faithful to his wife), and Frida had sat up, a hand pulling through her curly hair and said that the doctors had told her it would be tricky. That it would be fine, if he didn't have one. He pushed through the turnstile and onto the uptown platform. How long would it take for her to wake up and find him gone? Imagine she was pregnant off the back of this, something in his brain commanded him to think. Imagine she was in her hotel room right now and the beginnings of life were stirring within her already. Not for years, except for the rare times after he took cocaine, had John had thoughts like these – governed not by content but by their shape, their pattern. A thought that hurtled and then repeated, over and over. Imagine you got Frida Slattery pregnant, he thought again on the platform. He knew he couldn't make the thought stop. Imagine you got Frida Slattery pregnant, because you are a stupid idiot and a bad man. He pictured his brain swirling, like a liquid circling down a drain without end. Imagine you have to tell Kitty what you've done. The train slowed to a stop in front of him and he boarded. In his jacket pocket he found his phone, his hand shaking. He pulled up the email Frida had sent him a week earlier, arranging to meet. He typed a reply to her now.

Sorry Frida, had to leave for the theatre.

He couldn't think of what to say that would do the job without incriminating him. He didn't want to put it on the record, his own idiocy and immorality. Immoral! John suddenly felt Catholic, sitting slumped on the blue plastic subway bench. Confession, maybe, might help. He needed to call her and explain. Sorry Frida, he typed. Can we talk later? He pressed send.

5.

The first thing Frida was aware of when she opened her eyes was the pain in her head. Then the light streaming through the window, which was open. The noise of traffic on the street below. The smell of male sweat, alcohol. New York. John Reddan. And the time. An interview with a journalist elsewhere in the hotel in just over an hour. John was gone, and she wondered if maybe he'd left a note somewhere, but there wasn't time to look. She called room service for coffee. Ran the shower, used the hairdryer. Sitting on the edge of the bed, watching time slip by. Knock on the door from the concierge. Towel wrapped around her, getting cold. White shirt, blue jeans, lots of concealer under the eyes. Don't look too closely. Why did she do that? She wanted to pretend the last five years hadn't happened, that she was twenty-eight again and had time ahead of her to figure out what her life would be like. Mascara, lipstick, fuck fuck fuck this. Everything taking much longer than it should. Phone ringing. Front desk. Claire from *Vanity Fair* was waiting in the lobby downstairs. *Where are my shoes?* Frida left the room, took the elevator down two floors to the other suite Mel had booked, and waited for

Claire to arrive. She looked at her phone, checking to see if John had texted. He had not.

Every time Frida was in a hotel room such as this one, waiting for an interview to begin, the same thought ran through her head: Tank it. It was a ragged impulse, the sweeping, brief notion of pulling the car into the headlights of oncoming traffic, the urge to drop your phone into the crevasse below. It passed. Frida tended to behave herself, because it was in her own interest to do so. Her interest, the show's interest. Mel's, the Lunds', the wide network of talented, skilled people who worked on the show with them. Now these thoughts were starting up in her head once more.

Okay, go on, tank it, she thought. Put the Lunds in it, tell Claire they were inhumane, cruel, give them no choice but to fire you. Give Mel no choice but to fire you, too.

Tank it!

Tell Claire about the time Tobias took his penis out of his tight blue jeans at the table of the restaurant in Malibu, nudged you in the ribs lightly, drew your eyes downwards.

Tell Claire about the affair Sara had with the production assistant, Oliver, and how Oliver's contract was terminated unceremoniously once Tobias told Sara to ditch him.

Tell her enough that someone will be forced, in all seriousness, to take you roughly by the arm and say, Frida Slattery, you'll never work in this town again. Oh, she had always dreamed of that line. There was enough there, certainly, in her memory. There were so many stupid little stories she could have told. Frida hadn't realised that she had been keeping a list all this time.

Tank it, she urged herself. Take the whole thing and flush it down the toilet.

A knock on the door, and Frida rose to open it.

Claire was a small woman with pinched features who Frida thought looked very familiar. Maybe they'd met before. She extended a clammy, cold hand and Frida shook it, and they took their seats on opposite ends of a sleek grey couch with Claire's recorder between them. The terms of their conversation had been agreed in advance, and so Claire began by politely asking Frida what had happened in Georgia.

Frida arranged herself neatly, one leg crossed over the other, hands folded in her lap, shoulder angled towards her interviewer. And she told the story that she and Mel had prepared in advance – the stickiness of the weather, the sudden onset of excruciating pain that cut through the days of filming, the dreadful prognosis of the rural hotel doctor, the long drive through the night to reach safety. It already felt like this story had happened to somebody else, that Frida was merely recounting a grotesque personal essay she'd once read online.

Once she was in full flow, it became much easier not to tank it. She was just another actor reciting her lines.

'The Lunds were so supportive,' Frida said. She told Claire how Sara Lund had driven her to the hospital and played Fleetwood Mac. How the two of them had been there when Frida woke up after surgery, had barely left the building the whole time.

'Sara just gets it. Tobias too – I was blown away.'

Don't overdo it, Frida told herself. She smiled peaceably at Claire.

'I'm lucky,' Frida finished. 'I know not everyone gets to work with such compassionate people.'

'It sounds like it was a real emergency situation,' Claire said.

Frida nodded, closed her eyes. She readied herself. 'They said I could have died.'

'The doctors?'

'Yes.'

'Good Lord.'

'It was a dark time, and I was in incredible pain. You know, I had been lucky, I think, to have lived for so long without experiencing something like that.' Mel had prepared all of this for her. 'For so many women, it's not possible to live in ignorance of how our bodies work. For me, it had to get to a point where I was forced to acknowledge it – an emergency situation, as you said, something that interrupts everything. I mean, the way ovarian torsion works is that it could have been happening for weeks without my noticing, until the pain got too extreme to bear. When you're shooting on location, often I find you dislocate a little from your body, as a way to get through long days.'

Claire looked out the window, then looked back at her. 'I think that's something that women do in general, isn't it?'

Frida tilted her chin, smiling evenly at Claire. 'Sure.'

And then another line prepared by Mel. 'Our bodies – well, they're tricky, aren't they? And that was what I learned after my surgery, that there is so much we, even doctors, medical experts, don't understand about women's health. I thought, why is that? And what does it mean? Now that I'm recovering, it's something I'd like to do more to support, you know, charity work, activism.'

'Do you think female actors with careers like yours face a lot of pressure?'

'Of course. I'm so lucky, but we sometimes are treated like racehorses with short lifespans. I know from talking to my peers that it does seem to get harder to find the good roles, with every year that passes. And when you factor in things like motherhood, or even what happened to me this season—'

Claire tapped her pen on her notebook, leaning forward. 'Is motherhood a role you'd like to try?'

Frida thought of John the night before, patting down his pockets for a condom that she knew wouldn't exist. What was the phrasing Mel had drilled into her?

'Out of respect for my own family I'm not going to answer that.'

'Gotcha,' Claire said, nodding. 'One more question, before we finish. You grew up Catholic, right? I did too. Irish, Boston, you know.'

Frida nodded, unsure of where she was going with this.

'I'm wondering, and I ask this only because of my own thinking, my own upbringing. I'm wondering, when you were unwell that night in Georgia – did you ever think you were being punished for something?'

'Punished,' Frida repeated faintly.

'Yes,' Claire said, nodding eagerly. 'Maybe you didn't get this, but when I had a bike crash last spring, it was my first thought in the hospital. What does God want with me?'

Frida looked at her, the other woman's small blue eyes shining at her expectantly.

'I have to say,' Frida said. 'God doesn't play much of a part in my day-to-day life anymore.'

'Yes, I get that. I just thought I'd ask.'

After the interview ended, Frida watched Claire leave, then set a timer on her phone and waited for twelve minutes before she left, too. She didn't know where she was going. Unsteady on her feet, she made her way through the marble hotel lobby and out to the street. God, she thought, punished. She thought of last night, telling John about the abortion. Stupid, unnecessary confession. He had stared back at her blankly, like he didn't know what reaction she expected of him. Stupid thing to have done, Frida thought, shaking her head. She walked to a bar on the corner of the block and took a seat, ordered a white wine.

Who would judge Frida? When she made decisions like the ones she made last night, she felt truly alone in the world.

How would John judge her? She remembered suddenly the previous night, after they'd finished. Surprised, slightly, that he had actually managed to finish at all, given their history and the amount they'd both had to drink. They were lying together in the way they always used to, legs intertwined, talking nonsense.

John turned to face her, he was saying something about some actors he'd worked with lately. About screen tests, close-ups. He held her face in one hand and squinted at her. Their noses brushing.

'What are you looking at?' she said.

'What work have you had done?'

She blinked. 'What do you mean.'

'I know all about actors, Frida. I know about how it is in Hollywood.'

'Stop,' she said, ducking her head out of his grasp. She could feel his eyes on hers, scanning for tells.

'Come on,' he said, goading her, playing. He was pretending it was a joke. With one hand he skimmed her forehead softly, like a hairdresser might when spinning the chair around to face the mirror. 'I think you look beautiful, by the way.'

He'd said it like it was a surprise, a generosity, and Frida shuddered to think now that it had felt like one at the time.

There was an email from him on her phone, she noticed now in the bar. She opened it. Can we talk later? Hours earlier. Later was now. She sipped her wine, winced at the taste of yet more alcohol, and replied, Yes, free now and appended her phone number. John called her almost instantly.

'How was your interview?' he asked.

'Hellish, my God. Do you ever get asked about Catholicism? Sometimes I hate being Irish.'

'Oh yeah. That one. Well, try writing a play like *Ripples*. They tend to see whatever sin they want to in it.'

'Sin isn't the issue,' Frida remarked. 'I think with me, they're more caught up with shame.'

'That's because you're a woman,' John said, and she had nothing to say to that, and the thunderous silence hung on the line for a second.

'Sorry,' John said, continuing on. 'Nothing personal. Anyway, I wanted to speak to you after last night. I think we both know it was a mistake.'

'A mistake,' she repeated.

John cleared his throat. 'I'm married, Frida,' he said in a low voice, like someone might have heard him.

Frida's cheeks burned, like she was in trouble at school. 'I'm aware.'

'Look, I'm not saying ... Look. You know how important you are to me.'

'I know,' she managed, though she didn't have any idea. 'You don't need to explain—' Mortified.

'No, no, of course. I just needed to talk to you.'

Frida could hear the strain in his voice. How much he hated having to do this, and for a moment this felt good to her. She thought of the picture of his wife beside him in the in-flight magazine.

'Go on,' she said.

She heard John inhale sharply before he spoke. 'Do you think it would be best if you took the morning-after pill today?'

Frida's eyes closed and she gripped the wine glass in front of her.

'Look,' he said. 'You've done nothing wrong. I made a mistake last night. And you know that Kitty and the boys are my priority, and I have to put them first.'

'Yeah, yeah.' Frida's voice was small now and she hated it, how she must look to the tall young guy behind the bar, and if he recognised her from television or the Marvel movie she didn't care, because as far as she was concerned she mightn't ever be on screen again.

'And I want us to be able to work together in the future, you know.'

'I get it, John,' she said, wanting the conversation to finish now.

'I know you do. Of course you do. And I can trust you.'

In his voice there was the barest hint of a challenge.

In Frida's head, the old impulse again, lit up in neon. *Tank it.*

She sipped her wine, made him wait.

'Yes, John,' she replied at last. 'You can trust me. It was definitely a mistake. Look, I have to go. It was good to see you yesterday.'

'Yeah, of course, you too.'

'Stay in touch, yeah?'

After she ended the call she ran a hand over her cheek where the screen of her phone had been pressed, and it was cold and alien to the touch. How juvenile it felt, to have a grown man asking you to take care of things. Telling you how terrible it could be if you didn't. How disastrous for him. How much it felt to Frida like being a teenager. John was pathetic. A grown man, she thought, signalling to the barman for the same again.

9. Hiatus, 2017–2019

1.

In the kitchen, John was cooking beef bourguignon. In the dining room, Kitty, pouring wine for Barry and Joanna, visiting from Dublin while they sold the little house in Harold's Cross and moved up the road to a bigger home in Terenure. All the children watching an animated movie together in the living room with chicken nuggets and chips. From the kitchen, John could pretend that this part was simple. Family life. Domesticity. The countertops crowded already with plates and dishes, bowls of salad, marinating meats, dirty knives and spoons. John pretended to be serene, above it all. He'd shot a movie recently, his first, in the countryside in Hungary. His first day on set he'd been alarmed by the way the production stretched endlessly outwards, more wires, more trailers, more random people whose jobs he did not know or understand. The whole thing could not be contained the way it could in the theatre, bound by the walls of the building. So he'd done the same thing there as he was doing here in the kitchen. He'd pretended to float about what seemed to be chaos. Someone else could clean this up.

Barry came to him bearing two glasses of wine.

'The chef at work,' he said, extending one glass to John. 'The women are talking about schools.'

'Join me here in the lions' den,' John said.

'How's work?'

'Ah, you know.'

'No idea, actually. I'll remind you what it is I do for a living. You don't happen to need a mortgage, actually, do you?'

'Work's grand. We just finished editing the movie. It's out next year, at one of the festivals, we're hoping.'

Barry emitted a low whistle. 'The movies. Big time. You took your time getting there.'

John turned from the stove to look at him. 'I mean, not that long. I've been busy with the theatre. And there's not, like, a hierarchy.'

'Really?'

'Shut up, Barry. Go talk to the women about childcare.'

John ladled stew onto four plates and the brothers carried them to the table where the wives sat. Joanna was a buxom woman from Limerick with hair that John thought was too long and girlish for her age. She and Kitty gave the men a pair of pointed looks across the oval teak table.

'John,' Joanna said. 'We've got a few questions for you.'

John paused as he set the plates down onto the table.

'I was telling Joanna about Robert Macauley,' Kitty said.

Robert Macauley was a playwright from Edinburgh who both John and Kitty knew slightly. In recent weeks, Macauley's new play had been dropped by a West End theatre after the publication of a newspaper story in which a woman alleged that Macauley had promised her a job in return for sex when she was twenty-one. In a matter of days, Macauley went from one of London's most revered writers to social pariah, the kind of name that could kill a production by merest association.

'You know Barry and I don't know much about the whole theatre thing,' Joanna said to John. 'The entertainment industry. But I've been reading some of these accounts from Hollywood. I'm curious to know what you two think of it all.'

Kitty reclined in her dining chair. 'We had an argument about this the other night.'

John frowned. 'It wasn't an argument.'

'John thinks Robert shouldn't have to lose his job,' she added.

'That's not what I said.'

'Isn't it?' Kitty asked.

'I said that I don't understand how someone can go from being beloved and revered to utterly untouchable over a single uncorroborated story from one single woman. Overnight. I get it if some people don't want to work with him at the moment, but now they're pulling productions of his work in Germany. Productions he's got nothing to do with.'

'Kitty, what do you think?' Joanna asked.

Kitty tilted her head to one side. 'I think it's interesting that people are saying now that this sort of thing has happened since the beginning of time. I mean, you always heard tales, but—'

'What kind of tales?' Barry asked her.

'Well, the wardrobe department isn't that bad. The worst I ever got was some old queen trying to show me his todger.

But what I'm saying is that it's taken this long to listen to all these women. Maybe that shows that things are changing for the better.'

'So you two are at loggerheads,' Joanna said across the table. She looked a little bit pleased with the idea.

'We're not at loggerheads,' John said.

'Aren't we?' Kitty asked.

'Of course not. We're allowed to disagree about things, you know.'

'Do you find the whole thing scary, John?' Barry asked his brother.

John coughed. 'Scary, no.'

'John's got nothing to worry about,' Kitty said in a low, sweet voice.

'Let's eat,' John said, pulling his chair close to the table.

'But it is interesting, isn't it,' Barry continued, cutting a slice of sourdough. 'How it seems like different rules apply for one industry. For one set of people we regard as, you know, special or creative or talented.'

John was beginning to find this exhausting. 'Look,' he said. 'I'm not saying that you should be able to commit crime, actual crime, and get away with it because you're a quote-unquote great artist. Some of the other stories coming out at the moment are horrific, and Kitty's completely right that of course we should listen to and believe these women.'

'But,' Joanna prompted.

John continued. 'But I think what some people don't understand is how much of our work does happen late at night, in bars, or hotel rooms, or people's flats. Behind closed doors, you know. There's a grey area there sometimes. Sure even Kitty and I met at work. People sleep together, sometimes things get complicated. Not for me, personally, but I can see how some of these things might get confused in the retelling.'

'I think it's not so much about grey areas,' Joanna said, 'as it is about power dynamics. Kitty was saying that the woman in your man Macauley's case was just starting out, she was looking for a way into the industry. And he knew that and he took advantage of that.'

John closed his eyes. Had Macauley taken advantage? In a way, John thought, it could be argued that the woman was taking advantage of him. Using her youth and sex appeal and, he didn't know, her joie de vivre, to get ahead with a guy who was far past all of that. But he wouldn't say that aloud, not with the two wives giving him pointed looks across the table.

'Thankfully John has the added defence that he doesn't actually like collaborating with people, or mentoring young talent,' Kitty said, swishing red wine around in her glass.

John glanced at his wife across the table. She looked particularly beautiful when she was being like this.

'Maybe we should drop this,' Barry suggested. 'The beef's delicious, John.'

'I don't know,' Joanna mused. 'It's something I'm finding so interesting. Everyone I work with is talking about it. And obviously they're like, "Hey, Joanna, don't your in-laws work in theatre? What do they think about all this?"'

John looked at his sister-in-law and struggled to remember what kind of ordinary job she did for a living.

'Well,' Kitty said. 'Now you know what to tell them on Monday morning.'

'I'm going to get more wine,' John said, rising to his feet.

In the kitchen, the same mess John had created earlier in the evening. He found a bottle and opened it, then took his phone from his pocket. He leaned against the counter, which was sticky with grease. John has nothing to worry about, Kitty had said at the table. Almost like she was mocking him. Lately it felt like everyone was mocking him. He'd turned forty the other month. When did this start to get better? It had been starting to get better, hadn't it? And then this new dark wave emerged on the horizon. He was thinking all the time now, about these women and their stories. How delicate a person's career, a whole life, could turn out to be in the face of their stories. John opened the inbox on his phone. All the time he thought that an email might suddenly appear there, the way it had for Robert Macauley and for other men John knew. He heard plenty of stories about these emails. An address that ended in the name of a newspaper. Would you like to comment on the below, Mr Reddan? It was like looking out to sea from the deck of a ship, knowing the whole place was littered with bloody World War II munitions, but without any idea of how they could be avoided, if they could be avoided at all.

John almost wanted it to hurry up and happen to him already. Perhaps it could be precipitated by him directly, getting it over with. But then that was the other thing. When he cycled back through the timeline of his career, there was no one single moment that stood out to him. Some errors of judgement probably, some women he'd slept with who he cringed to think about now. A teenager he was too old for, doing the *Graceland* tour, but she was of age, wasn't she? And nothing more improper than that, surely. No particular woman who he'd wronged or one single incident that he could truly be hanged for. It was more of an air of malaise, a cloud of toxicity that John was certain he too was breathing in, and breathing out again, and that would suffocate him in the end.

'John?' Kitty appeared on the threshold of the kitchen, lovely in her long light-blue dress. 'Do you think you could put the kids to bed?'

The Head of the King was the first film John had managed to get made. It had taken a long time to get it going, to find a producer to raise enough money and bring everything together for him. So different from the theatre. Frustrating, to say the least. Originally he had a script of his own, something he'd been working on since he'd left New York after *Ripples*. It was classic Reddan stuff, estranged siblings, crossed lines, absent fathers, lots of infidelity. The producer didn't like it, though, and instead he'd been paired up with a guy called Mark who'd written a novel that won a few prizes. The novel was about an army veteran who goes off the grid. John's producer owned the rights to it. John read it, didn't think much of it. Read it again, thought he could make it very different. He met Mark a few times and found him to be stubborn, strong-headed, not one for collaboration. Was unsurprised to learn Mark was childless and unmarried. In the end they sent drafts back and forth 107 times. John knew it was 107 times because he could see it in his email inbox. Search 'Mark script', results 1–107. The two of them would both be credited as co-writers on the movie, and John was happy with that. They wouldn't speak again after it came out. *The Head of the King* was so different now from Mark's book. The veteran was much younger, less of the baggage of middle age and more of the young man's emotional torpor. By the time John flew to Hungary to start shooting, he felt good about how far it was from the original book. On the plane he flicked through the hard copy of the script with satisfaction, like he was leaving Mark to eat his dust. My movie now, motherfucker.

Shooting was exhausting, unparalleled, different from anything John had done before. So many people asking him questions all day long. The lead actor, a young British guy who'd been nominated for a Bafta the year before, was needy in the extreme. Treated John like the two of them were partners with equal shares in the production. What do you think of this, John? How about if I do it like this?

Just fucking do it, John thought. I'll tell you if you're doing it wrong. He resorted to taking himself off to the Portaloos for little breaks, breathing heavily while staring at his phone screen. Gritting his teeth and muttering a reminder to himself. You wanted to make this film, and everyone is waiting for you outside.

He was always someone else when he was away working. It was a discrepancy he had been aware of since *Ripples* in New York. On one hand, the feeling of freedom could be intoxicating, addictive. On the other, though. Halfway through the shoot in Hungary he started to lose his grasp on things. Sitting in his hotel room, staring at pictures Kitty sent of the kids, he found he barely recognised them. It was a relief to return home and see the three of them in the flesh, embrace the boys, smell the aroma of his own house, his belongings, his family. Bask in it. The rest of it ebbed away.

2.

On waking, it took Frida a moment to know where she was. A large bed, a warm room, rumpled cotton. Dim sunlight. Then the smell told her the rest. She was in a Palm Springs Airbnb.

The desert, she thought, smelled like air conditioning and dust.

Kara was already up. Frida could see her neon-orange swimsuit draped over the back of one of the chairs outside. A little puddle of pool water grew beneath it. The two of them liked going to the desert together. It was an easy way out, a couple of hours on the highway in Kara's silver BMW, a journey that always felt like an escape from something. Thelma and Louise. Once they arrived, there was all the space and quiet they could want. When they came here, Kara tended to get up early and log on for a few hours while Frida caught up on sleep. The routine made Frida feel like a little girl, asleep while the adults went ahead and got the day under way.

The desert was also where they'd met, almost two years earlier. Frida liked this, imagined telling people about the circumstances of their meeting. I was a thirsty man in the desert, and she appeared like a mirage on the horizon.

Two Januaries earlier, Mel's fortieth birthday party and Frida's first time in Palm Springs. A girls' weekend at a resort made up of a series of pretty bungalows clustered around a kidney-shaped pool. Kara had been in the next house over at the hen party of a friend from college, and when Frida had taken the lounger beside her, bleary-eyed, she hadn't realised that Kara wasn't part of Mel's group. Kara, for her part, had humoured her. 'I thought you were cute,' she teased Frida a few dates later. By the time Frida realised her error, she also realised that she liked this woman's company, that Kara was ten times easier to lie beside than any of Mel's coterie. The women in Frida's bungalow were a combination of talent professionals, Hollywood Brits and up-for-anything party animals in very short dresses and designer handbags. There was a lot of coke back at Frida's bungalow.

'Do you mind if I hang out here for a bit?' Frida said.

'If you don't mind me doing some reading for work,' Kara replied. 'One of my girls is getting married, but she doesn't understand that I've got a lot to get through first of all.'

It helped, Frida figured, that Kara was gorgeous, built like a pole-vaulter, with her hair cropped into a short pixie cut.

'You must work a lot, to be up and at it so early at a hen do.'

'You know, we call it a bachelorette,' Kara said. 'I'm a lawyer.'

'Do you like it?'

'Yeah, I do. What do you do?'

'I act,' Frida said, and was embarrassed for herself.

'Anything I've seen?'

'I actually play a lawyer. I'm on a show called *The Reason*.'

Kara closed her binder and sat up very straight. 'Oh my God. I've seen you.'

'Oh, gosh, have you?'

'Lawyers love your show. Wow, I didn't recognise you in your sunglasses. Really, we love your show.'

Frida took off her sunglasses, sliding a palm behind her head. 'Well, thank you.'

'Now, I've only seen a few episodes. Sorry, I don't watch a lot of TV. But believe me when I say the girls at my firm are so into it.'

'God, thank you. I think I needed to hear that. Usually when I meet fans, they're like, TV superfans, you know? They're not LA lawyers in cool swimsuits.'

Back in the city, Kara asked Frida out for dinner. After, they kissed in the car parked outside Frida's place, the engine still running, and Kara pulled away to laugh.

'Just like suburban kids,' she said, and Frida noticed that Kara's eyes had a penetrating quality, something Frida recognised from particularly compassionate make-up artists.

Kara's life was a revelation to Frida: a third-generation Californian with no connections to nor aspirations for Hollywood and the entertainment industry. Kara was an intellectual-property lawyer, though her work focused mostly on the pharmaceutical industry. She'd grown up in Berkeley with hippie parents, but the kind who had managed to combine principles and some level of material comfort through careers in academia. At Stanford Kara had studied social sciences but took classes in medicinal chemistry, briefly thinking she might go to med school. She was on the track team. She had a couple of serious girlfriends and was a member of a predominantly African-American sorority. She had had a wholesome young adulthood, one thing leading cleanly to the next, in a manner that Frida felt was foreign and appealing when she heard all about it. A spell out east at Yale Law School had been a mistake for Kara – she hated the cold and made zero friends – and only served to make her certain that California was, and would forever, be home. It was a surprise, then, to Kara when she fell for an Irish actress who was still new enough to Los Angeles to marvel at the Hollywood sign from time to time. Frida was surprised, too – struck by how impressive and self-fulfilled Kara was, and flattered by the other woman's interest in her.

Now two years had passed since they'd first met, and the desert had become their favourite place to be together. It was usually Kara's idea: a call on a Thursday evening during a stressful week, the suggestion that the two of them could leave before rush hour on Friday and make it here in time for dinner. Frida liked the version of herself she was in the desert: a more relaxed person, a person who could do nothing all day but read in the shade on the patio, smoke a little weed, eat in diners with her girlfriend, go to bed early with Kara and make her happy in the way she liked best. It made her feel good about herself. This time, though, it had been Frida who suggested coming out for a weekend. She needed the break. In recent months the atmosphere in LA had turned claggy, like one endless humid afternoon. It was good, obviously, that women were speaking out the way they were now. And at first she had found the change of climate invigorating. But it became deadening, hearing these stories over and over. Frida found herself irritated by the stories. She wondered why the women were choosing to tell them. Was it really cathartic for them to talk about the worst thing that had ever happened to them in public like this? Or maybe, she thought, these stories weren't the worst thing that had ever happened to the women. They were just one more in a long line of horrible things, the chain of grim events that could make up a woman's life.

It was exhausting, too, to have to reappraise every interaction she'd ever had with a man in her line of work. This was another benefit of life with Kara. She didn't have opinions on the industry beyond the basics reported in the *New York Times*. She asked Frida questions, certainly, but those questions were things like 'How's work going?' rather than, 'Have you ever experienced sexual harassment in your own dressing room, by a man further up the food chain than you, and if so, what was your reaction, and why?'

It also helped that Kara was Kara, and not dependent on Frida for self-definition. Early on, Frida had learned that there would be many evenings when Kara was not available and would not make herself available. She had lots of commitments. She had her work, which she really did love, and she had her sorority sisters, and her two nephews, the sons of her older brother Eric. This was not to say that Kara didn't get serious about their relationship: after six months, the two of them flew to SFO and spent a weekend with Monica and David, Kara's parents, and after a year together, Kara reciprocated with a trip to Ireland during one of *The Reason*'s production breaks and met Una and Edel.

Now, after the fact, Frida could regard the trip to Ireland as a turning point. Kara had been out since high school, and she was realistic about the situation Frida was in. The two of them had gone out for dinner with Mel when their relationship was new and Mel had been succinct in her feedback to Frida afterwards: a) Kara was lovely, and b) it was dicey, at best, for Frida to come out at this time. Frida's thoughts turned around this for several days. She agreed that the idea of 'coming out', as an actress, was not quite what she was looking for (an interview in a glossy magazine? Going on *Ellen*?). She was crazy about Kara, but it's not like they were about to get married. They had their own lives. Frida liked the way they could go several days without messaging and then see each other on a Saturday night, catch up and enjoy each other's company over a nice dinner. She wondered sometimes if their connection would persist if she and Kara decided to move in together. Probably the charm would wear off, she thought, picturing another woman's dirty laundry in her wicker basket.

Also, 'coming out' would mean, surely, that Frida was gay. And was she? She still had no idea.

'I think it's more that you've failed the compulsory heterosexuality elements of the curriculum,' Mel said.

'I have had relationships with men that I enjoyed,' Frida protested.

Mel laughed darkly. 'Have you? Which ones?'

Anyway, most of all 'coming out', to Frida, meant change, and when she thought about Kara she felt more comfortable than she had in years. It didn't feel like change so much as a burrowing down into the cushions of life, a more lavish hotel room than Frida was accustomed to.

That's Hollywood, Kara shrugged when Frida relayed Mel's feedback to her. Mel's decree (which was what it had been, really, since Frida still let Mel make most of her decisions for her) didn't really change Kara and Frida's day-to-day. They still went out to restaurants and parties, and Kara met the Lunds over dinner in Malibu. They just didn't go to big events together and when Frida did interviews to promote the new season of *The Reason*, which was tipped for a few Golden Globes this year, she still lowered her head bashfully when asked about romance. I'm seeing someone but it's early days, it's too soon to talk about publicly.

Could you call it an open secret? Frida thought that would be a bit much. Doing so would imply people really cared about Frida's sexuality. Frida was nominated for Best Actress in a Television Series that year, but otherwise she mostly flew under the radar of celebrity. *The Reason* had its fans, but Frida didn't tend to get tailed by paparazzi or stopped while shopping. A lot of that came down to personal choice, she figured. These days, she chose not to play with much of the publicity machine that went on around her. Since her surgery in Georgia and the wild, emotionally turbulent months that had followed, Frida had been considering what she really wanted from both life and work. After her trip to New York almost two and a half years earlier, she'd become a bit of a hermit, renovating her house in Los Feliz and trying to look after herself. She stopped drinking, stopped googling things that stressed her out. Less of the pointless networking, less of the pleading with casting directors for theatre auditions. The superhero movie had opened a few doors, but Frida didn't bother investigating them all that much. She preferred early mornings hikes, lots of yoga. Not all of her good habits stuck, but it was enough to make Frida feel in control of her life once more.

On their visit to Ireland last year, Frida had worn sunglasses and a baseball cap while she travelled through Dublin Airport. She and Kara had rented a car and gone straight to Edel and Ian's house. Frida was equal parts pleased with and pissed off by the way Edel was going out of her way to be completely fine with this new chapter of Frida's romantic life. But it *was* fine, she thought. When Edel asked what they wanted to do, Frida had answered for them both. We really just want to lay low, she said. After a long weekend of bracing sea swims, hill walks with the girls and takeaway dinners, Kara and Frida drove to Connemara, where they stayed in a cottage Frida had found on Airbnb. To call it remote would have been understating things. There was nobody around for miles, by the looks of it, and while Frida sighed with contentment and lounged performatively on the sofa, Kara was on to her.

'You're hiding us,' Kara said after they'd unpacked their bags.

'I thought it would be relaxing,' Frida protested. 'A change from LA.'

'It didn't occur to you that I might want to, you know, see Dublin?'

Frida grimaced. 'Sorry. It's just, you know, Ireland's not California. It's small, it's harder to fly under the radar.'

'You mean when one of us is a celebrity?'

'Well, one of us is Irish, yes. People do know me here.'

'And they don't know that you have a partner, and that she's a six-foot Black woman.'

Frida didn't say anything. She felt like a coward, and she supposed that she was.

Kara could never stay frosty for long. She had too little annual leave to waste it being angry at her girlfriend. But on their return to LAX, Kara turned to Frida and informed her that she needed a little space for a while. Frida nodded. What else could she do, really? This was Frida's doing, after all. Days went by, Frida studiously not texting or calling, and when Kara finally got in touch again a week and a half later, it was to tell Frida that she'd done some thinking. Kara understood the nature of their relationship, she told Frida. She was fine with them not being out, but it came at a cost.

'I'm going to be less available for you. We have fun together, don't we?'

'Yeah, of course.'

'Great,' Kara said with brisk professionalism. 'So let's just keep doing that.'

On hanging up the phone that night, Frida found her eyes filling with tears. Why had that hurt so much to hear? She liked the way she and Kara lived their own lives, and certainly she wasn't anywhere near ready for a more serious iteration of their relationship. She'd watched the scenes of jubilation on Irish news when marriage was legalised at home and felt emotional about it all, but had also felt removed from it, like it was a measure of freedom being allotted to someone else. The idea of it applying to her own life: marrying Kara, of buying a little vacation home with her or pursuing IVF with her – it all felt dizzying and crazy. It wasn't her own life. It was more like something interesting Frida was reading in a novel. But at the same time, Kara's recognition of Frida's reticence was painful in a way she could never have anticipated. She was being seen. It felt like ice all through her veins.

That had been a year earlier. Since then, Frida had found herself waiting for things to change. She thought that maybe if she quit the show, tried to do something else with her work, she might undergo some process of maturing into a different kind of woman – one who might even be able to offer Kara more. One more season, then. God, it was exhausting to live this way, waiting always for the next thing to begin. After seven years in Los Angeles, Frida had essentially given up on the idea of moving back home. This would have to be home, then, and she'd need to find a way to live with that.

The sliding patio doors of the Palm Springs bedroom opened and Kara came into the dark room.

'You awake?' she asked Frida, who sat up in bed.

'Yeah, sorry.'

'You slept late.'

'What time is it?' Frida reached for her phone. '11.17. Jesus, I really am sorry.'

Kara smiled at her, taking off her green terrycloth shorts

and changing into blue jeans. 'It's okay. I had work to do. You hungry?'

There was an email on Frida's lock screen from John Reddan. What the fuck, Frida thought, placing the phone face down on the bed beside her.

'Hungry, yeah. I am,' she replied. 'What are you thinking?'

'I'll go out and get us some lunch if you want?'

Frida looked up at her girlfriend, trying to smile normally. 'Sounds perfect.'

Once she heard Kara start the car outside, Frida reached for her phone again. The email had no subject line, but she could see it was sent just an hour ago. Early evening in London, she thought, doing the maths. She tapped it open.

To: Frida Slattery
Subject: (no subject)

Hey Frida,

I hope you're well over there in Hollywood.

I'm getting in touch because I've been thinking lately about what has happened between us over the years. There's been a lot of it in the air recently, talk about men and women in our industry, and I can imagine it's the same over there for you too. I wanted to say that I've thought about it a lot and I don't know if I always did the right thing by you. I'm curious to know if you feel the same way? If you've been thinking about us recently, too. Or if you have any other thoughts.

We were really young when we met and worked together and so many things are different now. It would be good to hear from you. Hope all else is good with you.

All best,

John Reddan

Frida wanted to laugh but instead found herself silent. Had he laboured over this email the way he did over his first drafts? The idea of John at work in his office, whatever that looked like, crafting this email as carefully as he had *Bird* or *Four and Ten*. Smoking a cigarette, ash falling onto his keyboard. They hadn't spoken since New York – was that the time he was talking about, not doing the right thing by her? Frida could imagine sleepless nights for John Reddan, as all the other men who resembled him were felled one by one by women's stories. How many emails like this had he sent? How many skeletons did he have in his closet? And he feared that Frida's was among them. Yes, she wanted to laugh. Her skeleton was here under her skin now. She could feel it, running her fingertips over her collarbone. It had never been his. She hadn't realised until now, the curls of spite that rose up like smoke when she thought of him. But it was nice, wasn't it? It was the thing about all these skeletons coming out of closets. That men who thought they could do anything were beginning to learn otherwise.

No, John Reddan was not the first name that came to mind when Frida thought about men and women and their industry. She thought first of the Lunds, both Sara and Tobias, and the way they ran their sets, their comfort with making others uncomfortable. How they seemed to almost get off on it, sometimes, Tobias looming over some assistant or other, and Sara's many in-plain-sight affairs. The power they held over everyone on their production, the casual and cruel way they both talked about their staff when it was just Frida and the two of them by the firepit in their garden. Frida thought of producers who'd propositioned her over dinner, actors who'd cornered her at parties, the time just a few months ago when Peter Wright (supposedly totally harmless, almost dangerously boring Peter Wright) had grabbed her arse while they were on camera doing press on a red carpet, so that the camera couldn't see but those around them doubtlessly could. Humiliating. Actually, to call what he grabbed her 'arse' was being polite, really. Some of the articles she'd been reading recently had taught Frida that other women call what he did sexual assault. When they'd left the step-and-repeat and were out of sight of the cameras she'd pushed Peter hard in the chest, and he'd looked right through her.

No, what happened between Frida Slattery and John Reddan had been so different to all of that. It was slippery, sure, like so many of the stories being told lately. But it was a kind of friendship, wasn't it? Maybe it was a kind of love. It was certainly collaboration. Would there be a John Reddan now if there hadn't been a Frida Slattery then? She thought of the first time she read his script for *Graceland*, marking lightly in pencil all the lines he'd lifted from their conversations. She remembered rubbing those pencil marks out, so John wouldn't see them and ask about them next time they met to rehearse. Like she had something to be ashamed of. When their relationship had eventually turned romantic, there was no end of consent. Asking each other constantly is this okay, do you like this. That certainly hadn't been the issue, had it? It was the very same as how they were when they were working on a play together. That summer in Dublin, writing *Four and Ten* together, or whenever you chose to begin their story, Frida and John were equal players in a script for two, a pas de deux that depended on both of them in order to keep moving. It was only when one of them pulled away, as Frida had, that things got complicated.

So why did Frida feel so odd reading John's email now? There was indeed a slipperiness. What would Kara say about the whole thing? That's what happens when you date men, Frida. But she and John had never properly dated. What a concept, dating. She and John Reddan had forged from nothing at all a kind of intangible something. She remembered him in Toner's pub, calling what they had *alchemical*. Their names on a poster together. God, in his way he had made her into an actor. Even though he was the one who got the credit for all the emotional excavation she'd done for those plays. She remembered a profile of him in one of the British Sunday papers not long ago, praising the generosity and nuance of his work, the way he understood men and women equally. Maybe he'd made Frida Slattery into an actor, but she thought that she'd made John Reddan into an empath. At least in the eyes of his audience, if not in actual fact. She had to think of this as a collaboration, a form of connection. Or else it all became too much. All that had passed between them. That had surely been why, Frida realised all of a sudden, she'd ended up sleeping with him in New York. It had been an attempt to keep that collaboration alive.

Maybe that was what this was about. John was worried about Frida tattling to his wife in the guise of the moment's feminist transparency. What had he said to her on the phone the next day. Take care of it, Frida, or we won't be working together again. The last time John Reddan had tried to direct her, and she'd ignored him, though of course it hadn't led to what he feared, not with Frida's mangled ovary. And had they worked together since then? Of course not! Frida read the email once more. It was impossible to tell what he meant. It's almost like he wanted to cover all bases (while apologising for none of them, she noted).

And when Frida put aside her phone and lay back down, closing her eyes, she saw the past. In London between understudying and getting the job in *The Reason*, Frida had taken a lot of acting classes to pass the time and get out of the flat. She would go online and look at listings, see what was on and just go along. At one of these classes, taught by a very hostile Englishman who had absolutely no patience, she was introduced to the Stanislavski technique for the first time. It seemed so obvious once it was laid out before her. That she, and every other actor, had a vast bank of emotional memories already within them, garnered from all of the little different things she had ever experienced, and that these could be called upon at any time in the service of performance. For a little while, she got very into it, the recalling of instances like biting into a particularly sour orange, or battling a migraine. She went back to the Englishman's class several weeks in a row, thrilling at all the little processes the class of ten actors went through. Receiving a brief, isolating herself to prepare for the performance and then finally, standing up in front of the class and pulling the memory out of her for public consumption. A form of productive regurgitation. It turned every shitty day – every time she missed the bus or argued with John or had a vexatious phone call with Una – into fodder for future performance.

It also gave Frida a superiority complex. She believed now, even though she had long since outgrown her Stanislavski phase, that remembering was a skill of hers. She was better at it than other people were. Her years of practice had paid off and she could do it more intensely. She was an auteur of memory. She had it mastered. Light falling on the back wall of a granite house, sitting in the emerald-green grass watching it. The sound of a football being kicked against the wooden fence. Or in the bathroom as a girl, perched on the edge of the bath as Edel pierced Frida's little ear with a safety pin and an ice cube. Their mother storming up the stairs when she heard Frida's wailing. Yes, she remembered all of it.

And John. She remembered John. The black eye he had the day of their first rehearsals for *Bird*. The bravado of him, trying always to outdo Chris in the tiny rehearsal room. The way he'd taken her wrist in his hand so tenderly backstage, right before their first show. It's running through your veins, Frida.

Oh, she knew she could remember every pint they drank together. Every last one. The way the light had changed on John's face as the hours had passed in the back room of some pub, the way Frida knew the contours of that face so well.

Like she could close her eyes and draw it in her mind. She could call on these memories at any time. The way he'd made her brain feel in those days, cycling home from an afternoon with him, her mind fizzing with excitement about the fact that they both existed in the same place, at the same time, and there was so much ahead of them yet to come.

It had never really been romantic, except in the way that two people could come together sometimes like that. Could reach some hidden part of each other, the thing that was out of reach for everyone else they might have met. It was never romantic per se, not like Hollywood romance, but it was the small romance of inner life. The sharing of private things. The only thing Frida had ever wanted, the thing she would swap it all for even now.

How long would John continue to have this influence on her?

And what was it that he thought he had done to Frida? She picked up her phone again, her finger hovering over Reply when she heard Kara's car outside.

Kara. What was she going to do about Kara? She knew that Kara thought Frida wasn't serious about her, and realistically she had to agree. So why were they still doing this? Kara came through the bedroom door now, pushing it open with her keys in one hand and a brown bag of groceries in the other, with her hesitant smile and excellent posture.

And Frida knew then that it was never going to be enough. She was not going to change, not by quitting *The Reason* nor by any other means of redirection. She wasn't going to be able to become a different person simply by wishing for it.

Maybe Mel had been right about Frida failing compulsory heterosexuality. What else had Frida failed? Oh God, you can't be thinking that way.

Kara was standing in front of her, waving a hand back and forth as if Frida was in a trance.

'Are you okay?' she asked. 'You seem a little lost.'

And Frida looked up at her from the bed, with her phone clammy in her hand and nodded at her and said, 'I think I'm coming down with something.'

3.

The day after *The Head of the King* screened at the London Film Festival, Alice Greer turned up on the doorstep of the Reddan house unannounced. Kitty arrived home from school drop-off and found her there, walking tentatively up the tiled garden path as if unsure how approaching a house worked. Kitty invited her inside, went to the kitchen to turn the kettle on.

'John's still in bed,' she said to Alice, who had sat herself primly on the edge of the high stool in her brown leather trousers.

'Kitty,' Alice said. 'Would you take his phone away from him before he wakes up?'

When John came downstairs in his navy dressing gown, he found his wife and his agent together in the kitchen, a pot of tea on the island between them.

'Christ,' he said. 'Why do I get the feeling there's about to be an intervention in here?'

Later he would think that an intervention would have been preferable. Alice Greer was sitting at his dining table because she wanted to deliver bad news. *The Head of the King* had not been well received. At the party the night before, John had received his share of backslaps and congratulations. He'd made a short speech that thanked all the right people, and after that the evening had blurred into an abstract mess of champagne and egotism. Kitty had left at ten to relieve the babysitter.

There were a handful of bad reviews in the morning's papers, Alice reported.

'Don't read them,' she advised.

'I can handle a bad review,' John said, and across the room he heard Kitty release an anguished little sigh.

'You're an adult,' Alice conceded. 'Read them if you want. But John, don't get hung up on this. You tried something new, and that's always a creative gamble.'

Could it have been as bad as she said? Upstairs in his study after Alice left, John opened his laptop and saw for himself. The critics were going to town on it. The movie was the work of boring men, apparently. Its themes were out of step with the cultural conversation. Stale, pale, male, one critic concluded. Her byline photo told him that she was a young, wan woman with a smug expression.

They were not even cutting enough to be truly devastating. It was something much worse than that. The flaccid disappointment of his peers.

As a result *The Head of the King* was in and out of cinemas in a fortnight. A month later, it was like the whole thing had never happened. John tried to focus on new writing, getting another play together, seeing where he might head next. This is the artist's life, he told himself to soothe his ego. Sometimes, it contained failure and rejection.

But by another metric of success, John Reddan was now doing just fine. Several months later, the film had receded in the rear-view mirror of his mind. It was rapidly being replaced by something much more exciting. The very fact of the film's existence, regardless of its reception, had had an unexpected impact on his career: John knew how to make a movie, so now he got booked to direct ads for luxury family cars, perfumes and high-definition televisions. Suddenly John was making very decent money. Broadly speaking, things were going well. Over a year had passed since women started speaking out and nothing had come out about him personally, so he began to think that he might be home and dry. When he'd emailed Frida Slattery in the middle of the night, months ago, her reply a few days later had been so curt and bland that he'd wondered if it had been written by an assistant. If Frida had an assistant who wrote her emails for her. Thanks for your email, good to hear from you, blah blah blah. I have enjoyed working with you over the years. Once he saw her reply John was forced to wonder what he'd wanted from Frida to begin with. A form of forgiveness, maybe, though he hadn't apologised for anything.

Surely he had nothing to apologise for.

He didn't write back, only archived the email and moved on with his life.

Now he was going out all the time – meeting producers, judging theatre festivals, attending any party he was invited to. Hungover in the morning on the school run, on the occasions John actually came home in time, depositing his boys at the school gates with sunglasses on, smiling a little too much at all the other mothers at the gate.

At first John only did it when he was away. A method of dealing with the weird dissociation he underwent when travelling for work. A night shoot in Paris, bringing a girl back to his hotel room after wrapping the Toyota ad. She worked for the ad agency, apparently. They didn't talk much. The rules were different when he was away. It was more respectful to Kitty this way. Also, it felt amazing to wake up with a young woman in his bed in the Hyatt, like he was a different man, like he'd managed to make very different choices over the years.

Soon, though, it was just another part of John's life. It came with the territory, he thought, the going out all the time, the cocaine, meeting all the interesting people who dressed well and wanted to talk about his work. Another evening spent in one or other of the Soho members' clubs his professional circle went to, missing bedtime with the boys, socialising with some actor or producer with good stories to tell. And then their table ended up merging with the table of beautiful, charming women beside them. And truly, John couldn't help it.

Did he even enjoy it? It was difficult to say. It was like his many attempts to give up smoking. He could happily go all week without a cigarette and then on a Saturday night he would be drunk on Greek Street and think, Why not? What could improve this evening more than a cigarette? And after that he was powerless to stop himself. It was the alcohol, he reckoned, that made him do it in the first place. A few drinks and suddenly he was always looking for a bit of skirt. He was chasing that illusion of freedom he'd had when abroad and away from his family, ever since *Ripples* in New York with the Quirke boys, Frida Slattery's hotel room. The power of that illusion led him to wind up in rooms in far-flung parts of London, beside a woman whose name he usually couldn't remember. And missed calls from Kitty on his phone. And the same fear that had dogged him that morning in New York, that he was going to get punished for all of this bad behaviour. Since then, as a rule, he always carried condoms.

Yes, it wasn't great, was it? And yet it felt like he had broken something inside himself and he couldn't go back now. Some tendon of his had snapped and it couldn't seem to repair itself. He was hurting Kitty and he knew that, yet he couldn't stop doing it. He knew this was complicated, this was probably hereditary for him. Thought of what his father had done to his mother. The years John had spent trying to hash it out in his notebooks, and now this. It wasn't even just about the fact he was being cruel to his wife. He was tired of feeling hollow, brittle, useless. He missed the way he'd lived when he was working on plays like *Bird*. The way he could look at the world, even the hard and painful parts, and think: this is good, I can use this.

The whole thing, the missed calls, the misery, the powerlessness of it, it was all bound up with Catholic guilt. In Foyles he bought novels about sex by young Irish women in an attempt to understand himself. He returned the next week and asked the bookseller for more recommendations, was met with an awkward stare in return. John knew there were questions he wanted answered. Why did it have to be this way? Couldn't he make his own decisions? Couldn't he just have a wife, and also a girlfriend or whatever? That was how people did it nowadays. He met young people on shoots and in Quo Vadis who were all in open relationships, and by and large they seemed to be pretty happy with themselves. Why did he need to feel such shame? In the waiting room of the sexual-health clinic around the corner, where he had an appointment to discuss the possibility of a vasectomy, he picked up a brightly coloured pamphlet on ethical non-monogamy. Surely Kitty knew by now. She knew when he didn't come home. She didn't say anything to him about it, but also, she barely spoke to him at all. The nurse called his name and John folded the pamphlet in half and slid it into the inside pocket of his jacket.

4.

Three weekends before Christmas, Kitty and John left the boys in the hands of Kitty's mother and boarded a Eurostar to Paris. Almost five years had passed since they'd gotten married in Islington Town Hall, a tiny ceremony on a grey January morning with the two boys squirming in the arms of Barry and Kitty's mother, then a long lunch in the French restaurant down the street. Kitty had made her wedding dress, a knee-length cream shift with a matching jacket trimmed with pretty Carrickmacross lace that had been sitting on top of her sewing table since finding three metres of it in an online auction when pregnant with Ru. They hadn't gone on a honeymoon. John had suggested Rome, or Barcelona, but Kitty told him she was too anxious to leave little Fionn, only seven months, for even a night. It was also obvious that she was preoccupied by the medical demands of Ruadhán's early childhood. That was a constant source of stress and unease in their household: the apparently endless paediatric cardiology appointments and rounds of testing that were necessary even when he seemed to be doing just fine.

Paris was Kitty's idea. The way she framed it made it sound

like a second chance at honeymoon. It was a rare evening that they were both at home, the boys in bed, but they found themselves lingering over the dinner table with a bottle of red. They needed to try something different. Ridiculous to pretend otherwise, she said, and the look of exhaustion on her face made it obvious that Kitty had been trying her hardest up until now.

'I know you've been having a rough time since the movie,' she said.

John's neck stiffened. 'I don't know if I'd say a rough time ...'

Kitty continued, playing with her dessert spoon. 'I thought that simply being here, making home a nice place, I thought it might be enough to help.'

Until this point, John had assumed Kitty knew. He worked on the basis that they'd come to a silent arrangement regarding his infidelity, a sort of don't-ask-don't-tell thing. To be honest, he thought it worked this way in most marriages, at least most happy ones. Looking at her now over the table John had the dizzying realisation that perhaps Kitty had no idea. The nights away, the drinking, his reluctance even to sleep in their bed when he was home, instead falling asleep on the couch in the living room in front of the TV, to be woken by Fionn clattering down the stairs at 7 a.m. It was possible, John thought, sweating now, that his wife took all of it merely to be evidence of John's own personal unhappiness, and nothing more malevolent than that.

'I don't know,' she said, pushing back her dark hair with one hand. 'I'm just tired of feeling lonely.'

John swallowed. He gripped the stem of his wine glass like it might stop him from tumbling to the ground. 'Okay, Kitty,' he said finally. 'We'll go to Paris.'

John felt something shake him awake. It was a change in the light. The train had just emerged from the dark of the tunnel and now he could see the bright, flat land and concrete of Calais outside. Beside him, Kitty was gazing out the window.

'You okay?' he asked.

She didn't answer, just smiled wistfully at her own reflection.

John sat up, stretching his sore back. 'What's up?'

'I was thinking about something my mother asked about you, when I told her I was pregnant with Ru.'

'Years ago now, Kit.'

She ignored him. 'She asked me if you were a good person. I said I thought you were. I think she had this idea about artists, about the kind of lives they led. She had this really concerned look on her face and she tried to rephrase her question. Is he ... you know, is he normal?'

'What did you tell her?'

'I remember laughing. I remember not knowing what to say. I didn't know if you were normal, John. I barely knew you at all.'

They checked in to the small, expensive hotel in Pigalle and while the receptionist prepared their room keys, John could see Kitty watching their reflection in the mirror behind the desk. Both of them took pride in how they made a handsome couple. Kitty was tall, but John was still a few inches taller, broad-shouldered and narrow of torso beside her graceful frame. He thought he was ageing nicely. Men like him tended to do better as they got older, became distinguished instead of weird-looking. And of course, he still had his all his hair – more than ever, he sometimes thought, still thick and coarse and sticking up at odd angles even now it was entirely grey.

He'd liked the look of Kitty from the outset, seeing her backstage at the Court. He'd been berating some junior member of the crew for being late, and she'd run past as if on tiptoe, her arms filled with garments. He had thought her so elegant, almost imperious, and so quick on her feet. When they'd started living together, Kitty took pleasure in dressing him up like he was her doll. Over the years she filled his wardrobe with nicer versions of the things he might otherwise buy for himself: dark T-shirts in heavy cotton, Chelsea boots in soft leather, black linen suit jackets from a tailor she used to work with in the theatre. Upstairs in the hotel room in Paris, he dressed for the evening in one of these suits and was lounging on the bed, watching in the mirror as she slipped into her deep-green silk dress.

'I think you were right about this, Kit,' he said, folding his hands behind his head. 'It's good to be away from London.'

'It is, isn't it,' she replied, turning her back towards him, inviting him to button her up.

As his fingertips brushed her back he could feel a shiver pass over her smooth skin.

'You look beautiful,' he told her in a low voice that made the room feel very still and quiet. She remained where she was and leaned backwards, and his fingers undid the buttons again and pulled the dress's straps away from her shoulders. His face burrowed into the space between her neck and shoulders, and he could feel Kitty relax against him. Maybe he could stop the rest of it and be the version of himself that she needed. It could be easy, he thought. It had always been easy with her. Gone was the *Sturm und Drang* that sex caused him in his twenties, the anxiety that led him to bad decisions with women and the perpetual dread that dogged him once he eventually started sleeping with Frida Slattery. At the time he'd worried that would follow him forever – the Frida-generated neurosis, failure to launch, the stop-and-start of it all. With Kitty, though, he found all that evaporated. From the first time, they moved together like they knew each other – no, John thought, actually it wasn't like that. They moved like they didn't know each other at all, like they were two strangers who owed each other nothing, and that was so much better.

The restaurant Kitty had chosen for the evening was one that they'd had recommended to them so many times, by so many people, that it felt inevitable they would go. It was a short walk from the hotel, through streets busy with Parisians wrapped up in winter wool and sat underneath heaters on café terraces. They hurried together, Kitty's heels skipping over the cobblestones. The restaurant was done up to look like a neighbourhood corner bistro, tall glass windows between the tables and the street, but John could hear American accents all around them. Kitty wondered aloud that perhaps they'd been seated in the tourist section, that maybe you were supposed to book under a French name if you wanted the real thing.

Jean et le petit chat, he offered in response, wiggling his eyebrows.

John was never comfortable when they first arrived in places like this – loud, bustling, enclosed. Immediately he flagged down the waiter for a bottle of red and once it arrived, poured both glasses and drank half of his before Kitty had had a chance to raise a toast.

'John,' Kitty said pointedly. His eyes met hers and he nodded at her, like he'd just noticed she was in front of him.

'Cheers,' he said, lifting his half-empty glass. 'Uh, *santé!*'

Kitty gave a minute roll of her eyes. He could tell that the little flame of intimacy they'd shared an hour ago in the hotel room had already been extinguished. He felt himself retreat at times like these. His wife, across the table from him, was trying nonetheless to reach him.

'How's work going,' she asked. 'Have you been talking to anyone recently?'

It was like they had a script. She always started by pretending she simply wanted the gossip, the way couples did when one half stayed mostly in the home and the other went out and gathered information.

And John answered, because he knew the script, too. He liked playing the role of hunter-gatherer to Kitty's homesteader. That had always been their way, the easy template into which they'd both slipped when she was first pregnant. He told her who was sleeping with who and which producing partners had fallen out. Who was buying the rights to which hit novels.

Who had gone off the deep end, left the wife. Kitty laughed at the right times, leaned in, stroked his wrist across the table. It was such a delicate process, the business of marriage.

The food came: two steaks, Kitty's much smaller than John's even though they'd ordered the same thing, a potato dauphinoise and a green salad heavy with vinaigrette.

'When are you going to start working again?' she asked, sawing into the piece of meat oozing on her plate.

'I am working.'

'Come on. You know what I mean. Working-working. Writing.'

She couldn't let things go, he thought. She couldn't ever take the path of least resistance.

'I think you should be thinking about another play,' she said with certainty, topping up his glass.

'I am thinking about another play.'

'Really?'

'You know I'm always working.'

She raised her dark eyebrows. 'Do I? I know you're always out. I know you're always off doing God knows what, leaving me at home with the boys.'

'It's work, Kitty,' he hissed in his arguing-in-restaurants voice. 'I can't just "do another play". I need someone to put it on, someone to produce it.'

She rolled her eyes, which made him feel unhinged. 'If you wanted to, if you really wanted, you would just do it.'

'Kitty,' he said. 'Of course I want to. I don't know why this has gotten you so upset.'

It was bad now, the way they looked at each other. It was

surely obvious to everyone in the restaurant that they were in the middle of something.

'I'm upset because I don't recognise you as the man I met back then,' Kitty said. 'Who the fuck are you, John? If you're not working, if all you do is go out and drink and you're never bothered with your family. Who are you? Because you're not the man I married.'

'The man you married? We got together after a one-night stand, Kitty.'

'The way you say it is like you owe me nothing.'

John raised his eyebrows and widened his eyes.

'Oh my God,' Kitty murmured. 'Do you actually want to be with me and the kids? Honestly. I have to know.'

He hesitated for just a moment. An American couple at the next table had stopped talking, were listening in.

'Really think about your answer, John,' she added in a low voice.

'Of course I want to be with you,' he replied.

'You don't act like it. I can't go on like this. I didn't want to have this conversation here, but look. Maybe I should go to Brighton for a while with the boys.'

'You won't do that.'

'I would 100 per cent be within my rights.'

John shook his head slowly. 'I'm not saying that – I'm saying that you won't. I'm saying that we need to stay together, all of us, that's how it works.'

He drummed his fingertips on the edge of the table in front of him. He was thinking. 'We need a change. I think that much is obvious.'

She was quiet for a moment. 'What kind of change?'

'I don't know. We could move. Leave London. It's London that's the problem, you know. It's not good for either of us.'

'Go to the countryside, you mean? Or Brighton?' she added hopefully.

John winced. 'What about Dublin?'

'Dublin,' she repeated.

'You've always liked it there, haven't you? It would be different, for sure. And Jesus, think, we could sell the house and get ourselves a palace. A house by the sea.'

'And I could work.'

'Absolutely you could work. Absolutely.'

John could feel beads of sweat forming on his forehead now.

'I could even take on looking after the boys,' he said, 'while you go ahead and get back into things. I could take a break from work, you know, we can probably afford it.'

'No,' Kitty said, balling up her napkin and tossing it onto her plate. 'You need to get back to the theatre.'

5.

In the end, it was Kara who broke up with Frida. On a Tuesday evening, while Frida was on a rest week from shooting, Kara drove over to Frida's after rush hour and ended things with her in the kitchen of the bungalow. She didn't even take her handbag from her shoulder. What she said was that she knew Frida wasn't serious about them, and probably wasn't serious about relationships generally. Kara said she wasn't sure Frida even liked women, really, when it came down to it. She said she had been fine with many aspects of their relationship, including the relative independence afforded to both of them, and even the levels of secrecy Frida's career demanded. But she had not been okay with Frida's half-assed attempts at caring for someone – anyone – other than herself.

Frida was floored by this last part.

'This isn't fair,' she managed to say.

'But it's happening,' Kara said, leaning back against the kitchen island with her arms folded.

This must be what she's like in the mediation room, Frida

thought. Aloof, intimidating, even cruel. Very effective. For the first time, she felt on uneven ground with Kara. Of course things like this never did end cleanly, though. After that there were late-night phone calls from Kara in the following weeks, and drunken texts from Frida. On one occasion Kara turned up at Frida's and the two of them went to bed together again. Frida asked her to leave before they fell asleep and Kara did so with a hurt expression on her face. In the morning, Frida got dressed for work and kept thinking, like a little girl: unfair, unfair, unfair.

Maybe Kara was right and Frida wasn't serious about anyone other than herself. Single again, alone, with not quite enough work to distract her. Frida had too much time on her hands to think about the vagaries of her life. At her annual birthday lunch with Mel two months later, she told her agent everything. The long and drawn-out break-up, how she'd driven to Kara's one night under the influence of the THC gummies she'd ingested after work, shouting into Kara's intercom, promising change, an explanation for everything that had happened. Kara talked a big game about not wanting to see Frida again, but that night she buzzed Frida up and the two of them ended up in bed again, talking and arguing and having sex until the sun came up. A frequent point of contention was the idea, expressed by both parties on different occasions, that Frida didn't really like women in the first place. When Frida conceded this point and said that it was perhaps true, Kara looked at her and laughed darkly in her face. Make up your mind, Frida. Time to shit or get off the can.

Often this season Frida had been late for work, which was not like her. She did not mention this part to Mel. Mel was empathetic about the break-up – that sort of thing, the emotional life, the perils of romance, she had a lot of time and energy for. But you didn't get through six seasons on a hit TV show by being late for work. Thankfully the show was in such disarray that the only people to notice were Jeanie and Robert in hair and make-up, who both got on well with Frida, and would always cover for her. Mel was compassionate, but she had her limits.

'What do you think might make you feel better, Frida?' Mel asked her, her brow furrowed like she was doing sums in her head.

Frida thought back to when she'd first met Mel and the two of them spent hours on the phone. Running around London together like a pair of shaky-legged yearlings.

'Can you get me some work to keep my mind off things? Anything. Really, anything.'

That was the thing Mel was good at, after all. There was a small role in an independent movie as the sister of the wife in a divorce drama, which took up a fortnight on location in Pasadena. Early mornings, long days, which Frida liked. She was most herself when there was work to be done, when she could lose herself in the warmth of studio lighting and attention. There had been a time, long ago now, when this made her feel alive, like something was on fire in her blood. Now it was sufficient to keep her from thinking about making mistakes, and that was enough for Frida.

She met with a director about a play in New York, a small

thing, an adaptation of Chekhov, but the director, Ella, was a chic young woman who'd won an award and had been profiled recently in *Vogue*. Her original Yelena had dropped out to take a big role in a superhero movie, and now Ella badly wanted Frida instead.

'I can just see this for you,' Ella said.

'I don't know why,' Frida replied with a laugh, trying to be casual.

'But I do.'

There was an urgency in Ella's voice that resonated with some hidden frequency in Frida. It awoke a concern she had that this might be her last chance to play the younger woman, the second wife.

'Okay,' she said to Ella, 'I'm in.'

Ella grasped Frida's hand, squeezing it tight as she grinned at her.

God, Frida felt old. Now if she skipped Pilates one week she found her hips ached when she climbed the slope of her street to get to the coffee shop. Were it not for *Uncle Vanya*, she would have taken a month off before the next season, go home to see her family. Sleep late, stop drinking so much. More green vegetables. There were problems now that even work couldn't cure. The thing to do was keep going, she thought. Finding a sublet in New York for two months. Packing a suitcase late one evening, tearing her Los Feliz bedroom apart while choosing the clothes she could wear for her life elsewhere. Who did she know who lived in New York? Who could take her out, show her around?

On the bed her phone vibrated with a call from Edel. It was early morning there. Very early.

'What's up?'

Edel's voice on the other end was tight, small. 'It's Mum. She's had a stroke.'

'Oh God,' Frida murmured. A few years ago, a round of cardiac tests on Una's heart that revealed atrial fibrillation. Some daily medication, Frida didn't know what, and instructions from her doctor to quit smoking, which Frida doubted Una had done. 'What happened? What's happening?'

Edel sighed. 'She was at ours for dinner when it happened. So that was lucky. She's in hospital now. We've been here all night. She's awake, she's talking, but I think she'll be here for a while. Then she's going to need care of some sort, I don't know yet.'

In Frida's stomach something roiled.

'We're waiting for the physio and the occupational therapist to come here. Ian's sister Lisa, you know she works here, she's being really helpful. She says that the kind of stroke Mum had, I don't what you call it. Obviously it's not good. But it's got the best long-term outlook apparently.'

'Okay, that's good.'

'When can you come home?'

'Uhhh,' Frida said, looking around her messy bedroom. 'I need to check with work.'

'But you're not filming until October, right?'

The way Edel said it, it was so final, so definite. Frida sat down on the edge of her bed and rested a foot on her half-packed suitcase.

'I'm actually on my way to New York to do a play.'

'A play,' Edel repeated.

Uncle Vanya.'

'Broadway?'

'Yes. Well, Off-Broadway.'

'Okay,' Edel said, like she had just been told by a waiter that the kitchen was out of the beef. 'So when can you come here?'

Staring out the window at her small patio garden, Frida ran the numbers in her head.

'I'll come as soon as I can,' she promised.

'As soon as you can?' Edel asked. 'Do you mean like, the next flight, or sometime next month?'

Why didn't Frida drop everything and go? What did she owe Ella, anyway? Anyone would have to understand her reason for leaving. 'Family emergency' – it was one of the big ones. It would be a legitimate escape, it would also be her duty as a daughter. Ugh, her duty as a daughter. How rarely had Frida thought of herself in that context in the years she'd been here? A daughter, a sister. Here she was just Frida Slattery, no backstory, like she'd emerged from a pod or a cabbage patch. It was so easy to retreat into one's selfishness this far from home. It was part of the appeal, for Frida at least, and she assumed, for everyone else who left as well.

'Edel, I can't get out of this contract. Let me see what I can do. I can come in a couple of weeks.'

'Frida,' Edel said, drawing her name out until it became an admonishment.

'I'll call you tomorrow. And Mum too. Give her my love.'

If she were a different person, perhaps, Frida might have been able to be better about things like this. But two days later, she boarded the flight to New York and started rehearsals.

6.

When *Vanya* finished its run after just three weeks, Frida went straight to Dublin to see her mother. Una was staying with Edel and Ian and the girls in Crumlin, a bed in the dining room. Her movements were slow, and she was not particularly talkative but otherwise Frida was pleasantly surprised by her condition. The daily phone calls she'd had with Edel had her anticipating the very worst. In the dining room Frida sat with her mother, talking about New York. Una looked much as she had the last time Frida had seen her, dressed in white trousers and a floral blouse and with her hair freshly trimmed into her chin-length bob. She sat with the newspaper crossword folded in her lap, a blue biro with the lid still capped in her hand. While Frida rattled on with her stories of yellow cabs, the reviews the play received, and celebrities she saw on the subway, Una nodded slowly, her eyes far away, always gazing out the window to the quiet suburban street where Edel and Ian lived.

On the flight home Frida cried behind large sunglasses. Back at work in Los Angeles, she was the recipient of frequent voice notes from Edel complaining about how difficult it was to work, raise two pre-teen girls and bring one's mother to hospital appointments. What was the weather like in Los Angeles, Frida? Don't answer that.

I will come after this season wraps. I will give you everything you need from me the moment this next season wraps. On her calls with her mother Frida could tell that things were getting worse since she'd left Dublin. She could see it through the phone's screen, the way Una's face was changing, the greying of her skin, the weight loss. She tried not to think that this woman was a different person from the mother she had known all her life. When she started thinking about it, it became hard to get her head around, the idea of a person with constituent parts, the idea that you could only change so much before something of the person themselves got lost.

Work was no longer a useful salve. The set was a nightmare. Everyone watching themselves, or else eyeing each other with suspicion. One day Frida went to her trailer and found Sara on the daybed with her shoes off, lying down with a cigarette in hand, ashtray resting on her sternum.

'I'm hiding,' she announced.

Frida went to open a window. 'Do you have to smoke in here?'

'If I smoke anywhere else, Tobias will yell at me.'

'You've never been afraid of him yelling at you before.'

'Yes,' Sara said, sitting up and nodding energetically. 'That's it. I'm not afraid of him yelling at me. I'm afraid that if he yells, the crew will start saying we're running a toxic environment here.'

Well, maybe you are, Frida thought to herself, sitting down at the vanity and examining the lines around her eyes. A typical day on set often did involve yelling, if not between Tobias and Sara then between Tobias and a cameraman or Sara and a production assistant. When the yelling started, Frida and George and Peter tended to clam up, keeping their faces perfectly still. Any sudden movement could attract the attention of the person doing the yelling, and the one thing the rest of the cast and crew enjoyed most was seeing the show's stars be on the receiving end of poor treatment. God, the place was a mess. Production assistants came and went so quickly; Frida used to try to learn everyone's names, but now it was pointless.

Except for the yelling, Tobias never talked to Frida anymore. For some time now, he had treated Frida like an extension of Sara. Frida often wondered why the two of them were still working together like this. At the catering truck on a night shoot one evening, Sara told Frida they were living separately now, Sara in the house in the Palisades and Tobias in a loft in Koreatown.

'It's a mess,' Sara said with certainty, squeezing a squiggle of ketchup onto her hot dog.

'I'm really sorry,' Frida replied.

'Don't be. It's better this way. I've been thinking we should throw our friends divorce parties when they break up. Because in order to get to that point, things must have gotten really fucking rotten along the way. A divorce can surely only be an improvement.'

Frida took a bite of her burger, thinking of Kara. Who in her life would have thrown Frida a break-up party? Friends were thin on the ground these days.

When she was filming, Frida usually tried to immerse herself in the world of the work. She was not talking about going method, no, of course not. It was a procedural TV drama, not Daniel Day-Lewis in *The Last of the Mohicans*. But usually she tried not to check her email too much. If something truly important was happening, Mel would let her know. At the moment, though, there were emails from Edel, forwarded things about family and appointments and the home help that Frida was paying for, always with the added line up top: Just keeping you in the loop x E. They were approaching a two-week break in filming and Frida had booked flights home.

It was while checking her laptop for these messages in her trailer that Frida saw the email from the reporter. Mel's assistant had forwarded the message to Frida without comment, and the whole thing struck Frida as odd. That she might actually receive an email like this in her personal inbox. The reporter wanted to know what Frida Slattery thought about allegations of sexual impropriety on the set of *The Reason*. There's a big story coming, the reporter wrote, with lots of other sources from inside and outside the production. Would she like to join them?

Frida pushed her laptop away from her like it was on fire, then closed it. There were real problems in the world, she thought with anger. There were terrible things so far away from this stupid maelstrom of power and sex. All of it was just a distraction, a thing we used to pass the time.

10. Exit strategy, 2019

The sleeping pill Frida had taken just before boarding her flight kicked in right on time. As the plane doors closed, she could feel the drowsiness begin to descend. This was what she hoped for. She'd spent an awful lot of money on this ticket. She was hoping that it would be the last time she made this journey for some time.

Welcome aboard this Aer Lingus flight, EI68 to Dublin.

The sound of her own voice came through the gauze of her sleepiness like the clear ringing of a bell. Of course. She had forgotten that the job she'd taken earlier this year might result in something like this.

It was one of the more elegant things Frida had done in her life, she thought, dozing off. She was proud of the way she had left Los Angeles, the way one thing had led smoothly to another. The voice-over work had come first. At that point, all Frida knew was that it would be wise to have ready cash. She had gone to Mel and told her that she wanted to generate some income to pay for her mother's care. Una had had another series of small strokes shortly after Frida's last visit, and on a long and difficult video call one afternoon Frida and Edel had made the decision to find a nursing home for her. Mel referred her to a colleague who specialised in voice-over work. For the three months she was shooting *The Reason*, Frida was also popping into recording studios on her rest days, reading into a mic for a few hours. She told nobody about it. She read audiobooks by Irish authors, trailers for big movies, ads for cars ('Imagine a world where ...'), the odd video game. Easy work and enjoyable. Frida had always been good with her voice, an uncanny mimic. She had her mother to thank for that. Rather, her own craven need for her mother's attention. The money was indeed paying for Una's care at Woodpark Healthcare in Rathfarnham, but there was enough of it that Frida was also able to start stockpiling an emergency fund of her own. The airline messages were just a fun Easter egg. Taking the job was a little like ordination into official Ireland, becoming the voice of the national air carrier.

By then, it was clear that *The Reason* was mortally wounded, a production stumbling onwards in the face of gossip and increasingly bad reviews. The reporter whose email Frida had initially ignored had gotten the story out eventually. Fifteen former crew members, as well as two unnamed cast members, claimed that the Lunds were presiding over a toxic work environment rife with sexual impropriety, favouritism, bullying and harassment. The article was published in the middle of filming the next season and Frida read the whole thing in her trailer on her phone before call time. When she headed down to set to start shooting, she had a ringing in her ears like she'd just been punched. The whole place was eerily silent and everyone stopped what they were doing to watch Frida cross the lot. Only Sara was behind the camera, sitting on a high stool, arms folded, jaw jutting forward with tension.

The jig was up. The thing that surprised Frida was just how long it had taken.

'You okay?' Peter Wright asked in a low voice as she sat down behind the desk in the set that was their office.

Frida looked at him, frowning, unsure what he wanted her to say.

The show would limp onwards until the mid-season break. Without warning to Frida or any of the colleagues she still spoke to, a press release from the network announced that *The Reason* was going on hiatus. Frida sat in her car in the driveway and called Sara. Sara's phone was off. Then she called Mel, who fell immediately into a recognisably polished patter, intended to reassure Frida about her prospects. The show would come back soon, in the meantime they were queueing up to offer Frida Slattery other roles. Who were 'they', Frida wondered, though didn't bother to ask.

Then Mel asked Frida, with audible trepidation, if she thought she'd be able to deal with a little downtime if necessary. 'Because this is a sensitive point in your career,' she said firmly. 'I don't think it's the right time for you to go rushing back to the stage or anything.'

Frida knew what she meant. Their careers were so linked by this point, and Mel couldn't bear the idea of Frida pivoting away from the work that had made them both money. To Mel's mind, a bored actress, especially one with pretensions, was a dangerous thing.

'Mel,' Frida said, trying to cut across. 'Mel, it's fine, I've got plenty to do.'

That was true, after all. There was the voice-over work. She was overdue a trip home to see her mother. She hadn't visited

Una since she'd left Edel's for the home in Rathfarnham, six months after her first stroke. Edel said to give it a little while, wait until she was settled before coming to visit. On this occasion, Frida decided she would book into a hotel just off Grafton Street rather than crowd in with Edel's gang.

The morning after Frida arrived in Dublin, Edel drove her to the home in silence. It was the nicest place Edel had been able to find, and it was paid for almost entirely from Frida's kitty, the money moving in and out of her checking account so quickly that she lost track of it. Nonetheless, Frida still found herself struck by a desolate feeling in the car park as Edel reversed into a space.

'The view is nice,' Frida said, gesturing to the sliver of the Dublin mountains visible from outside. Edel ignored her comment.

'I hope you know that she's very physically weak now,' Edel warned Frida while they got out of the car. 'Mentally she's there, but physically ...'

From the front, the nursing home was a big old Arts and Crafts detached house, with ivy climbing around the large front door. As they approached, Frida could see an ugly extension, more recently built and much bigger than the main building.

Inside, the building was quiet. Like a little girl Frida followed Edel, who got them signed in and negotiated the corridors with ease, greeting one or two of the staff en route. It was like when she'd started secondary school, and, lost in the large unfamiliar building, could simply trace Edel's own practised footsteps. Una was in a room at the back of the home, with a window that looked out onto a verge of lavender and fuchsia plants. Frida recognised some of her mother's things on the shelves by her bed: books, a framed picture of the two girls as teenagers in school uniform, another of Edel's daughters in sunglasses and shorts. Una was indeed thinner than the last time Frida saw her, and when Frida pulled her in for a hug, she felt her mother's weak arms try desperately to grasp her. She sat down carefully on a folding chair opposite Una's armchair while Edel busied herself opening the window, fussing over throws and checking surfaces for dust with the tip of her finger. Edel flicked into conversational autopilot, talking of the girls and of how fancy Frida's hotel was. Frida in contrast was almost as quiet as Una, who was trying to open a bottle of sparkling water with shaky hands. Frida leaned forward, taking the bottle from her mother's hands and doing it for her. A faint, uncertain smile passed over Una's face.

In the car, Frida leaned forward and put her head into her hands. She emitted a low moan, then placed her hands back into her lap.

'That was really hard.'

Edel turned on the engine and the radio automatically started playing dance music. 'Yeah, well. That's how it goes,' she said in a cold voice.

Frida glanced sidelong at her. 'Okay,' she said tentatively.

'I'm just saying,' Edel continued as she pulled out of the car park. 'Sometimes in life people have to do things they don't want to do, Frida.'

'Do you think I don't know that?'

'I don't bloody know. I know you're never here. You've completely checked out.'

'I'm here right now. I am literally sitting in your car with you.'

'Yeah, and you're gone again in two days. For how long this time?'

'I'll be back in two weeks.'

'You said you're not even working at the moment. You could be here all the time if you were actually bothered, Freeds.'

Frida said nothing. Turning the corner, Edel abruptly pulled the car onto the curb beside the Luas station.

'You're fine from here, right?'

'Sure,' Frida said, leaning in to give Edel a peck on the cheek. 'See you in the morning.'

In her hotel room, Frida lay down on the bed. Outside she could hear the sound of tourists and pub drinkers milling on the pedestrianised street. Edel was completely right. There was nothing keeping her from staying here for longer. She told herself that it was necessary to be in LA, that there were meetings and so on about future projects, but the reality was that Una was very unwell. Her mother and Edel both needed her here in a way that work did not. The knowledge of this came over Frida like a fever, and she gave into it without a fight.

In the morning, Frida went to Hodges Figgis and picked out some books she thought Una might like. She was going to Edel's for lunch, then the pair of them would visit Una again in the afternoon. She would change her flights in the evening, see if the hotel might have room for her for a little longer. It might even be nice to be in Dublin again, to pretend to be living here. She walked past the flower sellers on Duke Street, trying to remember what flowers Una preferred. Lilies or sunflowers? She opted for sunflowers, wrapped for her in white paper by the florist and bundled into Frida's arms like a newborn infant.

On the street outside Trinity she hailed a cab to take her to Edel's. She collapsed into the backseat with her shopping bags. As the driver turned onto South Great George's Street, Edel's name popped up on Frida's phone screen. A white flash went through Frida's mind at the sight of it. It was Una, of course. Edel said in a steady voice that she had had another stroke an hour earlier and an ambulance was bringing her to St James's Hospital.

Frida leaned forward and asked the taxi driver to divert to the hospital. He glanced warily at her in the rear-view mirror. When she arrived, the tote bag of books heavy on her shoulder, the flowers clasped to her chest with one arm, she felt as though she was in a dream. She stood there at the entrance to A&E, which was perhaps not where her mother was, and all around her paramedics trundled past and patients smoked. One in a hospital gown with an IV in her arm. Frida couldn't remember what time it was, what date, or if she'd ever been to this particular hospital before. Surely not, she thought, why would she have been here? She watched the taxi pull away, the driver raising a hand to her as he drove off as if the two of them were old friends, and she had the distinct sensation it was too late now, that if her mother was indeed dying, then that was it. Frida had chosen to spend her adult life away from home, in pursuit of ludicrous goals and foolish ambition (selfish!) and now she would have to account for everything that choice had cost her.

'You in the right place?' the patient smoking with the line in her arm asked her.

'Yeah,' Frida said, giving a small nod.

When finally she found someone at reception to tell her where to go within the hospital complex, her pace picked up and she walked with determination, like she did when the cameras were on her. Frida turned a corner to see Edel standing at the other end of a long corridor, grey-faced, listening to a tired-looking doctor in a white coat. Both of them turned to watch Frida as she walked towards them. She knew it already, but Edel confirmed it when she reached the pair of them. Una's heart had stopped about twenty minutes earlier while Frida's taxi was stuck in traffic on Thomas Street.

It was surprising to Frida how quickly things shifted after that. She was plunged so readily into the automatic process of preparing an Irish funeral that the actual mechanics of it were a mystery. Who pressed the button to start this? One thing followed another cleanly – the death notice, the funeral home, the priest – and Frida found she always had a job to do. She shuttled between her hotel, Edel and Ian's house and the funeral home. Huge taxi bills. Trying to communicate with her drivers through body language. I don't want to talk on this journey. There was a chasm within Frida, a dark entity that cursed her for not managing to see her mother the morning before she died. You're a bad daughter, it said to her over and over. It tore through the days, and kept her up into the small hours. At the funeral home, Ian's sister the doctor came with a little brown bottle of Valium and doled it out to Frida and Edel. Simon sent flowers from Dubai. Simon – someone Frida hadn't thought about in a long time. That was the theme of the week, apparently. At the service the next morning, Frida saw friends she hadn't in years, old faces from college and from theatres that appeared in a blur to shake her hand and deliver condolences, and then departed again without leaving a trace.

After the funeral passed, the rest of Frida's time in Ireland was spent going through her mother's empty flat in Dun Laoghaire with Edel, boxing and bagging things up. Quickly she and Edel ran out of things to talk about, sometimes just passing each other something they found in the flat – a photo of the two of them as girls, a cookbook they remembered from childhood – but more often than not they didn't engage with each other at all. Edel worked with her headphones in, occasionally chuckling at some podcast she had playing in her ears.

And the time to think turned out to be what Frida needed most. This was where her escape plan hatched. Something about the sorting, almost meditative, removing cups and mugs from the dusty kitchen cabinets. It helped that this was not Frida's childhood home – just the small one-bedroom flat her mother had bought once the girls had left home. Frida had stayed overnight here just once or twice, falling asleep on the couch after Christmas dinner. Waking in the dark of the early morning, uncomfortable and unsure of where she was. So for the most part she could go through the motions rationally, one thing after another. She was moving through the detritus of her mother's life. Detritus, she thought. Was that term fair? But what else was it now that her mother was gone? There were so few things of her mother's past in the flat, no photos of Una in her youth or old forgotten lipsticks or unfamiliar glamorous silk scarves. Una wasn't like that. She didn't hang on to old parts of herself. It was all more recent and less personal: receipts for the post office, blister packs of paracetamol and reusable shopping bags, the everyday clutter of a woman in her late seventies.

Inevitably this process made Frida think of her own detritus, the clutter that filled every corner of her bungalow in LA. Imagine packing it all up to come home. Where would she begin? In this way Frida did start the process of accounting that had struck her as so monstrously permanent on the threshold of the hospital's A&E. By the time she and Edel had their mother's flat emptied and cleaned, Frida knew what she would do next.

She would go back to LA one more time. She was free of *The Reason* now, her contract voided by the show's indefinite hiatus. Sara had sent Frida several emails after hearing about her mother's death. The first was the usual pleasantries, polite well-wishes. Then came more messages, less cogent, sent late at night. In one of these messages, Sara lamented that she and Frida rarely hung out anymore, and said she missed talking to Frida about work, about love, 'about the ways we tend to hurt those we care about most'. Frida was unclear as to what Sara's agenda was here. In her emails Sara wrote obliquely of conflict, of preparation. Were the Lunds splitting up? Was Sara trying to get Frida on side in advance of a legal battle? If so, Frida wanted nothing to do with it. Were it not for the loose ends to be tied up, she thought she might not bother going back to LA at all. What was there for her? An ex-girlfriend who had repeatedly told Frida she didn't want to speak to her. An agent – her only friend, really – who would always put earning potential over Frida's own creative ambitions or personal desires. Frida supposed that she liked her bungalow. But there were bungalows in Dublin. There were things much better than bungalows, which Frida saw every time she took the train back into town from Una's flat in Dun Laoghaire: beautiful Victorian houses with rambling gardens facing directly onto Dublin Bay, lovely Georgian terraced townhouses with the kind of stately urban grandeur Frida had never once seen in America.

Yes, so Frida was decided. She would go back, pack up the bungalow, sell it and move home to Dublin. First, she would need to fire Mel.

11. The dark times, 2020

1.

In the end the Reddans' new life lasted just over four months before Kitty decided that it wasn't enough. They were in the living room of the house they were renting in Phibsborough, having only recently unpacked the final box. The boys were in bed upstairs, Sunday evening, school in the morning. Almost Christmas holidays. They'd been out all day, visiting friends with children of a similar age in Rialto. Now the two of them were exhausted on the couch, Kitty in striped cotton pyjamas, her bare feet resting neatly on the needlepoint ottoman she'd found in an antiques shop on Francis Street.

'I can't do this anymore,' she said, her voice even and calm.

John turned from the television to face her. 'Do what?'

'I thought the fresh start would help. I thought I could try harder.' She paused. 'I have tried harder. But I can't live with you. I don't love you, John, and I know you don't love me.'

The way she was speaking sounded to John like a speech rehearsed in front of a mirror. It sounded to him like Kitty was acting.

'Why are you telling me this?'

'I want us to separate,' she said. 'I think we have to, for the boys. It's not right.'

He felt a thin red mist rise in him, and he stood up without thinking.

'John,' Kitty said. 'Don't shout.'

In the morning he helped get the boys up and dressed and Kitty took them off to school on their bikes. John had not slept. He stood on the threshold of the house in his dressing gown and boxer shorts, watching the three of them disappear down towards Cross Guns Bridge. Kitty was right. They didn't love each other. But to think that he must leave their home because of it, to think he must extract himself from the family life they'd built together, was enraging. Hadn't he been so good since last summer? Staying off the drink, keeping the head down, uprooting his whole life for them.

John viewed the last nine years as a series of sacrifices made in the name of family life. It had been this way ever since *Four and Ten*, watching that play go off into the world without him while he'd been at home with the newborn Ruadhán. Left to watch it all from the sidelines. Over these past four months, he had tried to frame the move to Dublin as a positive one. The more he thought about it, the more London was in fact becoming synonymous with the failure of his movie, which he didn't like to dwell on but which undeniably had happened. The TV work, the ads, the partying, all of it was salve. Distraction. Pointless. He needed to get away from all of that. He needed theatre again. This was supposed to be a return to his roots.

The problem was that everyone here hated him. At first they were all eager to set up meetings with him. When he bumped into them at plays and galleries, they were friendly, sometimes buying him a drink or filling him in on some industry gossip he'd missed over the years. And then afterwards, when he called or emailed to arrange a time, nobody got back to him. Even Katie MacGowan, who'd met him for lunch in Cornucopia like the old days, talked with enthusiasm about working together until she added, with an air of confession, that her three children at home meant she wasn't producing much these days. It was like the sensation of walking into a room and feeling the conversation about you die down on your arrival, over and over.

Since arriving back in August, John had been struck by a kind of confused nostalgia that was so deep, so permeating that it felt almost neurological. Like déjà vu or the onset of migraine. He tripped into chasms of memory on every street corner, like cracks in the pavements. There were ghosts of people he had known, and people he had been, everywhere in the city centre. It was impossible not to think about Frida Slattery here. He thought he saw her everywhere, in pub corners, queueing at the chemist, waiting for a bus. Riding a bicycle in one of the city's new cycle lanes. Nothing more than apparitions, the workings of his fretful mind. And when he did bump into someone he'd known back in those days, he thought, why is this person so old now? What happened to them? Have they been sick?

Certain times of day were particularly dangerous: damp autumn mornings, clear-skied dusks. It came on like a dizzy spell, flashes of memory of her, and of him too, that unsettled him so deeply. Time collapsing onto itself. He envied Kitty for having no memories of this city before they'd moved here. For John, it was impossible to separate the Dublin of his past from the Dublin of his present. The two lay awkwardly over each other like a pair of teenage lovers. Even when he saw an old pub that had been torn down, replaced by the shining glass facade of a new hotel or an office, he could also see the outline of what was there before.

Maybe that was why everyone in his industry was so cold with him. He reminded them of a different time. Or maybe it was just what Brendan Quirke had said to him years ago in New York: John, everyone in Dublin thinks you're an arsehole.

Kitty granted him reprieve until after Christmas, so the boys could have one last taste of normality. In the new year, the week before the schools went back, they dropped Ruadhán and Fionn at Barry and Joanna's for a sleepover and went to a hotel in Wicklow to talk things out. Kitty had everything planned already. She kept saying that she only wanted things to be easy for the boys. As if John only wanted things to be difficult. She knew of a couple who would be subletting their cottage in Stoneybatter for a few months while they worked abroad. She hadn't asked them about it yet, hadn't wanted to embarrass John. John wanted to laugh at this. Embarrass him. Okay, do your best, Kitty.

During their first four months in Ireland, Kitty settled into Dublin in a way that astonished John. So quickly, smoothly, she found friends to have coffee with after the school run, other parents with whom she actually had things in common. She made it look so easy. Early on she found a childminder named Beatriz, a very pretty young Brazilian woman with a sardonic way of speaking, who would do pick-up and stay until dinner time. Soon Kitty was having meetings about getting back to costume work, covering the holiday of staff at the Gate and the Gaiety and occasionally teaching students at the drama school that hadn't existed when John used to live here. Kitty's productivity was impressive. She said it was because she was making up for ten years of lost time. This arithmetic could only diminish John's own idea of his work, all his typing away at his laptop in the little study in the back bedroom. Writing was not going well, had not really gone well in years, since *Ripples on the Water*, probably, if he was honest about it. He had been trying to take meetings, to see if he could get something going. Eventually, with help from Alice Greer, he pinned down the manager from an independent theatre company more known for nurturing emerging artists. Over coffee, she agreed to put him forward for a play at the Gate in the spring. *The Tempest*. Shakespeare, he thought. Shakespeare is inescapable in the end.

The spring, though. Maybe things would change in the spring.

Nobody had ever said to him directly that the movie had been a flop, but God, it was obvious. Even the car ads the agency had been getting him had dried up since moving away. He no longer went out five nights a week in London, and so it was like he'd never existed. John did not like to think about *The Head of the King*. Good God. Those reviews.

John's work was stale, pale, male. He was barely in his forties. When had he stopped being 'promising'? Whatever promises he'd once made had long since been broken. All of them, he thought, driving back across the city having collected the boys from Barry and Joanna's. John felt a million years of age. Take me around the back and shoot me, he thought. Father of a teenager any day now. Ruadhán with his video games, the sound of gunfire incessant through the house. Fionn still his little lad for now, but that too was slipping away.

They'd tell them about the separation on Sunday night. Kitty had that bit planned out too. On Saturday John went to see the cottage in Stoneybatter, a tiny cramped terraced house of the kind he would've lived in as a student, though with a front door painted a sunny yellow. It reminded him of the thatch he and Barry had grown up in, only much smaller, damper and filled with the bohemian ephemera of the cottage's owners: pottery, houseplants and a red kilim rug on the old pine floorboards. Through the living-room window John could see a few teenagers milling around on their bikes. Not good for the boys, he thought.

'Yes,' he told the couple, both actors, who were going to Australia for work for six months. 'I'll take it.'

They should have bought a house by the sea, like he'd wanted to. Things would have stuck by the sea.

When John moved into the cottage the following week, he didn't manage to unpack his things straight away and the place quickly became cluttered and messy, his books and clothes piling up on every surface. He sat up in bed and stared at his laptop. He was trying to start writing something new, before *The Tempest* rehearsals kicked off. Already he was miserable in this house. Spent the first few days struggling to assemble IKEA bunk beds for weekends with the boys. Bought a secondhand car since Kitty had kept theirs. It got broken into the second weekend it was parked outside. The thief took all the small change in the dashboard, rearranged his old CDs in return.

When John went out and bumped into people he used to know, he pretended to everyone he met that work was good, life was good, moving home had been a good idea. He didn't know if everyone knew about him and Kitty yet. He'd downloaded a dating app alone in the cottage one evening, spent an hour or so selecting photos of himself, then had deleted it in terror the moment he saw a woman he faintly recognised. Worst time of year to end your marriage. Every day was January grey, bleak, cold in the old terraced house. He'd tried to chat up a woman at the bar in the Abbey one night. She was younger than him and dressed in tight black leather trousers and green cashmere polo-neck. You must be hot in that, he'd said, gesturing to her outfit. I mean, it's hot in here, he corrected himself.

The price you pay for fashion, she said, smiling up at him.

Her name was Mairéad and she worked at the National Library. Something very junior in comms. He'd gone to the bar to buy them a round of gin and tonics and was trying to catch her eye across the room, where he'd left her by the window. She saw him and he thought she might have winked – actually winked at him, the chemistry they had already! And then as he was tapping his card to pay he saw another girl appear at her side, clock him and lean in to whisper something to Mairéad. Mairéad shook her head and then, John couldn't believe it, the plastic cups of gin and tonic sweating in his hands, the pair of them left.

No, that hadn't gone well. Leave women to the side for a moment. Stay in, focus on the work. But John had no good ideas for new work, the blank white expanse of the Word document goading him.

What was John allowed to want?

He went back into the folder titled Old stuff and within it, another folder marked Old notes. A document not opened in years titled For Frida.docx.

What if John made something that was pure Frida?

He opened the file. It was ten years old, this document, and there was just one line of text there at the top of the page.

```
And the light in her face, the way she can
turn it on when she wants.
```

John read this text and could sense it setting him off. Sitting on the couch and imagining being sat in front of Frida and waiting for it. The room dissolved around him and he was there in the theatre again, her on the stage in front of him sitting on a stool. Smiling at him. Had it been fifteen years now, since the first time? It felt like longer. What was the thing he felt now when he thought about the light in her face? Something like love, or was it something more like desire? It was something he'd never had for Kitty. It wasn't like that at all.

The light in Frida's face. The change. The way you only noticed that winter had been so dark when the sun appeared in a rectangle opposite your bedroom window one morning, a rectangle halfway down the wall and you remembered then that the world is turning.

John wanted the chance to tell her what to do once more. Frida, look at me, John thought. Now, look to the very back of the room. But he wasn't allowed to want things like that anymore.

Throughout January, John went to the mediator with Kitty to talk about how they could separate and co-parent successfully. In a small room in a Georgian building near Merrion Square, it all came out. The infidelity, the abandonment. John tried to shy away from specifics, because those were the hardest parts to admit to, but overall learned that Kitty had already suspected the worst of him. It was very painful, this form of accounting. It was like taking off your clothes on stage, John thought, to have your innermost self judged by a legion of unknown faces in the dark. But each time he left the room, he did find that he felt a little lighter, and also thoroughly drained, like he'd been sat too long in a sauna.

The point of these sessions was not to air John's dirty laundry, though. They were trying to find a way to leave each other efficiently, in a way that didn't hurt the boys. John liked the idea of rotating custody within the house in Phibsborough: the boys would stay put while the parents switch in and out week by week. Kitty didn't. She didn't want to leave the family home while John got to play house.

For now they agreed that John would have them every other weekend until they arranged finances and he found a more permanent place to stay. Finances, he thought, picturing all the remittance notices his agent had ever sent him over the years.

Leaving the third session John and Kitty walked to where her bike was parked beside the iron railings of the terrace.

'There's something I wanted to bring up today, but we ran out of time,' she said, twirling her helmet by its strap. 'I think you should know that I've been seeing someone.'

'Jesus. Already?' John asked. Without looking at him, Kitty tilted her head in such a way that made John think that there had been an overlap along the way here.

'What's his name?'

'Niall O'Donovan.'

'Niall O'Donovan.'

Kitty nodded, not looking at him.

'I know that name,' John said.

'Yeah, you might.'

'He works in RTÉ. He's something important, isn't he?'

'He's the commissioner of drama programming.'

John made a noise halfway between laughter and spluttering. 'You left me for the commissioner of drama at RTÉ.'

'He's not why I left you, John. Grow up.'

What did disappointment feel like? In the cottage in Stoneybatter John knew he couldn't think about that. It might squash him, the weight of it: the marriage, the movie, *The Tempest*, even the boys. The living arrangement that Kitty had chosen for him. The fact he had to do everything for himself now, shopping for groceries, washing bedsheets. Every shirt he owned was wrinkled now. Disappointment abounded for everyone except Kitty, apparently.

And so he kept coming back to the Word document, all through the grey January weekday afternoons. For Frida.docx, like it was a love letter. It wasn't a love letter. Maybe it was a way of asking himself – asking the world – what John was allowed to want. What he wanted was to tell Frida everything that had happened, about all the disappointment in his life at the moment. How could he begin to tell her any of it, though? All their lives together, it had been her telling him. It had been John listening, John buying the pints, John laughing when Frida wanted to be laughed at. And then later, it had been John telling Frida what to do, but that bit was very different. That bit had been on a stage.

Now John didn't really have any other friends, either. Barry, maybe, the two of them watching the football midweek, eyes forward, talking conditionally about their lives, only ever in the second person. Joanna undergoing tests for breast cancer. You'd be feeling the pressure, you know, when the shit hits the fan. You'd be scared, in a way, of being alone. Like whatever it was wasn't happening to them. Happening to someone else instead.

No, he just had this: 3 p.m. on a Wednesday, rehearsals at the Gate not starting for another week. No Ruadhán and Fionn until 10 a.m. on Saturday morning. He started typing in the Word document.

`Maybe there's a woman on stage,` he wrote.

Frida in Los Angeles still, John assumed. Her show on hiatus, he'd read recently, and who knew what that meant for her.

And it's dark up there on stage, he typed, and the audience can barely see her, but there's just enough light to see the top of her head. Pale yellow hair in the dim light.

And it felt stupid, suddenly. Frida Slattery in Los Angeles. Frida Slattery starring in a long-running cable TV soap or whatever you'd call it. The two of them didn't speak anymore, for good reason. There were so many other actresses, John told himself. Stop fixating on this one.

But this was the only thing he wanted now. Now that things had started falling apart. He wanted another go at this. The cursor blinking at him on the page. If he and Frida had ... he couldn't finish the sentence. He wished she hadn't told him about that.

None of this would've happened if they had.

A little girl, maybe. A little older than Ruadhán. They would've timed things better. The sacrifices John had made wouldn't have felt like sacrifices. They would have felt right. You were supposed to want what you ended up with. You were supposed to say, Jesus, it's tough but I can't imagine it any other way. Even on the bad days you were supposed to be delighted with yourself.

John thought that surely these were the bad days.

The document was there on his computer, but soon John found himself distracted. All through February, something was happening that was beyond his or anyone's control. Every morning he stopped to buy a newspaper on his way to the coffee shop. Parts of the world were starting to come to a halt. Hospitals became crowded with the ill, and theatre began to seem less important. Perhaps things would all blow over soon. The boys' school closed for two weeks after two teachers become unwell. Beatriz went home to Brazil. John was back in the house in Phibsborough more often than not, taking care of the boys, talking with Kitty. One Tuesday morning he took the bus into town to meet with the theatre staff about *The Tempest*. In the meeting room they'd booked in the hotel across the road, he found himself blindsided. The theatre wanted to cancel the play, postpone it until later this year, maybe, if they could find a free slot in the calendar.

'But we've sold a lot of tickets already,' he said faintly.

The artistic director, an imposing woman named Sally who dressed in long, brightly coloured tunics and scarves, and who didn't like John, shook her head. 'It's just not a good idea, I'm afraid.'

And apparently that was final. There was nothing else to be said or done about it. Again, for what felt like the hundredth time in twelve months, John realised that he was powerless. Across the boardroom table, Sally said they were thinking about their options, and maybe it might be possible to do something like a 'table read' online, instead of in the theatre. John laughed at her, incredulous.

'You're not serious,' he said.

'Right,' Sally said, like she'd expected a negative response from him. 'Well, I just thought I'd run it by you, anyway.'

Leaving the theatre John stepped out onto Parnell Square into what was a surprisingly crisp, bright winter morning. A man around his age was rolling a cigarette at the bus stop across the road and eyed John suspiciously; John didn't think he knew this man, but gave him a nod of recognition just in case. This was happening more and more these days.

More reminders that John Reddan had moved back to a city where everyone had thought for years and years that he was an arsehole.

And apparently at the worst possible time in history.

He walked down O'Connell Street, then along the quays back to the house in Stoneybatter, where the cursor was still blinking at him on the screen. He thought about the cursor, if it was the same in every document he had ever opened. If it had migrated with him from one laptop to the next for these last ten years, had been watching him, for however long he had trying to write something titled For Frida.docx.

And then very soon everything was closed, all the schools and theatres and not just those affecting the Reddans' daily lives. On television in the cottage John watched the Taoiseach decree that life as they all knew it must stop. A few days later, as he started to go mad inside the four walls, Kitty and the boys cycled to his street in the cargo bike and waved at him through the window. It was clear the boys didn't fully understand the separation, and how could they? So young, John thought, younger even than him and Barry when they'd gone through the same thing with their own parents. He watched through the window as they left a loaf of sourdough bread for him on the doorstep, like he was a shut-in by choice. The man in the bubble. But it wasn't just John, of course. It was everyone in the country. Now John's parenting was limited to video calls at bedtime. Trying to kiss his sons through the screen. The ridiculous noise John made. *Mwah.* A noise he had never once made before. Goodnight, boys. The hopelessness of it, the dry silence of his living room after they hung up. He missed how they smelled, how all four of them used to smell the exact same, faintly dermatological and sweet. Now it was all just dust on his countertops, grime of his own under the fingernails. The same clothes every day. A stupid decision to move to Ireland, a stupid time to get divorced. Every single day the exact same as the one that came before it. And it could be weeks of this, months even, and Alice Greer called him from London and asked him in his professional opinion, what did he think the future of theatre looks like? She was canvassing all her clients, she thought, because she was bored and stuck at home with her teenagers for company. She asked John what hope was there for their world, if so much time was going to elapse before they could gather again.

And John told her that he didn't know. He told her that he didn't seem to have any original ideas at all anymore.

Hmmm, Alice said, like she was a doctor and his inertia was a troubling symptom she'd never seen before. Then they dropped the topic and stayed on the line for a while, trading professional gossip about productions cancelled and things moved online and people they knew who were stuck at home like everyone else, drinking too much, getting into arguments on social media because they couldn't deal with being out of work.

When she hung up, John called up Sally.

'Okay,' he said, rubbing the back of his neck. 'So maybe there is another way to do this play.'

2.

On a Friday night in late March, Frida sat on the couch in the flat in Monkstown, a blanket over her knees, her phone in her lap. A message from Edel popped up on the screen, followed quickly by another.

>Your man is on the telly
>
>The dickhead

Which one? Frida typed.

>John Reddan

Oh that one Frida replied. What channel

>RTE1. On the late late show

Frida reached for the remote on the coffee table.

>Is he ... sexy now? Edel messaged.

In the living room the television lit in action and John Reddan's face appeared large and slightly blurry, via what seemed to be a laptop screen. In the background Frida saw a small, sad-looking kitchen, tired pine cabinets with clutter on the countertops.

> I think he's sexy now, Edel messaged, not waiting for Frida to reply. When did that happen?
>
> I think you've been trapped in quarantine for too long, she replied.

The screen cut to the interviewer alone in studio, wearing a sharp blue suit, sitting on a brown leather armchair and talking to the air.

'So John,' the interviewer said. 'Like everyone else in the country, you're stuck at home right now.'

'Indeed I am,' John said.

'And tell me what it was you were supposed to be doing tonight, had we not found ourselves where we are now.'

John's face in soft focus. He laughed awkwardly. 'Ryan, right now I should be at the Gate Theatre, at the first night of my production of *The Tempest*.'

'And this play was to be quite special for you, wasn't it? Your first new work in Dublin in a long, long time.'

'Exactly, yes. And I know I speak on behalf of the whole cast, the whole crew, when I say how hard it has been, how disappointing to be pipped at the post like this. I know it's a feeling a lot of us probably have right now, this feeling of cancelled plans, the listlessness of it all.'

'So tell us what you have planned instead.'

John's face crinkling around the eyes, almost as if he were in pain.

'It's unorthodox, Ryan,' he said. 'It's not what I had ever imagined myself doing. But in the spirit of these new, strange times, we're going to give it a go. We're going to do it online – a virtual play, if you will. Our actors will log onto a Zoom call, not unlike the one I'm doing with you right now, and they'll act in their separate living rooms, kitchens, wherever. It'll require a little imagination on the part of the audience, but I think that's something we're all proving ourselves to be capable of at the moment.'

'Almost more like a radio play rather than a stage play.'

'Exactly.'

Frida thought about acting on a Zoom call, speaking with the tiny lens of the computer camera in mind. Not for her, thanks.

'Would this be a world first?' the interviewer asked. 'Do you know if other theatres will do similar?'

'I'm sure they are planning to. We have so few options in this current climate. But my intention, with staging in this way, isn't to be first, to be a pioneer. It's simply to give people some sustenance, some art that will feed them in these difficult times.'

'You think that's something we're in need of at the moment.'

'Absolutely. Absolutely.'

'Do you think in a year or two's time, we're going to see a whole raft of art – plays, novels, movies, what have you – about all of us being locked in our houses, being isolated from each other? Will there be a John Reddan play about quarantine at the Gate next year?'

John frowned, thinking about the question.

'Would that be so bad? Since the beginning of time, humans have made art about the world they live in, the situation they find themselves in, the challenges they face. It's something I myself have been doing my whole life. I hope you don't mind if I read a small bit of poetry now. It's from Bertolt Brecht, obviously someone very important to all of us in the world of the theatre. It's something he wrote in 1939, a time of unimaginable terror and darkness. It's something that I find inspiring.'

'Please, go ahead.'

John looked straight into the camera and raised his chin.

'"In the dark times,"' he began very slowly. '"Will there also be singing? Yes, there will also be singing. About the dark times."'

On the couch Frida rolled her eyes.

'Singing about the dark times,' repeated the interviewer in the studio. 'Wow. John Reddan, thank you so much for coming on this evening.'

'Thank you for having me.'

'After the break, I'll be talking to some of the doctors and nurses working at the frontline of this crisis.'

Frida switched off the TV, dropping the remote on the couch beside her.

> I'm thinking definitely sexy, yes, Edel wrote. But sadly that man would eat himself with a spoon if he could. Would we do a facetime with the kids tomorrow afternoon?

The flat Frida had rented in Dublin was on the ground floor of a large house in Monkstown, with a partial sea view and when she'd arrived by taxi, a cold and blue winter day in late December, the line that divided sea and sky looked to her like it had been drawn in a very fine dark pen. The effect was uncanny, unsettling her. Inside the flat, she found ceilings much higher than she was used to from living in Los Angeles. Looking at her two suitcases sat in the bedroom, it seemed ludicrous, the notion that she could pack years of her life into such a paltry baggage allowance. What had she forgotten? What did she jettison without realising? It was supposed to be a way to start again, the move here, an attempt at undoing some knotted strand of herself.

It had taken Frida two months after the death of her mother to wrap up her affairs in Los Angeles. She took Mel out for dinner at the Chateau Marmont. Mel looked so much at home in these places, dressed in a long gauzy orange dress and expensive wedge-heel sandals. It was dusk, and they ordered martinis and oysters to start. All around them on the terrace were beautiful people who looked famous or important in a way that Frida no longer cared about. Mel wanted to gossip, pointing subtly at a table near them occupied by two men she knew to be guilty of bad behaviour on set. Frida went along with it. She waited until they were well into their second martinis to break the news to Mel.

'You're firing me,' Mel said in disbelief, one hand on her breastbone.

Frida pursed her lips. 'I need to make some changes.

There are so many other things I want to do, and I have the opportunity now.'

Mel shook her head slowly.

'I know how much of my career I owe you,' Frida added.

'All of it.'

'Well, not quite all of it.'

'The parts that mattered most, yes.'

'This is what I mean,' Frida said. 'There are parts of my career that matter to me, you know, even if you think they're worthless.'

It was horrible, to have to do this to a friend, she thought. It was the price she was paying for all those hours spent confiding in Mel over the years, all the easy camaraderie they had shared together. And it was worse, she knew, for Mel.

'If you'd stuck with your little arthouse plays, Frida, you would not be sitting here right now enjoying all of this,' Mel gestured to the oysters in front of her.

Frida nodded. 'I know.'

'So if that's what you want ... If you want to give up your nice life in Los Angeles, then go for it.'

'That is what I want. I know that now.'

Mel crumpled her napkin and threw it down on the table. 'You'll never get back here, you know, if you go.' Her voice was angry, but Frida thought Mel's eyes looked sad more than anything else.

Frida's heart beat faster now. 'Fine,' she said.

Mel looked at her, saying nothing, arching one eyebrow.

Over the course of a couple of weeks, Frida sold the house and most of her furniture and culled her possessions to just a few crates to be put into storage. She visited her Los Feliz haunts for the last time, thinking already of Dublin and the cooler weather that awaited her. It would feel like relief, she thought, to get out of here, go home, start afresh.

She didn't know how painful it would be to settle back into the place where she had grown up. It was new, navigating a version of Dublin without her mother in it. It hurt much of the time. In that first month, Frida walked along the seafront almost every morning, even in the pissing rain, and thought about Una's life, and Frida's own life with her, nested dolls, the pair of them. What happened to it all after death, how could she and Edel possibly hold on to it. When clearing out the flat they had each chosen items of Una's to keep. Simple gold jewellery to give to Sophie and Sinéad. Frida had a mustard-yellow velvet armchair and Edel took a long rectangular painting of Dublin Bay that now hung on her kitchen wall in Crumlin.

The plan was to take a few months to sort her head out, then get back to work. Without an agent it was harder to set up meetings, but Frida tried to stay busy as much as she could. That was what the new start was about, wasn't it? Every time Frida went to the city centre she saw faces she recognised, running into old friends barely spoken to since their weddings five or ten years earlier. She wanted to be brave enough to go to the theatre alone, but knowing there would be people there with whom she would need to make small talk was nerve-wracking. Had Frida ever had friends here? She wasn't sure now. She was thinking about all the choices she had made to get this far. All the things she had foregone in the name of success (success, she thought, as Mel had defined it). 'Real relationships', being honest with herself, being direct and true with the people she cared about. Being courageous. Making real decisions. God. Even having people she cared about in her life. Had she ever been a person with friends? In Dublin in the old days, as a student and shortly thereafter, it certainly seemed like she had. She had rarely been alone in those days, everyone living in each other's pockets. But now the city seemed so different. Everyone had changed, hadn't they? She wished Catherine still lived here, anything for an ally against this strange new world.

Then as lockdown began, Frida found herself bored, like everyone else, and angry. She was angry about everything. She was angry about the plans she had had to cancel, a trip to London to meet casting directors and new agents. With that specific anger came the abstract anger at having had things taken away from her, like a child. Since leaving Los Angeles Frida's sense of time had changed. She was thirty-eight now, the age Una had been when Frida was born, and she was getting older every day.

And God, this interview with John Reddan made her angry. She hadn't known that he was here, and being caught on the back foot was always annoying. The way he got to act, the way he was treated like he was an artist, a man of substance and merit and perhaps even genius, with access to lucid quotations from Bertold Brecht. *The Tempest* at the Gate, she thought. Was she jealous of him? Of course. Or not exactly. She was jealous of men more broadly. All the unfairness of it. She wanted to go on television and give her opinion about the value of art in times of struggle. Of course Frida wanted that! Who didn't? She stood up from the couch, feeling her heart rate rise. She'd barely left the flat all week, but the groceries had been delivered today. From the fridge she took a bottle of white wine and twisted open the plastic cap. There was so much going on in her mind. In her bedroom, in the bedside locker she found a little pink flowery notepad Sophie had given her for Christmas. Just write everything down and see what happens, Frida thought, and took a seat back on the couch.

3.

After the interview ended, the producer appeared again on John's laptop screen, giving him the thumbs up.

'Nice work,' she said. 'You're free to go.'

He clicked out of the window and closed his laptop. The air in the kitchen suddenly felt colder, looser, like he had just entered a house that had been empty for a long time.

'There will also be singing,' he repeated in a deep, theatrical tone. 'About the dark times.'

He stood up from the table and turned around, looking for the bottle of whiskey. It was on the counter behind him and it occurred to John then that it might have been visible throughout the interview. Uncapping the bottle, he felt a ripple of shame skim over him like a passing cloud. Ah well. Surely everyone in the country was on the whiskey at the moment. He didn't want to appraise the interview that had just ended, yet the old feeling of adrenaline was buzzing through his blood. Hence the need for whiskey.

Once again, the weekend stretched out in front of him. Zoom rehearsals on Monday and before that, two days of nothingness. The previous weekend, the first of this new world, when Kitty and the boys had cycled to his house on their way to the park and waved at him through the window, it had somehow made things even worse. Left to his own devices, with the curtains drawn, John felt less alone. More contained. Happier now the alcohol was doing what it tended to do. He walked around the tiny cottage with glass in hand. This house was meant to be a temporary measure. After two months, he was beginning to think he would be stuck in Stoneybatter a little while longer. Texts from Australia informed him that the actors had no idea when they might be able to come home again, and they didn't sound like they were in much of a hurry. Summer there, and less risk of the virus. Could John keep their plants alive until they came home? Why not, he thought now, looking at the wilting potted ferns that lined the windowsill in the small living room.

How could two adults live here? It was claustrophobic enough for him alone, the tiny rooms, no storage space. He still hadn't gotten around to unpacking so the suitcase on the bedroom floor served as his wardrobe now. The two-seater kitchen table his desk. When the boys had first come to visit, before the lockdown, they had sat right down on the living room floor amid all of John's papers and books and started playing their Nintendo Switches. John opened the kitchen's back door now and stepped outside, patting the pocket of his jeans for his cigarettes. It was cold, the night unnervingly quiet. The cottage had a garden so small as to make a mockery of the word, little more than one metre by one metre of concrete that held his bike, albeit at an awkward angle, and a few dying geraniums. It was overlooked on three sides by other terraced cottages. On the fourth, a back gate opened onto the street, which led in turn towards the Phoenix Park. Imagine if he had to live here forever, he thought, lighting a cigarette. Maybe he would go for a run in the morning, the way people were doing now. Maybe, in the afternoon, he would reopen the Frida document. The Zoom read of *The Tempest* was going to be ridiculous, he knew, and the idea he'd put forward on the chat show that evening, that it would be a brave new step for theatre, an attempt to meet the audience where they were, was false. It was a cop-out. It was a pantomime of art, of performance. He was doing it only to have something to do, to keep his mind off things. The team at the theatre was over-zealous and also coincidentally had only recently hired an ambitious new digital director. If John was to turn on the television and see another director making the case for it, as he himself had done just thirty minutes ago, he would laugh. There was no art to be found on a video call! A ridiculous concept, he thought, dropping the butt of his cigarette into the pot of dead geraniums.

No, it certainly wasn't going to be art. But eventually John would need to find a way to do something that was. After all, he thought, what else was there now?

12. The auteur, 2020

1.

'What have you been doing with your free time?' Kitty asked John. They were in the kitchen in Phibsborough, drinking tea while the boys made last-minute additions to their overnight bags.

'Ah, you know,' John said. 'You find a way to fill the days.'

'I don't know, actually.'

'Well, pretend that you can.'

Informed by government guidance, he and Kitty had recently made the decision to combine their split household into a single phytosanitary unit. ('Romance,' John had said on the phone when it had been agreed. 'It lives.') Kitty had been feeling the weight of sole custody of the boys, and John found he was delighted, if somewhat apprehensive, to see them again. He drove over on a Saturday morning to pick them up for a long weekend, their first with him in months. The May bank holiday, a break so inconsequential it might as well not be on the calendar at all.

'Can we go to the park, Dad?' Fionn asked from the backseat of the car. There was traffic, inexplicably, on the North Circular Road.

John sighed. 'Are you not sick of the sight of the park?'

'We're not allowed to go anywhere else.'

'I know that. Would you not like to see the sea?'

He turned at the next lights and drove them instead to Sandymount Strand. It was the only bit of beach accessible within the new five-kilometre cordon, and even then he was probably pushing it. He'd use Kitty's address if the Guards stopped him. He almost wished they would, a chance to interact with a new human. It was a clear, fine day, and the sight of the sea had all three of them giddy as they got out of the car. Blue streaks of it under the endless sky, the tide out as far as it got. Dog-walkers and even a young fella with a red box kite.

Fionn was running around on the sand, head down into the wind, almost horizontal. Ru stood at the water's edge, collecting stones and throwing them into the sea. John thought to teach him how to skim stones, but he didn't know how. He remembered a time with Frida, a day off during the *Graceland* schools tour, the two of them driving around the west pretending they weren't in love with each other. Stopping the car near Liscannor one afternoon, driving back from Lahinch. Waves crashing along the jagged shore. And John walking along the rocky promontory, looking for the biggest stone he could find to chuck into the water. Frida, arms folded against the Atlantic wind. Do you think that impresses me, John Reddan? He had hoped it would. From nowhere two aul lads in trunks, grey wiry hair all down them like silverback gorillas, had clamoured towards the water to swim. One turned to John, beard curling like Poseidon and said, Would you stop, with the stones. This a swimming place. Are you six years old.

And now Fionn had just turned seven. They'd celebrated his birthday a month ago on video call.

On the rocky promontory Frida had turned away from John and the Poseidons, trying to swallow laughter at him. Noise all lost in the wind anyway. That kind of flat-out wind that made your ears hurt. Let's go, Reddan. Back in the car, fiddling with the radio. Her hand brushing over the top of his on the gear stick. Who had they thought they were fooling?

'Dad,' Ru said, holding out a large stone for him to take.

Fionn was the one who looked like John. Ru looked more like his mother, her elegant features like an old painting of a countess. They were going to move in with the commissioner for drama soon, the boys reported on the drive back to Thor Place. But they couldn't until later in the summer. They like him okay, they told John.

'What do you like about him?' John asked.

'He's got a red car,' Fionn said. 'But he's very old.'

'Older than me?'

Fionn examined John's face in the rear-view mirror. 'Maybe.'

They had to move into Niall's house, they said, because he had so many daughters and there wasn't room for them to visit from college in the house in Phibsborough.

'We don't like the girls,' Ru said.

'They're ancient,' Fionn added.

In the cottage he set them up with sandwiches and video games and sat in the kitchen to write. If there was a point in writing, he didn't know anymore. On video calls with his manager, with Alice Greer, with bored producers he knew who wanted a gossip to pass time, everyone said that theatre might be over. They said John should try writing for television now, that was where the future was. All of us in our little bubbles, watching the screen, not talking to each other.

A few people had watched *The Tempest* online. It had received a couple of decent reviews in the arts sections of the broadsheets, which, John reminded himself, had nothing else to write about at the moment. It all counted towards John's secret mission of public rehabilitation. Love me, please love me. I will write something that makes you love me. He glanced towards the living room where the boys had the volume up and carefully he cracked open a can of Tuborg. He had been clearing the Centra out of Tuborg lately. Usually only during the week, when the boys weren't there, but it was Saturday afternoon, wasn't it? This was what people called a trying time. He certainly hadn't known that the privacy that he once longed for could feel like this: the house so quiet during the week, the street outside so still.

He got the feeling that Kitty was enjoying the endless lockdown, despite her complaints about childcare. He saw her life in little snippets via her Instagram account: the boys in the cargo bike queueing for babyccinos at the coffee-shop hatch; the banana bread in the galley kitchen of what had briefly been his house; the hammock strung up between two trees in the Phoenix Park. Meanwhile another night on the beer for John over here. He started running in an attempt to keep him off the booze. Didn't work. Earlier that Saturday morning, he told Kitty he'd been running in the Park, since she loved it there now. She asked whereabouts, and he was too ashamed to tell her that he didn't make it off the main road through the middle of the Park, got surprised by the sight of all the deer, realised he had gone further than intended and would struggle to make it back. Went to piss behind a tree and accidentally made eye contact with a Garda in a passing car. All the while the running app's narrator in his headphones, telling him to keep going! Afterwards he'd gone back to the cottage, which he never called home, not even briefly in his mind, and opened a can of beer.

'Dad,' he heard Ruadhán call from the front room. 'What's for dinner?'

'I just gave you lunch,' John called back.

'Yeah, but I'm wondering. Can we have chipper chips?'

They never get chipper chips with Kitty, he thought. Only red pasta with secret vegetables. He called in the takeaway order and at 6 p.m. the three of them walked down to Manor Street to collect battered sausages, bags of chips, cans of Coke and a piece of cod for John.

'Hang on,' he said, pausing outside Centra and giving his phone to Ruadhán. 'Need a paper. You guys decide what film we're going to watch when we get home.'

Inside he queued at the till with the *Irish Times* under one arm and a six-pack under the other. By the automatic door he could see the boys debating the choices available on Netflix on his phone.

At home, the boys settled on *Home Alone 2* and took the couch, while John sat on the battered leather recliner with his chips and his beer. The magazine supplement fell out as he unfolded the paper, and on the cover was a large picture of Frida Slattery, leaning against a low wall, arms folded, Dublin Bay in the background. The headline across the image was:

Coming home: Frida Slattery begins again

Calm as anything, John flipped open the magazine. Another large photo of Frida, this time on a bench, hair blowing in the sea breeze. Carefully he moved his chips to the coffee table to avoid getting grease on the page. The pull-quote halfway down the article:

All my life it's been men who get to be the brilliant ones, who get to tell the stories. When do women get a chance at brilliance?

Jesus, how about that for public rehabilitation. Not that she needed it. Actresses like Frida were treated like minor royalty in this country, beautiful, apparently talented women who went out into the world to make a good impression on behalf of Ireland.

FRIDA SLATTERY GETS REAL

Frida Slattery has bad timing. Having spent the best part of a decade in Hollywood, the actress from Deansgrange finally made the decision to come home and return to her first love of the stage at the end of last year – just a few months before theatres everywhere shut their doors amid global lockdowns. Over Zoom, she smiles at the irony of this. 'I had it all planned out,' she says. 'I was going to take a few months off, get myself settled into Dublin again and then start working in the spring. And look what happens.'

Instead, Slattery says she's enjoying a bit of a sabbatical. Living near the coast in south Dublin, she has time to reflect on what she calls the 'heady rush' of the job that took her to Los Angeles in the first place. The lead role in *The Reason*, a hit US series set in a criminal lawyer's office. Slattery said goodbye to Kathleen Richards, her on-screen persona, the tough and yet fragile Irish-American lawyer, last year, when the show ended in some controversy after seven successful seasons. A non-disclosure agreement prevents her from talking much about the end of *The Reason* now, but she is quick to say that she learned a lot from her years working on it. 'It was a crash course in how television gets made,' she says from her living room, her soft features and blue eyes animated as she speaks. 'It was a merry-go-round, a rollercoaster of work and chaos and drama, and it was exhausting but always such good fun.'

Nonetheless, certain aspects of Hollywood life left Slattery with a bad taste in her mouth. 'It's been talked about to death by now, but I really can't get over the way men treat women in this industry. It took me a long time to get angry about it, and I've been lucky to work with some excellent directors, but still, you see some of these men with power – directors, producers, whatever – completely abuse it.' That relationship between director and actor is particularly interesting to Slattery, who first made a name for herself on the stage in Dublin and London before turning to television. 'Every director is different, and I really love getting to know them, how their approach can inflect my own, can make me a better actor,' she explains. But their influence on her isn't always a positive thing. 'At best the relationship can feel like a true collaboration, where both parties bring their own unique personalities and skills to the table. At worst, it's more like exploitation.'

Slattery says she's not interested in naming names – she says, with a wry smile, that she'll leave that for the book she's writing. But she does mention working with a director who brought a secondary school student back to their hotel. 'Part of me is like, well, you'd never get away with that today, at least. But part of me thinks things like that are probably still happening right now.' Another man in a position of power regularly exposed himself to her in the workplace, and she alludes to offers of work being dangled in exchange for sexual favours. 'The problem is the power and freedom we give to the male artist. We put these people on a pedestal and we tell them that the decisions they make are proof of genius. So of course, they feel they can act however they like in their private lives, too.' But doesn't she think that things are changing? She frowns, then smiles thoughtfully. 'I'd like to hope so. I want to be optimistic. But all my life it's been men who get to be the brilliant ones, who get to tell the stories. When do women get a chance at brilliance?'

Midway through our conversation, Slattery picks up her laptop and carries it outside to a sunny back garden. We're joined then by a local tortoiseshell cat who she says passes through every day. It's clear that there's a happy domesticity to her life here. 'I definitely wanted to be closer to friends and family,' she says of the move. The death of her mother last year made her more conscious of the distance involved in her life, and she has settled not far from where she grew up in Deansgrange. 'I've been waiting for so long to come back to Ireland. I think every Irish person who goes abroad looking for some kind of broader success is always thinking of how and when they can come home again.' Workwise, Slattery is hopeful that the move will turn out in her favour. 'I'm dying to get back to the theatre,' she says. 'There's so much to admire in Irish theatre and film at the moment. I want to do real work, good work here, collaborating with the artists I'm most excited by. People say there are no decent roles for women in their late thirties, but I think it's bullshit, especially in the theatre. There are so many stories that need to be told right now. I'm ready to start telling them.'

John placed the magazine back onto his lap and reached for his plate of chips. He glanced over to the boys, who were comfortable where they were. Was this what it felt like for the paranoid schizophrenic, he thought with a sweaty rush of panic, who watched the six o'clock news and thought the newsreader was speaking directly to him? He tried to stay calm. He could identify two things ringing in his mind from Frida's article. First there was her anger at his behaviour in the past – the way she misrepresented things he'd done, people he'd slept with years ago now. People he never even thought about anymore. A secondary school student, he thought with indignation. That girl had been an adult, and anyway, that was a misrepresentation of what had happened. But the way Frida talked, it made him feel on edge. It was a dangerous game, and one he'd assumed he hadn't been playing. And was he the director who she said had offered roles in exchange for sex? Surely not. Surely that wasn't at all a fair account of what had happened in New York.

And then there was also what he thought must be her desire to work with him again. To work in the theatre again, to tell her little stories. Could she have meant anything else? John stood up, walked into the kitchen, leaning his forehead against the cool glass pane in the backdoor. He opened his laptop, wrote her name in the search bar of his inbox. Their last emails from two years ago came up on the screen – the stilted, awkward exchange back when he was panicked about the women telling their stories.

No. Email wasn't right for this. He needed to talk to Frida the way they always had. The thing they had that night in New York, staying up late in the diner talking about everything, before they'd pushed it too far. Email was embarrassing. Imagine trying to explain all of this, the cottage, the boys, Kitty and the commissioner, within the rectangle text box of his inbox. No, he needed to be standing in front of her. He needed her to look him in the eye.

When they first met, Dublin had been a place where if you stood still long enough, the person you were looking for would walk right up to you. It gave life a tremendous feeling of fatefulness, of chance. But now they were older, and the city was sleeping. Frida was by the sea. He opened the magazine again and looked at the picture. Looked like Dun Laoghaire or thereabouts. Far outside his permitted radius. He would figure it out. He would circle the city all summer if he had to. He thought of himself in his running gear, cutting swathes through Dublin until he ran into her. John closed his email and went looking for For Frida.docx. Underneath all the stupid sentences he had written already, he started typing a new line.

```
What if she tells her story herself?
```

He could see her on the stage again. Alone, like when they'd done *Graceland*. Maybe no set. Maybe nothing but her and the light. Speaking about whatever it was that she needed to get off her chest. Speaking about him, if that was what she had to do. What might she say about him, given the chance? John felt nauseous at the very idea of it. But nausea was good, wasn't it?

2.

Summer, and thank God the shops had reopened. Frida took the Dart into the city centre to buy herself some new sheets, some towels. Lately she had been swimming in the sea almost every morning, dunking herself in the cold water like she was trying to wash something from herself. The shock of it had given her a decisive new taste for comfort. She bought herself one of the trendy insulated coats everyone had, as well as thick, expensive towels from Brown Thomas, and a new swimming costume in efficient, unremarkable navy.

The streets outside were half-quiet and she realised then what the difference was. No tourists. The crowds thinner, very pleasant. Like the city belonged to her and her alone. She had just chosen a bunch of dahlias from the sellers on Grafton Street and was heading down Duke Street towards the Dart when she saw him, John Reddan, sitting outside Davy Byrne's with a pint, a paperback and a plate of chips. For a second she thought to quicken her pace, but it was too late. His head turned and their eyes met.

'Frida Slattery,' he said, pronouncing her name low and slow. 'Fancy running into you.'

'God, John, how are you?' The words came out automatically, the way they did whenever she ran into somebody she knew on Grafton Street.

'I'm fine, very well.'

Frida clutched her flowers in their white paper to her chest. 'I was going to say I'm surprised to see you here, but I suppose I'm not surprised,' she said. 'Because I saw you on the television a few months back.'

He smiled. 'And I read your interview in the paper not long ago.'

'Some way we have of communicating with each other, eh?'

'Well,' he said with a roll of his eyes. 'I didn't choose to go on the *Late Late*. The theatre wanted me to try and drum up some buzz for the "Zoom play".'

He's so *important*, Frida thought. 'Oh yeah,' she said. 'I didn't catch that one. How did it go?'

'It went.'

'It's weird, isn't it? Work now. I've got nothing to do, I constantly feel like I should be doing something. But I don't know what it is.'

'We're all in the same boat. I heard your mum died last year. Sorry for your loss.'

She paused. 'Ah, thanks.'

'Had she been ill?'

'She'd had a stroke a few years back, and then a few more after that.'

'Jesus, horrible.' John leaned back on the bench, folding one arm behind his head.

'How's your family?' Frida asked politely.

'Barry? He's great, he and Joanna have managed to hole up in West Cork. That's the way to do lockdown, I reckon.'

'Oh right. I meant Kathy and the kids.'

'Ah, the boys are brilliant. Kitty and I are in the process of separating.'

'Jesus, I didn't know. I'm sorry to hear that.'

'Thanks.'

'A friend of mine, Sara, the showrunner on my old show, she used to say that you shouldn't apologise when people tell you're they're divorcing, you should congratulate them. Because if it's come to the point of divorce then usually things are so bad that divorce can only be a positive step.'

'I see.'

'But I'm guessing that's not really the case here.'

'Look,' John said. 'It is what it is. She seems happier now anyway.'

'She's in Dublin?'

'Yeah, they're in the house we were renting in Phibsborough. I'm staying in Stoneybatter but I'm going to need a more permanent solution soon.'

'You've both got custody?'

'It's being hammered out at the moment, but yes. Whereabouts are you?'

'In Monkstown. Also renting. Just thinking about what I want to do next.'

'Do you want to join me here?' He said it the way he always

used to say it. 'I think we're allowed to socialise as long as we're outside.'

'I don't know if it's a good idea.'

'What, having a pint? I don't have the virus, Frida.'

'John,' she said, smiling. 'Do you think we're old friends?'

'I would think that you could put it that way, yes.'

'Well, okay. I don't know if that's how I'd put it.'

'What would you say we are?'

Frida closed her eyes and thought. 'I think it's very complicated. When I saw you on TV, I felt really angry.'

He nodded. 'All the gender stuff, in your article. I get that. The whole male artist, male genius thing.'

'What? No. Not "the gender stuff", John.'

'Then what?'

She shook her head, exasperated. 'I don't know where to start.' She started rearranging her shopping bags in her hands as if to leave.

'Wait,' John said, standing up and stepping out in front of her. 'Wait a second, Frida. I read the interview. What you were saying about telling stories, other stories. I get it. I think I can help you.'

'Help me?'

He took a deep breath. 'Yes. Frida, I've been writing things for you my whole career. Even when we weren't talking to each other, I've always had you sitting there in my mind. And I'm writing something for you now. I want to show it to you. I think I can help you tell your stories, all the things that you want to talk about.'

'You can help me,' Frida repeated dryly.

'Yes.'

'Do you remember the last time we tried to write together?'

'Yeah. *Four and Ten*. It did quite well, if I recall.'

'Your *Four and Ten* did. That wasn't my play. You took me out of it entirely, and instead you made it about us in a way I never consented to.'

'Frida, I—'

'I just don't want to do this.'

'All of that was a long time ago.' There was, Frida thought, a hint of manic desperation in his eyes.

'Great bumping into you, John,' she said, and continued down the street.

On the Dart home Frida grinned behind her cotton face mask. Sometimes when washing the dishes or in the shower, Frida entertained elaborate fantasies of running into John somewhere, giving him an earful. It was undignified of her, but she indulged it anyway. Now she had just experienced the real thing, and it felt good, the image of him cowed, knowing that she was right and he was wrong. She had been measured, she thought as the Dart aligned itself with the edge of Dublin Bay. She had been, for the most part, reasonable.

His email arrived before dinner was ready. Frida wasn't surprised to see his name flash on her phone's screen. It felt inevitable. Pasta boiling on the stove, she sat at the table and opened it.

To: Frida Slattery
Subject: Today

Frida,

I am really glad that we bumped into each other today. To be honest, I'd been hoping we might since I found out we were both back in Dublin.

I want to apologise, but I don't exactly know where to start. I understand why you're angry. But I also want to know more about your side of things. From our conversation today I think it's clear we have different views of what has happened between us. When I think of the time we spent working together, and everything else that went with it, I think of good things, good work, good times.

I know I have made mistakes in my life. I am sorry that I hurt you.

I understand if you don't want to talk to me at all, but if you did, I'm here and I want to listen.

Yours, always,
John

Attached to the email was a document titled Frida Slattery Plays Herself.docx. Frida downloaded and opened it. It was not a script, really. She could see that immediately. She reckoned you might call it a treatment.

FRIDA SLATTERY PLAYS HERSELF

Summary

On a Dublin stage, the actor FRIDA SLATTERY has been cast in an unnamed one-woman play about trust, truth and creativity, in which she plays an actor named Frida Slattery. The unnamed play is written and directed by her former collaborator and ex-boyfriend, JOHN REDDAN.

SLATTERY brings her own motivations, secrets and desires to her performance in REDDAN's play. She has complex opinions and beliefs about art, gender and moral behaviour garnered from her own life experience.

When the curtain goes up, SLATTERY decides to go off-piste, ignoring the script REDDAN has written for her and instead taking this opportunity to reopen the cold case of their past and re-examine it on her own terms — their work together, the way they treated one another, the mistakes they've both made.

Character

Frida Slattery, age 39, white Irish woman 5'4", slight but strong frame, blonde curly hair, intelligent eyes, quick wit and razor tongue. Blue jeans and a white shirt, classical elegance. Bare feet on the stage. A woman who could convince any man of anything she wanted. One of the city's great beauties. Also an outstanding actress, much beloved by her peers and audiences. And, a startlingly good mimic. Maybe, perhaps, the second coming of Ingrid Bergman.

Frida's heart rate quickened. I'm thirty-eight, she thought indignantly. She exited out of her inbox and went looking in her contacts for John's number. She didn't have it. Back to her inbox, where she typed Can you call me please?, added her mobile number and hit send. She stood up and went to the hob, waiting while the saucepan of spaghetti bubbled away in front of her. Before the timer on her phone went off for the pasta water, John's number appeared on her screen.

'What is this?' she asked.

'What it looks like,' he replied. 'It's for you, obviously.'

'You want me to re-examine the past,' she said. 'That's what you wrote, right.'

'Look, I want you to go up there and talk about whatever you want. Drag me through the dirt if you must.'

'Why would you want that?'

'Frida,' he said. She could hear the urgency in his voice. 'Don't you think the best work of our lives has been the work we've made together? I'm not trying to dismiss your TV career, but come on. Think about it. Think about *Bird* and *Graceland. Four and Ten.*'

'You made *Four and Ten*.'

'I made it out of the thing you'd written. I made it out of us, sitting every day in a flat we used to live in together. A flat you left me in, Frida. I made it out of love for you.'

She said nothing.

'And all your best work has come from me talking about myself,' she said, thinking aloud.

'Yes. Yes. Exactly.'

She sighed, making a noise that was almost a laugh. 'Oh, God, John!'

'I know.'

'Can you hear yourself,' she said.

'I can. I can. Look, just meet with me. Let me know when suits you and we can meet and talk and figure this whole thing out.'

The alarm sounded on her phone then and they were both jolted by the noise of it. Frida switched it off.

'Oh God, John,' she said again, this time dragging out his name. 'I don't know. Let me think about it.'

She read through the document again while eating her anchovy pasta at the dining table. It was undeniably thrilling, thinking of the play that might emerge from a document like this. *Frida Slattery Plays Herself*. And they said there were no good roles for women her age. Frida would not have thought that she had the name recognition to appear in a show's title like that, but who was she to say otherwise?

Was this not the exact kind of theatre that she had been so keen to get back into? What was this if not a formal risk? She could only imagine what Mel would think, if Mel were still involved in Frida's career.

Okay, she typed to John in her email. Can you meet me at Seapoint tomorrow afternoon?

3.

When John arrived at Seapoint he could see Frida sitting on an orange towel on the concrete jetty, water dripping from her ponytail. She was wearing a navy-blue swimsuit, the kind that made her look like she was training for some kind of endurance event. Maybe she was. She spotted him walking towards her and stood up, wrapping her towel around her waist.

'Wait here,' she said, heading for the beach shelter to get changed.

John took a seat on a bench and looked out at Dublin Bay. The tide was in and the sea was busy with hardy-looking swimmers of all ages. It was not for him, this bracing open water, this earnest form of self-flagellation.

When she emerged again, Frida was dressed in a T-shirt and jeans. He thought that she didn't look at all remarkable here in this context, that probably nobody here knew she was someone who had been on television screens for years and who some people, not all people but certainly some people, would have considered a celebrity. She sat down on the bench beside him.

'Before we even think about any of this,' she said, 'there are some things I really need to talk about.'

John nodded.

She pulled a stainless-steel flask from her tote bag, unscrewing it to pour herself a cup of rust-coloured tea. 'I think my main concern is about your motivations in writing something like this. We haven't worked together or been in each other's lives for ten years. And my memories of those times are not exactly positive, you know. So I'm sitting here wondering, why have you started this now, what is it that you want to get from me?'

John crossed his legs at the ankle and leaned forward on the bench. 'It's what I said yesterday on the phone. I think we do our best work together. When we were young and writing together, I thought that we had the rest of our lives to keep going, to get better and better. And as it turned out, life wasn't like that. Don't you think the age we are now, Frida, this time in our lives, you can feel the clock starting to run down?'

Frida took a gulp of tea, starting straight ahead at the horizon. 'So, you want another go because you think it'll keep you young and relevant.'

'God, no. Nothing like that. I just want – the separation, the time I've been spending on my own, it has me thinking about what I want from my life. And I want to make work with you, Frida. I don't want to shoot car ads or make horror movies or operas. I want to make really fucking good plays with you.'

'So yeah, exactly. And I want to know why you want that from me.'

John glanced at her, brow furrowed in confusion. 'Because

it's real. When we work together we make real work, stuff that is difficult and emotional and yet still entertaining.'

'Well, we did once. Over a decade ago.'

He nodded eagerly. 'Yes.'

'But that work you made, John,' Frida said, then placed a hand on her breastbone. 'It took something from me, and turned it into something from you.'

'What do you mean?'

'I mean you didn't always treat me fairly. You treated me like something you could mine and extract and sell onwards. Now that I'm older and I have some distance from it – well, the whole thing feels a lot more transactional now.'

'So that's why you hate me,' he said. 'You think I used you.'

'Oh, John,' she said slowly. 'I don't hate you. It's not that. It's so much more complicated. You don't – you don't know what it's like to be an actor, to be a woman, even. You go through life thinking everyone is using you in some way. You get used to it quickly. And when you do complain about it, you feel like a bit of a bitch.'

John went quiet, folding his arms. 'You know I was heartbroken when you left.'

'What?'

'When you went to Los Angeles. I thought it would kill me. Watching your taxi pull off the curb outside the flat. Our flat. Your flat.'

'Don't try to guilt-trip me, John. I had to take that job.'

'I'm not trying to guilt you! I thought we were speaking openly here.'

Frida raked a hand through her hair. 'Fine.'

'Also hang on. You didn't have to take that job. You wanted to, which was fine, whatever. But nobody put a gun to your head. You were going to be in *Four and Ten*. It was going to be both our names on the poster again. Don't talk about it like you were backed into a corner.'

She said nothing, and he looked at her, waiting. She shook her head, like she was saying, so what?

'Frida,' he said once more. 'You really broke my heart. Just remember that when you're drawing up what you think is the complex power dynamic that exists between us. You were the one with the power. You were beautiful and charismatic and I was absolutely crazy about you. And I know you knew that.'

Leaning forward, Frida placed the flask down on the concrete between them.

John continued on. 'I know it's easy for you to believe that I was some evil patriarchal man who used you up and got to benefit from your good reviews. But I just think it's a lot more complicated—'

'John,' she said, interrupting him. 'In New York you told me if I didn't take the morning-after pill you wouldn't work with me again. Many people would consider that to be blackmail.'

John felt his face blanch. He swallowed hard. 'I don't think that was the conversation we had. That's not exactly how I remember it.'

'No. You called me up after my interview and said it would be best if I took Plan B because you wanted us to be able to work together in the future.'

From the next bench two older women in Dryrobes fell quiet, flicking their gaze over to them.

'I asked you if you were planning to take it,' he said quietly. 'I would never threaten you.'

'That is not at all how I remember it,' she said.

'Well, I remember it differently,' he said flatly.

'Okay, but bear in mind what I do for a living. I literally memorise things.'

'I don't know, Frida,' he said, his voice rising. 'I was just worried and I felt guilty.'

'Yeah, well.'

He watched as Frida took a pair of gold-rimmed aviator sunglasses from her pocket and put them on.

'Look, I'm sorry for that,' he said. 'I have behaved really badly over the years. I know that. To you, to Kitty. To countless others, probably.'

'John Reddan, the top shagger,' Frida said dryly.

Two seagulls landed in front of their bench, one fixing a large glassy eye on John.

'I suppose that comes back to what I'm worried about, too,' she continued. 'That you're here looking for absolution. Your wife has left you, you're out of work, you run into me. And you think that if you win my approval again, your guilt goes away. You get to be free.'

'I don't know if that's a fair appraisal of things.'

'But it's what it looks like from here. Look, John,' Frida paused, gesturing out to the open blue expanse of Dublin Bay. 'I've been swimming in there every single day the last few months. It's really, really cold. At first I kept thinking, well okay, if I come back tomorrow I'll have acclimatised a little more and it'll be easier. But do you know what?'

'What?'

'It doesn't get any fucking easier. I just get used to it. That's all.'

'I don't get it.'

'What's there to get? All my life I've been getting in the cold water of my work. I've been making myself uncomfortable so that the show can go on. So that others can get things made, and we can have a nice time. And it's just gotten to a point where all I can think of is, like, why not turn the heating on? Why not make things easy for myself? I thought that I'd get that from *The Reason* and in the end it just got so messy. I can't do that again with you, John. It can't be like how it was when we were together. I know there were two of us in it and it wasn't just you being a prick. And when you talk about making art the way you do, well, God, you know how that makes me feel. You know that I want to make good things with you. Oh, Jesus. I suppose what I'm wondering now, if we are going to do this, is how can we make it different this time?'

'You can go up there and say whatever you want. You can say all of this, if you feel like it.'

'But that's hardly a play, is it?'

John laughed, the noise hollow. 'Who fucking knows?'

Frida stood up, taking her tote bag. 'I'm getting cold. Okay, John. Every time I think about doing this, I get a sort of sick feeling in the pit of my stomach. But when I think about the alternative, you know, not working together, not talking to you, not seeing you. Well, that seems boring.'

She smiled at him but the smile seemed to be entirely for her own benefit.

'Send me over what you have,' she said. 'I'll start making some notes for you.'

In the cottage John opened up his laptop and started looking back over his notes. How was he to know what was in Frida's mind? It had been terrifying, hearing her talk to him like that. Accusing him of blackmail! Like all along he had been living two lives without knowing, one where he could oversee his actions and his consciousness. And another one, where he was cruel to all the people he loved most.

Maybe this was a terrible idea. The woman with the most knowledge of some of John's worst deeds, and he was inviting her to go up there and tell the world about him. What would his family think? He imagined Barry slapping him hard on the back of his head, calling him a fucking idiot. Kitty in the audience, curling her lower lip and leaning in to tell the commissioner something. Trying to take the kids away from him. Could the stakes really be that high? He remembered an early review of *Graceland* that he hadn't wanted Frida to read, one of the newspaper critics who'd thought the play he'd written was just gossip, or John enacting revenge on a man who'd bedded his girlfriend before him. He didn't care about reviews anymore, but what would they say about this? This idea he had was self-indulgent. That was undeniable. The whole thing was dependent on Frida lifting it to a new level, taking the audience with them as they rose. Same as it ever was, he thought.

In the evening Kitty dropped over the boys. The two lads fought in the kitchen while he cooked spaghetti bolognese. Over dinner Fionn kicked Ruadhán under the table and Ruadhán looked to his father, clearing his throat. The boys had decided that John should get a dog. Kitty would never get a dog, they reported, and so it was up to John to sort this out.

'I'll think about it,' he said, spooning parmesan onto his bowl.

'We'd like a labradoodle,' Fionn added.

'The curly things? Absolutely no way.'

'Dad!'

'Where would he sleep? On my bed?'

After dinner they all watched TV, John drinking a beer on the couch and texting Frida. He typed: I know you're not sure about this. Neither am I but I think that's a good sign.

It was an attempt to ease his own mind, but if it had the effect of easing hers, too, then that was a bonus. He was about to send another message along the lines of 'The making of good art requires the makers to be uncomfortable' when he read back over it and imagined Frida rolling her eyes at him in her empty flat.

It was likely that if they didn't make this play, Frida would talk anyway. She'd mentioned writing a book in the magazine interview, and maybe it was meant to be a joke but John could picture it. Someone would definitely publish it. That thought was even more frightening to John than sitting in front of Frida in Seapoint, listening to her listing his various crimes. Turn it into a Reddan/Slattery production, he thought, and maybe he had a chance to control the narrative a little bit. Or maybe he didn't. But maybe even if she made him look awful, tried to ruin him, he had a chance to get something from it anyhow, to earn a decent reception, a critic calling him brave or a boundary-pusher or an innovator. Other men wouldn't have the guts to do this, he thought with certainty, and the thought was a balm to all his insecurity. He felt physically strong, like the swimmers he'd watched in Dublin Bay that afternoon. Though maybe he also felt a little cynical.

Beside him Fionn clamoured onto Ruadhán, trying to pull the blue woven blanket over his little knees. Stop, Ruadhán said, and John leaned over, primed to tell them to stop fighting, when Ruadhán took the blanket and shook it out, pushing half over his little brother's lap and half over his own.

13. *Frida Slattery Plays Herself*
(Frida Slattery and John Reddan), 2021

1.

By the time *Frida Slattery Plays Herself* had been announced and tickets put on sale, the script had still not been finalised. To call it a script at all, Frida thought darkly as she sat at her kitchen table, staring at the latest document emailed by John, would be rich.

The process had been stop-start. In the weeks after she'd bumped into John on Grafton Street, they'd only managed to meet a couple of times, sitting in Frida's living room with the garden doors open for ventilation. Extra jumpers on as the weather began to turn. The stray cat she'd adopted passing through at her leisure. Work, if you could call it that, was mostly a case of getting to know each other once again. Filling in some of the blanks of the past ten years.

Then the country was ordered back under lockdown and Frida was alone again for most of the winter, staring at the Word document. It was little more than a bullet-point list of ideas, the vaguest gesturing towards the kind of person Frida Slattery might portray as herself on stage. Weeks passed this way, and she was grateful for the existence of the play, theoretical as it still was. The document, her daily swim, her video calls with her nieces. There was nearly nothing else in Frida's life that winter. But little progress was made, and when Frida and John spoke on the phone she felt further from him than ever. It was almost like she'd made the whole thing up.

In the spring, energy returned. Katie MacGowan found them a good theatre with a slot in the calendar for later in the year, tentative as it may be, and John was able to come over to Frida's once again. From the first visit, he was full of momentum. On the doorstep he went to hug her and they both pulled away suddenly, mindful of contagion. Not wanting to touch at all. In her living room, she watched John sit down on the armchair. His limbs as long and gangly as ever, making her normal-sized furniture look like it was made for children.

He told her that he wanted more input from Frida, that he wanted the script to be hers. So she did what she always used to do. She told him stories about her work, about Kara, about decisions Frida herself had made, all her complicated thoughts on what it was to be a woman telling stories about your own life, and he sat there on the armchair in front of her, recording on his phone so he could type her stories up later on.

At first it felt exciting, the wide-open possibilities of it. And to be working with John again was a little bit wild and strange, like getting dressed in the clothes she'd worn in her early twenties and finding they still fit perfectly. In a way she liked the changes they'd made, the fact that they were doing this in plain sight rather than under the guise of friendship like they had years before. Lately, though, the project had begun to feel deadening.

'Good,' John said urgently when she told him this while rehearsing in her living room one afternoon. 'That's good. We want to embrace all the difficult parts, not run from them.'

Frida frowned. 'After all this, don't you think that audiences are just going to want some straightforward entertainment?'

'Ha!' he said, rising to his feet from her armchair. 'I don't give a flying fuck what audiences want. They'll eat what they're served.'

'You must be a hell of a parent, John,' she said.

Frida had recently met the boys for the first time. He'd brought them swimming in Seapoint one sunny afternoon, and had texted her from the Dart. She came down with a roll of chocolate digestives and a flask of tea. The little one, Fionn, looking so much like a miniature version of John that Frida felt unnerved by him peering at her from inside his beach-towel cocoon, his hair all sticking up just like his father's. John did seem like a good parent, attentive, encouraging, reaching for one boy or the other with long arms to stop them falling off a curb or a bench. Frida was dying to know what Kitty's take on him was.

But good God, was John Reddan the adult man annoying. He cycled nowadays. That was his new thing. She'd never thought he'd end up a cyclist, but now he arrived at her flat most weekday afternoons, covered in sweat and wheeling the bike into her narrow hallway, leaning it against the wall. Then going through to the living room and sitting down immediately on her nice armchair. The armchair she'd taken from her mother's flat, which she now thought of mostly as Pádraigín the cat's chair, old worn mustard velvet against which John pressed his damp T-shirt as Frida watched with lips pursed. She offered him use of her shower, and only once had he taken it. She caught a glimpse of him through the chink in her bedroom door, his shirt off and one of her swimming towels around his waist. He was built now, in a way he'd never been when they were together. His shoulders and back were dense with unfamiliar muscle. She imagined him with a lockdown exercise routine, daily press-ups on the floor of his living room. The unchecked vanity of a man his age.

Usually, though, John just got on with things. Exhaled heavily, sat down and sweated directly onto her furniture while he took various papers from his backpack. Work to do, apparently. Had he always been like this? Had she just been charmed by it in the past? He didn't seem to think about people who were not John Reddan. Self-absorbed to the nth degree. Frida supposed that she'd once viewed this as a positive quality, the necessary trait for an artist to produce important work. Now she thought there was probably no work so important as to necessitate acting like a dickhead. He made fun of her for things like her diet and her daily yoga. You're like, *sooooo* LA, he told her in a stupid voice. She watched him rifle through her bookshelves, taking out a copy of Stoppard's *The Real Thing* and leafing through the pages. When he found the line he wanted, he slammed the book shut and tossed it carelessly onto the ground.

'Hey,' she said. 'Do you mind not fucking my books around the place?'

'It's the wrong edition,' he said. 'I'll have to find mine in Phibsborough later.'

John insisted on drinking coffee basically constantly, rinsing out the French press and refilling it all afternoon and into the evening. He left the coffee grounds in the sink for her to deal with. Frida drank one coffee a day, which she purchased from a van on the seafront after her swim and made last all morning. After that, she switched to herbal tea.

'I don't know how you sleep at night.'

'Whiskey helps,' he said, grinning at her while rolling another cigarette by the kitchen window.

God, he is embarrassing, she thought. So undergraduate. Far too old to be acting like this. Was he putting it on for her sake? She wished that he wouldn't. She poured hot water over a camomile teabag in her mug and went back to the living room, lying down on the couch that came with the flat. Outside the sky was starting to grow dark as the evening rolled in.

The small pink notebook Sophie had given her was filled with Frida's notes, dating back to the start of lockdown. She opened it on her lap now, tapping the end of a biro on the page. She was thinking of John's original treatment. He'd mentioned trust, truth and creativity. It was Frida's job to bring her own thoughts on all of this to bear. But that was the problem. Alone in her flat with her notebook, it was easy to think through the events of her life, the details of her work and her relationships.

But with John here, making coffee in the next room, waiting for her to come up with something brilliant, it felt impossible. What did he want from her? What could she reasonably give him? The story of their past, he'd suggested originally. But that wasn't interesting enough, was it? It was just a stupid relationship they'd had when they were young. And now Frida was here, trying to turn all of that into something people might care about. What was original or interesting about it?

John came into the living room with his coffee mug.

'I don't know if I can do this,' she said.

'What's the problem?' he said, sitting down in the armchair opposite.

'I don't think this is interesting enough. I don't think I'm interesting enough.'

He leaned forward. 'Good. Put that in. Instead of being worried about not being interesting enough, just put in a section about how it feels to need to be interesting enough.'

'You really think we can just make art out of anything at all.'

'Of course we can! Who is to tell us we can't? Put your whole self into it, Frida, say it with your chest, and we'll get away with whatever we want.'

'You are ridiculous.'

From the armchair he grinned at her. It was a look of utter confidence, so brazen that she had to laugh.

'You used to believe that all this stuff meant something,' she said. 'I just realised that.'

'Oh, I don't know if that's true.'

'No, I remember that guy. He used to think that if you wrote something and put it on stage and it all worked together, people would feel changed by it. He went on and on about it.'

'I'll let you in on a little secret, Frida. That guy was just trying to impress you.'

Frida looked at him. He had one leg over the arm of her armchair, sitting like a lanky teenage boy.

'Did it work?' he asked.

'John,' she said, shaking her head. 'Can we try to do some work here?'

It was getting weirder, she thought, doing the washing-up after he'd cycled off into the night later on. At first the two of them had been so cagey around each other, treading carefully as if the ground between them was littered with old landmines. But with each afternoon spent in each other's company, things were changing. John was more comfortable in her presence now. Not just the way he smoked in her kitchen and sat in her armchair. It was just like he said: he wasn't trying to impress her anymore. He was less careful with her, with their connection. He said things that he must know might hurt her – off-hand comments about her acting, about the way she kept her flat, about the love she had for little Pádraigín. She had thought that the thing that linked them after all this time was gossamer thin, delicate as silk. John was treating it like the heavy coil of rope that kept an ocean liner attached to the dock.

And funny all the same that he wasn't trying to direct her.

That would have been the return to form that Frida anticipated. But no, he was keeping a distance from that side of things, instead just egging her on, always encouraging her. Frida thought she was being cynical, maybe, but it seemed suspicious. Like he was trying to coax something out of her without her knowing. The other day he suggested that if she got stuck on stage, she should just start talking about their relationship.

'Tell them all about the two of us, right from the very beginning, and leave nothing out,' he said, his voice urgent and probing.

When she went to bed, turned off the lights and listened to the quiet street outside her window, Pádraigín curled at the end of the bed, she couldn't get John off her mind. Not the John of a few hours ago, but the one who had taken up space in her thoughts her whole adult life. Regret, maybe, about the decisions she'd made, the way she'd left, the space *The Reason* had taken up. Because he'd been potential, hadn't he, the thing you have in spades when you're that age, the thing you have so much of that you can't see it at all until it has gone and you're thirty-eight, alone in bed in the dark with a tortoiseshell cat you found in the back garden.

And was that John one and the same as the divorced dad with the bike she knew now? They looked so alike. The same rangy form that she had found herself enveloped in, the same doormat-thick spiky hair, though grey all over now. The same gentle, coaxing interest he'd always had in her. Tell me Frida, tell me, tell me.

She was always going to worry that he was using her, she

thought. That meant their relationship would always be odd in some respects. Could Frida live with that? Or even, could she work and act under those conditions? She could, she thought. But she'd need to do some things her way.

2.

They were standing at the traffic lights at D'Olier Street one afternoon when they saw it. A bus was passing through towards College Green and on the side of it was a banner ad that John and Frida had signed off a couple of weeks earlier. On one end there was a picture of Frida's face in profile, mouth set in a firm line. Then the title, in block capitals: *Frida Slattery Plays Herself*. At the other end, Frida's face again in profile, facing back towards herself, this time her mouth in a wide, sinister grin.

'There,' John called, fumbling with his phone to open the camera.

'Oh God,' Frida said, turning away from the bus. 'No, no, no.'

'What? It looks amazing.'

She went to the doorway of a nearby newsagent, wobbling a little on her legs like a small deer. There she sank into a squat against the shop door.

'Frida,' John said. 'Are you okay?'

'Yep,' she called, her voice muffled. Her head was buried into her knees. 'Just a little light-headed all of a sudden.'

'The ad looks really good,' he added, trying to show her the image he'd managed to snap on his phone.

'Mmhmm.'

'What's wrong?'

'Nothing.'

'Is it all just a bit ...' he trailed off, looking for the right word. 'Overwhelming?'

'Mmhmm.'

With one hand he leaned down and stroked her soft hair, the way he did to the boys when they were sick. It's the delay, he thought, it's not good for a person's disposition to deal with so much change and delay. It made the thing you were working on seem larger than life, divorced of all the context that would usually surround it. The play had been pushed back once more, but this time everyone seemed certain that this was it, that when it opened it would coincide with a great, society-wide reopening. This made the delay a good thing in John's eyes. He felt that the production was lucky, maybe even slightly blessed. He thought that he and Frida were part of something much wider than themselves. It was an uncommon feeling to have at this stage of a new work.

The other thing that was special about this play was that it was Frida's. His name had sailed by on the side of the bus, yes, but in much smaller text, so small you'd barely see it unless you were looking for it.

'Okay,' she said. Slowly, she rose to her feet, grabbing his forearm for support.

John wrapped an arm around her waist for support as they crossed the road. 'I gotcha. You know the show is going to be fine, right? We've been blowing it up into this huge, life-changing, earth-shattering thing for so long now. But fundamentally it's just another play.'

'Ugh, I know,' Frida said. She tilted her head, resting it for a moment against his side and John was surprised by the immediate flicker of his heart rate, like the switching-on of the electrics in some old derelict house. Zip into life again, and then her head was back upright and they were not touching at all.

For months in that stupid bloody cottage John had stared at his laptop alone and thought about watching Frida Slattery at work. Now he did the real thing almost every day, sitting in her yellow armchair, almost drunk on it. Like a young man again. The way her face changed. She was older now, still so gorgeous that it was distracting. Constantly John wanted to kiss her when they were in her living room, but he was very aware of how it could ruin things between them again. But then sometimes she acted like she wanted that, too. The night a few weeks ago when she'd brought out a bottle of wine to celebrate the script being 'finished'. She'd turned off the top light and lit a row of candles along the mantelpiece; wasn't that romantic? Wasn't that a way of marking a prelude to something? And soon they were listening to old country music that he knew she loved, whining voices and gentle guitars. The two of them on the couch together, her feet poking out from the edge of the woollen rug draped over her knees. He knew he couldn't kiss her, no, it would be far too much of a risk. But he could always talk to her.

'Do you ever think about what might have happened if

you'd stayed in London?' he'd asked when they opened the second bottle.

She stared at him from the other end of the couch. 'I don't know if there's a point to wondering about that,' she replied.

'Okay,' he said, and they both fell quiet.

'We could maybe put it in the script, though,' she added, gazing out the window. Then she extended her legs out on the couch so they were touching his, like they were two old friends so comfortable with each other's bodies that they could just sit like this. For a while, the two of them sat there like that, not talking, making their way through the bottle.

3.

A week before rehearsals at the theatre were at last scheduled to begin, Frida went away with Edel and Ian and the girls. It was the August bank holiday, and Ian had borrowed a house in Kerry for a few days. On the long drive down, Frida sat beside her nieces on their phones, staring out the window while her mind went blank. She needed this break so badly. For weeks now she had felt addled, wound up, with thoughts about the play. The best part of a year thinking about it, rehashing years of her life spent in John's orbit. Seeing the poster on the bus the other day – awful. She'd gone home that night and tried to book a flight to London. The airline website kept telling her there was a problem with her card details and when she tried again, she got a text from her bank to say her card had been compromised somehow and frozen. What were the chances, she thought. She'd lain down on her bed beside the cat, staring at the ceiling.

And still there were things yet to be decided. Even now the script was no more than a series of bullet points and suggested topics, segues and the most abstract of stage directions. John was so happy about that. Frida was terrified by it. Katie MacGowan thought the pair of them were insane, but she declared that she'd long since given up on trying to talk sense into John Reddan.

What John kept saying was that the fear was a good sign, the fear meant they were on their way somewhere important. The thought that she continually came back to while she was in the sea or washing her hair or trying to read was that John meant they were on their way somewhere together. Frida was unsure about whether that was a good thing. It was an uncertainty she'd had ever since she'd run into him on Grafton Street the previous summer.

She tried to explain that to Edel while the five of them were walking through Killarney National Park the next day, the sisters a few paces behind Ian and the girls.

'I feel like I've been listening to you talk about that man for half my life,' Edel said.

'In fairness, Edel, there was a long period there where I didn't mention him at all.'

'Well, you're making up for lost time now, anyway. Do you know what I think?'

'What?'

'I think he's in love with you,' Edel said to her in the offhand and devastating manner particular to sisters. 'And I think you know that, and maybe you like that.'

Frida kicked a clod of dirt in the path ahead of them. It broke up on impact, dusting the toe of her white trainer.

'It's okay if you do,' Edel said. 'I'm not judging you. Life's way too short for that. And I think his attention is probably very flattering, right?'

'I don't know if that's how it is,' Frida said with irritation. 'I don't think you understand what it's like to be an actor.'

'I certainly don't.'

'Hmm.'

'I'm just speaking as your sister, Free. But maybe I shouldn't have said anything.'

Since the death of their mother, Frida and Edel had reconfigured how to act around each other. Grief had had different effects on the two of them. Edel said she was going through a second adolescence; on the other hand, Frida felt a hollow kind of independence that she thought must finally be the mark of adulthood. Maybe other women felt this way when they had children of their own, she reasoned.

The five of them reached a café by the lake's shore where they ordered toasted sandwiches and chips. Frida had the feeling she often had with Edel's family, like she was pressed up against glass peering through at something she herself would never have. Most of the time it didn't bother her anymore. Edel had started her family so early that it had always seemed foreign to Frida. For years she had flickered back and forth on the topic of whether or not she herself wanted children, but in her early thirties found a lot of comfort in the idea that she 'just hadn't met anyone she can really see herself with yet'. The rupture and removal of her left ovary hadn't necessarily rendered Frida infertile, but it did mean that conceiving would be at least 50 per cent more difficult, according to the consultant, and to Frida it was as if the door had started to close at that point. Maybe if she'd stayed with Kara, but there were so many reasons why that hadn't worked out. Now she was sat at a picnic bench with two teenagers, both of whom looked quite a bit like Frida, actually, and one of whom, Sophie, had her same capacity for mimicry. It is good to be their aunt, she thought, aware that she repeated this in her head often.

In the evening they made pizzas with an array of different toppings and the three adults went off down to the pub on the main street while the girls stayed home to watch TV. Frida got the first round in.

'How are you feeling about your play, Frida?' Ian asked. 'The great return to the stage.'

'That's a sensitive question, Ian,' Edel said.

'No, it's okay,' Frida said. 'I'm nervous. But also I guess I'm excited about getting started.'

'You're working with John Reddan again? I didn't like that movie he did. Shite, actually.'

'Yeah, it wasn't good, was it? Well, I didn't see it, but that seems to be consensus.'

Edel moved the ice around her glass with her straw. 'We think John is in love with Frida.'

'Aha!' Ian said, looking at Frida with a big grin.

'Edel thinks that,' Frida corrected. 'I think we are two people working together in a complicated industry.'

'But wait, he's divorced, right? And he wrote a play for you, with your name in the title?'

Frida nodded at her brother-in-law. 'Well, we wrote it together, but yeah.'

'Yeah, that is all pretty damning, I have to say,' Ian said. 'I'd say that lad is in love with you.'

'But how do you feel about him,' Edel asked. 'That's what I want to know.'

'Yes, will the play end with the two of you driving off into the sunset together?'

Frida put her hands over her face. 'I don't know! No! I don't know how the play ends but it's definitely not that kind of thing.'

'Sorry,' Edel said. 'Did you just say you don't know how the play ends?'

'I don't want to get into it,' Frida replied.

'Well, I can't wait to see it,' Ian said, raising his pint glass in salute.

Frida found herself smiling now, almost chuckling to herself. It was such a lovely surprise, to have this time with her family. A simple break from John and the play was providing a form of relief that she hadn't realised she'd needed. And it was clarifying something in her mind, something about the work. It was dripping slowly through her mind now, the idea of it. In the dark corner of an old pub in Kerry, she began to realise what it would take to play Frida Slattery.

4.

'I still don't understand it,' said Kitty in the kitchen of her new house in Rathmines. It was Ruadhán's tenth birthday, and they'd just returned from a picnic in the park. 'This play. Is it a play or is it like, stand-up?'

'Jesus, Kitty, it's definitely not stand-up,' John said.

'But it's not scripted,' she said, pouring tea for both of them. 'So she just goes up there and talks, and much of what she says is about you.'

'I don't know what she's going to say.'

'So how is it a play then? God, John, of all the work you could've made with this woman.'

He could hear Kitty's dislike of Frida in her voice. During their relationship John had always tried to mention Frida as little as possible, the way you were supposed to do with the big ex-girlfriend. In retrospect, his reticence to discuss her had only drawn more attention to how big this ex-girlfriend was in his life. In their mediation sessions, when John was busy admitting to the infidelity of the last few years, he had managed not to name Frida specifically. But when he looked at his ex-wife now, he thought that somehow, surely, she must be able to tell.

'When you see it you'll understand,' John said with unearned confidence. He himself was almost as unsure about the play as Kitty was, and far more anxious, considering all the possible things Frida might do or say on stage. 'Look, there's a play within a play. So what you'll see is an actress, in this case Frida Slattery, about to go on stage in a play, which you won't see. And she's killing time backstage by talking about herself and her work.'

'Okay,' Kitty said slowly.

'You're not the only one a little confused. I did an interview yesterday and the journalist's eyebrows were disappearing into her hairline. But when you see it, I think it'll all come together.'

'What does Alice think of it?'

John looked to the ceiling and let out an ironic laugh. 'I think her words were, "I can't stop you, John."'

'Well, I'm looking forward to it,' Kitty said in a cool voice.

Since they'd entered into a formal separation agreement, things had been easier between them. It was painful, still, to see Kitty in the new house she'd bought with Niall O'Donovan, whom John had no choice but to hate. But he found that he could tamp the emotion down for long periods. Nobody would know how it made him feel. The work was helping, as was the time he spent on his new bike. The fear John had had when they'd first separated, that he would become a man utterly alone in the world, had dissipated. Funny how a few healthy distractions could do that. He was in the process of buying a house in Harold's Cross, near where he had once lived with Barry. He found he could mark time by the way the boys changed and grew. Something outside of himself, for once. It was only on these pickups and drop-offs, these hinges in his daily life, that he even needed to talk to Kitty. Maybe she would resent him forever, but if so, he found he didn't really care. Her life was almost unrecognisable: this big red-brick house, the sprawling garden where the boys played, this man, Niall O'Donovan, who apparently really loved her. Niall was about ten years older than John, gregarious and yet almost contrived in his friendliness, with a halo of grey curls on top of his head. He had a deep laugh and a clammy, tight handshake that John dreaded receiving. But he supposed that all of this was what Kitty had always wanted, and now she was able to have it with someone who was actually there with her, wanting it too. For so long John had been lying to her in one form or other, keeping much of his inner life from her. Now he could do so without guilt, without worrying about hurting her, and in that way he thought that Kitty had given him a wonderful gift. It was a second chance at being himself.

5.

Alone in her flat, Frida dialled John's number. She needed to tell him that she was having a little wobble. Three days until opening and it was more impossible than ever, the idea of her going out on stage as herself. 'Herself', whoever that was. When John eventually picked up the phone she could hear the kids in the background. He said that he was about to drop them back to Kitty's, but he could meet Frida in town after that.

'Kehoe's?' she suggested, pulling on her denim jacket.

On the Dart into town, Frida ran through all the times in the past when she'd had a little wobble. Usually it was picking up a script for the first time, meeting someone she knew she needed to impress. She had the same concern as always. Do I really know how to do this?

But wasn't this all she had ever done? Since she had been a girl on the bike home from school, lines from *Macbeth* or *Hamlet* echoing in her head from English class before the bell rang.

A girl on the bike, the wind dancing in her hair because she never bothered with the helmet back then until she got within sight of the house, pedalling and thinking of the world outside the school. Frida hadn't wanted fame or stardom or name-in-lights or the gold statuette in those days. She just wanted the feeling. The feeling she got when she came off stage. Like she was on fire.

Like she was the fire.

But it had been so long ago. Now all Frida could think about was herself. That was the problem with this play. She thought of herself when rereading the script, herself when her back ached on the rolled-out yoga mat, herself on the Dart now, the coastline zipping by, the pale reflection of her face in the carriage window. The lines on her face, like a child had gone over her reflection with black crayon. Hadn't bothered to keep up the fillers since leaving LA.

And it used to be easier, didn't it?

What had happened to Frida Slattery?

Age. Years. Decisions. Too much to enumerate. The Dart pulled into Pearse and she got off, walking down the long ramp to Westland Row. Was she the same girl she'd been on the bike? What parts of her had changed? She rarely had to think about this question in California. In Dublin, though, Frida couldn't hide from it. Every street she walked down held some ghost version of her, younger, more naive or maybe less, more hopeful or maybe more scared. The version of herself who had been in love with someone whose surname she couldn't recall, or jealous of a woman who was dead now. She saw a bar in which she used to drink, a theatre where she once worked, the pub where she'd met the man who made her into Frida Slattery for the very first time.

Frida's breath caught in her throat and for a second she felt it again, the feeling of falling, the edges of her vision flickering black for just a split second. And she regained herself and tried to remember what it had felt like when all of this was new to her.

A teenager cycling home from school. The thing she used to tell herself before she got on stage in front of everyone in the school concert hall. I can go out there and pretend.

Trick them, fool them, convince them of my worth. Trick them into thinking that Frida was confident or interesting or valuable.

She did it over and over, every time she went to work. Get up there before the cameras and pretend.

Trick the Lunds into thinking she was better than a cable TV actress. The summer after Una's first stroke, she'd returned to Hollywood two weeks later and told them they should write parental grief into the next season for Kathleen. The Lunds exchanged a look like, would that really be okay? Sara clearing her throat, tapping her pen on the script in front of her.

Do you need more time, Frida? We can always write you out for another few episodes if you want to go back to Ireland.

Absolutely not.

Frida was fine. Unhappy but here, anyway. She always took whatever happened to her and put it on the stage beside her. Like a wheelie suitcase dragged through an endless airport terminal. Me and my emotional baggage, ha.

Was it normal? No, but it was Frida Slattery. Remember John Reddan in the backroom of some pub years ago quoting Nora Ephron at her. Everything is copy. How funny, that there was a time when she could hear a quote like that and just decide to make it a part of her. That there had been a time when she had the choice of what to take on and what to leave behind.

And in the present moment she was walking through town to the pub, probably that same pub where John was waiting for her right now.

Always her life had been one foot in front of the other. One job, one day at the office, one day at a time. One more person to impress. Frida had never bothered to look past it. Why was she doing it? Where did it come from? Why was she a success, if she was one at all? Why was she here now?

John Reddan had once thought she was decent. Her whole career, these last sixteen years, because a man named John Reddan looked at her as she sat on a stool in an audition room, reading a script and he thought, She's decent.

But was she decent? Frida didn't think so.

Maybe it was like Edel and Ian said. John was in love with her.

And wouldn't that be mortifying, if she got up on stage in three nights' time, and as the play unfolded it became clear to the world that this was just a director in love with an actress. Nothing more to show for themselves than that.

She remembered the first time in the room for *Bird*. Him losing interest as she'd fumbled through the script. Devastating script, so much of John the little boy poured into it. And the other actor, Chris, so good, so delicate with all the raw pain of the grown man there in the lines as he read through the pages.

But when it got to Frida, Reddan wasn't sure.

She saw him chewing the end of his biro.

She saw him jiggle one of his legs, sneak a look out the window.

She remembered thinking, I have to get him on side.

He said that they should take a break, the three of them taking out their tobacco and papers in sync. Turning on the radio. Talking about something on television the night before.

She remembered trying to do her impressions, cycling through a couple. Trying to make him laugh.

And John Reddan did laugh.

Frida thought, Well, that is nice. Having John Reddan think that I'm funny or interesting or valuable, yes that feels very nice.

She didn't realise she'd end up trying to do it for sixteen more years.

And now she was pushing open the door of the same pub where they'd first met, going to meet that man again and here he was, sitting on a barstool, resting an arm on the counter looking at her.

John rose to give her a hug of greeting, signalled to the barman for a pint.

Here he was, waiting for her to sit down on the stool beside him, waiting for her to start talking. Frida was so tired of talking. Always trying to convince someone of something, always pretending to be something else.

'You okay?' John asked her.

She ran a hand through her hair uneasily. 'I don't know if I can do this. The play.'

'You're still on that.'

'It's not the play,' she said. 'It's us.'

He shifted his weight beneath him. 'What about us?'

'When I'm with you,' she said, 'I don't know who I am.'

'Go on.'

It was so much easier to talk to him when she wasn't looking at him. Frida let her eyes drift to the row of whiskey bottles on the wall, lit from behind. 'You asked me the other day if I ever think about what would've happened if I'd stayed with you in London,' she said. 'And I don't, not really. But I think a lot about what would've happened if we hadn't met when we did. When we were young. I was thinking about it on the way in here. I wonder if I would've had the career I've had. If I would've had an acting career at all. I worry sometimes that you're the only reason I ever got anywhere.'

John was shaking his head. 'Absolutely not. You're very, very talented, Frida.'

'And I knew you'd say that now, because all you've done since we started working on this play is egg me on, plámás me, keep me going so that the play keeps going. I didn't come here looking for compliments from you.'

'But you did call me. You did say you were having a wobble and wanted to see me.'

Frida sighed through pursed lips, frowning. 'I don't know what I want anymore. I don't know why I ever wanted to act. I think after this, I'm going to cut my losses and quit and just, I don't know. Make quilts.'

'It would be a crying shame,' he said in a low voice.

'Shut up, John! Shut up for one moment. You convinced me

to do this because you said that all your best work was made with me in it. But that's not true. The one in New York, the one with the ghosts. That was so good.'

'Frida, if you're trying to tell me that you want to give up, please, can I just say, just stick with it. We're almost there.'

She ignored him. 'I need to know something,' she said in a clear and serious voice. 'I need to know if you're in love with me.'

The firm line of John's mouth erupted into laughter. Open-mouthed, his bad back teeth showing.

'Frida Slattery,' he said, shaking his head at her.

'You're not answering my question. I'm aware I sound ridiculous,' she added.

He continued shaking his head slowly, like he couldn't believe her. He picked up his pint and swilled what was left of it around and around, watching the viscous brown liquid cling to the sides of the glass. Then he looked at her again.

'I've been in love with you since the first day we met.'

Quickly they left the pub. They took the Dart home and walked up the hill to her flat. In her bedroom they both undressed and when she looked at him, looked over his body, the greying hair on his chest, Frida tried not to think about herself. The Frida she was the very first time she had done this with him, the Frida she'd become in the intervening years without him.

In the morning he woke first, rising to go and make coffee in her kitchen. When he brought her a mug, they sat together in the twisted sheets and she rested her head against his belly.

'I hope that did it now,' he said in a low tone. 'Was that enough to stop you threatening to walk out on us?'

Frida could feel herself smile. 'That might be the worst reason to sleep with someone I've ever heard.'

'Oh, you'd be surprised,' he said. 'In the past I've found sometimes I don't even need a reason.'

'You know you're so annoying. You know I might actually walk out on us just to spite you.'

He tilted his face downwards to find her gaze. 'I can't tell if you're joking.'

6.

It had been a while since John had taken the Dart back from Frida's house. Nowadays, he cycled everywhere, and anyway, with the play about to open there had been less call for working from her living room. They'd rehearsed in the theatre just the other day, with John sat in the middle of the stalls, watching Frida moving about, talking, pretending to be a version of herself cast in a play about herself. This morning after their coffee, she'd gone to get ready for her swim and when she was dressed and ready to go, she looked at John and asked if he planned to stick around. He could tell from her tone that she wanted him to leave. So he got dressed too, walked with her as far as the pedestrian bridge that ran over the train tracks, and then watched her cross to reach the seafront. Her fair head bobbing as she walked away from him. It made his whole body feel like it was glowing softly, to think about how he and Frida had come back to each other the night before. He wanted to follow her down there, stay long enough to watch her take off her jumper and jeans, watch her slip down the concrete jetty and into the sea. He wanted the reassurance of it, to know where she was and what she was doing. He always wanted that. Instead, John swiped his pass at the station turnstile and waited on the platform for the next northbound train.

7.

Frida started with a brisk breaststroke out to the buoy, then came back towards the shore and trod water, looking at the blue sky above her. Two young women in wetsuits nearby were laughing and talking as they floated on their backs. They were practising, one of them said to Frida as she bobbed nearer to them. This was what you were meant to do if you ever got into difficulty in the water: float to live. Try it, the girl said, and Frida did, kicking her legs forward and spreading her arms wide.

'See, your body's instinct is to struggle,' her friend added. 'But it's actually safest to just tilt your head back and let the water hold you up until help comes.'

'I've never been any good at going against my body's instincts,' Frida said, hoping she sounded sardonic and not silly.

'That's why you need to practise,' said the first girl, giving her a wry smile.

Dressed again and with the feeling beginning to come back to her toes, Frida sat on the bench with her flask of tea. What she knew now was that the role she'd been given was that of a ghost. She could see that clearly. 'Herself' was going to be the director's madness and misery and regret made manifest, no matter how she played it. She was backed into a corner.

As she'd gotten dressed that morning, John had reclined on her bed watching her. He asked what she'd thought of the night before. She turned to look at him over her shoulder – he was shirtless, hair unkempt.

'Are you asking me for notes, John Reddan?'

'No,' he said with a chuckle. 'I just – I enjoyed myself. I wanted to make sure you did too.'

Already now she had forgotten the details of the night before. It was like when she'd come off stage as a teenager, all the adrenaline occluding the actual performance in her mind. But she knew one thing. When they were sitting at the bar in Kehoe's the night before, and he had said what he said, it had felt like the most real and permanent moment of Frida's life. It felt true, as indelible as genetic material or a mathematical proof. It was the sum of everything that they had done with their lives, both together and separately. It was inevitable, and in a way it made her believe she loved John Reddan, too.

'Of course I enjoyed myself,' she told him, and pulled her jeans on over her swimsuit.

8.

It was far and away the most expensive production the two of them had done together. Set designer, props master, hair and make-up, costume, even though Frida would only be wearing a white button-down shirt and blue jeans that she'd taken from her own wardrobe. Bare feet. John supposed this was all a sort of luxury, but of course Frida was probably well used to this after ten years of TV work. Opening night had sold well, around 70 per cent of the tickets gone. Theatre, it turned out, was back. John had spent so long trying to calm Frida's nerves, trying to keep her on the level, that he hadn't had time to be anxious himself. Now he was walking along the quays with a coffee he didn't need, the long evening setting in over the Liffey, seagulls diving and cawing overhead. In the theatre around the corner, Frida was backstage now. He would like to be sitting there with her as she had her eyebrows plucked or whatever they'd do to her, but Katie had asked him to take himself out for a walk.

'You're putting everyone on edge,' she'd said. 'Even me.'

And he'd always thought Katie was unspookable. Anyway, here he was now. Kitty and Niall would be there tonight, having recently discovered that Niall's daughter made an excellent and convenient babysitter for the boys. Barry and Joanna coming in the following evening. Frida mentioned her sister Edel, her husband and their two teenagers, too. God, it was a lot. That was just immediate family, never mind the legions of people he or Frida knew from work, old friends, 'friends', various people who John thought would probably be quite happy to see him fail. Of course he was anxious! There were always a great many things that could potentially go wrong on opening night, but tonight there were countless more. He still didn't know exactly what Frida would do or say when she went up there. He thought she'd start at the beginning: her first forays into acting as a student, before reaching the point where she met John Reddan. He wanted her to be honest about everything, even if the idea of what she might say about him still turned his stomach. They'd talked about him being on stage, sitting silently in an armchair, interacting with her in some non-verbal way. Or else standing in the wings so the audience could see that Frida was addressing him. They'd worked through each of these permutations in rehearsal and neither of them could choose one that was better, cleaner than the rest. Frida said she'd decide on opening night, and so at 5 p.m., John still didn't know exactly what his role would be.

Regardless of whether or not he would be involved, Frida would talk through her CV, would tell the audience that John had come to her and said he wanted to make a play about female suffering. The audience would probably laugh here, that was the intention. And Frida would riff on the commodification of female suffering in the arts, the fact that a woman couldn't speak about what happened to her without asking for her experience to be valued and redistributed in some way. This was the thing that Frida had a lot of opinions about, John had learned over the last year. And depending on her mood, on how open and honest she felt, she would talk about John, too. There was always the risk, of course, that she might be too honest – turn it into an excoriation of his bad behaviour as she saw it. But John hoped not. Instead, she might tell them how she felt about the plays they had made together, and while the two of them didn't expect the audience to be all that familiar with a handful of plays first produced over a decade ago, John thought that she'd tell it in such a way that they'd find themselves caring. He hoped this was true, anyway. He thought this was the magic of Frida Slattery, and if everyone else saw it they'd have to agree.

Through the whole seventy-minute performance there was the idea that Frida was an actress who was about to go on stage in another play. That the clock was running down. The stage was set to look like a theatre's backstage. And it was supposed to be like an off-hand private moment that an actor had with herself, looking in the mirror, pacing around the corridors. There were beats they had to hit regardless of what Frida decided she would or wouldn't talk about. Through much negotiation with Katie, they'd convinced her to come on at the final moment and call Frida onto the off-stage stage. Katie didn't like this, but she came around to it eventually. She said she thought the moment might be worth her own discomfort.

Ah, God. There was so much that could go wrong, for the performance and for him personally, too. All the things she could say about him if she took a fancy. He found himself now back at the stage door again, coffee gone cold. He stepped inside and walked down the corridor, where he saw that the door to Frida's dressing room was ajar. She was sat at the mirror, looking at herself. The place was a bombsite.

'Frida,' he said, closing the door behind him.

She turned to face him, smiling as if a photographer had told her to.

'How are you doing?'

'I'm good,' she said. She was wearing her blue jeans and white shirt with a black fuzzy fleece on over it. 'I'm a little cold, to be honest.'

'I'll get them to turn the heating on.'

'Thanks.'

'You're feeling okay about everything?'

'Yeah,' she said, stretching her legs out and pointing her toes in their grey Birkenstocks. 'I'm getting there.' She paused. 'I think I'm still a little worried. It just feels like such a gamble, John.'

He leaned back against the counter under the mirror and placed one hand down on Frida's knee. 'It's a gamble that I'm so happy to be making with you.'

Frida gave the tiniest of nods and stroked the back of his hand gently. 'I think I want to do it on my own tonight. I think you can be in the audience, not in the wings.'

'Are you sure?'

'Yeah. It's how I see it in my mind.'

'Okay, whatever you want.'

A knock then on the door, and Katie popped her head around. 'Thirty minutes, Frida.'

'Thanks Katie,' Frida said. 'John. Thank you for doing this with me. Do you think I can have some time on my own before I go on?'

He stood up and took a step backwards towards the door. 'God, yeah, of course. Whatever you need.'

'Cheers,' she said, reaching for a small tub of cold cream on the counter, rolling it around between her palms.

'I'll see you afterwards. I'll be back here as soon as you come off.'

'I know.' She smiled at him in the mirror. She looked so beautiful, more beautiful than ever. 'See you later.'

As John ambled down the corridor, back towards front of house, a little wave of terror came through him. If he sat in the audience, he needed to believe that Frida would actually go on stage. He wouldn't be there to make sure of it. But of course she would go out. They'd spent so long talking about her desire to bail, and that was all sorted now, wasn't it? Of course it was. Grabbing the arm of one of Katie's assistants, he asked the girl to get him a drink from the bar. A gin and tonic.

'Two,' he said. 'Actually, get two.'

They found a seat for John three rows from the front, right on the aisle so he could dash backstage in time for curtain call. The view here was good. While the auditorium filled, John saw familiar faces who waved to him as they took their seats. Edel and her daughters, all three of them looking like

Frida, four rows back. John raised a hand to greet them. He was thinking about what Frida was going to say when she came out. He was glad that she'd suggested he sit down here, because he realised now that he needed to see her from this angle in order to make all of it real. The months and months they'd been working on this, through two rounds of postponements and cancellations. Pacing around Frida's flat, trying different things out. Listening to her talking about him, about what had happened between them. Her twisting the story of how they met, how they started working together and how they ended things into different conflagrations each time. Omitting different things, leaving new blank spaces for the audience to fill in their minds. And then the events of the other night, like she'd decided to tie a bow on the whole thing. It was true, all of it. He had been in love with her all this time. How could he not have been?

He didn't know what would happen between them after the show ended in four nights' time. But he knew what he wanted her to say tonight. John wanted Frida to step out of the wings and start talking about the play that they could have made together, had things gone another way. The play that would have been their lives.

John loved when she told this version. She had told it only once, on the Dart home from Kehoe's three nights ago. She had been doing it jokingly, trying to show off her range, like a singer practising scales. But when she was finished, John found that his eyes were wet. Embarrassing to realise how badly he wanted for it to be real, for it to be more than a story.

But the train rolled into Seapoint station and Frida abruptly stood up, leaving the monologue behind as she disembarked. John followed her wordlessly.

And now, when the theatre was 70 per cent full, with all the ticket-holders in their appointed seats, murmuring with anticipation among themselves, the house lights went down. John found that he was holding his breath. An old feeling: his chest tight, sweat on his palms and under his armpits. He regretted the coffee of an hour ago, still cloying in his breath. He regretted not kissing Frida once more on her sweet mouth there in the dressing room. He drained his first gin and tonic, the ice cubes rattling in the plastic cup. The room went dark and the audience was sitting there looking towards the proscenium. John was among them and they were all the same there in the dark, all waiting for the curtain to rise, for Frida Slattery to step out on stage and begin.

ACKNOWLEDGEMENTS

I can't thank my agent Seren Adams enough for her constant support and belief in my work, and in this novel. Thanks also to Kat Aitken, and to the rights team at PFD. I am really grateful to my editors Sophie Missing and Rachel Sargent as well as all their colleagues at Scribner and Ecco, for their work on this book.

Bryan Moriarty provided invaluable insights on the working life of a West End actor. Dr Laura Casey and Dr Ross Foley shared with me their expertise in the workings of the human heart. My broader thinking on theatre, audiences and what it's all for has been deepened through conversation with Dr Emma Bennett. Jessica Stanley, Lisa Owens and Rosalind Jana read early drafts – thank you for your encouragement to keep going. It wouldn't have gotten finished without you.

Thank you to Museum of Literature Ireland and its staff for use of the Writer's Room which gave me the privacy and focus to finish this novel. A grant from the Dublin City Arts Office allowed me to take time off work to write at the same time and I am grateful to them, and also to the staff of the Dublin City Archives on Pearse Street for their help during my research. I believe that state funding for the arts enriches life on both on a personal level and a societal one, and this novel owes a debt to many of Ireland's beautiful public cultural spaces, including the National Library, where parts were written, and the Abbey Theatre.

Thank you to Tess Brady, Annelise Berghenti, Eleanore Hutch for friendship and encouragement, as well as Clíona, Camilla, Sadie, Sarah, Stevie, Leanne and Jeanie who all heard so much about this novel along the way through our book club – I'm sorry it doesn't feature a gunfight in the woods.

Thank you to my parents, Eilis Boland and Patrick Kinsella, and my family. Finally, thank you to Karl McDonald for your love, your conversation, and for always being willing to sit beside me in the cheap seats.

Ana Kinsella is an Irish writer. Her work has been published in *Granta*, the *Guardian*, the *Financial Times*, *Frieze*, *n+1* and many others. Her time spent as a magazine journalist, interviewing Irish actors, has informed her writing of this novel. She is also the author of *Look Here: On the Pleasures of Observing the City*. *Frida Slattery As Herself* is her debut novel. She lives and works in Dublin.